PRAISE FOR MARYJA
UNDEAD SERIES

Praise for the *New York Times* bestselling series

"MaryJanice Davidson's Undead series is laugh-out-loud funny."
—Heroes and Heartbreakers

"What can you say about a vampire whose loyalty can be bought by designer shoes? Can we say outrageous?"
—The Best Reviews

"[Davidson] never disappoints, delivering plenty of smart-ass dialogue and wacked-out adventures."
—RT Book Reviews

"Think *Sex and the City*—only the city is Minneapolis, and it's filled with demons and vampires."
—*Publishers Weekly*

ROAD QUEENS

OTHER TITLES BY MARYJANICE DAVIDSON

Fred the Mermaid series

Sleeping with the Fishes
Swimming Without a Net
Fish Out of Water
Sirena: An Undersea Folk tale
Underwater Love (omnibus of the first three stories)

The Insighter series

Déjà Who
Déjà New

Alaskan Royal series

The Royal Treatment
The Royal Pain
The Royal Mess

Gorgeous series

Hello, Gorgeous!
Drop Dead, Gorgeous

Stand-Alone Stories & Short Stories

Beggarman, Thief: A Boston Mutes Story
Carrie

Keep You Brave and Strong: A Hurricane Harvey short story

LTF: A Satirical Romance

Medical Miracle

A Contemporary Asshat at the Court of Henry VIII

Collections

A Snicker of Werewolves

Doing It Right

Dying for You

Hickeys and Quickies

I Have a Tapeworm: And other ways to make friends (nonfiction)

Really Unusual Bad Boys

Undead and Underwater

Under Cover

Undead and Unmistakable: An Anthology of Nonsense

Anthologies

Wicked Women Whodunit (with Amy Garvey, Jennifer Apodaca, and Nancy J. Cohen)

Bad Boys with Expensive Toys (with Nancy Warren and Karen Kelley)

Bite (with Laurell K. Hamilton, Charlaine Harris, Angela Knight, and Vickie Taylor)

Charming the Snake (with Camille Anthony and Melissa Schroeder)

Cravings (with Laurell K. Hamilton, Rebecca York, and Eileen Wilks)

Dead and Loving It (with Janelle Denison and Nina Bangs)

Dead but Not Forgotten: Short Stories from the World of Sookie Stackhouse (edited by Charlaine Harris and Toni L. P. Kelner)

Dead Over Heels (with P. C. Cast, Gena Showalter, and Susan Grant)

Demon's Delight (with Emma Holly, Vickie Taylor, and Catherine Spangler)

"Tall, Dark and Not So Faery," in Faeries Gone Wild (with Lois Greiman, Michele Hauf, and Leandra Logan)

How to Be a "Wicked" Woman (with Susanna Carr and Jamie Denton)

In Other Worlds (with Angela Knight and Camille Anthony)

Kick Ass (with Maggie Shayne, Angela Knight, and Jacey Ford)

Men at Work (with Janelle Denison and Nina Bangs)

Merry Christmas, Baby (with Donna Kauffman, Nancy Warren, Erin McCarthy, Lucy Monroe, and Susanna Carr)

"Alone Wolf," in Mysteria (with P. C. Cast, Gena Showalter, and Susan Grant)

"Disdaining Trouble," in Mysteria Lane (with P. C. Cast, Gena Showalter, and Susan Grant)

Mysteria Nights (with P. C. Cast, Gena Showalter, and Susan Grant)

No Rest for the Witches (with Lori Handeland, Cheyenne McCray, and Christine Warren)

Over the Moon (with Angela Knight, Virginia Kantra, and Sunny)

"My Thief," in Perfect for the Beach (with Lori Foster, Kayla Perrin, Janelle Denison, and Erin McCarthy)

Surf's Up (with Janelle Denison and Nina Bangs)

Valentine's Day Is Killing Me (with Leslie Esdaile and Susanna Carr)

Titles by MaryJanice Davidson and Anthony Alongi

Jennifer Scales series

Jennifer Scales and the Ancient Furnace

Jennifer Scales and the Messenger of Light

The Silver Moon Elm

Seraph of Sorrow

Rise of the Poison Moon

Evangelina

MARYJANICE DAVIDSON

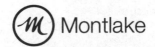

Published by Montlake, Seattle

www.apub.com

Amazon, the Amazon logo, and Montlake are trademarks of Amazon.com, Inc., or its affiliates.

ISBN-13: 9781662510359 (paperback)
ISBN-13: 9781662510366 (digital)

Cover design and illustration by Elizabeth Turner Stokes
Cover image: © Omnart / Shutterstock

Printed in the United States of America

For the pioneers: Sally Halterman, Bessie Stringfield,
Anne-France Dautheville, Theresa Wallach, Dot
Robinson, and all the other women riders who refused
to be excluded.
And me, maybe? For writing about them? That's kind
of pioneer-ish. No, never mind. It's gross to dedicate a
book to yourself. Right? Right.

AUTHOR'S NOTE

At the time of this writing, the Minnesota Correctional Facility in Stillwater is for men only. For the purpose of the terrific book you're about to read, I made the prison coed. Like college dorms! Except with more shivs and worse food.

The history of women motorcycle riders is vast and fascinating. I was surprised to discover that there weren't laws back then specifically forbidding women to get a motorcycle license. Instead, when a woman wanted to take the required exams, the men in charge would close the door: "There's no law against it, but there should be." (Don't worry; the ladies prevailed!) See the bibliography at the end for my sources and reading suggestions.

The $400 platinum urn that Amanda describes exists, if you find yourself with $400 on your hands and a need for an urn.

Unfortunately, so does the late Virgil Abloh's holographic duffel bag, if you've got $4,000 on your hands and a need for a truly hideous bag.

Prescott is a real river town in Wisconsin at the confluence of the Mississippi and Saint Croix Rivers. It's stuffed with parks, beaches, and great restaurants, and well worth a visit.

The Port of Prescott hotel in Prescott is also real, and also worth a visit.

The Schoolhouse Square town houses in Hastings, Minnesota, are real, and they're lovely.

Amanda's "Motorcycles and Mascara" T-shirt exists! You can get it at Amazon if you're so inclined.

Dinner for breakfast is a thing, and it's ridiculous.

Harold Perrineau's Mercutio is the definitive Mercutio; no one else comes close. Fight me.

PROLOGUE

Sonny finally had to blink, since he could feel his eyeballs drying out. There she was: Cassandra Rivers in the, um, flesh. All six feet of flesh. Parking her Norton Commando. Coming around the front. Coming inside. *Inside his place of business.* Sonny knew this because his nose had been pressed to the windows as he followed her progress from back to front—there was a horizontal line of grease where he'd pressed his nose to the glass and tracked her movement across the big window. As soon as he realized she wasn't lost, he raced behind the counter so he could (try to) look unconcerned AF when she walked in.

He knew her, natch. Everyone did; Prescott wasn't that big, about . . . four thousand people? Out of which maybe a dozen were cool? But Cassandra Rivers had never come into his shop, for obvious reasons. And after today, never would again. For obvious reasons.

"Morn—ack!" He coughed, tried again. "Morning, uh, Cassandra." Not for the first time, he wished he'd inherited his dad's bass instead of his mom's contralto. Then he remembered it was 5:00 p.m. "Afternoon, I mean. Good afternoon. Uh. Welcome. To my store." He coughed again. "More of a shop, though."

She didn't say a thing. Just strode up to his counter, held out a fist, opened it. Her key plunked down on his blotter. The

Heath-Ledger-as-Joker blotter he told his mother-in-law he didn't need because it wasn't 2010. But she'd had a crush on the late lunatic.

No hesitation either. Just clunk, right there on Heath's face. Like she was dropping off dry cleaning she was in no hurry to get back, when Sonny knew it had to be like cutting off her feet.

Worst of all was his scumbag brother's delight in her downfall. The little wiener set the standard for schadenfreude.

"So, um, Cassandra. I'm guessing you don't want a receipt."

She just looked at him with brown eyes so light, they were like whiskey. The good stuff. Angel's Envy bourbon. Maybe Four Roses. Her hair was short and wavy and deep purple. It should have looked ridiculous on such a tall woman. (It didn't.)

She was dressed the way she always was, since she planned to ride every day, even when it didn't happen. (She was like Beatrice Tarleton that way. Also, it was his mother-in-law's fault he knew the name of the twins' mother from *Gone with the Wind*.) Black jeans with armor padding at the knees and hips, good boots, a navy-blue crocheted tank top under the black leather jacket. He'd seen her parked on her bike more than once, crocheting away. Hell, maybe she crocheted while she was riding; wouldn't surprise him one bit. She and her friends were all degrees of crazy.

Or they used to be.

He tried again. "We were. Uh. Sorry to hear about, um . . . y'know. Just a real shame."

"Thanks."

This close, he could see the scar that bisected her left eyebrow, snaking up and past her temple like a white wire. He bet guys asked her about it all the time. He also bet they didn't get an answer. Or at least not a straight one.

He reached out and picked up the key, half expecting her to change her mind and stick a knife through his fist, retrieve her key, grab a Dum Dums lolly, kick him in the plums, then leave his shop, never to return.

But none of that happened.

"I'll, uh. Make sure it gets to a good home."

"It doesn't matter," she replied, which was the most shocking thing ever uttered in his shop since his uncle announced Biden maybe hadn't done *such* a bad job. Then, as now, he didn't know what to say. How to answer the unanswerable?

He cast about, finally came up with, "We're, uh. My wife and me. We're prayin' for you. And the others."

"But not your brother, I bet."

He almost laughed. "Well, no."

She smiled! No, that was a grimace. "There's no need for prayers. And the one who could have used them is dead." Excruciating pause. "But thanks."

Then she turned away and marched out all dramatic and cool, just like in the movies, except for the one detail movies never had to worry about.

"Wait, do you need a—how are you getting ho—"

Nope. Nothing. Not a pause. Not a backward glance. Just the shop door closing with a decisive clack.

Maybe she'd called an Uber. Or one of her deeply nutty pals. Maybe she was just gonna keep walking until Prescott was far, far behind her. It's what he woulda been tempted to do in her situation, especially if he'd been cut free the way she was. "Well. Bye."

He stared down at the key. "Now what to do with you?" he wondered aloud, and he was glad nobody was there to hear him talking to a key.

Besides, he knew exactly what to do.

CHAPTER ONE

Five years later . . .

"You're wrong."

"I'm right."

"You're wrong, and you should just sit there and simmer in your wrongness and accept being wrong, because you're super-duper wrong."

"But—ow."

Amanda Miller brandished the pen cup at her favorite customer. "Plenty more to throw where that came from."

Dave Conner: indie bookshop aficionado, golf handicap of sixteen, tall women his kryptonite. "Y'know, some people go to their local bookstore every week and never get hit with anything."

"Then it's not a real bookstore." Amanda Miller: proprietress of the Hobbit Hole, ride-or-die enthusiast, terrible basketball player. "And that's what you get for casting doubt upon my tale."

"I'm not—ah!—casting doubt." Dave dropped his left shoulder, and the pen sailed over it. "I just don't buy into your theory that all things motorcycle have always been—ah!—misunderstood."

"Listen. The first motorcycle wasn't even a motorcycle, it was a velocipede."

"See, you've already lost me."

"Shut up, please. Anyway, the inventor, a fine fellow named Pierre Lallement, called it the 'boneshaker,' possibly because it didn't have brakes. Not that this deterred him in the slightest, because like all riders, he—"

"—had more nerve than brains?"

"Okay, that might be a fair point. Anyway, he was test-driving the thing down a hill—"

"With no brakes. My point stands."

"Shush! Y'know, sixty years ago, you'd have been one of the people who insisted we'd never make it to the moon. Anyway, he realized he was about to smash into a horse-drawn wagon, so he bailed into a ditch. And the guys he almost hit, they took off running."

"With or without the horses? Or the carriage?"

"How the hell should I know? Could you not get me mired in minutiae?"

"I . . . think so?"

"Anyway, Lallement struggles out of the water-filled ditch that probably saved his life and limps into town and goes right for the tavern."

"Understandable."

"Who wouldn't want two or five shots of rum after the morning he had? Here comes the best part: the men he nearly crunched beat him to the tavern and were in the middle of describing the first motorcycle and the first motorcycle rider as—get this . . ." She picked up *Driving Bitch: A History of Female Motorcycle Riders.* "'A dark Devil, with human head and body half like a snake, and half like a bird, just hovering above the ground which he seemed no way to touch.'"

Dave blinked. "They thought he and his bike were Satan."

"Yes! And it stuck. Not just to Lallement. To bikers of all stripes. From day one, we were crazy and misunderstood."

"Y'know, I really only came in to pick up the new *Golf Digest*."

"Which you may have, not that you need it, *and* you got a fabulous history lesson. No need to thank me. Though it would be nice." She handed over the magazine. "Still looking for the One?"

"There's a putter out there for everyone," Dave replied, already flipping through the magazine. "And I will find mine."

"Still can't believe you went from zero to *Oh my God, I misplaced my range finder* in five months."

"Thought it was silly, all that putzing around with a little ball in rich people's backyards. Hell, I've been on jobsites right next to golf courses, and I couldn't believe some of the assholes walking around in pastels—"

"Don't shade shame."

"—and barfing Bloody Marys."

"Don't booze shame. Or barf shame."

He ignored her, still paging through the mag. "We did softball and bowling in my family. But in some ways, golf is even more challenging than bowling."

"In some ways, huh?"

"Anyway. It's hard but I like it."

"I think that's *why* you like it. Hey, no criticism from this quarter. I love you're trying new things. It's just, you don't look like a stereotypical golfer." Amanda leaned in, squinting. "You're like Curly in *City Slickers*: a saddlebag with eyes. And you've heard my mags rant, right?"

"Yeah. Not sure why you're going into that again or what it has to do with my saddlebag eyes."

"Because magazines are the biggest rip-off in the history of rip-offs! So expensive! Price 'em out by the page and then compare that to a paperback—you'll be horrified."

"Y'know you sell magazines, right?"

"It still makes me feel dirty. Hey, I'm as bad as anyone. You should see the stack of mags upstairs. They're all packed with pics and only need about twenty minutes to read. Then you're stuck with a stack of shiny paper getting more outdated by the second and realize you're stuck. 'I paid thirty bucks for two magazines full of recipes I'll never make.' Scam. Scam. Scam."

"They can't be all that—"

"The one exception is *Vogue*. I respect an unabashedly thick magazine that's been around forever. Like those old-fashioned phone books, it's a bazillion pages of gorgeous nothing."

Before Dave could respond, the bronze frog over the door let out a series of ribbits as a customer came in. Amanda stretched up on her tiptoes and waved from behind the cash register. "Welcome to my Hole!"

The customer in question groaned. "You've gotta stop that."

"Never." Amanda grinned as Sidney, her favorite customer, hurried up to the counter after a brief pause at the "Dinosaurs didn't read, and now they're extinct" book display. "So you've finally learned to read. That's just excellent, Sidney! How can I help you? Self-help? Cookbook? The latest celeb tell-all? An autographed copy of *Go the Fuck to Sleep*?"

"No to all of—wait, do you really have an autographed copy of that? If I ever have kids, it'll be just so I can read 'em that book." Before Amanda could answer, Sidney cut her off. "Never mind. Have you been on social media this morning?"

"Ew. No."

"Regular news then, you determinedly oblivious twit?"

"Again, ew." To Dave: "I get most of my news from fortune cookies."

He nodded. "That would explain how you failed to notice the pandemic."

"I didn't 'fail to notice.' I was just a little slow to catch on. And don't talk to me about the pandemic. I'm sick of hearing about the—"

"A-*hem*." Sidney smacked her hand, palm down, on the counter. Amanda didn't react, since Sidney had been doing that since she was in diapers, but Dave flinched so hard he knocked over the pen cup he'd been moving out of Amanda's reach. "Cassandra's in the tank as of a couple of hours ago."

"Weirdest phrase ever for a police station. Makes it sound like she's drunk. Wait." Amanda took a second to process. "Our Cassandra?"

"No, a rando stranger also named Cassandra got pinched, and I ran over here to tell you for no good reason."

Amanda blinked as Dave cleared his throat and said, "I'll just mosey four feet over here and look at a book I'm not going to buy in order to give you the illusion of privacy."

"Or you could leave," Sidney suggested, "and give us actual privacy."

Amanda barely heard them; she was too busy gaping like a goldfish. "Cass has been arrested? For . . . for what?" She cast about, physically and mentally. "Not for what happened back—I mean, she didn't do anything, so why—"

"I don't know for what. Like a dumbass, I thought you might have an idea." Sidney Derecho: fern enthusiast, wicked tennis serve, poetry prodigy.

"That *was* pretty dim of you," Amanda observed. "I also like how you pretended to insult yourself while actually insulting me. Never change, Sid."

"You know I hate when you call me—"

"You're not here for news. You're here to give *me* news. Mission accomplished. Cassandra's cooling her heels in a holding cell." Amanda spread her hands and shrugged. "Consider me caught up."

"Cold."

"So was she. Five years and nothing, not even a Facebook post. After . . . after everything. Everything we went through and suffered for and made happen and . . . nothing. For years."

"You don't use Facebook."

"Well, it's the thought that counts. Or something."

"That's how I found out. That whole check-in thing. 'Cassandra Rivers is at Precinct 2, City of Minneapolis.'"

Amanda laughed; she couldn't help it. "So it's a version of 'It's complicated'? Wait. How'd you even find out? Are you guys still Facebook friends?"

". . . no."

"You *are*! What the hell, Sidney? First, Facebook is problematic for too many reasons to go into. Second, she slashed us out of her life like the fat on pork tenderloin."

Sidney shrugged. "I just like knowing what that bitch is up to. And where she is. Better than not knowing and then getting caught in more fallout."

"She ran. And for nothing. There was no fallout."

"And you don't cook. How do you know how to prep tenderloin? How do you even know pork tenderloin is a thing?"

Amanda was still shaking her head and letting out a few tsks.

"Amanda . . ." Sidney reached out, took Amanda's small hand, squeezed.

Amanda stared down at their hands, her teeny pale paws and Sidney's perma-tanned, long, slender fingers. If she turned Sidney's hand palm up, then she'd see the scar Amanda gave her the day they met Cassandra. "This is an unsettling way for you to admire my manicure."

"Knock it off; you wouldn't get a manicure on a bet. She's in trouble."

"I wish I had a dollar for every time we said that about Cassandra 'Goddamned' Rivers. Oh, wait, I do, all three of us do, and I sunk it all into this place." As Sidney shook her head and Dave sidled away, Amanda sighed. "She didn't reach out."

"Well, no. She didn't. She shouldn't have to."

Amanda extricated her hand with minor difficulty. "You said it yourself, Sid; you found out on social media. If she wanted us, she would've called. That whole you-only-get-one-phone-call thing is a TV lie."

"I don't need a lect—"

"Cops *want* you to call people for help; it keeps the machinery in motion. Cassandra could have called either of us. Multiple times. And then ordered pizza. With multiple toppings. And multiple delivery times. Breakfast pizza, lunch pizza, supper—"

"Amanda . . ."

"But she didn't. Well, she might've ordered pizzas, that hypoglycemic jerk. After she had ice cream, probably. But she didn't reach out to either of us. Ergo, she doesn't want our help. Ergo, she can just deal. She made it clear five years ago and every year since, and the deafening silence from her this morning *also* made it clear: she's dead to us. Pardon the cliché."

"She came running quick enough when my marriage—"

"Your fake marriage to your scammer husband."

"—Imploded."

Hmm. It wasn't like Sidney to bring up He Who Shalt Ne'er Be Named under any circumstances, never mind to make a point. Not that she'd named her husband in so many words. "Yeah, and then she turned her back on us."

Sidney just looked at her.

"What?"

Nothing.

"Whaaaaaaat?" The swearing and sarcasm she could take, but when Sidney Derecho went all quiet and thoughtful? Torture.

"Again, she shouldn't have to."

"If we're gonna do the shouldn't-have list as it pertains to Cassandra 'Goddamned' Rivers, I want to find an armchair and get comfortable. Oh, look, there are three, because my bookstore kicks ass." But she stayed behind the counter. "Could you stop looking at me with your huge pretty eyes? It's like staring down the Little Match Girl, for God's sake."

Sidney said nothing, just widened her (small, squinty) black eyes and ruffled her curly brown hair until it was a thorough mess. It made her look still more imploring, which was as radical a departure from her everyday demeanor as Amanda had ever seen.

She sighed. "Fine. I guess we could . . . I dunno, look in on her? Find out about the charges and when they're gonna remand her antisocial ass. Maybe even . . . go for a ride? The three of us? If we can spring her?"

"You know she ditched the bike after . . ."

"So maybe all the other stuff I said. And then you and I could go for a ride, maybe hit Nordstrom's and check out the Tory Burch flats."

Sidney beamed, frown lines smoothing out in an instant, her eyes nearly disappearing as she grinned. "Aw, shit, yeah! That's great, let's do that. All of that. I know you just opened, but maybe we could head over to the station at lunchtime?"

"I could watch the store for you," Dave offered. He waved his phone at Amanda: "I thought I had a meeting with the Maplewood guy to give him a project update, but he canceled a few minutes ago."

Amanda shook her head. "Sorry, refresh my memory. The Maplewood guy?"

"Yeah, he booked me a couple of months ago. We went golfing, do you believe it? First time I golfed with a client. He could've gone with a construction company closer to where he lives, but he tracked me down specially." Dave puffed up a little as he said it, which was adorable. "The point being I can hang around for a bit. And y'know I've done it before."

Amanda beamed. "It's why you're my favorite customer!"

"You say that about every customer."

"Hush up and watch the register—ack!"

Sidney had already grabbed Amanda's elbow and hauled her out from behind the counter, intent on the door.

"Pitch pens till the cup's empty, knock over the Books That Should Be Banned display, put metal in the microwave, whatever. We'll see ourselves out." Sidney blew her chronically too-long bangs out of her eyes. "C'mon, let's book. No pun, et cetera."

"Is that even a pun, though?" Amanda asked.

"You won't be sorry."

"I'm already sorry, Sidney, not to mention upset, because I keep spouting clichés. Bye, Dave! All *right*, I'm coming, don't *yank*."

CHAPTER TWO

"What d'you mean, where's my bike?" Sidney asked. They were on the street in front of Amanda's Hole, squinting in the summer sunshine. "It's not here. Obviously."

"Then you'll have to ride bitch."

"You insisted we never use that phrase."

"I don't make the rules. Or the vernacular. I just arbitrarily enforce them. Sometimes. When I can be bothered."

"Or I could, I dunno, drive my car?" Sidney gestured to the dark-blue vehicle parked across the street. "Like a grown-up?"

"I thought it was weird when you came into the store in shorts and a T-shirt." On a bike at sixty-five miles per hour, shorts and a T-shirt might as well be made of Kleenex. Ninety-five and so humid it's like breathing through hot, damp cotton? Too bad; get your leathers.

Sidney treated her to a patented Sidney Derecho eye roll. "God forbid I dress appropriately for the weather."

"Is that a minivan?" Amanda gasped. "In a legal parking spot?"

"You know it is. Lots of space," Sidney replied defensively. "My hockey gear fits."

Amanda was still goggling. "Did you feed a meter this morning, you domesticated bitch?"

"Oh, like there's something wrong with not getting a parking ticket," Sidney snapped.

"You've changed, man." Amanda shook her head. "You've chaaaaanged."

"I've been driving minivans for the better part of a decade, you twit. Starting our senior year, when I gave you a ride home pretty much every day. And you own your own business, for God's sake! You pay taxes! Don't deny it."

"Oh, right. Taxes. I forgot. But if we're driving longer than fifteen minutes, I've gotta change," she said, pointing to her "Motorcycles and Mascara" T-shirt. "And we should stop for gas and cream puffs. Those errands don't need to be in that order."

Forty-five minutes and two cream puffs later, they were on the road, and the ride from Prescott, Wisconsin, to Minneapolis, Minnesota, was quick. Thirty miles in July heat—delicious! Or at least not entirely miserable. Amanda could countenance nearly all weather conditions except for extreme heat, which would kill her immediately, or so her mother (a redhead prone to heat exhaustion) warned her. She'd ride in rain before she'd ride through humidity; that was how God engineered her.

She wasn't in leather today; she'd only planned to motor two miles between her home and the grocery store, so her SPIDIs (which looked like leggings but were armored at the knees and hips) and a light jacket were sufficient.

Speaking of sufficient, riding for half an hour behind Sidney's minivan . . . wasn't. Nothing against Sidney. Or minivans. But it was impossible to shake the feeling that one of them was missing, possibly because one of them *was* missing, and had been for years.

Never mind! Amanda would focus on the joy, allllll the joy. She'd live in the moment, because she wasn't missing the old days at all, and she *definitely* wasn't wishing there were three of them, headed for a park or the Mall of America or the river or nowhere. Ah, nowhere. Those were the best rides, the ones with no fixed destination.

It had taken her a while to reclaim her joy after . . . after all that had happened. So Amanda was always happy to find more.

All that to say it was a quick thirty minutes, including parking time and a smidge of angst.

"Now that we're here, I'm wondering why both of us should go," Sidney said. "I don't know if it's at all like Stillwater. Maybe they won't let us see her."

"Why wouldn't they? Also, moot!" Amanda declared. "It's a team vibe. Did Carrie go anywhere without Samantha, Charlotte, or what's-her-face?"

"Pretty sure she did. The show ran for half a dozen seasons, y'know. They weren't *always* talking about banging while gobbling goat cheese pizza in various high-end restaurants before going home to their implausibly pricey apartments."

"It's gross that you know how many seasons there were before the revamp," Amanda replied.

"Almost as gross as you knowing there was a revamp."

"And who knew a weekly freelance column netted seven figures? Or at least, high sixes . . . not that she needed to worry about dinero once she landed Big. Again, I mean. She had to land him at least twice, right?"

"Why is it that whenever more than two and fewer than five women get together, *Sex in the City* comparisons come up?"

"*Sex* and *the City*," Amanda replied. "Did you use 'why is it' ironically?"

"No. My point is the relevance. And how terrible they all were. Carrie was a self-absorbed shithead, Charlotte never grew a pair, Miranda was a bitch to the one guy who worshipped her, and Samantha was too good for all of them."

Amanda laughed. "Your point? Samantha should've gotten her own show?"

"Who the fuck *cares*? That's always my point. Though if Samantha had a spin-off, I would've watched. Now come on."

"What's the rush? Are you afraid I'll change my mind and—*yeek!* Jeez, I'm coming . . . my legs work, y'know. There's no need to keep hauling me around—ow!"

CHAPTER THREE

The cop shop (Precinct 2, City of Minneapolis) was as welcoming as such a place could be: low brick building, trees, the Eastside Guardian statues (two policemen, one from the early twentieth century and one from 2009, and a girl-child looking up imploringly at both).

"What does it say about us," Amanda speculated as they mounted the steps, "that we know exactly what to do and where to go when a friend gets arrested? And if that friend got arrested in Seattle or Moscow or Luxembourg, we'd *still* know? Well, maybe not Luxembourg."

Sidney shrugged. "That we're living interesting or illegal lives."

"Or both," Amanda replied, flashing her dimples at the officer, who saw them and obligingly held the door open.

They had unconsciously fallen into the formation they'd used since they were fourteen: Sidney marching ahead, Amanda not quite abreast. And Cassandra would be bringing up the rear soon enough.

Or not. That would be fine too.

◆ ◆ ◆

"I'm not leaving anytime soon."

"Cassandra, you haven't even been arraigned yet," Amanda protested.

"There's no need because—"

Amanda cut her off. "And they've only got—what? Fourteen more hours to do it?"

Sidney turned to the detective around whose desk they were gathered and tapped her wrist. "Tick-tock, Clarice."

Cassandra laughed. "That loses some of the drama if you aren't wearing a watch, Sidney." Cassandra Rivers: six feet tall, crocheter extraordinaire, maaaaybe didn't murder anyone.

"Watches are extinct, Cassandra, you stately dumbass. Except Apple Watches. Maybe."

Funny how they (well, Sidney) had been soooo worried about Cassandra, only to find her leaning against a desk, long legs crossed at the ankles, sipping Cup-a-Soup and listening to whatever the hell the cop was saying. The look of amazed happiness on Cassandra's face when she spotted them was, it had to be said, pretty satisfying.

And speaking of pretty satisfying, the cop upon whose desk Cassandra's rump was parked wasn't bad to look at in *any* way. Tan jacket over a sky-blue button-down that matched his eyes. Chiseled jaw and stubble, right out of central casting for Brooding Hero. Or Brooding Psychopath No One Knows Is the Killer Until It's Too Late. Either way: yum.

Aw, the dark circles under his eyes are the exact color of a Godiva salted-caramel truffle! If he's tall, I'm done for. Might have to overlook the whole arresting-a-former-friend-for-murder thing.

"I'm waiting on some paperwork from the DA," Detective Chisel McJaw volunteered in response to Sid's reference to a cannibalistic serial killer. "Processing's a little backed up."

"Then it's back to the hoosegow," Cassandra said. "Only not really."

Waiting on paperwork? How delightfully vague. And processing could be "backed up" to last Tuesday; it didn't mean the arrestee gets to slurp soup while hanging in the bullpen.

"Thanks for your patience," Detective Jawman added, like he was a waiter instead of a homicide detective.

He wasn't surprised to see us either. Cassandra was, but not this guy. Were we expected? Why? And why is he treating Cassandra more like a guest than a suspect? I've seen her get ruder treatment at a Burger King drive-through.

"Well, Cassandra, we've got your back," Amanda announced, which might not have been entirely true, depending. "Or whatever hackneyed cliché you want to pick."

Cassandra nearly choked. "Why?"

"What d'you mean, why?"

"I mean—" Flustered, Cassandra tried again. "You didn't have to come. Is all I meant."

Sidney let out a snort. "Believe me, we're aware."

"What did I tell you?" Amanda asked, stretching her arms in a vindication V. "We're super superfluous." She would have kept rubbing it in but was distracted when Detective Jawman stood. "Yay, you're tall!"

He stared at her. "I'm sorry?"

"She has a thing for storks and stubble," Sidney explained, which was all kinds of aggravating.

"Anyway. You guys should go." Cassandra straightened; Jawman was only an inch or so taller. "Please don't misunderstand."

"Too late," Sidney grumped.

"I'm grateful you went to the trouble to come see me . . ."

"First, we just got here," Amanda pointed out. The cop was still staring at her. Was he challenging her for dominance? Because if so, he should have been glaring at Sidney. If they had a pack leader, she was it. "Second, there's usually a 'but' after a lead-in like that."

"Not this time. Grateful and goodbye." At their silence, Cassandra added, "Should we, um, shake hands?"

"Jesus Christ." From Sidney's expression, one would assume Cassandra had tried to hand her a dead possum. "No."

"You haven't heard all the news," Amanda said, wondering why she was prolonging this. Cassandra didn't want them. Going by the heavy eye contact, the cop didn't either. The obligatory check-in could be over. Whatever trouble this was, it didn't seem to implicate her or Sidney. If they left right that minute, they could hit Muddy Waters before the lunch rush. "Our news, I mean. We, um, know what you've been up to." Kind of.

"Yeah, well." Cassandra turned to look out the agreeably large windows, unconsciously rubbing the scar over her eye. "Nice day for a ride." Her smile was wistful, or the onset of acid reflux.

"Gorgeous," Sidney agreed. Then: "Really? We're gonna talk about the fucking weather?"

Proof you can't go back, Amanda thought. Five years was too long. The gap was unbridgeable, even if Cassandra hadn't been arrested. No point in prolonging any of it.

So! They'd go back to their lives. Amanda would resume the campaign to get Edward Gorey to come for a signing (the man's death *would not* stop her), Sidney would get banned from another hockey practice and fume about her soon-to-be ex-husband, and Cassandra would try yet again to undo her childhood, which would end in blood and pain. Or whatever else she'd been up to for five years.

Done. Over. And the time to move on? Now.

"Sidney drove her minivan here!" she yelped for no reason.

Cassandra blinked. "But it's beautiful outside."

"I know! But she sold her bike!"

Sidney rubbed her temples. "Fuck's saaaaake . . ."

"And she paid for parking!" Amanda tattled.

"For shame, Amanda. We should always abide by traffic ordinances," Cassandra said with a straight face. "I fully endorse Sidney's lawful action."

"Die screaming. Both of you."

"A minivan," Amanda added. "Full of hockey junk. She just needs the Karen Kut, and the transformation will be complete. It's awful."

"Yes, it's almost as bad as being pinched for murder," Sidney snapped.

Ah, yes. The felonious elephant in the room.

"Way to bring down the room, Sid."

"We are in the cop shop, Amanda!" In her agitation, Sidney was waving her arms like an irked windmill. And for the first time, Amanda realized Sidney was wearing a shirt Cass had crocheted for her five years ago. It fit like a dream because Cass's crocheted gifts were the opposite of prêt-à-porter.

Did Sidney grab that shirt on purpose? Or naw?

Meanwhile, Sid was still yowling. "The room was already down! Our friend—"

"Estranged friend," Amanda put in. Actually, "former" was more accurate, but she decided to be tactful in front of the cops.

"Ouch." From Cassandra.

"—is in the clutches of—uh—"

"Detective Beane," Jawman said, because Cassandra wasn't going to introduce them.

"Yes!" Sidney pointed, and looked great while doing so because the red ribbed top brought out her small beady eyes. Probably just a coincidence, then. "Him!"

Cassandra held up her hands like she was soothing a mad beast so it wouldn't trample her. "Here's the thing. Sean was telling—"

"Wait, what?" Sidney turned to Lawman Jawman: "Your name's really Sean Beane?"

"Sure."

Sidney zeroed in on him while Amanda pinched her lip so she wouldn't giggle. Amanda looked into his blue, blue eyes and had the odd sensation she'd seen them before. Which made no sense; if she had ever met *this* specimen, she would have remembered.

"You never thought about changing it?" Sidney asked.

The cop grinned, which made him look even cuter. Which was irritating. Amanda had zero time for a crush. Or even a date.

"Why? I'm not the one who keeps getting killed off in movies and TV shows. If anything, he should change *his* name. Maybe things will turn around for him."

"Maybe." To Cassandra: "I knew this had the potential to be surreal, but not to this extent."

Cassandra cleared her throat, which she always thought was subtle, though it sounded like a truck shifting into low gear: *grrrrhhhMMMM.* "Like I was saying, thank you for coming down."

"It's up," Amanda pointed out. "Technically."

"They don't have to leave on my account," Lawman Jawman said, because he was a helpful, hot, helpful cop. "You're welcome to stay."

Is this a police station or a wedding reception? Thank you for coming? So, definitely expecting us but didn't call or send anyone to fetch us. Allows Cassandra to roam free with impunity and soup. What. The. Fuck?

"I know this is a silly question," Amanda began, since the three of them—four if you counted the cop—knew the answer. "But who do they think you killed?"

Cassandra rubbed her scar again and grinned at the floor. "Franklin Donahue."

After a puzzled pause, Sidney asked for all of them, "Who the fuck is Franklin Donahue?"

"No idea." Cass shrugged. "They wanted to question me about the premeditated murder of a man I've never met."

"*Bum-bum-bummmmm,*" Amanda intoned because what the hell else was there to say?

CHAPTER FOUR

Detective Sean Beane hadn't been so excited about a case in years. Not that Cassandra Rivers had hired him, per se, but still—progress! Finally. He felt like doing a victory lap around the parking lot in sheer delight. He felt like making Cassandra another Cup-a-Soup. He felt like

(Get a grip right now.)

taking this all very seriously, as it involved serious crimes and serious people. And wonderful people. But yeah, also at least one scumbag killer.

He managed to cork his giddiness long enough to wave to Officer Dora Schoen, formerly of the Violent Crimes Investigations Division's family violence unit, currently riding a desk to accommodate her last trimester. One would think the paperwork alone would be suicidally depressing, but not only did Dora plow through it, she'd also found the time to pick up the phone and pass on the tip about Cassandra. Plenty of cops knew about OpStar. But not so many knew about Sean's long-term interest in the shuttered initiative.

So the elegant Officer Dora had tipped him off. And with the dignity befitting his professions, both new and old, Sean obeyed all parking ordinances and didn't almost break both legs to get to the precinct. He even had a few minutes to spare, which he'd used to good advantage, introducing himself to Cassandra and politely prying, which people tended to put up with in a police station.

She greeted him with: "This isn't like the movies."

"Not many things are." He stopped and considered. "Well. Documentaries, maybe."

"I haven't set foot in a police station since my mother . . ." Cassandra trailed off and rubbed her scar. "Uh . . . sorry, who are you again?"

He told her. The utter lack of recognition was both expected and a bit of a bummer.

"And you're here because . . . ?"

"Because I want the same thing you do: information."

She tilted her head to one side. "No, I mean, you, specifically, are here for what reason?"

"Information. It's not a riddle to solve. I genuinely want to find out what happened. And don't worry about the low-energy vibes you might be picking up from Precinct 2." Sean gestured to the dozens of police officers bustling back and forth. "They're getting it done. Well, most of it. You see, Ms. Rivers—"

"Cassandra."

"—at first glance this could be an ordinary business office. Or a FedEx hub. Or a waiting room! Except for all the sidearms. But instead, it's a building stuffed with men and women sworn to uphold the peace. It's why crime doesn't pay. It's why everything's going to be made right."

"Wow. You should write propaganda pamphlets." Cassandra narrowed her eyes. "You don't believe that. Not with *your* job."

"I believe most of it," he allowed. "Depending on the day. Now! Let me set up a conference room for you and your friends—"

"Not necessary. And not friends. They're not coming."

He waved away her prediction. "Oh, sure they are."

"They absolutely aren't."

"They are. And I can't wait to meet them either."

"Wanna bet?"

"Which part?"

"The part where they don't walk in, and you're crushed and hand me five bucks. Want to bet on it?" She grinned. "Don't let the fact that we're in a police station deter you from gambling."

"Fine, you're on."

"Also, should I be concerned about how you 'can't wait' to see Amanda and Sidney?"

"Not in the slightest."

Before he could elaborate, here came the other two who had saved his sister and niece from predations, justifications, and all-around douchbaggery. And he saw at once that they didn't recognize him either. The same could never be said of the three of them, especially Cassandra: the height, the hair, the scar all worked to make her unforgettable to pretty much everyone who crossed her path.

Which raised the question: Would Cassandra Rivers have committed murder in a town where she'd be recognized within seconds? People committed murder in their hometowns all the time, but . . . he couldn't see it. Not this woman. Not yet at least.

And he couldn't stop staring at Amanda. Her hair was different, longer than last time, a mass of red that tended to frizz. He had no idea how she avoided helmet hair; add that to the bundle of questions he wanted to know but likely would never ask. And she wasn't as pale as last time, which made sense given that it was now midsummer. Her dimples flickered depending on her mood; he'd never seen someone pull off a dimpled scowl before. Odd, the traits that stood out.

Her eyes were exactly the same.

"Detective?"

"Uh?" He glanced around and hoped he didn't look as dazed as he felt.

Amanda and Sidney had just left, and Cassandra was examining him with raised eyebrows. "You okay?"

"Of course. Just thinking about the case. And how you owe me five bucks."

She was already going for her billfold, then fished around and handed him Abe's picture. "You knew they'd come."

"Of course."

"Okay, now I'm a little embarrassed I bet against them."

"As you should be," he teased, and pretended to smell the bill.

"It's just . . ." Cassandra stared at the door her friends (?) had used to leave. "We didn't part on good terms. And I haven't been here in the station that long. They must have hauled ass to get up here from Prescott. Same as you. Wherever you came from, you didn't waste time either." She was shaking her head. "I didn't—I can't believe they came. It doesn't make any—why would they come?"

He shrugged, though he knew. "Listen, I know we just met again—"

"Again?"

"But . . ." He dug around in his suit-jacket pocket and came up with half a dozen business cards. Even better, one of them was his. "I'd like very much to sign you as a client."

"Client? Aren't you a cop?" She didn't wait for an answer before jumping ahead. "And why? I didn't kill anyone. But if I did, you don't think my first move should be to call, I dunno, a lawyer?"

"They can be simultaneous moves," he admitted.

"What's all this to you? No offense." She'd crossed her arms and had gone back to studying him like he was an intriguing manner of bug she'd never seen before. "I'm just wondering why you popped up out of nowhere and want me as a client."

"A colleague tipped me off. I know I'm coming off a little, err—"

"Like an ambulance chaser. A cute one, but still."

"Fair. The thing is, it's not out of nowhere. We've all met before. And I'm familiar with your work. Your, um, earlier work."

"Could you just spit it out, please? This whole stammer-ing-while-cute thing is coming off a little Hugh Grant–ish. D'you know how many times my mom made me watch *Four Weddings and a Funeral*?"

"No, I—"

"So much British spluttering."

Horrors. "You guys helped my sister a couple of years ago."

"Oh." Cassandra's eyes widened as she absorbed his words. *"Oh."*

"Yeah. So I've kind of kept tabs on you guys. Um. In a good way," he added.

"Sure, sure. Ambulance chasing coupled with mild stalking. Excellent."

He shrugged. "Sorry. But . . . y'know. Full disclosure."

"Is it full, though? And who did we help? If you don't mind my asking. Because there were so many—" But before he could answer, she was shaking her head. "I still can't believe—sorry, I'm kind of all over the place here. I can't believe they came. We haven't spoken in years. Why would they come?"

It was telling that she was more rattled by Amanda's and Sidney's appearance than she was about learning of his close connection to OpStar. *Should have bet twenty bucks instead of five.*

"Why?" He chose to take the question at face value and began digging for his keys. "Let's go ask them." *Only this time, Sean, keep your shit locked down. Good God, man.*

"Wait." Cassandra held up a hand like a traffic cop, which was cute given where they were. "Your plan was to pop in, reintroduce yourself—kind of—and remeet the three of us."

"Yes. And I have to say, my plan worked perfectly."

"But now you want to follow Amanda and Sidney, who just left, but not before making it clear they're not inclined to help. And you want to do that so you can . . . go talk to them some more?"

"It wasn't the plan until you lost the bet," he replied. "But now you know. Your friends—"

"Former. I think."

"—cared enough to come. It stands to reason they'd be amenable to further chats. You've got questions. As it happens, I do too. So let's go get some answers."

"I haven't hired you yet," she warned.

"We can talk about that too."

"Jesus." Cass stared at the door her (former?) friends had just left through. "You're right. It wouldn't have been a good idea if I'd won the bet. I'm just not convinced it's a good idea even though I lost."

"One way to find out."

"You got any references, guy-who-just-showed-up?"

"Dora!" Sean called. When the officer looked up, he pointed at Cassandra. "She wants a reference. Tell her I'm not a creep."

"By definition, you kind of are. Whether you're taking pics of a cheating spouse or tracking down a missing person, creeping is in the job description."

Sean rolled his eyes at Cassandra's snort. "Fine, tell her I'm a nice creep."

Officer Dora Schoen considered him for a long moment. Her big glasses and mop of reddish-brown curls, so ruffled they almost looked like goose down, made her look like a formidable Little Orphan Annie, if Annie had access to Smith & Wesson M&Ps. "Yeah," she said. "I can do that." To Cassandra: "He's not entirely objectionable. And pretty good at his job. So . . . I dunno."

Cassandra let out another snort. "As far as character references go, that's not the worst I've heard."

"Sidney and Amanda are getting farther away by the second," he reminded her.

"It's fine. I know where they're going." She looked him over one last time. "Let's go if we're going."

Yes! "Thank you, Dora!" he called, already grabbing his keys.

"Go away now, Sean." But she smiled as she said it, and the smile, coupled with the halfhearted reference, seemed to put Cass at ease.

"Yes, ma'am." Some people might want to fuck with an armed pregnant woman. Sean Beane was not one of them. He jumped ahead and pulled the door open for Cassandra. "After you, Ms. Rivers."

"Oh, stop it." But she walked through. And he'd take what he could get.

CHAPTER FIVE

"Well, that was dramatic," Amanda observed. She paused to take another sip of her iced tea, then added, "Also, why does Cass think that vaguely soup-flavored water is soup?"

"Let's focus on one disaster at a time."

"That better not be a segue into my lack of love life."

"It's not, Amanda. Like I give a shit you haven't gotten laid in the last few months?"

"Er, yes, 'months.' Sure, sure."

"Don't expect me to feel bad for you. Thanks to your bi energy, you've got twice the dating pool to draw on than I do. And technically I'm off the market."

"Technically" was dead right. Sidney's grifter spouse had wedded and bedded her, then promptly went on the run. But as the lady herself said, one disaster at a time.

They had fallen into old habits the way people slid into old jeans: they didn't have to think about it. So they'd left the precinct, Amanda on her bike and Sidney in her minivan, went right for Muddy Waters, ordered their respective meals, and took them to Prescott's Freedom Park. Though the thought of sucking down deep-fried cheese curds at 11:00 a.m. left Sidney feeling somewhat unwell, it was, as Amanda pointed out, lunchtime somewhere.

"Should we get her a lawyer? Or a CAT scan?" Amanda had temporarily abandoned her curds and was poking through the onion rings. The Muddy did 'em right—thin slices of ripe, battered sweet onions flash fried in boiling vegetable oil, then fished out, sprinkled with sea salt, and served smoking hot. Teeny-tiny mouth blisterers: the calling card of the perfect onion ring. "The only lawyer I know is the one who handled her parents' will after her dad was killed. I don't even know if she's still practicing."

"I'm not sure. This is happening irritatingly fast. Isn't that the way it is? Quiet winter, dull spring, a snooze of a Met Gala, and now we can watch Fourth of July fireworks while our friend is neck-deep in a murder investigation." Sidney took a bite, chewed, and then: "CAT scan?"

"Murdering someone you've never met sounds a smidge unhinged, Sidney."

"Obviously, they've got the wrong person."

"Yep, yep, sure. Cass would never *ever* be moved to a killing rage for any reason. And she definitely doesn't have a documented history of assault. Or triggers. Or a criminal record."

Sidney dug into the Muddy Waters salad: everything in the fridge thrown in a bowl and topped with grilled chicken and house-made ranch. And she took a swig of ginger beer. Not sickeningly sweet ginger ale. *Beer.* "What's your point? That she killed a guy she never met?"

"I have two points. One, I don't think she killed Franklin Donahue, whoever that is. Two, an accused murderess is coming up behind you."

"You should narrow that down. This town is a haven for sociopaths." Sidney turned in time to see their lanky erstwhile pal heading for their picnic table. "Hey. You should've waited until the sun was at your back. Way more impressive."

Cass checked her (typical) stride, then just stood there and fidgeted (atypical). "You guys left so quick, I wasn't sure . . ."

"What? That we wouldn't remember your weird penchant for dinner for breakfast? That's just silly." Amanda ate four more onion rings

("Ow, *ow*! Hot.") while simultaneously picking up a grease-spotted lunch bag and waving it at Cass.

"I didn't anticipate this," Sidney admitted.

Amanda gave her second-oldest friend a look. Why Sidney made a habit of downplaying her fine brain she would never understand. Bad enough she hid her intellect with profanity (when you call a defrocked priest a "limp-dick motherfucker," some people assume you're not bright). "Sure you did. You're the one who reminded me Cass likes extra onions and tomatoes with her beef tips, because she's a weirdo."

"Oh, look who's talking."

"Shush, Cass. And can I say it's hilarious that you still do the whole dinner-for-breakfast thing? The bar didn't have French onion soup this early, sorry. Oh. Almost forgot." Amanda handed over the last bag, which was Cassandra's first course: a piece of cheesecake the size of a brick.

"You're out?" Sidney was still goggling. "They just let you go?"

"No one 'let' me go. Well, maybe that guy." Cass jerked a thumb over her shoulder while taking a seat at the picnic table. Amanda craned to see around her and saw the yummy peace officer who should change his name before he got killed in "Baelor." "And he gave me a ride."

"He's back?" Amanda lowered her voice. "He was staring at me the whole time in the cop shop, and now he's here. Staring! Again!"

Sidney grimaced. "Stop, you're getting shrill. Which is a good trick when you're whispering."

"He's staring at me like he thinks I'm a criminal mastermind. Isn't that the cutest?"

"Oh, please."

"Don't roll your eyes. That's so mean, Sid. I could be a criminal mastermind," Amanda replied, stung.

"Or he thinks you're the weak link. Crack you to get the goods on all of us." Sidney paused. "If there were goods to get. Which there aren't." She let the silence stretch for a few seconds. "Right?"

"Or it could be because you're super cute," Cassandra pointed out. "That's a lie and you know it. All right, let's figure this out. Detective Sean Beane is either a caring, sensitive fella who understood he nabbed the wrong gal, or he's just really bad at his job," Amanda declared. *Or he's stalking me to get to Cassandra. Wouldn't be the first time.* Cass stood out in every room. Every. Single. Room. Even hungover. Even back when her scar was still livid stitches across her face. The rotten bitch didn't even try, and Amanda had lost count of the times some jerkoff chatted her up to get close to her Amazonian (former) pal.

"Or both," Sidney pointed out. "He can be both."

Amanda was already waving him over. "Hi, Detective Sean Beane who is going to change his name to Brian or Jeff or Agnes or Beverly and squash the curse once and for all." Then lower: "There aren't enough curds and onions to go around."

"What are you talking about? You've got two bags fu—"

"Shush, Cass!"

"Sorry," Beane said as he approached the table. "I'm not changing it. And it's way too early for onion rings and salad, but thanks anyway."

"Nobody offered you salad," Sidney muttered.

"Have it your way, Detective." Amanda again had the sensation she'd seen him before, which was no less puzzling than the first time it happened. "Welcome to Freedom Park. Want the tour? Here's the park. End of tour."

"My family used to live forty miles from here. I'm aware Freedom Park exists." He took them in with a half smile, detritus and all. "I hope I'm not interrupting your weird breakfast."

"Nope." Sidney speared more salad, then chewed same. "We were just talking about Virgil Abloh."

Amanda rolled her eyes. "No, we weren't."

Sidney ignored her rebuttal. "I've got nothing but respect for a trained architect who turned to fashion because he wanted to hang out with Kanye."

"Actually, I think he prefers to be called—"

"Don't care. Okay, fine, you got us; we weren't talking Abloh."

There was a short silence, broken by Amanda: "We were . . . um. We were reminiscing about the time Cass lost her virginity under that tree."

"Dammit, Amanda! How many times? It was *that* tree."

"Sorry, Cass. Got my *Pinus strobus* mixed up with my *Betula pendula*."

Cass crossed her arms and glared. "Not to mention we didn't even go all the way."

"Did too. We settled this while we were in high school, Cassandra. Getting and/or giving head counts as sex." Amanda looked up at the cop, who—was that a blush? Naw. Probably the heat. "It was nice of you to drop Cass off in the middle of your shift. If that's what you did. Are you side hustling as an Uber driver?"

"Naw. He wants to sign me as a client, thus the free ride."

"You need a lawyer, not a dick," Sidney pointed out.

"Not a dick," Amanda corrected. "Dedicated officer sworn to uphold the peace."

"Not really." He smiled at her, which was devastating in all the right ways. "You don't remember me, do you, Ms. Miller?"

So it wasn't my imagination. Amanda threw a triumphant glance at Sidney, who just took another bite of her salad and masticated, blank faced. "Of course I do. We met an hour ago."

"I meant before today. You don't, right?"

"Of course I do. I never forget a face," Amanda lied again.

"You called me Sarah for two months," Sidney reminded her.

"Sure, but I didn't forget your *face*." To the cop: "Yeah, I remember you. And as a test, why don't you tell me where I met you before? And I'll tell you if you're right."

Cass laughed. "Actually, we've all—" She cut herself off, and her smile fell away. Amanda guessed why, then turned around and had the (dubious) satisfaction of being right. *Behold, the world's first sentient skin tag. How'd he even know she was in town? Must be an awful, awful, awful coincidence.*

"The hell you doing here?" Shrill *and* nasal, the vocal calling card of the asshat. "You don't live here anymore."

"And as everyone knows, you're only allowed to exist in the town, city, or stretch of woods where your house, trailer, or shack is located." Amanda showed her teeth in what only an idiot would assume was a smile. "Good God, are you getting shorter?"

Jeff Manners spat, because the dichotomy of his name and his nature was beyond ironic, and focused his venom on Cass, who looked equal parts amused and wary. "You know your dad's still dead, right? And your mom got run out of town? So nobody here wants you around?"

Amanda snickered. "It's so cute that you think you speak for four thousand five hundred people."

Undaunted, Manners finished with: "So you should just get the fuck lost."

Amanda smirked. "Projecting again, Jeff?"

"I'm not a projector!" Jeff Manners: petite, terrible dancer, thinks bachelor's degrees are for pussies. Jeans out at the knees, denim vest, no shirt, motorcycle boots that made him two inches less petite. "I just wanted to know why you're still riding that baby bike."

It was a Triumph Street Twin, and he damned well knew it. Amanda popped a curd in her mouth. "My mistake; you're not projecting, you're sulking. Time to face up to the cold fact that we effortlessly outbid you. And not for the first time. So here's some more free and friendly advice: maybe upgrade from your sadass pussymobile before shitting on my ride?"

Detective Beane swallowed a laugh as Jeff flushed. Manners had been a bully since elementary school, likely because of his unfortunate domestic situation, too bad, so sad; he was in his late twenties now and responsible for his own actions. Thank God he hadn't yet reproduced.

The only good Manners was Sonny, who owned the bike shop on the edge of town.

The best part: Manners was a walking, talking, farting example of raging short man syndrome. The worst part: His fair skin and (thinning) carrot-colored hair meant that when he was angry, he resembled a denim-clad fire hydrant. Strangers occasionally mistook his tantrums for strokes.

He had one thing going for him—he was a dealer who didn't use. She admired the discipline. But still, dealer.

"I don't gotta take shit from you. You're so fucked up, you can't decide if you wanna fuck women or men."

"The bike you desperately want but will never have runs like a dream," Amanda continued, smiling, smiling. *I really think I could give him an aneurysm. A snark-based aneurysm. I must only use this power for good.* "Love that 900cc engine. A bargain, really. Too bad you missed out. Again."

The Triumph had only one real drawback: Larger riders felt cramped. Which wasn't a drawback if you were shorter than five feet five and weighed less than 150 pounds. It was small but looked badass, which was why Jeff wanted it so badly, and it was so light, it often didn't trigger stoplights.

"Are you all right?" Beane asked, perhaps prompted by how quickly Jeff's face was beginning to resemble a wet Red Delicious apple.

Mmmm . . . empathy is the new sexy.

Manners ignored him. "Nobody wants you here," he informed Cass. "You should just motor the fuck away."

"That's fine," Cass replied, unperturbed. "I don't want me here either."

"Your mom had the right idea," Manners said, adding, "she just didn't take it far enough."

Amanda leaned over and held Cass's arm so that the other woman wouldn't rise, grab one of the plastic utensils that came with their breakfast, and perform a tracheotomy on Jeff Manners, despite the fact that his breathing wasn't impeded in any way.

"Hey, Manners. D'you know what's sadder than peaking in high school?" Sidney was looking him over with an expression that suggested she didn't like what she saw. Not even a little. "Not peaking *ever*. Thanks for stopping by, now go suck somewhere else."

"You—you fu—you—you mother—fu—"

"Sir, do you require an ambulance?" Sean had his phone out in half a tick. So brave! Or at least quick. "It's possible you're succumbing to heat exhaustion."

"No, no," Amanda protested. "If anything, it's a snark aneurysm! And I get the credit!"

"Should we pull a betting pool together?" Cass asked. "I'll put ten on snark right now." And just like that, the three women were laughing together like there'd never been a crack in their trio.

"Stay the fuck out of my bro's shop," Manners commanded.

"Why the hell would I need to visit your brother's shop?" Cass asked with honest curiosity. "You know there's no point. The whole town knows."

"Get the fuck out of town." Manners seemed determined to stick to his script. Wise. It's not like he had the mental acuity to take any one of them on. "I see you again, and . . ." He snapped his pale, delicate hands into baby fists while Amanda giggled.

Then he spun on his tiny heel and marched back to his Honda NX650 Dominator, one of the worst bikes in the history of bikes. Shifting through the gearbox felt like shifting through gravel; the uncomfortable seat made long rides borderline torture; the teeny tank and soft suspension were an embarrassment. Couldn't top one hundred miles per hour, had a laughable forty-one miles per gallon, and needed servicing every other month. And good luck finding parts in a reasonable timeframe. *Ha. Ha. Ha!*

"What kind of a dumbass buys a bike just for the name?" Sidney speculated as they watched Manners scamper back to the parking lot.

"That kind," Cass replied, then giggled, which got Amanda going again. Cass was so big, her high-pitched Tweety Bird giggles always set Amanda off.

"He wasn't worried about me at all," Detective Beane observed, bemused. "I can't decide if that's irritating or emasculating."

"It can be both." *You didn't identify yourself as a cop either. Just watched. Him and us. Hmm.* "And did you notice, he not only didn't talk to Sid, he didn't even look at her? Possibly because she's repeatedly handed him his ass?"

"Pussy," Sidney muttered, and speared a cherry tomato. She looked up at Cass, pointing the tomato-laden fork at her. "What's the plan?"

"I—"

"Because now that Manners is outta here—"

"Don't say his name out loud!" Amanda yelped. "He'll reappear like Voldemort. Or Chrestomanci."

"   we need to get back to the important stuff."

"We do?"

"Yes, Cassandra," Sidney replied with unusual patience. "And you should definitely have a fucking plan."

Cass tried again. "Well—"

"What with the whole arrest thing."

"I wasn't—"

"And the whole murder thing," Amanda added. "Not that we think you did it." *Most likely. Or at least not without good reason.*

Cass reminded her of her grandpa's old coffee pot: Worked fine, though it took forever to get hot, and if you weren't careful, it would suddenly start spitting hot liquid everywhere. You took it for granted all the times it *didn't* make a big mess, so on the rare occasion it went up, the chaos was considerable, and it was like you were seeing it for the first time. *That's a reasonable metaphor, right?*

Eh. Needs work.

"Can we even talk about this in front of . . ." Sidney jerked her head in Sean's direction.

"Don't mind me," he replied, smiling.

"Let's go back to my Hole," Amanda suggested, then nearly giggled again at how the cop's eyebrows arched so high they looked like they were trying to crawl off his forehead.

"Oh, Amanda." Cass looked at her with warm affection, and for half a second, it was like the last five years had been an awful fever dream. The kind that makes you scared to go to sleep, because what if you wound up back in the nightmare? "Still?"

"I'll never, ever get tired of it," she declared. Then, to Sean: "You can come, too, but the second you hear something incriminating, you have to leave."

"Done," he replied at once.

"Be it on your head. Okay, everybody, my Hole is nigh!"

"Jesus Christ," Sidney muttered, but didn't turn her face away quickly enough, and the others saw the smile.

CHAPTER SIX

The Hobbit Hole was perched on downtown's eastern edge in an incongruously bright-blue Victorian home a few blocks from Prescott Beach. Like most Victorians, it looked like a dollhouse made real, with turrets to spare and stick work galore.

Amanda, who'd lived in trailer parks and Air Force housing until she was seventeen, always had the niggling feeling that the place wasn't really hers. The treacherous part of her brain would whisper that she was an impostor, and the cops would one day be waiting for her. "Sorry, this isn't really your life. Come along quietly, squatter."

And she'd comply. Because she'd know they were right.

She grinned every time she saw the place. The bright-blue exterior, the dark wood interior. The location—between one of the town's six liquor stores and a tattoo parlor—made it look like a giant had swept up the building from a country lane in 1862 and plunked it down as soon as they saw an empty spot, and who cared if the fit was perfect?

Amanda parked her bike in the alley and stared at the wall, unseeing.

Remember when you had "No parking except for the Bobber, the Hardtail, and the Tuck" back here, and people actually obeyed the signage?

No, I don't, that was years ago, ancient history. You know you don't get overtime, right, irritating inner voice?

She looped around and got through the door first. *Ha, losers, too slow! I win again!* Though it was possible the others had no idea they were in a race.

Dave Conner looked up as the bronze frog croaked her entrance. She could've come in through the back, but there was no frog in the back. *Is a door even a door unless a frog ribbits when it opens?*

"Hey, Amanda." Dave flipped the magazine closed, and they both pretended he hadn't been skimming *Catster*. "How'd it go with your friend?"

"Ask her, she's eight feet behind me. Also the cops. A cop . . . Did Edward Gorey call?"

Dave squinted at her through his reading glasses. He maintained he was too young for them (she pegged his age at early thirties), so by unspoken agreement, she never mentioned them. "Gorey's been dead for decades, so . . . no."

"Dammit."

Sidney stiff-armed the door open and marched in and, as she often did, pretended they were in the middle of a conversation. "We weren't racing, you lunatic."

"Loser talk." Amanda sucked in a greedy breath through her nose: books, coffee, and that smoky-woody smell of old buildings. She loved her Kindle—who wouldn't love six hundred books on a tablet that could fit inside a purse?—but some things they were no good for. The Hobbit Hole had been her singular goal since she was old enough to lust after books, and she needed the store if for no other reason than to feed her bibliosmia. "That's all I'm hearing."

The detective was on Sidney's heels; Cass was on his. *Oof, he's even cuter here than he was in the park. Is it the lighting? Or does his proximity to my lair make him somehow hotter? Do I just need to get laid? It's been a few months.*

Well. Sixteen. No. Twenty-six. Wait, thirty? There was snow on the ground but was that last winter or the winter before last winter?

To distract herself from Cop Cutie and her sadass sex life, Amanda pointed at Cass. "Buckle up, Dave, she comes bearing the calamities of the Greeks."

From Cass: "I'm sorry?"

"What? Don't pretend you didn't know what the pope said about his niece." In the short silence, she added, "Catherine de' Medici? Madame Serpent? No? Read more. And not just *Cosmo* and *RoadRUNNER*."

"Or you could give us a little more context instead of blarping out something about a pope and his niece," Dave replied, because he was a fiend. "Which pope? Which niece?"

"Read. More. All of you."

"To what end, you ridiculous bim?" Sidney was pouring herself a cup of coffee from the old-fashioned pot (Amanda's Hole was a Keurig-free zone) keeping warm in the corner behind the register. "You're the best read person I ever met, and you're so . . ."

"Carefree? Stuffed to the brim with joie de vivre? Freethinking? Wise ever so beyond my years? Don't hesitate, Sid; give me all the compliments."

Sidney heavily creamed and sugared the brew so that it was closer to a dessert than a breakfast beverage. ". . . immature."

Amanda laughed. "You're just saying that because I order anything with the word 'muff' in it."

"You might even be the smartest person I know," Sidney went on in a tone that was hilariously void of praise. When Sid listed people's virtues, she tended to sound irritated. "But yeah. The 'muff' thing is weird. I didn't even know what a muffuletta was until you ordered one." To Cass: "It's just a sandwich! And d'you know there are mints called Muff Divers? Guess how many packs Amanda has?"

Beane chuckled. "So you're a foodie?"

Sid jumped in before she could answer. "No. Foodies are irritating as shit, but they at least have taste. A discerning, um, whatever the fuck you call it . . . palate. Amanda will eat *anything*."

Amanda let out an affronted gasp. "That's a lie!"

CHAPTER SEVEN

A PARTIAL LIST OF THINGS AMANDA MILLER HAS PUT IN
HER MOUTH
    Savory oatmeal
    Jellied moose nose
    Oreos
    Pierogi
    Gazpacho
    Deep-fried Snickers
    Deep-fried butter
    Mock crab
    Actual crab
    Oysters
    Rocky Mountain oysters
    Canned bread
    Dental floss
    Tums
    Everything McDonald's has ever served
    Ditto KFC
    And Dairy Queen
    Popcorn
    Lutefisk

Allllllll the sushi
Except fugu
Leeks
Beets
Neeps
A paperclip
Thread
Pez
Peas

CHAPTER EIGHT

When in doubt, double down. "I have a discerning palate! Super-*duper* discerning."

Dave, meanwhile, had ignored Amanda's protests and extended a hand toward Cass. The tall, lean, suntanned thirtysomething man started his own construction company two years ago, and Amanda figured he must do wonderful work because he was getting contracts from places well beyond Prescott. He could stay in the business office all day, but he wasn't afraid to pitch in with the newbies. The palm of his hand was like leather, and he had fists like bowling balls. "Hi, I'm Amanda's favorite customer."

"Aren't we all?" Sidney muttered.

"Nice to meet you," Cass replied.

"I think you must've moved away before I got here." *Moved away, ran away, fled the consequences of her inactions. However you want to describe it.* "I'm Dave."

"Cass Rivers."

"Yeah, I know." Wait. Was that a blush on the construction guy's face? Dave was eyeballing Cass like she was a lasagna sundae. "You're, um, gonna be in the news again, prob'ly."

"Great. Because it was so much fun last time." Excruciating seconds ticked by until Cassandra added, "Yeah, I moved before you set up shop here, but I hear good things about your work."

Amanda doubted that very much. Cass had a longtime habit of lying to strangers to make them feel included, a result of her disastrous home life. *Please don't let Sidney call her out for it just now . . .*

"But not *too* far away." This out of nowhere from Detective Sean "I'll Get Around to a Name-Change Eventually" Beane, who was flipping through *Roald Dahl's Revolting Recipes*.

Amanda rounded on him. "Sorry, what?"

Sidney's antennae went up too. "You wanna elaborate?"

"You didn't move *too* far away," he said again. To (*ulp*) Cassandra. "You couldn't. Because of your mother."

"Leave my mother out of this, please," Cass replied very, very calmly.

Amanda wasn't aware she'd taken a step forward and to the right until she bumped hips with Sidney, who had also moved to step in front of Cass. So silly, the habits of childhood. Cass rarely needed protecting and had gotten into and out of ridiculous amounts of trouble without their help.

This would be a good time to make sure all the fire extinguishers work.

"Because your mother, she's part of it," the guy who couldn't read the room continued. "Right?"

"She's not a part of *this*," Cass clarified, still calm, but her knuckles were dead white as she clutched a copy of *Don't Make Me Pull Over!*

"I think you're wrong," Beane went on quietly. "I think the three of you know more about what's happening right now than you'll say, despite claiming not to know the murder victim—"

"We aren't *claiming* we don't know him, we *actually* don't know him," Amanda replied. She eyed Cass and Sidney, both of whom looked as puzzled as she felt. "None of us do."

"—and I also think what's going on now—"

47

"What *is* going on now?" Sidney put in sharply. "Specifically?"

"—has something to do with what happened five years ago."

There was a short, difficult silence. "Well, you're wrong," Amanda finally said, thankful that Sidney was now a few feet away from the hot coffee. "Entirely wrong."

It doesn't have something to do with what happened five years ago, you gorgeous dummy; it has everything to do with what happened five years ago.

"Speaking of my mother," Cass said, cupping her elbows and hunching over a bit like she had a cramp that wouldn't quit. "I need to get going."

Detective Beane held up his hands like he was being arrested. "If I overstepped—"

"You did."

"—I'm sorry."

"No." Sidney fixed him with the Glare. To his credit, he didn't burst into flames. "You aren't. In fact, I'm betting you got what you came for." To Cass: "Want some company?"

"Huh?" Cass looked thoroughly taken aback and straightened at once, Amanda was pleased to see. *Begone, phantom cramp!* "Sure, you can—I mean, I didn't think you'd—sure. Sure, you could—I'd love some company. That'd be . . . great. Very good and great."

"Well, I've had warmer invitations," Sidney sighed, scooping her keys up and shaking them at Cass. Sidney often did that, treated people like amiable dogs ("Wanna go for a ride? Huh? Do ya?" <Shakes keys> "We'll go to the parrrrrk . . .").

Because she couldn't resist, Amanda added, "Technically, that wasn't an invitation." But it was nice all the same. Sidney didn't want Cass dependent on a ride from Beane, and who could blame her after he dropped the mom bomb?

"Technically, you're a dumbass. A well-read dumbass." But she softened the snark with a smirk, slapped Cass's back—

"Ooooof. Careful. Sunburn."

—and began steering her toward the door.

"I should probably be going, t—"

"Not a chance, Beane." Amanda stepped in front of him like she had a prayer of stopping him if he wanted to vamoose. She *could* stop him, if so inclined. Slow him down, at least. But she had no time for the fallout from felony assault. "I have questions."

"Uh-oh." From Cass, still being steered. She had the grace to look alarmed on Detective Beane's behalf. "In for it now."

"May God have mercy on your soul, you poor bastard." As a departing line, it was pretty great. Trust Sid to cleave through the nonsense. Then she ruined it: "And why the hell is your back sunburned, you Nordic bitch? You should be bathing in SPF goop every morning of every day. Are you *trying* to get skin cancer? Jesus Christ. The two of you are killing me with stress, and it's awful."

Thankfully, the door closed on Cassandra's rebuttal. Beane, meanwhile, looked wary and amused at the same time. The minute the frog croaks quit, Amanda was all over him. Figuratively.

"All right, 'Detective' Beane."

"Huh. I could actually hear the quotes around 'Detective.'"

"Who are you and what are you up to?"

"Who are *you*? Who am I?" Again with the disarming grin, *God*, the man's ridiculous good looks were distracting. Why couldn't he have a scar? Or terrible teeth? Dirty, sagging, run-down picket fence teeth? "Who is anyone, really?"

"Knock it off, Beane. You're not the Sphinx, and I'm not looking for riddles."

"Okay. Now that we've established I'm not the Great Sphinx of Giza, what do you want from me?"

Okay, points for knowing the location of the Sphinx. But don't tell him that.

She stepped in close and restrained herself from jabbing a finger into his chest. He smelled like sunshine and cotton and . . . God *damn*, she needed to stay focused. "Show me your badge."

The faux cop pulled out his wallet, flipped it open, and handed it over.

"This is a library card."

"Oh. Right." He poked through it, handed it back. "Here."

"This is a Cold Stone Creamery rewards card." *I didn't ask to see his ID or his badge. Why would I? He was in the middle of the police station!*

"Careful, that's precious to me. Two more scoops and I get a BOGO coupon."

She tore it in half, ignoring his yelp. "That's for being a disingenuous stooge."

"I'm not *that* disingenuous." Beat. "What gave me away?"

"Besides your lack of righteous ID and badge?" Amanda flipped through his wallet. She approved of the library card and deplored the Apple card. About the Jersey Mike's card, she was neutral.

And . . . there it is. All the way in the back for some reason. Behind his driver's license. Who prioritized digging out a Cold Stone rewards card over digging out a badge, which provided a lot more cover than a Like It–size sundae with multiple mix-ins?

The weirdo in her sight line, that was who.

"I knew there was something off." *The second I saw Cass slurping soup, I thought there was something weird happening right in front of me. But I let myself get distracted by the reunion because God* damn *it!*

"Yeah, besides that." He hadn't stepped back, though they were nearly nose to nose. She liked/hated that. He leaned in a bit closer, and she wasn't sure why. Making a move? Trying to intimidate? Hard of hearing and needed to be closer? Slow-motion swoon? "What else gave me away?"

"I shouldn't tell you, but I get off on telling people how wrong they are. And like literally everyone in the country, I've watched cop shows and thus know all there is to know about being a cop."

"You're being sarcastic, but you'd be surprised how often people really do th—"

"Who are you and what are you up to? You used to be a Minneapolis cop, as evidenced by the badge you sort of but don't really keep hidden. You do some of the by-the-book stuff, but then you go off script. You're used to keeping your cool in the face of dangerous nonsense, and you don't seem to mind being interrupted."

"All of which indicates . . . ?"

"Like, you're used to being in control when dealing with excitable people who may or may not be interested in shooting you in the face."

"'A soft word turneth away wrath.'"

"Stop it. And you didn't arrest Cass."

"No one arrested her. She's a person of interest. She came in voluntarily. And so did I."

Amanda closed her eyes at the monumental stupidity of Cassandra "Goddamned" Rivers politely putting her head into the lion's mouth. *I didn't check social media because* ugh. *So when Sidney came in fussing about Cass being at the cop shop, I assumed she'd been arrested. Hell, Cass tried to tell me she wasn't going to be arraigned, but I cut her off. Stupid, stupid.*

"At the station, you said you were waiting on paperwork."

He didn't even blink. "That didn't mean Cassandra was under arrest."

"What. Is. Going. On?"

He shrugged. "That's what I'm here to figure out."

She waited, but maddeningly, he was done. "*Because* . . . ?"

"Uh . . . guys?"

"*Agh!*" Amanda turned away from "Detective" Beane. "Jesus, Dave. Wear a bell or something."

"I've been sitting five feet away this whole time."

"Not quietly enough," she snapped.

"Anyway, you don't need me to watch the register anymore, and something weird and intense is happening right in front of me, which is making me uncomfortable, so I'm gonna mosey."

She barely heard the frog croaking as Dave scuttled out. "Why are you here, Beane? Why are you interested in what's happening?"

He just stood there and looked at her. And after a long few seconds, answered: "Because of what happened five years ago. And because of my sister. And Cassandra's mother. And because of Operation Starfish—whoa."

She had slapped his wallet shut and shoved it at his chest. "Out." Taken off guard, he struggled not to drop it even as she had a hand flat on his chest and was propelling him, backward, to the door. He let her, thank God. "Right. *Now.*"

The frog announced his departure. Then she locked the door. Then she kicked the door. Then she went upstairs to suck down a pint of Häagen-Dazs Vanilla Swiss Almond and plot.

◆ ◆ ◆

Idiot.

You. Fucking. Idiot.

Sean looked at Amanda's store, at the blinds she'd hurriedly yanked down, the door she'd quickly locked. He could still feel the warm spot on his chest where she'd shoved him back, back, back onto the sidewalk. He was still trying to process how efficiently and ruthlessly she'd gotten rid of him. He'd run across bar bouncers who weren't as skilled at the drunk toss.

All because he couldn't keep his mouth shut.

Will you make a decision? Either tell her everything or withdraw and let events play out. But enough of the bullshit. Okay, champ?

Right. Because it was that easy. Because it wasn't complicated at all. Because everyone was who they appeared to be, all the time. And because none of them had anything to hide.

Shit.

CHAPTER NINE

He went home.

Of course he went home; where else was he going to go? Loitering in the alley and staring longingly at the door now locked against him, while a fine way to kill six hours, was a terrible plan. Getting drunk and subsequently dealing with an Uber, also not a great idea. Checking out a bookstore Amanda *didn't* own? Sacrilege. Grocery shopping?

Last one's the charm. He pulled off Highway 61 to hit Kowalski's, then loaded up on pancetta, cream, a chunk of good parm, garlic, butter, an Oreo pie crust sans filling, dark-brown sugar, a box of cavatappi, eggs, and whole milk.

Then he realized he'd bought ingredients to make two of Amanda's favorite dishes and nearly groaned. Last year, he'd made a conscious decision to pull back from following the remains of OpStar on social media. He'd told himself it was well past time; it had been years since OpStar had disbanded. It had been still more years since he'd seen Amanda. Time to move on. Not that there was anything to move on from. So even better! And maybe if he went through the motions, he'd eventually feel it.

Spoilers: not only did that plan fail, but he couldn't delete what he'd already read. He couldn't unremember she loved carbonara, butterscotch pudding, and every kind of Oreo. Just like he couldn't stop himself from keeping an eye on the three of them over the years, partly out of insatiable curiosity and partly so that if they ran into a jam, then there'd be a chance he could help them.

Fine. No biggie. It's not like he wouldn't use the groceries. Because he also loved carbonara and custard! Amanda Miller did not have a monopoly on adoring rich, cheesy pasta and creamy, buttery pudding! He would make her favorite things and devour them alone, and oh, hell, while he was being pathetic, he should sit in the dark too. Yes, perfect: gobbling pasta and chasing it with pudding. All he needed was Gollum's ratty loincloth and then he was set for a magical Saturday night.

Never mind. Time to focus. Now that he was in his neighborhood, it was crucial that he come to a full stop at the intersection, and not just because of the stop sign. He lived in the Schoolhouse Square town houses in Hastings, Minnesota; the place was newish (it went up about a decade ago) in a mostly quiet neighborhood. His town house was at the end of the block, just past the blind corner, which set up the illusion of having a much bigger yard than his neighbors'. The perk was offset by his actual neighbors, who had a way of coming out of—

WHAM!

"How 'bout *that*?"

—nowhere.

Sean didn't scream (this time). Benny Sol was still learning to master his inline skates; it had been a grueling thirteen weeks. "Check this, Sean!"

"Hi, Benny." The kid had come out from the blind corner and fetched up hard against Sean's car. "Not to be discouraging, but is it possible you're getting worse?"

"Anything's possible," Benny grunted. He was doing that beginner thing where he groped along the side of Sean's car while his skated feet scrabbled to find purchase on the pavement as he simultaneously struggled not to do involuntary splits while trying to remain upright. "Played hockey for three years; how is this so hard?"

"I tried to explain; it's not the—"

"Wait'll you see," Benny puffed. "Y'won't be—*waaggh*!" Sean could hear the squeaks of Benny's fingers clutching and grappling for purchase. "If I had any fingernails, I woulda just snapped 'em all off. Agggghh, my adductors!"

"Please stop and stand still, and let me help you," Sean begged. The boy's dogged will was awe inspiring and not a little terrifying. It was the same strength of focus that brought Hastings hockey to state finals and Benny to the University of Minnesota's premed program on a full ride. "Before this gets so much worse. It counts as skating by yourself if a full-grown man holds you up. I promise."

"Liar!"

"It's true. Ask your mom if you don't believe me."

"Pass. Now look!" Benny had somehow straightened to his full height of six feet six, then pushed away from Sean's car with tented fingers. For twenty-four glorious inches, Benny Sol was skating backward. Well. Rolling backward.

Annnnnnd then he wasn't.

Sean already had his seat belt off and his feet on the pavement, checked again for traffic, then hurried over and heaved Benny to his skates. "Y'know, a lot of guys your age would be trying out their graduation present."

"Driving's easy," the college freshman retorted, waving away the mere mention of his red Mazda. "This is a challenge. I've got knee and elbow pads; why don't they make butt pads? And don't tell me about subcutaneous fat. I know all about subcutaneous fat. Whee!" Sean had gotten him up and wheeled him to the cushion of grass between the sidewalk and the street. Benny pinwheeled his arms like every luckless cartoon character about to fall, then . . . fell. Face first. On grass this time, so Sean took it as a win.

"Well," Sean began, then stopped. The platitudes ("Keep at it!" and "You're getting the hang of it!" and "Gosh, you're getting better each day!") were all lies. "Uh."

"I'm not just out here mastering my skates along with my destiny," Benny said to the grass.

Might be time to scream again. "You mean there's more?"

Benny heaved himself over onto his back, sprawled in the grass like a scarecrow about to be crucified for the good of the harvest. He puffed shaggy brunette bangs out of his eyes; the kid always looked like he was overdue for a trim. He wasn't; his mop of shaggy brown waves just grew fast. "My mom wanted me to ask you to dinner."

"I'm not taking your aunt out again. Sorry, that came out wrong. And way too fast."

"No, it didn't," he replied cheerfully, dark eyes almost disappearing as he smiled wide. "No worries, Mom's off that plan. She still feels bad about Aunt Anne going through your wallet and then barfing on your wallet."

"Definitely the highlight of the Fourth of July picnic."

"On the upside, it was the last push my aunt needed to go to Hazelden. Not the DUI. Not her marriage imploding. Not shoplifting Kahlúa. Barfing on your Cold Stone Creamery card."

"I had to get a new one." Which Amanda destroyed. Was it possible the universe was telling him to stay the hell away from Cold Stone Creamery?

"That was her rock bottom, which . . . I don't get. I was sure the DUI was gonna do it, but . . ." Benny shrugged, still prone. "Whatever does the trick, right?"

"Glad I could help." Hazelden was a rehab center about two hours away in the middle of a Minnesota marsh. There weren't many activities to be found in the middle of a marshy slough, but sobriety was one of them. "Seriously, that's great news."

"She loves that place, man. Mom's already seeing glimpses of the girl she grew up with. Prebooze Anne. A creature of legend." Benny held out a long arm, and Sean began levering his gangly, amiable neighbor up off the grass. "You know they've got a sundae bar? I'm not in rehab, and I don't have access to a sundae bar."

"You have access to a car," Sean reminded him. "Which you drive very well. And which takes you anywhere you want to go. Including the sundae bar of your choice."

"Boring."

"So there's really no need for you to keep risking your—"

"Borrrrrrrrring."

"Tell your mom I'd love to come," he said, surrendering. "I'll bring dessert again."

"Yes, you will! Those little strawberry-basil hand pies were the shit. And I gotta tell you, man, I *dream* about your Rice Krispie bars. What'd you do to them?"

Sean had to smile. "Brown butter and homemade marshmallows."

Benny snapped his fingers with the air of a man remembering a word that had escaped him for a few hours. "Dammit, I knew that. Well, chef's kiss or whatever the hell people are doing now to express appreciation without bothering with vocab. Now watch out, I'm going to the end of the block."

"No!" Sean nearly sprinted back to his car. "Let me get inside first. I can't in good conscience watch you without calling first responders of some kind."

"Oh, please. You overreacted the last time."

"Stitches, Benny! On my watch. I thought your mom was going to shoot me in the face."

"She overreacted too. It's why I'm swaddled in so much protective gear I look like a Michelin Man."

"It's the only way you'll learn. And maybe not die during the learning."

"It wasn't my fault! I really thought you were going to catch me."

"From ten feet away, Benny?"

"So it's my fault you're slow?"

"Go drive your car!" he shouted, then put his in drive and went straight to the underground garage. He glanced at Benny in the rearview and was treated to the kid giving him a big smile and a pageant-winner double wave, both middle fingers extended.

He laughed so hard he nearly ran into the pillar. *If his mom catches him flipping all the birds, he'll need more than protective gear.*

"The pleasures of owning a home without the hassle of yard work!" Sean had to hand it to the board; the town home was as advertised. He'd never had to sweep a lone leaf or shovel a speck of snow. Part of that was thanks to Benny; his mom managed the complex. He might be shit on inline skates, but he could clear the sidewalk in about five minutes, a good trick when a squall dropped two feet of heart attack–inducing heavy snow.

The garage elevator deposited him at the back of his kitchen, where he dumped his bags on the island and grabbed the mail. It was the work of a minute to put away the groceries, and then he pored through the mail using all his senses, like a red fox hunting for voles. Though it was mostly catalogs and cooking mags (he paid his bills online), he once hadn't noticed an invitation to his niece's birthday party until the day of. His sister's irritation wasn't as devastating as his niece's sweet understanding when he showed up four hours late: "It's okay; Mommy said you were busy catching bad guys!"

Not really.

Not since that summer.

Maybe never again.

He shook off the grim thought and, having ascertained there were no sibling-inspired time bombs lurking behind the Duluth Trading Company catalog, grabbed a Coke and wandered into his living room. As with most of the town house, it was all wooden floors and throw rugs. The fireplace worked, but as often as he used it (twice since signing the mortgage six years ago), it might as well have been purely decorative. He'd never fucked in front of the fireplace; he'd never even snuggled in proximity to the fireplace. He'd had three women in his home in the last couple of years, and only one of them had made it to his bed. And she had been a one-night stand, which ended when the lady in question wolfed down both their breakfasts, then bounded out the door while bidding him a tender farewell ("Bye, Sam!") on her way back to her life.

They were lovely women, and he felt lucky to have been in their company, however briefly. But they shared the same flaw. They weren't Amanda.

It's not even like I want her specifically, he told himself. But her qualities were important, and the lack thereof would always be a deal-breaker for him. He wanted a partner as brave as they were smart, who wouldn't ignore an injustice, who would risk their personal safety to help someone.

Then you should try going out with cops.

He pondered the irony of wanting a risk-taking partner while knowing he'd worry himself into an aneurysm whenever she was in danger. He'd been sorry to see OpStar disband, but a small part of him had also been relieved. No more worrying that a disgruntled abusive spouse would empty a shotgun at the three of them. Or track them down one by one when they were vulnerable.

Not just vulnerable. Cornerable. Easy prey.

His sister and niece were safe. OpStar, while fractured, was safe. Cassandra had left town. Amanda and Sidney would carry on. He had told himself to follow their examples and put it all behind him.

Except he hadn't. And the reason was right in front of him: the second bedroom, which contained the time-honored tradition of the obsession board. Or, in his case, wall. On said wall was every clipping about OpStar, a few maps, some mug shots, articles about Cassandra's mother (not so many now, but back in the day there'd been dozens), et cetera. After a year of not setting foot in the office of obsession except to vacuum, he'd updated it yesterday with the clipping of Franklin Donahue's murder.

And then he'd met them on his own, without anyone in crisis.

So much for putting all of it behind him, or even part of it. Who was he kidding? He wanted them all safe—the least he could do for his sister. He couldn't bind them in Bubble Wrap for any number of reasons, but if Cassandra was innocent, he wanted to help. If she wasn't, he . . . didn't know what he wanted.

Better hope she didn't do it, then.

Yep. But regardless of who did it, Sean couldn't allow Donahue's murder to be the thing that came lurching out of OpStar's past like a fairy-tale giant to swallow them whole.

Have you been in a holding pattern all this time? For this very reason?

No idea. Also, moot. His focus now: figuring out a plan to help them, whether they wanted it or not.

CHAPTER TEN

Sidney's first thought each time she visited Minnesota DOC offender #266782 was to marvel at how Iris Rivers wasn't aging. At all. The whole family was like that; Cass occasionally got carded at movie theaters. Or at least, five years ago she had.

All that to say the Rivers's genes were top notch. From a physical standpoint, if nothing else.

"So fucking aggravating," Sidney said by way of greeting.

"Only my prison hairdresser knows for sure," Iris replied, patting her silver-streaked brown hair, which, it had to be said, was impeccably cut. Iris Rivers: convicted felon, Capricorn, regular contributor to the *Prison Mirror*. "Hi, sweetie! And you've brought Sidney." She smiled at both of them as they took seats across from her. "Which one of you lost a bet?"

MCF-Stillwater was, according to their website, a "level 4 close-security facility." The place housed about eight hundred offenders and was a half hour motorcycle ride from Prescott. Sidney and Amanda had visited semiregularly with Cassandra when they were teenagers, and they continued long after Cass's departure. They didn't coordinate. There wasn't a schedule. Every couple of months since Cass had left them, Sidney would go see Iris, mostly to make sure she was all right but also to do the casual *So, heard from Cassandra lately?* follow-up. Amanda did the same (though she professed not to give a ripe shit what Cassandra was up to) whenever she ran across new reading material Iris might like.

Visiting an offender wasn't like in the movies. There wasn't plexi-glass between them; the visitor and their offender of choice weren't yakking into a phone. They weren't searched; they weren't hassled by corrupt, brutal guards; they just had to show ID. Iris Rivers, displaying years of docility before and after her crimes, wasn't considered danger-ous enough to relegate her few visitors to a separate, safer visiting room.

So Cass and Sidney got to wait in a room that looked very like a bus station, complete with stubborn vending machines and fantastically uncomfortable plastic chairs with mint-green seats. And Iris was thrilled to see both of them, which meant Sidney had to endure an embrace. Hugs, unfortunately, were allowed. Maybe kisses too. Nightmare.

"Nobody lost a bet," Cass replied, squeezing her mom so hard the older woman's feet dangled four inches above the tile. "I needed a ride and Sid obliged."

"Just like that?"

"Well, I *am* awesome," Sidney deadpanned. "How you been, Iris?"

"Well enough, dear. And it's so nice to see a familiar face."

"What, instead of strange faces?" Sidney joked.

Iris didn't smile. "Yes, exactly so, Sidney."

Cassandra cleared her throat. "You look great, Mom."

"Aggravatingly great, according to Sidney."

"I said what I said."

"Are you okay in here?" Cass asked, looking around the large room. To the staff's credit, it could have been a conference room in an office building, except for the guards and warning signs. "Anybody giving you shit? Any gang wars we should be worried about?"

"For shame, Cassandra. They aren't gangs. They are 'security threat' groups. Just like this isn't really a prison. And I, not a prisoner." Iris leaned forward a bit. "I don't even have to look at Sidney; I can sense her rolling her eyes from here."

"Everyone in this facility can sense her eye-rolling."

Iris Rivers looked like a smaller, grayer Cassandra, especially when she smirked. She was wearing the summer uniform of the general female inmate, a navy-blue shirt and pants that looked much like scrubs. Iris had joked that the first year was the worst, as she'd had to endure the blaze-orange version.

"It's remarkable how relaxing the place can be once you settle in. My worries are few. No taxes, no rent, no grocery shopping, no cooking, no great big house to try and keep clean, no worrying about whatever the new black is."

No doors, no unbarred windows, no say in ninety-five percent of your daily routine . . . yeah, sounds like a dream.

Well, good for Iris for seeing the cafeteria glass as half full. She'd always been able to do that. The one time she couldn't . . . well. That was why she was here, and would be for years. It would have been longer if she hadn't spent a lifetime presenting as politely nonconfrontational. Turn the Other Cheek should've been tattooed on the woman's shoulder blades.

For all I know, it is.

Naw. No way. Iris was not a fan of body adornment. She didn't even have pierced ears.

Iris beamed at Cassandra, then looked at the table, then back up at Cass. Her smile faded when Cassandra sighed. "Mom, the only thing more irritating than your inability to look at my scar is pretending I don't have one."

Oh, shit. Yes, Iris had a tendency to do that. Still. Sidney held out hope that someday Iris would drop the habit, then reproached herself for major naivete. Yeah, it had been years since the, um, inciting incident, since euphemisms were all the rage this year. But Iris's crime was essentially on her kid's face, and always would be.

"I apologize," Iris said with simple dignity as Cass started to unconsciously rub her scar, caught herself, and let her hand drop to her lap.

"It's fine, Mom."

Iris leaned forward and tapped the back of Sidney's hand. "I haven't seen you since New Year's. How are your folks?"

Sidney ignored Cassandra's arched eyebrows. "Good, they send their love. Or they will when I tell them I saw you. Mom's selling the salon, and Dad wants to buy an RV and inflict himself on unsuspecting state parks."

Iris ignored the information to focus on her kid. "Cassandra, dear, you look surprised."

"I, um. Didn't know Sidney was still visiting you on her own. Is all."

It's not like it was a secret. You could've come by anytime and asked. Or called. Or texted. But naw. "Not always on my own. Amanda comes, sometimes. She likes bringing your mom books that skate up to the line of contraband without actually scooting over it. And she likes breaking her own magazine rule, so she also drops off *Marie Claire* and *ELLE*."

"She does, yes!" Iris clasped her hands together. "Tell her I loved *A Modern Guide for the Perplexed*. And I'm halfway through *Driving Bitch: A History of Female Motorcycle Riders*. Fascinating history. I fancied myself somewhat knowledgeable on the subject once I realized Cassandra had her heart set on a motorcycle, but there was quite a lot more to learn. And the women profiled were fascinating . . ."

She'll want to talk about Robinson or Stringfield or Halterman, Sidney guessed.

"D'you know, I'm just now reading about the founder of the Motor Maids? Dot Robinson? Fascinating woman."

Cass opened her mouth, but Iris rushed ahead. "The first to win an AMA national competition. Twice! And she spent decades empowering women to ride, because it fit nicely with her agenda: to prove you could be an award-winning biker who held your own with the big boys, without being a man-hater."

"We know, Mom. She—"

"She'd ride through mud and muck with the big boys, then clean up and put on lipstick and a pillbox hat—can't you just picture it?—and come down to the bar for some elegant martinis, just as ladylike as you please. It confounded the men." Iris smirked. "Which was the frosting on the cupcake."

"Yeah, Mom, we—"

"And a great deal of her fine accomplishments can be laid at the feet of her husband," Iris added, then shook her head. "No, that's not right. I expressed myself poorly. Not the credit for her actions, of course. Those are hers alone. But her spouse was extraordinarily supportive of her work. That makes a difference anytime, but especially back in the thirties and forties. He must have been quite extraordinary too."

Sidney and Cass knew all about Mr. and Mrs. Robinson. Thanks to Amanda, they knew about Robinson and Halterman and Stringfield and Dautheville and Wallach. Cass had dressed up as Sally Halterman for Halloween three years in a row, for God's sake.

The moment Amanda realized that her lifelong goal of owning her Hobbit Hole aligned with Cassandra's goal of owning a bike, she made sure the three of them knew all about the pioneers.

"Given your silence and polite expressions, you two knew all about Dot Robinson," Iris observed, because she was a shrewd bitch. "And possibly her supportive husband. What a pity we weren't all so fortunate in our spouses."

Ouch. Upside: it took Iris five whole minutes to bring him up. New record.

"I'm glad you're loving the books." Cass cleared her throat and turned to Sidney. "It's nice that you guys visit my mom. I didn't know."

"Still fighting? You girls need to straighten this out for good or ill," she ordered.

"What's the 'for ill' part?"

Iris ignored Sidney's relevant question. "At once. Five years is long enough."

Not quite five. After the mess imploded all over their lives, Cass indulged in a three-week bender, spent another three weeks detoxing, spent the summer moping, then abruptly sold her bike to Sonny Manners and fell off the world.

Four years, ten months, two weeks.

"We're working on it," Cass lied.

"Very good. So then, what's new with you two?"

"Not much," Cass lied again.

"I see." Iris's perfectly penciled eyebrows lifted as she leaned back in her chair. "It was kind of you both to take the trouble to come see me to tell me there's nothing of note going on in your lives at this particular time."

"Are you setting up a this-meeting-could-have-been-an-email joke?"

Cass chuckled as her mother threw up her (manicured!) hands. "Never mind, then. On your own heads be it."

Iris said things like that all the time, and Sidney should have been able to laugh it off, but this time, the words had weight. Like Mercutio's dying shriek: "A plague on both your houses." Much more impressive onstage or on screen than the written word. Which was probably blasphemy, but whatever. Like it was her fault the second she saw Harold Perrineau's turn as Mercutio she was ruined for any other Mercutio?

"So your folks are looking into retiring, Sidney? Good for them. *Gah*, I cannot believe I am so old my contemporaries are retiring." Iris leaned back, smiling. "I think it's lovely that they'll be driving around to parks together."

"Lovely, inflicting, retiring, giving up . . . tomato, potato."

"Sidney Derecho, you stop that. You have a lovely family. Well, most of them are lovely. Is your husband finally an ex? Stop doing the slashing motion across your throat, Cassandra."

"Might as well," Cassandra muttered. "Since you ignored it anyway."

"He's the thing of whom we do not speak," Sidney warned. "And no. He's not an ex in the same way he's not dead: that's a temporary condition."

"Did he truly use you to secure his Permanent Resident Card?"

"It was a green card—"

"Same thing, dear."

"—and yes. For which he will pay. And pay and pay and pay."

"He wanted you to come back to Canada with him," Iris volunteered for some reason. "I remember that. And I remember Amanda and Cassandra were so relieved when you didn't go."

"He *wanted* all kinds of things, some of which he got."

"Did he want an ass kicking on the way out the door?" Cassandra asked. "Because that's what he got."

"It's all water under the bridge he blew up. Change of subject, please."

"Very well. In nearly all ways, you are terribly fortunate to have such a lovely family. The blood relatives, at least. And your parents are perfect for each other."

"Iris, you've always tried to make it into this epic love story, and it wasn't." Small wonder, given that Iris and Cassandra's dad had suggested the opposite of an epic love story. "My folks banged; my mom got pregnant; my dad stuck around. They put up with each other. Soon they'll be trapped together in an RV. After that, God knows. The end."

Cass pretended to dab away a tear. Then said "Ow" when Sidney smacked her on the arm.

"You wait, Iris. My folks will pull Amanda's parents into their scheme too."

"They still take vacations together?" Iris asked. "How sweet."

"No, it's off-putting. It's just weird when your parents are friends with your friend's parents." Sidney threw up her hands. "I can't explain it. But there it is. Back me up, Cass."

"I think it's nice," the useless twit replied.

"It can be nice *and* weird," Sidney replied.

"I think it's also, the Millers love to travel," Cass continued. "What with Amanda's dad being in the Air Force and moving their family how many times in ten years? Amanda hated being new in town, but not those two. And since her dad just got out a couple of years ago, I think they miss the moving. So Sidney's folks started plotting these three- and four-week vacations and lured the Millers into their web."

"Weird," Sidney reiterated. "It's weird."

"You'd rather our parents all hated each other?"

"I'd rather all sorts of things."

"Ow!" Cass rubbed her arm. "You and the pinching. Cripes."

Iris's smile widened like she'd won the lottery. Not a big lottery. One of the little ones where you won a year's supply of Coke. "See? Just like old times."

Oh, sure. Cass is suddenly a person of interest in the death of someone she doesn't know, there's a cop sniffing around Amanda's Hole, Manners is on the warpath again, and we're visiting an incarcerated parent. Totally "old times."

"You just have a soft spot for Sid's folks, Mom."

"And why wouldn't I? During the . . . during all the difficulties, they opened their arms, home, and refrigerator to my girl. For years. A second family." Iris paused, then came out with it: "In many ways, a better family than the one she was—"

"Stuck with?" Cass interrupted with faux brightness.

"—born into."

Difficulties. *Way to ride that euphemism, Iris.*

"Are you still doing your transcripts from home, Sidney?"

"Yup. It's perfect. I set my own hours, transcribe clinic notes in the privacy of my own bathroom—"

Cass let out a surprised bark of laughter. "Good God, Sid."

"—and I don't have doctors in my face all day the way I would if I still had to work at the hospital. I save on gas and don't have to think about my wardrobe, and I never, ever have to sign a birthday card or cough up my hard-earned moolah for a cake every week."

"Well, that sounds just—"

"Elaine Benes had the right idea. When every day is someone's special day, nobody's day is special."

"Nice, Mom. Now Sid's gonna yell about *Seinfeld* for the next half hour."

"Don't be stupid. I can air my *Seinfeld* grievances in five minutes."

"How is everyone else? Is Amanda seeing anyone? Whatever happened to that gal she went out with last year? Mindy? Mandy?"

"Theresa," Sidney corrected. "Jeez, Iris, you weren't even close. And it was almost two years ago. Amanda broke up with her, big surprise. She goes through partners like cats through cat litter."

Amanda's problems with dating were exacerbated by her profession. She spent twenty hours a day in her building, so her partners du jour were almost always customers. Which made it awkward when she dumped them a few days/weeks/months later.

"Good for her for focusing on her business," Iris replied. "Is Amanda's family still doing the Christmas Meals on Wheels?"

"It's worse than that," Sidney grumped. "They somehow sucked me into their altruistic nonsense. Gotta give her credit, though; it was kind of fun."

"Sucked you?" Cass asked, delighted. "Doubt it. I'm betting Amanda casually invited you along—"

"Naw."

"—and you jumped at it—"

"Not fucking likely."

"—and loved it but were too proud to admit it."

"Nothing you've said makes any sense, and it all sounds wildly out of character."

For that, she was treated to Cass's helium giggles in stereo, since she'd inherited them from her mom. "Oh, yeah, Sidney? Did you do the Meals on Wheels things once?"

"Yes. Once. And maybe once or twice more; what are you, my biographer?"

"She could be," Iris said. "She's a wonderful writer."

"Both of you can go straight to hell," Sidney announced.

"Admit it! Admit you had fun being charitable all day, Christmas Day!"

"Nope. Taking it to my grave."

All right, all right. It had been fun. Not getting up at 6:30 a.m.—that could never, under any circumstance, be considered fun. But the assembly line had been kind of cool. Runners—usually kids not old enough to drive—would take the bamboo plates down the line, pausing in front of Turkey Guy, Mashed Potatoes Lady, Gravy Person, and Cranberry Gal, who sealed up the meal packages and gave them back to the runners, who would dash out to their parents' cars and fill the backseats. They had to watch their feet; in their zeal to deliver hot meals, if the runners were a little too slow after loading the meals, they risked run-over toes.

It wasn't just the "on Wheels" part either. About 150 people came for a sit-down Christmas dinner in the meeting house. Most of them were elderly, though the church invited anyone who was alone on Christmas.

And yeah. Maybe it got to her a little. All those elderly faces lighting up to see so much good food. But the best part was how they each got a wrapped present to take home. Cheap stuff—soaps, boxes of candy, mugs, games, slippers—but still.

And Amanda's family thought nothing of it. Their attitude was that it was weird if you *didn't* spend Christmas Day slinging cranberries. And the old folks, they appreciated it so much. They were always hugging and patting and even stroking Amanda's face. Sidney had come *this close* to a face stroking but managed to duck away in time. Luckily, her reflexes were better than those of any of the grateful geezers.

All that to say, yeah. It was fun. And yeah, she went back the next year. And the next. And maybe the next seven or eight years. She might even have donated a bunch of stuff for presents. But that was nobody's business, goddammit!

There was another half hour of chitchat, and to hear Cass tell it, her life was one mellow, stress-free day after the next. The pressure to profanely and repeatedly correct her was mounting, and Sidney was on her feet before she realized she had stood. "Welp, this has been a gas. And speaking of gas, I'm gonna fart pretty soon, so we should get going."

"You think I want to be in a van with your farts?"

"I think you have no choice, Cass," she replied. "Unless you want to hitchhike home." Wherever that was. Cass hadn't said, and Sidney was too proud to look it up or ask.

Cass got to her feet with a show of reluctance that didn't fool Sidney, or even Iris probably. The cold truth: Cass loved/hated her mother and enjoyed/dreaded these visits. She hugged Iris and said, "I'll see you next week, okay?"

"No need if you don't want to make the trip again so soon."

"It's half an hour, Mom. No biggie."

Iris held her younger doppelgänger at arm's length, scrutinizing Cassandra's face. "There now, see? No dropped gaze. My eyes remain on your face. And you'll always be beautiful." Then she leaned in and whispered something Sid couldn't hear. Whatever it was, it made Cass go bright red and stare at the floor, smiling.

"That's not her just being a mom obligated to compliment their offspring's face," Sidney said to break the silence. "Iris is seventy something and still looks great, so you will too."

"Fifty-three, dear. But thank you."

Sidney submitted to a last embrace, then coaxed another Snickers from the sad vending machine, and they headed out. The door was still hissing closed behind them when Cass turned to her and cleared her throat. "Thank you for visiting my mom. I, um, didn't know you did that." Pause. "So thank you."

"Don't be such a dumbass. I love your mother. She got a raw deal."

Cass smiled thinly. "Didn't we all?"

Well. Yeah.

CHAPTER ELEVEN

Operation Starfish, six years ago . . .

Cass gave her kickstand a boot, then came up behind Amanda, who'd just dismounted, and hugged her hard enough to pull her off her feet. "Stop it!" Amanda cried, because her worst fear was Cass finding out how hilarious she found the manhandling. Being friends with a gorgeous tactile giant was great good fun. "I'm not a maraca!"

Cass chuckled and plopped Amanda back on her feet, her heels hitting the sidewalk with a double thump. "Last time, you said you weren't a dog chew toy."

"And that stands as well!" Being tossed around by Cass wasn't just fun, and it wasn't just distracting; it made Amanda feel safe. Which was silly; she *was* safe. She was the rescuer, not the one who needed rescuing. And she suspected the reason their friendship had only gotten stronger since the day Jeff Manners made Sidney bleed was because they weren't just friends. Corny as it sounded, they were a sisterhood. And that relationship penetrated every facet of their lives, in all the best ways. Whether they were enduring a messy breakup, or giving Cassandra shelter after her mom went to prison, or trying not to be nervous about Starfishing, they were never, ever alone.

Such things, Amanda suspected, were a bit beyond Sidney. Or she didn't need to ponder the way Amanda did.

"Ha! Next time, Cass, just hold Amanda by the ankles and shake until her pockets are empty. I get the cash and you can keep the ring."

"The ring stays on my finger, and all my cash goes into my Hole, Sidney; you know that."

"I did know that," she admitted, and fidgeted, which was unusual. Sidney was the one who would usually grab Amanda's hands and demand she cease all unnecessary movement ("Argh, sit still, you're vibrating the whole seat, just watch the movie!").

"Right. You knew that. Okay." Amanda almost started fidgeting herself, then shook it off. She didn't have to ask. She knew Cass and Sid were thinking about all the things that could go wrong. But they who hesitate are lost, or whatever. "Now come on, both of you."

They were in front of the Schoolhouse Square town house block in Hastings, Minnesota, a small city on the Mississippi just across the river from Prescott. The new condos were all uniformly neat, with brick exteriors, white trim, and small porches big enough for two chairs or a medium-size grill.

Their client, Jen Johnson, came out hand in hand with a child who resembled her so closely that Amanda assumed she was a clone. What a time to be alive! "Hi, hi! We're almost ready."

Amanda knew that etiquette demanded a self-effacing reply ("No rush, take your time"), which, in this case, was a lie. Their first OpStar still haunted her: blood, fists, taunts, blustering, blood.

"We'll help you finish," Sidney said. As usual, she had driven her minivan, while Amanda and Cassandra rode their bikes.

"There's only two bags, and Emily has hers all ready. My new neighbor helped me pack everything up."

"Good." Sidney set the parking brake and jumped out.

"I guess his sister went through something like this?" Jen was continuing. "He left last night to go see her. He offered to move me himself when he gets back."

"That's fine. Looks like you won't need him. Since you're all set, we should get moving." Sid was already coming up the stairs to follow Jen back inside.

"He'll be surprised when he gets back, and I'm not here. But I didn't think my husband would do anything this—" Jen cut herself off, and Amanda realized the woman's nostrils were an angry pink, like she'd scrubbed her face too hard for too long. *Nosebleed. He got pissy about something and popped her in the face and then rushed off to work. Won't he be surprised when he gets back tonight?* Amanda had to make a real effort to keep the smirk off her face.

"C'mon, bags, bags!" Sidney was like a demented bellhop. "We should be out of here in not quite sixty seconds. Right? Right."

"Got it, we hear; tick-tock, Clarice." Cass bounded up the porch steps, greeted the child with an exuberant "Hello!" and then bent and scooped the child into her arms. She had her mother's blue eyes, glossy dark-brown hair, and epicanthal folds. "Ready to stay in the big blue house across the river?"

Emily slung an arm around Cassandra's neck like they were pals of old. "Blue's my favorite color."

"Mine too! Only not really, it's purple."

"Purple's nice," the child allowed. And then in one of those abrupt segues peculiar to children: "We have to go because Daddy broke his promise."

"That's okay. Your mom kept *her* word. And maybe your dad will come around."

"He loves us and will get help," she parroted. Through some alchemy Amanda never understood, every child in the world took to Cassandra without hesitation. And proximity to Cass increased their natural curiosity. Case in point: Emily reaching out and tracing Cassandra's scar with a small, chubby finger. "What happened to your face?"

"Emily May," Jen Johnson hissed, coming back out to the porch with Sidney. "Don't be rude."

"It's fine," Cassandra replied easily. "This?" She traced her scar up through the hairline and tapped her forehead for peculiar emphasis. "This is what happens when you're fishing and not paying attention."

Amanda nearly dropped the box of Emily's toys. *That's . . . an explanation, I guess. The way in which "There was a war and a bratty belle got married a lot and in the end promised to never give up and probably didn't but who knows?" sums up* Gone with the Wind.

Emily jerked her finger away. "Does it hurt?"

"Not anymore. How about this?" Cass stuffed the child's fist into her mouth. "*Dzzz izz hrrrt?*"

"No, ick!" Emily giggled and freed herself from Cassandra's maw. "Mom says it's time to go, and we're gonna sleep in the big blue house and then go stay with Grandma."

"That's a good plan."

"But we heard your motorcycles and thought it was scary people."

Amanda stifled a smile as she loaded the last bag into the van. *Go with that first impression, Emily May.* She didn't mind being seen as tough, even if only by a first grader. OpStar's reputation preceded them, but said reputation only pissed off the abusers, who pegged their rescues as unwelcome meddling.

"But it's just you," Emily finished. "And you're nice!"

"No, no. I'm the nice one," Sidney insisted. "Ask anyone! Well, maybe don't ask anyone."

◆ ◆ ◆

"Much better this time, don't you guys think?"

They were decompressing at Muddy Waters again, carrying over the habit from their adolescence. In high school, the three of them had dodged seventh hour for Muddy Burgers more than once. And why not? College wasn't in the cards for any of them. Sidney was heartily sick of classrooms and made a decent living as a telecommuting medical transcriptionist. Cass's entire focus was on OpStar, and Amanda would be damned before she'd use any of her cash stash for college. A business degree could come in handy, but if it meant putting off the acquisition of her Hole for four years—or even two—then it was a nonstarter. On the infrequent occasions they were caught ditching seventh-hour study hall, the school knew about Cassandra's situation and cut her loads of slack . . . and her accomplices too.

So the Muddy was their default decompression zone, which suited them. And to see Jen Johnson as they put Hastings in the rearview and crossed the river was to see a woman getting younger by the minute. Or at least less fretful. Amanda noted that Jen wasn't sporting any bruises or other signs of injury, but the young mother's relief at her and her child's escape was unmistakable. *Another fucko who's careful not to leave marks. Lovely.*

"She was perfect," Cassandra declared. "And her mom was great too. God *damn*, I love Starfishing."

"It's the ideal, right?" Sidney asked. The waitress swung by and dropped off Amanda's scrambled-egg platter, Sidney's breakfast charcuterie plate, and Cassandra's prime-rib sandwich with a side of last night's gravy. Cassandra loved everything about the Muddy except their refusal to make gravy for her at 8:00 a.m.

Cass looked up. "What's ideal?"

"Her whole situation. The shitheel that Jen married finally crossed whatever her line was; she reached out; she's got other family members backing her up; she just needs a place to stay where she feels safe while she finishes making her arrangements; enter us, exit all of us, and now they're safe."

"Thanks for the recap."

"Get bent, Amanda. That's how you saw it, right, Cass?"

"I didn't mind how the first time went." Cass grinned, clearly in the throes of violent nostalgia. "But, yeah, the Johnsons are the ideal. I don't think we should expect that every time, though."

"I don't even expect Cub Foods to keep my fried chicken hot. I'm sure as shit not expecting every OpStar outing to be perfect."

"It's insane that you have fried chicken for lunch almost every day and suffer no ill effects," Cass observed.

"Yeah, it's almost as off-putting as someone guzzling Mountain Dew at seven o'clock in the morning," Sidney scoffed. "With a gravy chaser."

"You're really onto something," Amanda told Cassandra in all seriousness. "You're really helping people."

"We, Amanda." Cass opened her sandwich to pile on the horseradish. "There's no OpStar without you and Sidney."

"Awww. So fuckin' sweet."

"She's being sincere," Amanda added, then let out a squeak as Sidney whipped a cold cut at her, too fast to duck.

"Don't translate for me, Amanda."

She peeled the slice of provolone off her forehead. "Noted."

"Yeah, sure. Until next time. You ever thought of being a teacher? What with all the lectures and how you can never stop yourself?"

"No." Truth. Amanda had only ever wanted her Hole; other career paths never entered her calculations. She hadn't spent years of her childhood fantasizing about one day being a teacher. It was always about re-creating the feelings of safety and continuity. It was about *owning* something, about making a place where she belonged, a place no one would question was hers. A place where she knew everyone and everything . . . or, at least, a place that would help her learn everything.

And not just for her . . . she envisioned the Hole as not just a place to buy books but OpStar's HQ. A place to hang out, to plot, to research. Free coffee and cocoa in the winter, spa water and lemonade in the summer. *Their own place.*

When she was being hauled around the country each time her father's Air Force orders changed, when she went to four schools in seven years, the only places that felt like home in all those years of blurry strangers were the local libraries and various secondhand bookstores.

"What about you?" Amanda asked. "What do you want to be when you grow up?"

"A shut-in." Sidney leaned back and smiled. "I'm not worried; it'll happen eventually. And we already grew up; we're drinking age and everything."

"Oooooh," Amanda teased. "And before we know it, we'll reach the pinnacle of utter adulthood and be allowed to rent a car."

"A cherished dream, and pass the ketchup."

"I will never understand that combo," Amanda commented as Sidney squirted ketchup on her scrambled eggs. "You don't even like ketchup."

"I don't like plain scrambled eggs either. But something about combining two things I hate turns it into something I love. Don't read into it, and don't you dare pontificate."

"I can't promise I won't do either of those things," Amanda admitted.

Cass waved at the waitress for more horseradish. "We've got Dr. Bimmerman to thank for the Johnson referral. I knew she'd be an asset."

"As long as she can help us without getting into trouble herself, I'm on board in every way," Amanda replied. While Bimmerman couldn't come to any of them and discuss a patient's medical history, she could recommend OpStar to patients she knew or suspected were being battered. "Are you visiting your mom this week? She'd love to hear about what you're up to." Cass made no reply. "Oh. Like that, huh?"

"You haven't told Iris about Starfishing? Why the fuck not?"

"Because it's *ours*. It's *our* thing that we started for our own reasons."

"Sure, sure." Amanda looked at Sidney for help, but the cowardly wretch just shrugged. "So, um, your mother's been locked up for a few years now. Maybe it's time to forgive her and let her know what you've been up to? Or maybe just one of those things, and you can . . . work your way up to the other?"

Cassandra simply sat as the silence got heavier.

"Or I could mind my own business."

"Just for a change of pace." Sidney smirked. "Just to see if you like it."

"One day, I will," Cassandra said. "Forgive her, I mean. And I like it when you mind my business, Amanda. It shows you care . . ."

"I hear a 'but' coming," Amanda warned.

". . . in a nosy and obtrusive way."

"Dammit, Cass!"

"All I know is, I'm not ready to do either of those things just now." Cass leaned back and crossed her long legs at the ankles. "And it's not like my mother's going anywhere."

"True dat," Sidney said, and dodged a clump of scrambled eggs.

"I warned you never to say that again," Amanda said. "It's dated, and you're too Midwestern to pull it off."

"Don't hate the playa, hate the game."

"You stop that right now, Sidney Derecho."

"For God's sake, Amanda," Cass said. "You might as well be flapping a red cape in her face. All you're missing is the double-dog dare. I'm gonna change the subject now because this is getting louder and even stupider. Are your folks still going to Tuscany together? Next spring, I think?"

Sidney nodded. "Burning their passports didn't work. The trip is still on, I'm sorry to say."

"Please tell me you're kidding about the passports."

Sidney ignored Amanda's horrified query. "It's so *weird* that your mom and dad and my mom and dad are still friends."

"By 'weird,' do you mean a natural occurrence? What with all their chauffeuring while we were still in school, they all got to know each other. Plus, Cass lived with you guys for a while once her mom went to prison."

"Don't remind me," Sidney grumped. "She kept stealing my toothpaste—"

"Sid! Borrowed. I borrowed your delicious Tom's of Maine because Crest is vile."

"—and I couldn't go a week without finding a long blue hair in something."

Cass grinned and ruffled her recently chopped and dyed hair, poison green this time. "You don't have to worry about that anymore."

"Yeah, no shit, but thanks for waiting years to take my advice. Anyway, our folks may have gotten to know each other when they were driving us around, but they haven't had to schlep any of us in years. Shouldn't they have outgrown each other by now?"

"Why?" Cass chased her last sweet potato fry with a gulp of Dew. "We haven't outgrown each other. Why should they?"

"True," Sidney said. "We're all just as immature and dim as the day we met. And speaking of dim, my folks want both of you to come to supper tonight."

"Yay! I haven't had any of your folks' cooking in forever."

"You had dinner with us last week, Cass, you gaping dumbass."

"Plus, watching your mom and dad cooking together is consistently entertaining. I'll never understand how they can get in each other's way and trip and stumble in that teeny kitchen while screaming and screaming at each other and then pop out of the kitchen with a gourmet meal. It's goddamned necromancy."

"Nobody understands. Don't think about it too long or you'll give yourself a headache. D'you know, people have been predicting their divorce for years? But they always make up, and I guess they love each other or whatever."

"'Or whatever,' Sidney?" Amanda teased.

"Pretty sure they decided to stay together just to spite the other person. There's a lot of 'get out' and 'no, *you* get out.' Plus, they hate paperwork. So I don't see a divorce happening."

"As long as they're not breaking each other's ribs or spraining each other's wrists, they're ahead of the game."

Amanda sighed. "And now I'm once again forced to point out that your bar for marital bliss is pathologically low."

"Only according to some." Cassandra closed her eyes and hummed. "I still dream about Sidney's dad's osso buco and her mom's hasselback sweet potatoes with that maple glaze that I would drink by the cup if I could."

"I'm not sure I can come tonight," Amanda said cautiously. "I'm looking at some commercial rentals."

"Again? Did a relative die and leave you a pot of money?" Cass asked. "Last we talked, you still had to save up at least another ten grand."

"I'm not ready to buy a place just now, but when that time comes, I don't want to waste time on guesswork or redundant research. I'll know what I want in terms of footage, location, access to parking, blah-blah. So I can't make it this time," she finished with real regret.

Sidney laughed. "Oysters. Paella. French silk pie."

"I'll reschedule."

CHAPTER TWELVE

Sidney: JFC I just sat across from Iris fucking Rivers and watched Cass lie to her face for HOURS mighty fuck I need a drink

Amanda: Who is this?

Sidney: KNOCK IT OFF!!!

Amanda: I haven't seen Iris in a couple months; is she still lovely?

Sidney: Yeah and JFC focus bc Cass didn't tell her anything!

Amanda: Did you think she would? "How's prison life, Mom? Also, I'm a person of interest in a murder investigation and our hometown still hates me and there's a cop sniffing up my backtrail but not to worry, how is your shiv collection coming along?"

Sidney: It's not a prison apparently. And they're not shivs they're contraband makeshift knives or whatever the fuck

Amanda: We can talk about your loathing of euphemisms if you like but that would be an entirely different conversation. Also, punctuation is a thing. Just saying.

Sidney: . . .

Amanda: Or we can stay on point: don't you think Iris has enough to worry about? I wouldn't have said anything, either.

Sidney: . . .

Sidney: . . .

Amanda: ???

Sidney: Ok fair point it was awkward AF tho

Amanda: It's always hilarious when YOU complain when someone makes things awkward.

Sidney: STFU.

Amanda: There it is. Listen we've got bigger problems. Detective Beane knows about OpStar.

Amanda: Sorry, I forgot the comma after "Listen."

Sidney: Jesus Christ!

Amanda: Don't rub it in. It's really hard to edit a text after the fact. Most of the time I can't be bothered. I resent your judgement, Sidney. I resent it heartily.

Sidney: FUCKIN SEAN BEAN KNOWS ABOUT OPERATIN STGARFISH WGAT THE FUCK??????

Amanda: . . .

Sidney: I'M NOT CORRECTING MY TYPO YOU RIDICULOUS TWAT

Amanda: Typos. Plural. And it's "Beane" with an extra "e." But don't fret.

Sidney: I AM FUCKING FRETTING AMANDA BE RESIGNED TO AN ASSLOAD OF FRETTING

Amanda: I fixed it so he has to come back to my Hole.

Sidney: Doomed we're fucking doomed

Amanda: I'll bring him upstairs and since he isn't handsome or anything I won't lose focus. I will find out what he knows, what he wants, and then we can figure out a plan.

Sidney: . . .

Amanda: Ok?

Sidney: . . .

Sidney: Since he isn't handsome????

Amanda: Fine, you got me, he IS handsome.

Sidney: We're fucking screwed. Your sexual dry spell is gonna doom us all. I'm coming over

Amanda: No, you are not. It's not time to gang up on him yet. What I need you to do is grab Cass and come over to the store tomorrow for lunch. I'll let you know what I found out and we can formulate a nifty plan. Also, please bring breakfast.

Sidney: I'm not a chauffeur or a chef and I don't do nifty. Taking her to the prison was a one-off because I felt sorry for her but I've gotten over that and how would I even know where that distant bitch lives?

Amanda: First, ouch. Second, you're still the worst liar in the history of liars. She was working from home even before the pandemic; it stands to reason she's still an independent contractor. So where did you drop her off? The bus station? No, a house or apartment. So you do, in fact, know where she lives.

Sidney: fuck

Amanda: Beane was right. What's happening NOW is because of what happened THEN. So the three of us have to fix it.

Sidney: We don't tho.

Sidney: Not really

Sidney: That whole you break it you buy it thing is overrated

Amanda: Tough nuts.

Sidney: Wait, what'd you do to make sure he comes back? Tell me you didn't fix the brakes on a cop car. You wanna room with Iris?

Amanda: He's not a cop. And I'd never be so drastic. I leave that to you.

Sidney: We're fucked. This is fucked. Everything's fucked.

Amanda: That's the spirit.

Sidney: Wait, what do y mean he's no a fucking cop now???????

Amanda: We'll get into it once you've calmed down. I gotta go—we'll catch up later.

Sidney: Why did you bury the fucking lede???? WHY DIDN'T YOU LEAD WITH THAT????

Sidney: Amanda???????

Sidney: Amanda???????

Sidney: fuck me 'til I cry.

CHAPTER THIRTEEN

When he knocked, Amanda didn't even pretend to *not* be lying in wait. Instead, she hurried down, let him in through the store entrance, then led him up the back stairs to her apartment.

"There!" she burst out when they were in her living room. "That's enough of the silent treatment."

He laughed, the jackass. "I thought the silent treatment would last longer than thirty seconds."

"Don't mansplain the silent treatment, you ridiculous fraud of a stooge. What have you got to say for yourself?"

He spread his hands

(Guy's got the long strong fingers of a professional violinist, oofta.)

and shrugged. "Er . . . that I haven't done anything wrong?"

"This is a bad beginning," she warned.

He smiled at her, which was kind of devastating. He couldn't be missing his front teeth or have trench mouth like a normal villain, oh, nooooo. He had to have a big perfect HMO grin. Like, Cheshire Cat perfect. It wasn't weird that she had a smidge of a crush on the Cheshire Cat when she was a kid, right? Right. Who wouldn't be into a chatty catty who disappeared yet left their smile behind?

"This isn't a beginning. Though I'm glad to be here; I wasn't sure you'd let me back into your store, never mind your home."

"No, *you* never mind my home." Then she contradicted herself: "This is the living room, kitchen's over there, bedroom's in the back." *Why the hell did I tell him where my bed is?* "And the toilet! Also in back."

"Thank you, I'll keep that in mind if I need to pee or nap."

"Grown men shouldn't say 'pee.'"

He ignored her demoralizing observation and strolled around the room. "Not a lot of books. Odd for someone who owns a bookstore."

"Where do you think I *keep* my books, faux detective Beane? I'm not going to reinvent the wheel up here."

"Snark is the new sexy."

"What?"

"This place is great," he replied absently. The stairs from the store led to what was mostly an open plan (save for the bed and bath in the back), complete with a reading nook in one of the turrets. The living area was filled with mismatched, comfortable furniture (Amanda prioritized comfort over looks just about every time), including the red velvet fainting couch in the left turret, which she'd practically stolen from a HOM Furniture we-lost-our-lease sale.

The nook also boasted a stack of magazines (*RoadRUNNER*, *Motorcycle Classics*, *InStyle*), books (*The Book Lover's Cookbook*, *Harley-Davidson Memories*, and *The Women's Guide to Motorcycling*, which Amanda was editing for fun), a soon-to-be-devoured bag of Chex Mix, and a view of Prescott Beach.

The dark wooden floors gleamed from irregular waxing; the walls were cream colored and studded with framed photos and demotivational posters ("True love is when two people lower their standards just the right amount"). There were plush throw rugs in jewel colors of deep red and blue, and a working fireplace, which she'd scrubbed like Cinderella, then used to store her candles.

"Look at all the windows," he marveled, eyeing her windowsill herb garden, which took up the opposite turret. She didn't have a green thumb—she could never muster the patience—but mint, basil, and parsley were so hardy that they could probably thrive on the bottom of a lake. "From the outside, it seems like it'd be dark up here."

As tense as she was, she had to smile to see he liked the building she loved best. "Okay, tour's over. Now, d'you want red wine or white, and you'd better say red."

"Whatever you're having is fine."

"I'm having a chocolate malt."

His face brightened, and at once, he looked young enough to be carded. "Really? That sounds great, I'd love one. You ever notice, malts are one of those things where you normally don't think about them, but when you see one, you want it?"

"Malts and popcorn and ballet flats, yep."

He followed her into the small galley kitchen, which wouldn't have suited Martha Stewart but was perfect for her. She loved *food*. Cooking, not so much. The stove, microwave, oven, and dishwasher were small and well used but in good repair. Most of her money was tied up downstairs in the store, which meant when things needed repair (and in an old house, when didn't they?), she was on deck. Thank God for YouTube videos.

She pulled out whole milk, Breyers chocolate ice cream, her homemade vanilla extract (once Iris Rivers had shown her how easy it was to make, she'd never looked back), and the malt powder. Her ancient blender sounded like a jet engine in distress, so conversation was impossible. It didn't seem to matter to Beane; he stood close, clearly approved of the caliber of ingredients, and watched everything while practically drooling. She kept catching him staring at her; then his gaze would skitter away, and he'd pretend he'd been admiring the cupboard or the hideous throw rug or her penguin salt and pepper shakers.

In three minutes, they were both struggling to suck thick shakes up into not-quite-wide-enough straws. *Mental note: pick up some of those fat metal straws Sidney's always babbling about. Except she mostly uses hers to poke things. And people.*

"God, this is wonderful. I love ice cream. Got a freezer full of the homemade stuff."

"You make ice cream?"

He nodded and sucked.

"That explains the Cold Stone Creamery fetish," she teased. "So how long did it take you to realize I hung on to your ID?"

"I'd tell you, but the answer is embarrassing."

"Detective," she snorted.

"Well, not anymore. Or at least, not on the force. Still a detective, though. I went private."

"I figured." Eventually. After missing a dozen clues. It irked her just to think about it. She pulled his driver's license out of her back pocket. "Here."

"Thank God. I was worried I'd have to wrestle you for it."

"Wrestle? You and me? Ha ha ha ha ha ha ha!" She coughed. "Ridiculous."

"I noticed your ring the other day. But you're single, right?"

"Right." She raised a hand and spread her fingers, showing him the wide steel ring. "I bought this for myself; it's not a gift and I'm not engaged. It's got a concealed razor in it for box cutting. I use it in the store and also the dance floor."

He laughed. "Oh, okay. Thanks for explaining."

Okay, he's displaying an astonishing level of relief right now. Why does he give a shit about my marital status?

"How about you? No flies on you, or a wedding ring either."

He shook his head, managed to suck up a mighty slurp, then replied, "No. Single. I'm—it's the job. And the hours. I don't really have time for . . . for activities that aren't the job."

"Those were several words when you could've just said, 'I'm single and ready to mingle.'"

"But only one of those would be true," he replied, and she had to laugh. She watched his cheeks hollow as he sucked in more malt, and it was fucking absurd; the man could've been a model. That was probably the real reason he'd quit the force—to follow the shallow dreams of the perennially handsome. She could tell by looking at him that he'd never be ugly or even old, only "distinguished." He'd go silver, not gray, first at his temples and then all over, and would retain his hotness, like Clooney or Selleck or Neeson.

"—Starfish?"

Oh, hell. He *was* responding, in addition to sucking. "How do you even know about Operation Starfish?"

He made a show of wiping his (perfect) forehead. "I thought you might've thrown me out again for bringing it up."

"The night is young," she warned him.

"Everybody around here knows about Operation Starfish," he replied, which was just about the most alarming thing she'd heard in all that long alarming day.

"My ass," she replied, because she was busy sifting through

(Everybody knows.)

the import

(EVERYBODY!)

of what he'd said to come up with something better.

"Your ass?" he asked. "I, um . . . it's nice. It's very nice."

She ignored the tentative compliment. "And when you talk about 'everybody,' you mean . . . ?"

"The people you helped. And the people who got angry when you helped. Lethally angry."

"Uh-huh." It was hard to hear him, what with all the screaming

(EVERYBODY!)

in her brain. "Which category are you?"

He dropped the teasing tone and replied with a simple, "The former."

Assuming he's not full of shit, it's someone he knows, as it's statistically unlikely we helped him. Plus, I'd remember if we met before. Sister? Neighbor? Absurdly young mother?

She realized they were leaning against her counter, hip to hip. He wouldn't look at her; his arms were crossed over his chest and his eyes were focused on the floor, and she could feel the tendons in her neck strain as she turned her head to stare at him. "Why are you in the 'former' category?"

"Because of Dinah Beane. That's what she calls herself now. But seven years ago, she was—"

"Dinah Linquist." The penny dropped. Dinah Linquist (five feet one, expert quilter, gourmet-jam maker) was the only Dinah she'd ever met, a petite brunette with blue eyes exactly like her brother's. Her build was so slender and small that the fat red cast made her broken arm look like a corn dog slathered in ketchup. Domestic violence was always awful, but the size disparity between Dinah and the man who'd broken her arm almost on a whim was frightening ("He hates the way I fold the fitted sheets, but those are impossible to fold!").

Scared to stay, scared to leave, but the positive pregnancy test and his habit of punching her in the stomach (like when she put flannel sheets on the bed in January instead of the tacky silk ones he liked) helped make up her mind. She'd expressed her gratitude to Cass, Sidney, and Amanda with a case of pear-apple butter, blueberry-thyme jam, plum jelly, and lemon curd. Each. It made Amanda picture Dinah's garden as a wasteland, stripped of absolutely everything that could be used to make jellies, jams, curds. Place probably looked like a tornado had whipped through by the time Dinah was done in the fall.

No wonder I thought I knew him. Amanda began putting away the ingredients as she pondered. "You said your family used to live forty miles away."

"Yeah. I settled in Minneapolis after the academy, and my folks, who split when I was younger, both retired; my mom moved to Missouri, and my dad went to Florida. And once she was out, Dinah never went back. Not even for her clothes."

That's right. We ended up going back and doing all her packing.
Amanda nodded. "Good, that's very good. I wish they all did that."

"Me too. She lives up in Fargo now. She had her baby, making me
an uncle, and found a great guy."

"That's wonderful," Amanda said with total sincerity, since not all
the people OpStar helped were saved. Or were saved, then went *back*.
Like poor Debbie Frank. They got her out and away. Unlike many
abused wives, Debbie had the resources to keep her distance and start
a new life. Once she was clear of that house and that husband, she was
more or less safe.

This is why we do this, Cass had said. *To save the starfish we* can *reach.*
And in their smug stupidity, they'd all given each other figurative high
fives.

But Debbie Frank returned to her husband, who demonstrated his
displeasure by beating her to death. She believed his promises. Maybe
he believed them too. And for all Amanda had studied the reasons
women went back to their abusers, for all her attempts to try and understand what was essentially a POW mentality, she would never, ever
understand the impulse to, not just return to the lion's den, but stick
your head in his mouth.

"Dinah never said, y'know? Not one thing to me. Not until it was
over. If she had—I was in college when it happened, but I'd have come
home so fast. I would have helped her. I would have done anything."

She saw his knuckles whitening on his malt glass, reached out,
relieved him of it, set it down. "Of course you would. You strike me as
a good-looking brother. Good, I mean. A good brother." Her blunder
made him laugh, thank God. "Is that why you became a cop?"

"Yeah. How's that for stupid?"

"What?" She drew back, surprised by his bitter tone. The guy had
done nothing but smile and shrug and give off casual vibes for all the
hours she'd known him; the mood shift was interesting. "I don't think
that's stupid."

He picked up his malt, pushed the straw aside, and just gunned the rest of it down his soon-to-be-frostbitten throat. "You're just being nice," he slurred.

"I promise I'm not."

"*Agggggggghhhhh.*"

"That's what you get for bolting a malt. Open your mouth."

". . . what?"

"I can fix it. Open your mouth."

"You can fix brain *frrrrrrrrrn?*"

She had leaned in and pressed the ball of her thumb to the roof of his mouth. "Okay, if you do this to yourself—"

"*Nnnnnnn?*"

"Stop trying to talk; there's a thumb in your mouth. When you try this at home, hold your thumb there for a good fifteen seconds, and it'll speed up the recovery. I don't know why. Probably a thermal energy thing."

"*Nnnnnn?*"

His mouth was warm, and his lips were soft, and up close, he smelled even better, like cotton and chocolate, and she was doing her darndest not to wonder how his lips would feel on her neck, the tender spot behind her ears, her nipples. Other places. "But it's not like we need to understand the science to enjoy the benefit. Right?"

"*Nnnnn.*"

"Right. See? My friend's mom showed me when I was a kid. Iris Rivers, as a matter of fact. She was a physician assistant before she went to prison; maybe this is a trick they all learn in school."

"*Nnnnn mmmmm.*"

"Doesn't it feel better already?"

"*Mmmmmfff.*"

Good God, her thumb was still—"Sorry! Sorry." She retrieved her digit. "But it does feel better." She waited. "Right?"

"Yes." Excruciating pause. "Thank you."

"So you became a cop to help people like your sister. Noble intent!"

He rewarded her enthusiasm with a snort.

"Let me guess: you found it unfulfilling because the nature of the job dictates that cops are reactive, not proactive. You can't stop someone from getting hit; you can only try to fix it so it doesn't happen again."

"Nutshell," he replied glumly.

"I stand by what I said: noble intent."

"Shouted," he said with a small smile. "You stand by what you shouted."

"Don't tone police me. Or volume police me. When did you chuck the badge?"

"June of 2020."

"Oh. *Oh.* George Floyd," she guessed at once.

He sighed and looked at his hands. "He wasn't the reason. He was the last straw." His head came up, and now they were hip to hip and staring at each other. "Don't get me wrong. There are incompetent, lying shitheads in every career in the world."

"Well, maybe not every—"

"*Every* career. In the world."

Except independent bookstore owners. We're always the exception to the rule.

"Even independent bookstore owners," he added, and she had to giggle. Which was evidently the right move, given how his expression lightened. Just a bit, but she was glad to see it.

"Like I said, it wasn't about Floyd, or even Chauvin. It was about the shit that happened before. And then it was how the Minneapolis Police Department's first official action was to put out a press release full of lies. And then they fucked up the protest response. And then a bunch of aggrieved white guys came to town and made everything worse. Every step we took, every move the brass made, just . . . kerosene on a blaze."

She was a little embarrassed that she never thought about it from the point of view of good cops. "I'm sorry; that sounds awful. Your jobs are hard enough without your bosses making it worse."

"Thanks. And when things finally started to settle down, I had time to think. And it occurred to me that we weren't fighting crime. We weren't fighting anything; we were strictly janitorial, so."

"So now you're in the private sector."

"Yes."

"Okay. That explains a few things. I've been wondering about you—"

"You have?"

"Don't sound delighted. You should sound intimidated."

"You have?" he whimpered, and cowered before her.

"All right, not that intimidated." But she laughed anyway. "I've been wondering why someone who isn't a cop and who hasn't been hired by anyone was so invested in looking into this. I'm right, aren't I? Nobody's hired you?"

"Not . . . officially."

"But here it is, Beane—"

"You could use my first name if you like. I would love if you'd use my first name."

"I'm not that kind of girl. Also—and stop me if you've heard this—"

"Oh God."

"—but your actual name is a death sentence that you're going to change; my God, man, go watch some Sean Bean movies. As I was saying—"

"I'm not changing it, Amanda."

"*As I was saying*," she reiterated, ignoring the mini thrill of hearing her name come out of his mouth. "If Operation Starfish was once a thing, it isn't anymore."

"I'm aware. Listen, I've been meaning to ask, why is it called Operation Starfish?"

"Was, Beane. Past tense." When he nodded, she continued. "It's from the starfish story, by Loren Eiseley."

"Ah, yes. A classic."

"You've heard of it then."

"No."

She sighed. "You're like a child."

"I am not!"

"Okay, okay. It goes like this: There's an elderly man walking on the beach, and he sees a boy picking up trash and throwing it into the ocean. But when he gets closer, he realizes it's not trash. There's about a trillion starfish all washed up on the beach. And the kid keeps picking them up and tossing them back in one at a time.

"So he asks the kid, 'What are you doing?' And the kid says, probably with an eye roll because duh, 'Throwing starfish back into the ocean. Surf's up, tide's going out; if I don't chuck them into the big drink, they'll all die.' Asked and answered, right?"

"I like how Loren Eiseley talks exactly the way you do."

"Shush. Anyway, the man points out there are miles of beach and loads of starfish, so what's the point when he can't really make much of a difference? And the kid listens to the buzzkill geezer, then bends down, picks up another starfish, pitches it back into the surf. And he says, 'I made a difference to that one.' End of parable."

"Ah. Thanks for satisfying my curiosity. I've wondered for . . . for a while."

"You didn't have to wonder. Sean, you do know if you wanted to see us again, you could have, right?"

He shrugged. "There never seemed to be a way to pop up in your life without coming off . . . um . . . without alarming you."

"Sure, sure, I can see that. I mean, you definitely don't want to *alarm* people. Much better to go the long-distance-stalking route."

"Well, when you put it like that . . ."

"Please tell me you don't have an obsession board in your bedroom."

"It's not a board and it's not in my bedroom."

She stared at him for a beat and then giggled. "Oh my God. I can't decide if I'm horrified or amused. Or both. Horramused? Hamused? Amorrified?"

"You can see it whenever you wish."

"Sure, sure. Who *wouldn't* go to a second location with a man who may or may not have an obsession board somewhere in his apartment?"

"Well, the invitation stands."

"As does my natural and understandable caution. But to get back on topic, Operation Starfish is strictly past tense." Amanda began rinsing the blender. "And you can probably tell me why."

"Something mysteriously dreadful happened five years ago, and you guys had to hang it up. Which is why Franklin Donahue was murdered this week."

"I'm not following."

"Yes. You are."

Dammit. He's right.

"So you're in this not so much because of the dead guy—"

"Franklin Donahue."

"—as you are because you feel gratitude and want to keep Cass out of trouble?"

He was already shaking his head. "No. I do feel gratitude. So does my sister; I'm betting she still sends you jellies."

Amanda took two steps, opened the cupboard opposite them, and gestured like a game show host pointing out a dazzling display of prizes. Both cupboard shelves were jammed with jams. They showed up regularly, ensuring Amanda thought about Dinah all the time. This made her failure to recognize her brother seem especially boneheaded.

He laughed to see the jars, gleaming with dark blues and reds like liquefied sapphires and rubies. Then he shifted mood again, back to intense. "If Cass killed him, she needs to be held accountable—"

Cass didn't kill anyone. I'm at least ninety-five percent sure.

"—and if she didn't kill him, someone did, and we should find out why."

"What 'we'? If it wasn't Cass, it's none of our business. *We're* not investigators, private or otherwise. Besides, if we knew who, we'd know why. I've got a whole mystery section downstairs that backs that truism. So what do you want from us, Beane?"

"I—"

She waited.

"I guess I want to make sure the right people are punished this time."

This time?

"Whoever that ends up being," he added.

"Whomever," she corrected absently. "So here you are."

"Here I am."

"Helpful, but only to a point."

"My curse, apparently." He shrugged. "I can be more than helpful, but I'd need information. And you brought up Iris Rivers."

"I did," she admitted. All right, so he wasn't a crusader for justice. But he could still be useful. Though before they took this any further

("This"? Are you talking about the investigation?)

she'd need to regroup with the girls.

"Let's start with something small," he coaxed. "Cassandra Rivers's scar."

"Cass would be the first to tell you it's not small. So would her mother. Also? None of your business."

"Not even for backstory?" he coaxed. "Because Iris Rivers was notorious for never calling the cops no matter how bad it got. So there's no official record of the inciting—"

You're wrong about that. "You'd have to ask her."

"But it's related, right? Since—"

"No," she said shortly. "This isn't a Q and A for your benefit. I'm not serving up malts and dishing hot goss so you can be predisposed to turning Cass in."

"I'm not predisposed to anything!" he protested. "If she did it, I want to help, and if she didn't, I want to help."

"She didn't. So don't fret."

"My God, I could never—if anything, I'm predisposed to—" Then he cut himself off so quickly that she heard his teeth click together.

"What?"

"Nothing."

"Whaaaaaaaat? You might as well answer me. You don't want to know how long I can keep up the whining."

"It's not important."

"And that's your call because—oh, You're, um. Leaving, I guess?"

Good guess, since he was already halfway down the stairs. She was so surprised by the abrupt departure that it took her a few seconds to follow him out of the kitchen. *And here I thought he was riveted to my every utterance, when, really, he just wants to get gone.*

"Thanks, I've—thanks for the malt," he called up from her entryway. "And for letting me up."

"You're welcome." She came closer and was amazed to see that her proximity was making things worse. "Are you all right? You're acting like a diabetic who can't find his insulin."

"Insulin! No! That's ridiculous! I'm not diabetic! No need for a shot!"

"Oh. Well. That's a relief. There's nothing more reassuring than a grown man screaming denials as he scrabbles at my door in his rush to escape."

"I'm fine! Nothing to worry about!" He was fumbling with the knob. "I've been taking up too much of your time as it is!"

"Not really."

"And I have to check the mail!"

"Okaaaaaay."

"Fine! I'm fine!"

She crept closer. "Sure, sure. Anyone seeing what you're up to right now would think everything's okey dokey. I'm not trying to hinder your escape, but could you take it easy on the door? Abraham Lincoln was still walking around when this house was built. Don't *claw* at it. Thumb the button *above* the doorknob while simultaneously *turning* the . . . annnnd you're gone."

She listened to his footsteps as he bolted. Then she went back to the kitchen to finish her malt and plot their next meeting.

CHAPTER FOURTEEN

The door was still closing behind him when Sean booked around the corner and leaned against the wall, unable to go a single foot farther. Amanda's Hole shared the alley with a liquor store, and when the rear door slammed open beside him and someone chucked half a dozen empty booze boxes into the dumpster, he still couldn't move. He idly wondered if they were going to go back and break down the boxes or file that chore under "It's the garbage man's problem." Then he wondered what the hell was wrong with him.

Are you all right? You're acting like a diabetic who can't find his insulin.

Christ, if she only knew. To be so close to her after all this time! He had a thousand questions but could think of no quicker way to scare her off than to appear obsessed.

"Appear" obsessed?

The roof of his mouth still tingled from her touch, which was the most ridiculous thing. The roof of his mouth had *never* tingled like that, not even the time he sucked down a ghost pepper. Then, as now, he thought he'd need to sit down very, *very* soon.

And it all came back to a kindness she and her friends did his sister years earlier. Another battered spouse to them; a darling baby sister he couldn't protect to him.

◆ ◆ ◆

He'd run into Amanda years ago, when OpStar was packing his sister's belongings. His scumbag brother-in-law was in lockup. Rumor had it that the shithead showed up for the booking rocking two black eyes, which saved Sean the trouble of a couple of punches, but Operation Starfish didn't waste any time. There was no telling when the asshat abuser would show back up. So in, pack, out, gone. Often (but not always) never to return.

"I know this is opportunistically gross, but she's got Jimmy Choos! In. My. Size! Oh my God, they're purple! You *know* purple clashes with my hair, which is why I get off on wearing it, and also, I think she should lend them to me because wouldn't they look great?"

"You're right," her friend said, tossing a box marked "winter gear" in the back of the van. She had the most dour expression Sean had ever seen on a teenager; he wondered if she was an old high school senior or a young college freshman. "It's opportunistically gross. And you're babbling, which makes my head hurt. Heads up, pal."

"What—" He rubbed his elbow as the shoe gal bustled past and clipped him with a stack of shoe- and cardboard boxes. "Oh."

"One side, sunshine," the petite dynamo sang out. He steadied the boxes; they were piled so high that he couldn't see her face. "Time is money. Money is money, too, but that's beyond obvious, which is why it's not a saying."

"*Way* too early for your babble, Amanda." But her friend was smiling a little.

"Well, that's just a lie."

He realized who they had to be: the women who got Dinah out of the House of Fists. They had a code name of sorts . . . Operation Meteor? Star? No. Starfish.

He'd come by just to get a look at the place before Dinah put it on the market. He wasn't even sure why he'd come; Dinah wasn't there. Neither was the SOB she'd married.

Guess I just wanted a look at the scene of the crime. Crimes. All the crimes.

He pulled the first three boxes from her stack and put them in the back of the van to be helpful and to get a better look at her. The slight redhead looked to be in her late teens, with skin so pale he imagined she'd burst into flames if she even thought about going to the beach. Her pointy chin, wide-set, pale-green eyes, and cheerful grin made her look like a cross between an elf and an alien, in all the best ways.

"Thanks, we've got it covered." She plopped the last of the boxes into the rear of the van, then climbed inside and started organizing the boxes. "Sidney? Are you still outside or did you go back in the house?"

"Since I can't teleport, and it's only been three seconds, yes. I am still outside."

"Sidney!"

"Jesus. *What?*"

"This is the second to last load!"

She'd had to raise her voice because another rider pulled in on a Norton Commando, parked perpendicular to the van, and cut the engine. "Ha! Perfectly timed."

"Oh, look who the fuck it is. Nice of you to show up after we finished ninety-five percent of the work, Cassandra."

The other woman grinned and shot her the finger. "Good morning to you, too, Sid. And like I said. Perfect."

Amanda hopped down. "You're buying lunch, you tardy tart."

"Done. But I would've paid for lunch anyway; I sold another article!"

"Yeah? Well, I probably slipped a disk with all this bullshit, but hey, good for you."

"Good for all of us, Sid," Cassandra corrected. "It goes into the pot along with what Amanda's making at the library and your paychecks from the long-term care facility."

"It's a nursing home!" Sid practically screamed. "Nobody calls things what they are anymore!"

"And your grumpiness can't hide the fact that I'm your hero. Go ahead and try."

"Oh, fuck me."

Cassandra pulled off her helmet and gave him a once-over, which was fair. He'd been gaping like a rube. All three of the women were striking, not just in looks, but in their lively personalities. They didn't seem to have much in common besides their partnership. And he wasn't sure how three very different women could work together in (relative) harmony.

I'd think their differences would make things harder, but maybe their differences complement each other? Or is that too Hallmark Channel?

And oh, now look at this. Bad enough he'd been caught staring, now he was standing there gaping like a rube at her scar. Was it an accident? Or assault? Jeez, she could've lost an eye. And now he was stuck in the don't-stare-but-don't-look-like-you're-trying-not-to-stare-while-not-staring loop.

Even as he worked on not staring, the gal with the scar he wasn't staring at made a sound like a truck struggling uphill in low gear: *hhh-gggghhhKKKMMMM.* "Help you with something?"

"No." He realized he had to elaborate when she raised her eyebrows. "I just came by to . . . I mean, I was in the neighborhood. This neighborhood. School break. I'm on break from college. Saint Olaf." *Why did I tell them that?* "I came by to see . . . to see . . ."

The caustic one (Sidney?) slammed all the doors, gave him one more distrustful look, and then climbed into the driver's seat.

"I still think it's weird for a teenager to have a van."

The window instantly slid down. "Shut the hell up, Cass; I don't have to justify my choice of transportation to you. You gotta admit it came in handy today."

"It's true. I *do* have to admit that. Aw, you're so cute when you're grumpy."

"Then I'm the cutest bitch any of you have ever seen."

"It's true! Paralyzing levels of cuteness!" Amanda called.

"Yep. Don't worry, I'll only remind you of that a few thousand times." Cassandra popped her helmet back on just as the redhead (Amanda?) swung a leg over her Triumph. Both engines rumbled to life.

"Sure we can't help you with something?" Amanda asked.

"What? No. Um. What? No. I'm fine. It's fine. No thank you." Before he'd finished speaking, he promised himself that if any of them needed help, then he wouldn't hesitate. He wouldn't be a student forever. He could be an asset. He'd have to work out how he'd know they needed help, but that was a problem for another day. For now, he was happy in the knowledge that his brother-in-law would have to spend the next five to ten years picking on people his own size. Which was entirely due to these three women. He didn't dare tell them his name. He might start sobbing on their necks in sheer gratitude, which would be, at best, alarming. "Thanks anyway."

Amanda shrugged, Cass nodded politely at him, Sidney probably gave him the finger (the window was back up, and he couldn't see her anymore), and they were gone.

The entire encounter had taken under two minutes, and they'd been so busy and bustling that they'd barely noticed him.

Which, though he didn't know it then, would come in handy seven years later.

CHAPTER FIFTEEN

Their meeting had been brief, but she'd made a crater-size impression on him. He went back to college, his parents went back to Missouri, his sister had her baby, his incarcerated brother-in-law had an accident that left him partially blind in one eye. Life was grand.

And quiet. Which was good! After what his sister had endured, quiet was a blessing. She deserved it. His whole family deserved it.

Yep. *Total* blessing. In fact, he appreciated the blessing of quiet so much that he showed up at the police academy two days after he graduated college. Nobody had it quieter than cops, right?

And sometime between his sister's rescue and Cassandra Rivers selling her bike and moving away (but not too far away), something happened. Something worse than Cassandra's injury, something so shattering that Operation Starfish imploded, and the trio was fractured. And maybe the rift was permanent.

And then Franklin Donahue showed up dead. And the three of them claimed he was a stranger. They were wrong, but he wasn't sure if they were lying.

Fortunately, there was a way to find out.

Mind made up, he pushed away from the wall, left the alley, and strode to his car, wondering for a moment what Amanda was doing now.

You've got it bad.

Yeah, yeah. It'd be nice if his inner voice ever told him something he *didn't* know.

CHAPTER SIXTEEN

"Look. *Look*. These shelves are filled with stories of gutsy heroines— actually, mostly heroes because patriarchy—leaping into danger and solving mysteries despite their utter lack of training or experience. And a lot of them are kids. What the *hell* was Carolyn Keene thinking? Also note that this is the *fiction* section, because in real life, all that gung ho garbage does is get you killed. Or indicted. Or sent to juvie. Maybe all three."

Amanda clapped. "Now do a dramatic reading from the cookbook section."

"Jesus Christ, it's like talking to a redheaded log."

It was the next morning, and Sidney was in the process of providing dinner *and* a show. Well, breakfast and a show, close enough.

"Nobody's solving anything, I promise," Amanda soothed. She was behind the register, making sure there was ample coffee. Though since caffeine made Sidney more . . . Sidney, perhaps that was an error. "I'm aware we're amateurs with no lawful authority except for the ability to make a citizen's arrest in a limited capacity."

"Wait, that's a real thing?" Sidney slumped into one of the over-stuffed armchairs. "I've only seen it in the movies. And always as a punch line."

"Is that a *Who's That Girl?* reference? Your mom really likes Madonna."

"My mom *and* my dad. They met at a Madonna concert in the nineties. And we're getting off track, Amanda."

"Right, right."

"Though it's tempting to track down my husband and citizen arrest him right in the face."

"One calamity at a time. Once we get this solved, we can go hunt down your hubby."

Sidney let out a snort.

"Yeah, I know. Listen to me saying 'we can hunt him down' like it'd be easy to catch a con man. Still. Doesn't mean we can't try. But again, one personal disaster at a time. So to sum up, nobody's in danger; we're not solving shit . . ."

"Good."

"But . . ."

Sidney sighed. "Fuck."

". . . we need to get as much info out of Sean Beane, pee eye, as we can. Don't worry, though."

"At no point in our lives has 'don't worry' ever been followed by anything good."

"Always so negative, Sid, you ferocious wench. I'm just saying, I think I'm figuring him out a little. It can be hard to get him talking, *really* talking—"

"Like he could even get a word in edgewise around you," Sidney snapped.

"I'm going to pass over the cruel irony of your unkind and unsolicited opinion and reiterate that I've got this."

"*Mmmmm.*"

Amanda rejoiced (quietly). "*Mmmmm*" was Sidney for "my concerns have been temporarily appeased, though I reserve the right to revisit this conversation at any time."

She really is a big bag of mush under the gear. Pretty sure her worst fear is public exposure of that tender heart. That and moths.

Sidney had shown up, dressed like she was going to hop on her Yamaha XSR900 Roadster and ride to Alaska: black jeans with armor padding at the knees and hips, purple and black textile jacket, and her HeartBreaker boots, also purple and black. Even the most experienced riders took a tumble now and again. Dressing for disaster was the way to go, and screw the heat.

And a helmet, needless to say. Sidney had recently traded up to a carbon solid. It had set her back eight hundred dollars—she'd transcribed extra clinic notes and decided against buying Coach loafers—but a decent brain bucket was crucial. Amanda and Sidney were in no rush to part with their kidneys, lungs, hearts, retinas, livers, and/ or pancreases. Eventually, sure. But there was plenty of time for that. God willing.

Once upon a time, Sidney had always dressed like she was going to ride that day. But Amanda hadn't seen her in head-to-toe regalia in some time. She doubted it was a coincidence. The real question: Did Sidney do it on purpose or naw?

Before she could ponder further, the frog announced Cassandra's arrival.

"That fucking frog is the least annoying thing about this place. Hey, Cass."

"Hi, guys." She shrugged out of her old motorcycle jacket, and no wonder: outside it was seventy-five and climbing. Why Cass was in her old leathers when she'd gotten rid of her bike years ago might also bear pondering. "Something smells good."

"Yeah, that's your breakfast," Sidney replied. "But I'm not sure I'm ready to watch you slurp up French onion soup at eight thirty in the morning. Again, I mean."

Cass smirked. "Aw. You missed me."

"She said nothing of the sort," Amanda cut in. "Also, you missed a spellbinding rant from Sidney, but I can give you the highlights."

"'This is dumb, you're all dumb, I can't stand all the dumb, everyone should go fuck themselves all the time'?" Cass asked.

Amanda giggled.

"Fuck you both."

"Thanks for breakfast," Cass said, all teasing gone from her tone. "Really. You didn't have to."

"I got you some cake too. You still do that thing where you eat dessert first?"

"Life is short, and we can't know the day or the hour, or however the saying goes. Yeah, I still eat dessert first. Thanks again."

Sidney flapped a hand at her in response. "Like I could face your mom and tell her I left you to starve."

"That's—er—thanks." To Amanda: "Sidney came to see Mom with me!"

Amanda was a little startled by Cassandra's bright-eyed enthusiasm. "Just because you bailed doesn't mean we decided to let your mom twiddle her thumbs in lockup."

"'Bailed.'" Cass nibbled her lower lip. "Yeah, I guess that's one way to describe it."

"Oh, you don't like 'bailed'?" Amanda asked sweetly. "Is there another descriptor you want to swap in?"

"No."

Another of those hateful, short silences followed. Probably one of those careful-what-you-wish-for paradoxes: Cass was back in their lives—hooray, probably! But their easy camaraderie, so effortlessly established in middle school, was splintered. Amanda had to fight the urge to take Sidney's left hand and turn it over, palm up, to see how much the scar from the day they'd met had faded.

But she had an equally compelling urge to boot Cassandra out of her store, lock it, and never speak to or of her again.

Except that would jettison Detective Beane from her life.

So?

Then her traitorous mouth popped open and, to her horror, words came out: "We can't move forward until we go back."

Sidney nudged her aside with a hip bump as she went for coffee. "Yeah, that's one of those comments that sound cool until you think about it for five seconds and realize it's nonsense."

"C'mon." Sidney was concentrating on sugaring her vile brew, and Cass was flipping through a copy of *I'm Glad My Mom Died*. Nevertheless, Amanda had the sense they were both listening hard. "A lot has changed, but the three of us still hate elephants. We saw too many women who ignored the pachyderms in their boudoirs, then got smacked around for it."

Sidney shook her head. "Pachyderms and boudoirs. It's like you don't want people to understand what the hell you're talking about."

"My point is, can we just . . . just . . ."

"Fix everything?" Sidney suggested. "Abra-fucking-cadabra?"

"Nothing so simple. Obviously."

Cass was already shaking her head. "We can't. It's too—there's been so much—just bring me up to speed, and we'll come up with a plan or we won't, and it's okay if we don't."

Having no plan is okay? Who *was* this creature? Amanda threw up her hands. "Fine. We'll play catch-up. Guess where my new piercing is?"

"For the love of fuck, don't answer that," Sidney warned. "Also, I'm still married to that Canadian shitheel; Amanda's still obsessed with her Hole; you probably didn't kill anyone, but the dead are still dead; your mom's still locked up; my husband still needs hunting down; and it's all a fucking disgrace. There. Now you're caught up."

"Nice," Amanda said. "You should write plot summaries for the AV Club."

"You haven't gotten a divorce?" Hilariously, Cass sounded more shocked about that than anything else.

"I have to catch him to divorce him, the slippery motherfucker."

"Why? Besides bloody vengeance, I mean?" Amanda asked. "Can't you get a divorce for desertion? In absentia or whatever? Is that still a thing?"

"Or whatever. Yes. And I will," she vowed, and Amanda felt a bit sorry for Sidney's soon-to-be-ex, a rogue who'd charmed them all back in the day. And then disappeared, leaving his wife-in-name-only holding the emotional equivalent of a Hefty bag full of diarrhea. "That's a problem for another day, thank fuck."

Amanda sighed. "And here I've been hoping you two crazy kids were going to make it."

"No, you weren't. This time next year," Sidney vowed, "I'll be a divorcée or a widow. His choice."

"So! On that cheerful note, let me tell you what I found out last night."

She did. It didn't take long—

"He's *not* a cop? Fuck."

—and the commentary—

"Fuck, fuck, fuck."

—was what she anticipated.

"Son of a fuckity fuck! *What* is going on?"

"That's what we're going to find out, Sidney," Amanda replied with utter (maybe misplaced) confidence.

"The best part of the story is all the jelly you've squirreled away in your cupboard," Cass observed with a grin.

"Ease up, she sends it faster than I can gobble it down. Think of the number of bread loaves I'd have to get through in a week. I'm only one person, Cassandra!"

"Dinah's homemade stuff is so good," Cass replied wistfully. "And her lemon-cranberry curd. I get homemade jam at the farmers' market, but hers is ahead of the pack."

"First, keep away from farmers' markets; they're hotbeds of haggling, and you're terrible at it," Amanda commanded. "Second, Dinah would have been happy to keep you in jelly. You could be in curd up to your tits right now if you wanted."

"Yeesh." Sidney snickered. "That's quite the mental image."

"But you're not, and it serves you right for not leaving a forwarding address."

Cass's mouth tightened. "Well. Yeah."

Sidney was giving Amanda the a-little-harsh-doncha-think look, which was deserved. As soon as the words were out, Amanda wished them back. *You hate her and never want to see her again. Or you missed her and want to help her. Or you hate her but want to help her. Make. Up. Your. Mind.*

Give me a break, internal nagger. It's been all of two days.

Just so. Because it wasn't simply a matter of forgiving Cassandra and weaving a spell, and abracadabra, they would all be friends again, riding and living together.

The only problem with that was that they weren't friends. They had never been friends. Cassandra and Sidney and Amanda had been only children. Not a single one of them had a sibling or even a cousin. So they created a sisterhood. They made their own family, and that family created OpStar out of nothing but the pictures in Cassandra's mind.

And she shit on all of it. People always assumed Sidney was the mean one, because they were unobservant idiots. Sidney was a pile of sentimental mush, which she camouflaged with smirks and profanity. By contrast, Amanda held on to grudges like dragons hoarded treasure. Small wonder Sidney had been ready to haul ass to the Minneapolis police station, while Amanda would have been fine staying in her Hole.

"So that skinny little fuck who bopped up and watched us pack Dinah's shit," Sidney was saying, "that was college-age Sean, prebadge? Huh."

Cassandra nodded. "I see it now, but . . . if he hadn't reminded Amanda where we saw him, I wouldn't have remembered him either."

True, but that was more because when Cassandra was Starfishing, she reminded Amanda of a line from *The Other Boleyn Girl*: "Anne always had a vision like a lantern with the shutters down. She only ever shone in one direction."

In Cassandra's case, she was always entirely focused on the abusee and getting them out. And then moving on to the next and the next and the et cetera.

And if the abusee went back? Well. Cass tended toward the you-had-a-chance-and-you-blew-it-so-best-of-luck-and-we're-out-of-here mindset.

Cassandra Rivers's upbringing was responsible for her best *and* worst qualities.

"So in addition to a stalker alert—"

"He didn't come near us for years," Amanda pointed out. "He didn't seek us out until Cass was in trouble. How is that stalking? Although there may or may not be an obsession board in play."

"—we should see this as good news," Sidney finished. "Cass was never under arrest; the cop isn't a cop; Cass doesn't know the dead guy; we don't know the dead guy; they've got nothin'; the end. And nobody's even hired this guy, right?"

"Not so far."

"Okay then. This is good. Things are starting to make sense, a little. We didn't think you killed anybody, Cassandra."

Amanda coughed. "Sidney's not speaking for me."

"But we were worried you'd go down for something else. From, um. Earlier."

"Thoughtful! And nothing at all to do with protecting yourselves from five years of fallout, hmm?" But Cass said it with a grin.

"Right. Nothing to do with that. So . . . we good?"

Amanda blinked. "Is that it, then? We all go back to our lives? Our bikes, our obsessions with dead writers, supper for breakfast, dessert first, clinic notes addressing the heartbreak of incontinence?"

"Hey, don't joke about that," Sidney said. "Incontinence isn't funny if you're the one pissing yourself in the grocery store in front of a feral pack of giggling nose pickers."

"Noted. Sorry." *Shit. I forgot how zealously Sidney guards her clinic patients and their dignity.* "So we're agreed? This is done?"

"Yeah. I mean, I did just give a whole lecture on how we're not detectives; we're the embodiment of amateur."

Cass smiled. "Sorry I missed that."

"Let the real cops handle it," Sidney finished.

"Not sure that's the best idea either," Amanda muttered, remembering what had driven Beane to quit.

Sidney read her mind. "Oh, come on. Hashtag 'not all cops,' right?"

". . . right. Okay, so I'll let Beane know and that'll be that."

"You'll let him know?" Cass asked.

"Yes. As I said. I will let him know." When neither of them responded, she sighed. "Whaaaaat?" *That didn't sound defensive, right?*

"We've agreed we're done, we agreed we don't have to do anything else, but you still want another face to face with Beane to . . . tell him we're done?"

"Well, Sid, he might have more intel."

"'Intel'? Stop talking like you're in a movie. And we just agreed we don't need to take this further. Don't call me Sid, and don't let your dry spell steer the car," Sidney warned.

Amanda blinked. "What?"

"Dry spell?" Cass was staring at her with utter astonishment. "You?"

"Yes, *me*," Amanda snapped. "I'm a smidge busy these days, what with running my own business and doing all the repair work this ancient building requires and visiting incarcerated moms and looking up old friends who have been accused of murder."

"Didn't we already work this out in high school?" Sidney asked. "You're bi, which means your dating pool is double."

"That would be a good point except it's about my schedule, not my preferences. Not that it's any concern of yours, but I have a date next week with a discerning lady I met via snatch.com."

Sidney burst out laughing. "You're making that up."

Amanda shrugged. "Well, okay, I am. But don't you think snatch. com should be a thing?" David Rose from *Schitt's Creek* was her lodestar; like him, she loved the wine, not the label.

"I still don't get it," Cass confessed. "You could be with anyone. In the world. You've always had a girlfriend or boyfriend."

Amanda could feel her cheeks getting warm. Cass was one of those people who thought her (former?) friends were more fuckable than they really were. It was flattering, if inaccurate, to be seen like that.

"Amanda, how are you gonna corner this guy—"

"'Corner'? You make it sound like I have to set a trap."

"—and serve him an aggressive helping of 'We're out, buh-bye'?"

"Easy-peasy." Amanda held up her ace. "The gorgeous dummy forgot his driver's license."

CHAPTER SEVENTEEN

His phone was chiming, and Sean Beane didn't give a ripe shit. Then he remembered what day it was and fumbled in the general direction of the nightstand. The water bottle fell (he always capped them after he'd taken a swig for this exact reason), followed by the keys, followed by his phone, which was now buzzing on the hardwood floor like an irked hornet.

He peeked over the edge of his bed. No phone in sight; it had vibrated itself under the bed. Of course. His bed was absurdly high, the bedding ridiculously fluffy, so when anything hit the floor, it was always just out of reach.

He wriggled farther over the edge, following the vibrations. His detective work bore three pieces of fruit: (1) his phone was back at hand, (2) as was his water bottle, and (3) he needed to dust under the bed.

"Hey, sis," he croaked.

"Yikes, drink some water right now," Dinah ordered.

"*Nnnfff*," he replied, then took a few swigs. "Be glad we're not on FaceTime."

"Listen, we both agreed this was an excellent alternative to your Thursday pop-ins."

Sean didn't say anything. He'd talked to Dinah plenty of times in her old life, and she'd never once let on that her shitpoke "partner" was smacking her around. He found out later that on more than one occasion, they'd spoken on the phone while she was sporting a splint.

But she had a point; the pop-ins were stressful and expensive. He tended to spend the visit prowling around bedrooms, poking through medicine cabinets ("Whoa! Who needed the ACE bandage? *Who got hurt and had to wrap something?*"), giving his (current) bro-in-law severe side-eye, and politely interrogating his niece ("Has Mommy been to a doctor since my visit two weeks ago? Or an emergency room? You can tell me. Uncle Sean promises not to beat your stepfather to death.").

"And you've gotta get a new bed, Sean," Dinah continued. "You've been sleeping on that pile of polyurethane for a decade."

"I like it," he lied. "Got it broken in and everything. Because I've got the sheets."

The sheets! Egyptian cotton, Mayfair Linen, 800 thread count. He had them in four colors: teal, burgundy, taupe, seafoam. Bedding and high end ingredients, like real vanilla, were his only splurges.

"They can be the greatest sheets in the world—"

"They are."

"—but you're putting them on a pile of garbage."

"You're a pile of garbage," he muttered, because he was still half asleep, and it was the best he could do.

Dinah snorted. "That'll teach you to stay up half the night making eight kinds of custard."

"Four. And that's not why I was up late. But thanks for reminding me I'm out of bittersweet chocolate." He sat up, scratched his head, yawned. "Guess who I've been hanging around with all—"

"Amanda Miller." He was surprised into a temporary silence, broken by his sister's giggle. "Well, yeah! Who else? She knows you're an obsessive horndog, right?"

"I have thus far hidden that aspect of my personality," he lied loftily.

"My ass. So, what? Did you run into her in midstalk? Please tell me you're not calling from a lair you made in her attic."

"I ran into Cassandra Rivers," he replied. "Who's in some trouble. I got a tip-off from Dora Schoen that Cassandra was a person of interest in a murder, so I'm trying to help them—"

"Them? You're talking about OpStar! Are they getting the band back together?" Her pure delight came through every syllable.

"No, I don't—I mean, I'm not sure what their plans are. Y'know, after."

"After . . . ?"

"After my investigation wraps." *After we find out whether Cassandra Rivers killed anyone. After we find out who did. After everyone goes back to their lives. Including me.*

"So keeping half an eye on them all these years has paid dividends."

"I'm not sure 'dividends' is the word we're looking for here. And yeah, I've kept my ear to the ground." He heard his tone shift from sleepy to defensive and made a mental note to tone down the whining. "Why wouldn't I? I just want to be there for them the way they were for you."

"No argument on my end, big brother."

"I'm your little brother. By two years, if my math is right."

"Your math is fine, and you act like a big brother, so that's what I call you. So who'd Cassandra kill? Sorry, sorry, who did she *allegedly* kill?"

"Someone who deserved to die."

"Oooooh, cryptic."

"But I don't think she did it."

"Even more cryptic."

"It's too soon to—I mean, I've got some investigating to do. Which I'll be working on the second I get out of the shower. They all love your curd and jellies, by the way."

"Good thing, since I just sent Amanda a box of cranberry-rosemary."

"And me, too, right?" he whined.

"You hate cranberries *and* rosemary."

"Right, so make mine lemon. Or blood orange! That was really good."

"Blood oranges are tough to come by this time of year, but I'll keep an eye out. Anything else for you this morning?"

"Give my niece a kiss and my brother-in-law a firm handshake. Or vice versa; what do I care? Now if you'll excuse me, I need to launder my sheets and replenish my homemade ice cream supply. And investigate a murder."

"Who knew being a private investigator paid so well?"

It didn't. He cleared about thirty thousand dollars last year, and if he didn't have contacts in the MPD, he wouldn't have made even that much. By contrast, when he'd worked for the MPD, his salary was forty-eight thousand dollars. Worth it—he liked the work a lot more—though he missed the health plan, which had been outstanding. And he was between cases, so the timing was optimal.

"And then see Amanda," he finished as he scratched his chest and yawned.

"Careful. Keep this up, you might not be living an incomplete life much longer."

"Dare to dream, Di."

"Give them all a big hug from me. Or just keep lurking in the shadows, only to spring forth when someone needs help. That seems to work for you, little bro."

"Finally! Didn't think you were ever gonna get it right."

"I was referring to your IQ."

"Just for that, I'm coming for another unannounced visit, and I'm making pistachio gelato."

"Don't even joke about that. Any of that."

"Love you, sis."

"Of course you do! I'm incredibly lovable, while you're just tolerable. Now go knock Amanda Miller's socks off. And don't make any jokes about how her socks aren't the only thing you want off."

He closed his mouth and cursed sibling telepathy. "I'll talk to you in a couple more days."

"Good. I expect to be regaled." She made noisy kissing noises into the phone. Or she'd begun eating her way through a brick of brie. "Bye!"

Sean put the phone down and surveyed the mountain of linens he'd swaddled himself with. Time to switch out the dirty sheets for the clean. He wondered if Amanda preferred burgundy or seafoam.

Getting a little ahead of yourself, don't you think?

He was. And it was pointless to speculate about Amanda's color preferences. He needed to stay focused, and why speculate about something he'd likely never know?

CHAPTER EIGHTEEN

"This has crossed the line from cute to incompetent."

Amanda handed Beane his license. "It was never cute. Also, did you really resign over the Floyd debacle? Are you sure it wasn't because you misplaced your gun or badge or cop car?"

"This is a great store," he murmured.

"It sure is and, apropos of nothing that just happened, have you been tested for ADHD?"

He laughed. "Repeatedly."

She watched him prowl amid the shelves, heading for the cookbooks, then pivoting to military history. "Ignoring the true crime section, huh? I don't blame you. You've probably seen way too much of it."

"I have," he replied. "So I'll never buy true crime. It's the same reason cooks never buy cookbooks."

"You could've just said, 'Naw, not a fan of the genre,' but you had to unleash the snark. Careful, that's a game for two. Or more."

"Got it."

"While you're here, Jelly Man—"

"That's my sister, not me. Maybe you should try calling me Sean?"

"Maybe you should already be in court making arrangements to change your name for your own safety? I don't want anything to happen to you."

"Why?" He swung around and speared her with a stare. "You barely know me."

Good question. "I don't want anything bad to happen to anyone," she lied. She hoped any number of awful things would happen to Jeff Manners, and had cherished the same hope for Cassandra's father. On that point, at least, her wish had been granted.

"To sum up, thanks for your help, but we are no longer in need of your, uh, help." *Good God. Could not have sounded dimmer or less confident.* "So . . . goodbye?"

Nooooo! Why did I make that a question?

He was still looking at her. "I haven't really helped yet. Which isn't to say I don't want to. But you're neck deep in a confusing mess, and I hate confusing messes."

"Then stay out of my basement. And I'm knee deep at most," she protested. "Besides, there's nothing confusing about a mysterious dead guy turning up in the wake of various domestic disasters."

His gaze sharpened. "'Wake'? Is that a joke?"

"Not that I know of." She thought about it for another few seconds. "No. Not a joke."

"Because Franklin Donahue was found in the river."

"The river" usually meant one particular river. In Prescott, it meant two: the town was located at the confluence of the Saint Croix and the Mississippi. The rivers were so different, the sparkling deep-blue Saint Croix against the Big Muddy Mississippi, that if you were in or on the water you could see the line of demarcation.

She frowned, processing. "He drowned?"

"No. Shot in the back of the head, then dumped."

Amanda tried to picture Cassandra shooting someone, lugging a corpse to a boat she would've had to procure in advance, motoring to a desolate spot (harder to find than you might think), then tossing said corpse overboard, not caring where it washed up. And alone for all of it.

"There's no way Cassandra did that."

"Because she hates boats. And the water."

"Well. Yes." Cassandra had no use for rivers, ponds, lakes, beaches, creeks, streams, brooks, boats, or the accoutrements of the same. And she cordially despised fishing. "How did you know that?"

"People in town talk about her."

"Well, yeah, but they're bound to—"

"A lot."

"Really?" *Not sure why I'm surprised. Constant, speculative gossip is the nature of small towns.*

He had given up on military history and was now standing in front of her. She thanked God for the counter between them. Otherwise, who knew what foolish sexual escapade she might pull him into?

His head was tilted, and he was studying her like she was the most interesting map in the world. "Didn't you know? You guys are legends. People are going to be talking about you a decade from now, even if Operation Starfish is done."

"There's no 'if.' Operation Starfish is done."

"As you say."

"My point," she continued, and then stopped. *What was my point again?*

"I know you don't want to talk about Operation Starfish. And we don't have to. But we could start with something easier. How did you guys even meet?"

"Digging into the background leading to Operation Starfish is still getting me to talk about Operation Starfish."

Sean shook his head. "Hey, I'm saying this as a fan, not an investigator. You're all pretty different, right down to your bikes."

"We met a bazillion years ago," she replied. "And it's nothing to do with Franklin Donahue."

"Oh, so his name you remember, but not mine?" he teased.

"It's not about my memory; it's about how you, Sean Beane, are walking around with a target between your eyes until you change your name." *Your beautiful dark eyes.*

"Is that what it's about? Because I'm not following your, ah, logic."

She waved away his irrelevant comment. "Like I said, we met a bazillion years ago. We clicked, we came to be best friends, the end."

CHAPTER NINETEEN

A bazillion years ago . . .

"Ow! Fuck! Get off me!"

"Let go. Leave her alone."

Amanda froze in the act of rooting through her backpack. The first voice, that was Sid whatever-her-last-name-was. The other one—New Girl? Hard to tell; she didn't talk much. But who else would be dim enough to jump into . . . into whatever it was?

Rather than her usual oh-my-God-I'm-late-I'm-late-stupid-snooze-button White Rabbit–inspired gallop up the steps that led to the school's double doors, Amanda pivoted

(Enh, what's one more tardy? I'll tell the 'rents I was framed. Or doing a good deed. Something.)

and followed the voice around the corner to the parking lot.

Smoker kids picking on somebody again. Ugh, think they've figured out they're clichés yet? And how do they not have frostbite? It's twenty degrees, and every one of them thinks winter-weather-appropriate clothes are uncool.

Just as she got close, she saw Jeff Manners

(Ugh.)

in his winter getup

(Vest with sleeves, T-shirt, faded jeans.)

hanging on to Sidney's wrist ("Get the *fuck* off me!") and the new girl

(Whoa, tall.)

walking right up to him. Zero hesitation.

Before she could say anything, Jeff jerked Sidney's wrist close to him, hocked a loogie into her palm, then slammed it against the streetlight

(Ewww ewww ewwwwwww!)

where it stuck fast.

"Later, bitches."

Walking, talking cliché. Jesus wept.

"Don't run off just yet," the new girl said with a smile, then stepped into Manners so they were chest to chest. Well, boobs to neck. Which was bad. People underestimated Manners's pure viciousness because he wasn't much bigger than a fire hydrant. Unfortunately, he was three-fifths stone muscle, one-fifth belligerence, and one-fifth loogie. And he never minded mixing it up.

Ask Lane Carlson, who had four inches and twenty pounds on Manners; Jeff managed to break his wrist anyway. No basketball for Lane last season. It was a miracle the squat shithead wasn't expelled and indicted.

"'Don't run off'? No time now, bitch, but I'll fuck you after."

New Girl's smile widened, and she brought her knee up. Hard. Manners hit the pavement like he'd been tossed from the roof, and Sidney started laughing so hard, she almost lost her balance, pinned in one place as she was.

"Jeez, that's nasty," the new girl—Cara? Cassie?—said, motioning to Sidney's hand, still stuck like a fly in glue.

"*Real* nasty," Sidney chortled. "Keep up the good work."

"Who spits?" New Girl seemed equal parts amused and taken aback. "We're in high school next year, and you've gotta worry about getting spit on?"

"We don't worry, because we're not responsible for anyone's spit. Wow, you really nailed him."

"I'm shocked he didn't see it coming. I mean, why *else* would I step in close like that?"

"He didn't see *you* coming," Sidney chortled. "Most people know not to mess with him. So he wasn't ready."

"This is gross," Amanda declared, examining Sidney's hand, still stuck fast. "But amazing! It's thermal conductivity in action."

"This is not the time for a science lecture, Amanda!"

"Agree to disagree." Amanda cleared her throat. "Jeff's twitching. Is he gonna choke on his puke?" And as Sidney craned her neck to see Manners, who was still writhing and groaning, Amanda yanked her hand off the streetlight.

"Fuck!"

"Sorry, Sid. I figured it's easier if you don't know it's coming."

"Well, that's a goddamned lie. And don't call me Sid. How many times do I hafta tell you?"

Amanda blinked. They knew each other and had a couple of classes together, but she'd never spoken to Sidney beyond "Can I borrow a pen?" "This is the first time you've told me."

"Oh. Well. Going forward, then. Name's not Sid. It's Sid-*nee*." To the new girl: "Hey. I'm Sidney Derecho. Thanks."

"Glad to help."

"You're in our grade, right? You and I don't have any classes together."

"We do," Amanda piped up. "She and me, I mean. We've got fourth-hour health and seventh-hour study hall." Where she'd observed Cassandra behaved the same way in each class: kept her head down and read *ELLE*, *Vogue*, and *Cycle World*. Teachers loved to try to trip her up by calling on her when she had the mag out. So far, New Girl had shown she was a handy multitasker. Hadn't missed a question yet. If she kept it up, then Amanda might have some real competition for valedictorian.

Cassandra, rangy and lean, with shoulder-length dark-brown hair and light-brown eyes, reached out, picked up Sidney's hand, turned it over. Her mouth tightened as she saw that it was shiny with spit and blood. "I think you'd better see the nurse—you lost some skin. I'd take you, but I'm still having trouble even finding the bathrooms in this place."

"Fine, *I'll* take me and give you the tour at the same time."

"I'll come too."

"Oh, we're all going?" Cassandra tried to play it cool but couldn't keep the delight out of her tone. Amanda, child of an Air Force master sergeant, knew how she felt. Being the new girl was scary. She herself had been to four schools in seven years. Only her mother's promise that this time, *this* time, they were staying put through her senior year had given her the courage to be a bit more outgoing.

In other words, maybe Cassandra's head-down attitude wasn't about being snobby.

"Yeah, we're all going," Sidney replied, nodding. "This is Amanda, by the way. You probably recognize the top of her head."

Cassandra laughed. "About as well as she recognizes mine."

"New Girl's a sneak reader too," Amanda told Sidney.

"Weirdos. Sounds like you guys haven't officially met. So, meet. Officially."

"Hey."

Who knew Sidney Derecho was such a stickler for intros? "Hi, it's nice to meet you." Curious, Amanda asked, "How come you're always reading a motorcycle mag? And fashion mags?"

"I like bikes. And I like reading a magazine founded over a century ago that covers fashion *and* stays relevant. In the most fickle industry in the world! Plus, Anna Wintour is a delightful bitch."

Damn. That's the first time I've heard her raise her voice and say more than five words in the two weeks she's been here. That's what turns her crank? Bikes and ball gowns and bitchery?

"No shit? *Vogue's* been around over a hundred years?" Sidney asked. "Not that I care. But that's kind of cool. And the bike mags?"

"Cheaper than cars, much, much cooler than cars, and when I'm sixteen, I can just climb on . . ." Cassandra sliced the air, miming taking off. "And go." Cassandra paused, lowered her voice, then added, "I've been saving up for my own since I was ten."

"Cool." The new girl had made that confession with the air of someone . . . well, making a confession. Like it was a dark secret she didn't want getting out. Maybe her folks didn't like motorcycles? Why would they even care? You had to be sixteen to drive anything, and Cassandra was three years away from that. "I started saving a year ago for my own bookstore."

"You have? That's . . ." Amanda saw Cassandra deciding which word to use. ". . . unusual."

"I'm an Air Force brat. First place I find when we move is the library. And I can't own my own library, obvs. So I want my own bookstore. One where anyone can come in and get all kinds of things."

"That sounds—"

"Not just the stuff on the bestseller lists. Rare stuff like out-of-print mysteries and good coffee, and the coffee will be free. And I'll put art by locals up on the walls, and there'll be big soft armchairs to read in. And extra space for book clubs to meet, and a kids' corner for story time."

"Sounds like you've—"

"And I'll give discounts to people who donate their used books, which I'll turn around and donate to local schools. It'll be a total safe space for anyone who crosses the threshold. And I've only got eighty thousand dollars to go."

Cass waited, and when Amanda didn't continue, replied, "That sounds awesome."

"No, wait, my math is wrong." She snapped her fingers. "The sweater! My mom offered to go in with me, so I only had to pay half price for a cashmere sweater. Cashmere, guys!"

"That gorgeous purple thing you were wearing last week?" Sidney asked. "Nice."

"Yes. Worth it. I mean, I have to have clothes. So only seventy-nine thousand eight hundred dollars to go."

"That's a great goal," Cass said. "But it sounds expensive. And hard. And expensive."

"Well, yeah. It's not much of a goal if it's easy."

"Point," Cass conceded.

"Come on, my palm isn't getting any less bloody and spitty." And as Amanda and Cassandra fell into step on either side, Sidney continued. "So is it a white knight kink with you or did you have a score to settle with Manners or what? I'm not criticizing," Sidney added, which was wholly out of character. "Just curious."

Cassandra shook her head. "None of that. I just hate bullies."

"I think that applies to everyone who isn't one. Anyone ever say, 'You know who I think are great? Bullies.'"

"No. I don't mean dislike; I don't mean I think they're a pain. I *hate* them. I hate them the way people hate plague. I hate them like famine."

Sidney blinked. "Listen, my folks are gonna lose their damn minds when I walk in the door all bandaged and shit. You wanna come over to my house after school? I could use a corroborating witness."

"I—yeah. That'd be great. I'm Cassandra."

"Yeah, I know," Sidney replied. "New Girl from New York."

"I'll come too," Amanda decided.

"You weren't invited, but whatever."

"So invite me, you grumpy bitch." Which got Cassandra going, and her mouse-on-helium giggles were contagious. By the time they got to the nurse's office, they were laughing so hard they were staggering like drunks.

It took Amanda a year to notice that Cassandra never invited either of them over, and another year to figure out why. But that was . . .

CHAPTER TWENTY

". . . embarrassing," Sean asked, "given how smart you are?"

". . . a story for another time."

"Oh. Well, that works too."

"I know it 'works,'" she snapped. "Anyway, from such things—loogies, thermal conductivity, *Cycle World*'s February issue—lifetime friendships were forged. Well. Not lifetime, I guess."

"Having met every person involved in that fracas—"

"'Fracas'?" Amanda said, delighted. "I only get to hear that word when I use it."

"—nothing in that story surprised me."

"How about this, then?" She fussed with the old-fashioned bulletin board behind the register, took out pins and put them in different spots, moved the calendar out of the way, and from underneath it all, she extracted a photo, turning it around to show him.

He took it, looked at it. Grinned. "Oh, my."

"That right there is a photo that drips eroticism."

"That was my first thought too," he replied with an admirably straight face.

It was a snap from their first Halloween, taken about eight months after they'd bonded over Manners and his penchant for loogies. By then, they were too old for trick-or-treating (the realization of which is one of the saddest days in a kid's life) but never too old for costumes.

Sidney was dressed as Anna Wintour. Who knew she'd grow to love hate-reading *Vogue* so much that she glommed all Cassandra's back copies? Cassandra went as Sally Halterman, and Amanda was in a head-to-toe Jersey cow costume complete with bright-pink udders.

Sean tapped the picture. "This should be blown up to poster size, copied, and mounted in every room in this building."

"You're preaching to the choir, pal. I spent the whole night running around saying, 'My eyes are up *here.*'"

He handed it back. "Wish I could've been there."

"You do? Why?"

He didn't hear the question, or ignored it. "Who's Cassandra dressed as?"

"Sally Halterman, the first woman to get a motorcycle license in DC."

"Oh, yeah?"

"Uh-huh. She was a four-foot-eleven, eighty-eight-pound spark who wasn't having any sexist nonsense. And she'd been riding nearly a decade before she decided she should get a permit."

"I'm sure that went smoothly."

"Alas, the man—of course a man—decided she shouldn't have one. Not that there was a law against women motorcyclists—there wasn't. But the cop giving her the exam thought there should be."

"Is this a good time to throw in hashtag 'not all cops'?"

"Hush. Anyway, the cop first insisted she was too small. Then he decided—though she was pushing thirty, which, in 1937, was like pushing, I dunno, one hundred?—anyway, he decided she was too young. He looked forward to failing her; except she passed the written exam. Twice.

"So the way she explained it—I'm paraphrasing here—'I passed the written examination . . . twice. The first time I got eighty, but that wasn't good enough for him, so I took it again and got ninety-two, and when that didn't satisfy him, I got my lawyer.'"

"Ha!"

"This should have settled things, except it was 1937, so the cop tried a few more ploys to deny her a lawful license. In the end, he not only passed her, he had to admit, 'Lady, you handle it as well as a man could.'

"Anyway, I told Sidney and Cass all about her, so that was Cassandra's costume that year. And the next. And the next."

"But why d'you keep the picture buried on a bulletin board? Never mind," he added kindly. "I know why."

"Yeah, yeah, because you're a former cop *and* a telepath."

"All former cops are telepaths," he replied with a straight face.

"Anyway. We met, we clicked, we bonded, shit happened, the end. None of which is any of your business."

"Debatable," he acknowledged.

"The reason I brought you here—"

"You didn't. I brought myself."

"'To get your license back. *I brought you here* just to tell you we're out. Nobody killed anybody, thanks for everything, later tater."

"Got it."

Amanda nodded. "Okay. Great."

"Could have been a phone call, but that's fine."

But then I wouldn't be able to see you. "Yes."

"Anything else?"

Wanna make out in the graphic novel section? Ack! Down, libido. "No."

"Well, I've been dying for another chocolate malt."

"Ooooh, me too!" She caught herself. "Dairy Queen has them. And the ingredients aren't expensive."

"Ah."

"So . . . bye."

"Goodbye." She let out a slow breath as he turned and headed for the exit. *Almost gone. Almost . . . gone . . .*

Why aren't you asking him out?

Because ex-cop or not, if he gets the chance, if something comes out that we don't know about, he'll have her arrested.

So?

He looked back as he reached for the door. Was he . . . ? Would he? She held her breath. Movie? Dinner? Naked malts? She wouldn't ask him out, but if he was determined to stick close until his curiosity was assuaged, then she could tolerate a romantic pseudodate. She'd wear a bra and everything.

"Do you and your friends want to see a corpse?"

CHAPTER
TWENTY-ONE

"So! Your plan to tell Detective Beane that we're done with all of it has somehow led to the four of us going to a morgue to eyeball a dead body."

"You're saying that like it's a bad thing," Amanda muttered.

"I told you not to let your libido drive," Sidney warned.

"I know what you told me!"

Sidney drew back a little. "Whoa."

"You also told me UGGs are sexy and would make an inevitable comeback, so you might not be the best source for advice, so how about that? Huh? Huh?"

"Touché."

After Sean left Amanda's yesterday, they'd all agreed via text to meet this morning at the Ramsey County Medical Examiner's Office, Cass and Sidney showing up together.

Amanda had given it some thought and eventually decided to take her Triumph, despite the fact that she'd parked it in the alley overnight. She had a used 2009 Ford Escape hybrid, but compared to her bike, it was indifferently maintained, and with 164,000 miles on the odometer, she only used it for winter chores when the bike was impractical.

The problem with keeping a motorcycle outside overnight? Bugs and spiders could—and would—crawl out at the worst possible moment. Nothing worse than trying to focus on the road, only to look down and see the queen of something crawling on your thigh. So she was damned careful when she put the bike through the T-CLOCS pre-ride inspection.

CHAPTER
TWENTY-TWO

T-CLOCS (Check Every Time Before Ride)

"The number of fatalities per vehicle mile traveled was 37 times higher for motorcycles than for cars," per the USDOT site Amanda checked regularly.

Fortunately, steps could be taken to reduce the chance of winding up a mangled statistic.

T—Tires and wheels. Visually inspect to make sure they're properly inflated; check your brakes. Brakes that do not slow the vehicle in question are bad brakes.

C—Controls. Check all levers and switches, check all cables, and test your throttle. Check and double-check to make sure everything's right and tight.

L—Lights. Super-duper important for obvious reasons. Check headlamps, brake lights, turn signals. It's hard enough for drivers to notice motorcycle riders; don't give them an easy her-lights-were-out-and-she-came-outta-nowhere! excuse.

O—Oil and other fluids (brake, coolant, etc.). Check levels; be alert for leaks. Leaks = bad.

C—Chassis. How's the frame? Loose? Anything rattling? Cracks? Breaks?

S—Stands. Make sure both (side *and* center) work.

CHAPTER TWENTY-THREE

Detective Beane strolled out from wherever he'd been lurking—as an ex-cop, he seemed to have a penchant for getting in / popping up everywhere—and had the gall to pretend to be happy to see her.

"Hi!"

"*Mmmmm.*"

That checked him, she was glad to see. "Ms. Derecho. Ms. Rivers. And . . . Amanda."

Amanda ignored Sidney's arched eyebrows. "We're here, just like you wanted."

Just like he wanted? Suuuure, babe. Whatever you need to tell yourself.

"I'm glad," he replied simply, because he was a manipulative schmuck who *killed it* in those chinos, dammit. And the pale-blue dress shirt made his eyes look still bluer. And he'd found time to shave in the last twenty-four hours. If she had hoped she wouldn't find a clean-shaven Beane attractive, that hope was now dashed. Dashed and smooshed and ground into the dust.

"Dashed!" she cried aloud, then restrained the urge to clap a hand over her own mouth.

Sidney took her hand, patted it absently. "Keep it together, Amanda. I've gotta admit," she added, looking around the small, almost-cozy room, "a field trip to the morgue is not like in the movies."

Sidney had a point. The place was devoid of drama. There wasn't a grizzled detective pacing back and forth, barking questions at the ME. (Beane wasn't currently grizzled and definitely wasn't pacing. Or barking.) There were no dramatic reveals and, best of all, no sinister mounds hidden under long white sheets. Sheets were not a thing in modern-day morgues (maybe not even in morgues of the past; who knew how many lies TV had told her?), and thank fuck for that.

When she was little, her dad, an avid *Star Trek: The Next Generation* fan who had Counselor Troi's face tattooed between his shoulder blades, let her watch several episodes. All good clean fun until season four, episode seventeen (those numbers would be carved into her shrieking soul until she died): "Night Terrors."

A not-so-long long story: the intrepid *TNG* crew finds a stalled ship, tries to fix it, ends up getting stuck themselves. No biggie; is it even a *Star Trek* episode if they don't get stuck or stranded or amnesia or blown up?

Except something in that part of space was interfering with their REM sleep. Which everyone needs. So after a few days, the crew starts hallucinating.

There was a happy ending, but first Amanda had to sit through the worst, most terrifying, and awful, *awful* part: Dr. Crusher was in the morgue, fiddling with her tablet (another example of tech that Team Roddenberry predicted would come to pass), when she turned and saw *every single sheet-swaddled corpse sitting up and looking at her.*

Ye fucking *gods.*

She felt someone take her other hand and was surprised to see it was Cass. "Don't worry," she whispered. "You're getting your REM sleep. Nothing to see here."

It hit her like a slap. How could she have forgotten? Cass was strictly *no touchy* until she let you in. Then it was hugs and hand-holding and dozing off on a shoulder and using each other's laps for pillows while sprawled in front of a TV, watching great scary movies like *Unfriended*. And terrible scary movies like the sequel to *Unfriended*. Cassandra Rivers would drop every wall she'd spent her childhood building . . . for a friend.

Amanda squeezed back, then let go and reclaimed her other hand from Sidney. "You're right," Amanda said to both. "Nothing like the movies."

Although Beane was somehow finagling to get them into the morgue, most visitors had to stay in the small waiting room just off the morgue proper. The walls were painted pale, peaceful blue. The chairs were dark brown, stain resistant (smart!), plush, and immaculate. The carpet was deeper brown (smarter!) and had been recently vacuumed. The place smelled like bleach and air freshener (smartest!).

There was even a little coffee table, which was oddly jarring because there were no magazines artfully fanned out on it. How could there be? If there was such a thing as *Morgue Weekly* or *Country Morgue*, with articles like "The Ten Best-Dressed Funeral Directors" and "Formaldehyde: The Ultimate Botox," she didn't want to read them. She couldn't imagine anyone outside the profession who would.

Beane wasted no time bringing them to the back. She'd expected the place would look like a gigantic operating room and be chilly and reeking of cleaning products and corpses, and she wasn't disappointed. At least no one (living or dead) was in the middle of an autopsy.

"Thanks for agreeing to have a look," he said, pausing before a bank of drawers.

"We'd never turn down the opportunity to stare down a dead guy," Sidney said straight faced. "Also, Amanda mentioned we're done, right? She said something to that effect? Last night? About how we never needed to meet again? And we could be of no further help to your fake investigation that no one asked you to undertake? Right? This sounds familiar to you? Yes?"

"Yes." Beane flipped a couple of latches, yanked on the handle, and the dead, sheetless stranger rolled out. Not even a body bag. So . . . yikes.

Amanda stared at the corpse, a tall man with a cleft chin, glaring gray eyes, and a mouth gaping in . . . what? Horror? Shock? Midbite? Fish-belly white, limbs puffy and swollen. Chin-length, deep-black hair. And the stench wasn't great, either, though it would have been worse without the body coolers.

At least it was on its back. Amanda had no interest in ogling the bullet wound in the back of the dead guy's head. This must be Franklin Donahue.

Ha! Sucks to be Beane, because there's no dramatic reveal here, just a stranger none of us—wait.

She held her breath and bent closer. Something about the chin . . .

"Shit!"

Amanda thanked God the outburst had come from Sidney instead of Cass. She tried to speak and could only manage a minuscule croak. It felt like someone had reached down her throat, grabbed her stomach, and made a fist. She cleared her throat and tried again. *Calm, calm, go for calm.* "That's not Franklin Donahue."

Sidney was making a face like she smelled something bad. Probably because she did. They were probably all making that face. "It sure as shit isn't."

"It can't be!" Amanda cried. "The hair and eye color are wrong." But hadn't she read somewhere that . . .

"Yeah, but being in the water does that, I think. Especially if he was in the river for a few days. There's no question. That's Jonny Frank." When they all looked at her, Cass shrugged. "What? It's not incriminating to know who he is. I still didn't kill him. I didn't even know he was out."

"None of us knew he was out." Amanda stared hard at Beane, who returned her glare with a steady gaze. *Oh, you sneaky POS. Later for you, pal. And later for me for falling for it. Again.*

"No, I didn't think you did," Sean "Who Wants to Ogle a Corpse?" Beane replied. "It wasn't in the papers. Not even his family knew he was—"

"He *killed* his family—Debbie Frank," Sidney snapped. "And got five years. Jesus fucking Christ with this system."

"It sucks," Cass agreed. "But if we start to talk about the inherent suckiness in our sucky system, we'll be here for days, which will also suck. And we'll all feel better for venting, but nothing will get done, and nothing will get done, and nothing will get done, because some shit never changes."

Sidney found a thin smile from somewhere. "That's the spirit. And like I said, this guy killed his family. His first *and* second wives—Wanda and then poor Debbie. There wasn't anyone to notify. No wonder we didn't hear he was out."

Killed his families, yes. That was Jonny Frank's legacy. Killed his wives. Killed their friendship, decimated Operation Starfish. Blew up everyone's lives, including his own.

Now dead on a slab and still causing trouble.

LOCAL WOMAN'S DEATH RULED ACCIDENTAL

The death of Wanda Garner has been ruled accidental, according to the coroner's report released Friday.

Garner, 23, was found dead at the foot of a short staircase in her home. Cause of death was a fracture at the base of her skull and intracranial hemorrhage.

Foul play was initially suspected, but as the victim was

apparently alone, there were no witnesses, and police were unable to make any arrests.

Garner is survived by her husband, Jonny Frank, and her brother, Marcus Garner.

CHAPTER TWENTY-FOUR

"Didn't think it was possible to bring the room down *more*, but here we are," Sidney observed. "In our defense, how could we have predicted that a field trip to the morgue would be such a downer?"

Cassandra was rubbing her temples. "This. Isn't. Happening."

"Feel free to kill Beane," Sidney said. "Because how sneaky was this?"

"Way ahead of you," Amanda retorted.

"Ow. Wait!" Sean yelped. "Ack, that one almost went in my—wait!"

"You. Sneaky. Piece. Of merde." Amanda had found a cup of pens on the coroner's desk, which meant it sucked to be Sean Beane. Amanda punctuated each word by tossing another missile. "You. Set. Us. Up."

"That's one interpretation." *Damn. Beane's quite the Artful Dodger.* "If it . . . hey!" He caught the next one, then ducked as another one flew over his head. He closed the distance between them and caught her wrists gently, shaking them in a futile attempt to get her to drop the cup and pen.

They were. Um. Very close. Close enough for her to resent his ridiculous good looks all over again. Close enough to glare into his blue, blue eyes.

"Hands off," she managed through clenched teeth, and was furious with herself because she didn't entirely mean it.

"Please listen," he said. His grip loosened but he didn't release her. "If it makes you feel better, I don't think any of you killed him."

She let out a breath that was closer to a hiss than a sigh. "Oh, we're all suspects now?" *Using me. The way I am using him. But my motives are somewhat more pure! Maybe!*

"Actually, I think he just said the opposite," Cass put in helpfully.

Oh. Shit. The two of them weren't alone. *How could I forget Sidney and Cass are RIGHT THERE?*

Sidney was holding up her hands like a traffic cop trying to intimidate a bus. "Beane! Let go of her. Amanda! Put down the cup of tiny projectiles." To Beane: "Prob'ly should have warned you about her penchant for this stuff. Except you didn't warn *us*, so fuck it; hope she puts out one of your eyes."

Sean obeyed, but Amanda ignored the command. She'd put the pen cup down when she damned well felt like it. "Cassandra has been *nothing* but cooperative, Beane! You didn't even have to track her down; she came in willingly! And you do this. Some sort of stupid reveal so you can gauge our reactions. Like it's a talk show ambush instead of real life and real death."

"Which worked," he pointed out. "You were all astonished. You're either Oscar-caliber actors—"

"Well, Cassandra *was* Pugsley Addams in our senior play," Sidney volunteered. "There wasn't a wet eye in the place."

"—or had no idea Jonny Frank was shot to death and dumped."

"Guys, guys!" Cassandra was making the time-out gesture, which looked stupid no matter who did it. "It's fine. Calm down."

"This is no time to calm down, and I fail to see how any part of this is fine," Amanda snapped.

"Love the attitude, though, Cass," Sidney said. "That's a story you should stick with. It's fine, you're fine, we're all fine, everything's fine. Unless your name's Jonny Frank. Or Franklin Donahue."

"I didn't kill him when his name was Jonny Frank, and I didn't kill him when he was Franklin Donahue . . ."

"So, what?" Amanda asked. "He legally changed his name? Is that why nobody knew who Franklin Donahue was at first?"

"Who cares? Nothing's changed, okay, Amanda? I didn't kill him, no one here killed him, so please just settle. I know he's an *ex-cop*, but there are still penalties for assaulting one."

"A few things have changed," Amanda corrected. For starters, instead of the dead guy being a stranger, he was someone all three of them had a motive to murder. Shit, at one point, they'd had a sit-down and discussed the various ways Jonny Frank deserved to be folded, spindled, and/or mutilated. Sidney even volunteered to be the getaway driver, and Cass reminded them she could get her hands on her dad's guns (two 12-gauge shotguns, a 20-gauge shotgun, a Beretta APX Carry, and the always-popular .38 Special) anytime she liked. "More than a few, now that I think about it."

"Not really," Cassandra replied. "Not at the fundamental level. I didn't kill anyone."

"That's all very well, but—"

"And I can prove it."

CHAPTER TWENTY-FIVE

OpStar, six years ago . . .

They met in Lilydale, on the wraparound porch of a Victorian with a hideous paint job.

Puce? Really? It must be like living inside a bruise.

"Hi, Amanda."

"Hi, Paul. These are my friends, Cassandra Rivers and Sidney Derecho."

"Hey," they said in unison.

"Nice to meet you both. I know that's what everyone says, but it is. Nice meeting you, I mean. And right on time, thank God." Paul Banks's handshake was firm, his gaze direct. Glasses magnified his small, smiling dark eyes and laugh lines, and he had the broad shoulders and trim waist of a pro swimmer. If Amanda hadn't seen his ID (5'8", 165 lb., age 29), she would have put him at forty. There was a wedding ring on his left hand and splints on the last two fingers of his right.

Amanda was now used to schooling her face when meeting clients. She made no mention of bruises, breaks, burns. She didn't evince surprise or even sympathy when she saw signs of the battering-equals-love mentality.

Sidney . . . not so much, as demonstrated when she cleared her throat. Cass recognized the phlegm warning too; she and Amanda traded "oh, shit" glances. *Maybe I can distract her with—*

"So here's a thought . . . and don't you dare interrupt me or 'translate,' Amanda . . ."

Dammit!

". . . I'm not a shrink or anything, but maybe hit her back?"

Paul blinked. "Why would I do that, Ms. Derecho?"

"To, um, get her to back the fuck off? Keep her slapping and punching and breaking and burning and all the other 'accidents' to herself?"

"Sidney—"

"Uh, Sid—"

"And where does that end?" Paul asked, and to Amanda's relief, he sounded curious, not angry. "You think brutalizing my wife in response will de-escalate the situation? Because I think that would end with one of us breaking a glass and eating the pieces."

Good GOD.

"Right. Duly noted." Cass clapped her hands together. "And on that note—"

"Yeah, I guess." Sidney sounded doubtful, but even she could tell this wasn't any direction for a sane conversation. Because Paul Banks had a point. Say he broke his wife's arm. Then what? She's sorry? She never hurts him again? They live happily ever after, and the only bruises they get are from gardening mishaps and enthusiastic sex on hardwood floors?

Or she heals and bides her time and then arranges another trip to the ER for Paul Banks. Followed by disaster. Destruction. Anything and everything except de-escalation. Divorce court would follow if they were lucky. If not . . . another kind of court.

"Sorry, it's none of my business. Well, it's a tiny bit our business, maybe. I've just never—" Sidney cut herself off, which was the only way *to* cut her off. "Where's your shit? I'll help you load up."

Amanda understood the confusion. It was one thing to research and come to intellectually understand that women abused and men *were* abused, but seeing it in the flesh, so to speak, was something else. She'd never expected to meet a man routinely brutalized by his smaller, lighter, weaker wife. A young man—only a few years older than she and her friends—in decent shape, capable of putting up a fight. And would, so long as he didn't have to hurt someone he cared about.

All that to say, the broken fingers were only the latest I-hate-when-you-make-me-do-this gift from Mrs. Banks.

"Now what's this?"

Swell. Speak of the devil. Well, think of her.

"In our defense, we've only been here forty-five seconds," Sidney observed. "No matter what, we wouldn't have been out of here when she got back."

Mrs. Banks had pulled into the driveway, and Amanda could feel her glare from thirty feet away. She braked, parked, and her car door flew open hard enough to rebound shut on her shin as she tried to climb out. Even with the windows up, her howl of pain was perfectly audible.

"Oh, shit," Paul muttered. "Whatever you do, don't laugh at her."

A timely warning, given that Mrs. Banks's attempts to escape her car were an exercise in Three Stooges–esque comedy. She'd gotten the door open again, only to knock her head as she tried to get out.

Mrs. Banks finally freed herself from the vehicle—

"Hon, you promised you were going to wear your seat belt."

"Fuck off!"

—then came bounding across the lawn like a pissed-off gazelle. Honest to God, a fucking gazelle. Mrs. Banks ran like the lawn was three feet high instead of trimmed to golf-course specifications.

Amanda didn't have to look to know Cass and Sidney were wearing the same stunned, trying-not-to-laugh expressions. As sometimes happened, the inherent danger heightened the giggle factor.

"Uh, hon, it's okay; you don't have to worry about walking on the lawn—I already picked up the dog poop this morning." Then, sotto voce: "We don't have a dog. But the neighbors do."

"Heard *that* before," Gazella snapped. "What, you need these girls to protect you?"

"Naw," Sidney replied with a wicked grin. "We're just here to hold you down while he kicks your kidneys up into your lungs."

Amanda bit back a groan. De-escalation and Sidney Derecho: nope.

"They won't touch you, and neither will I," Paul soothed. "But I've got to go."

"I knew you were up to something! Your lie was stupid and clumsy."

"As was yours. You never take Saturday-morning shifts," Paul replied. "But it doesn't matter. It doesn't change anything."

"I said I was sorry!"

"And I believe you. I believe you every time."

"You know what'll happen," she growled. "You know what I'll do."

"It doesn't matter."

"Keep off him, Banks. We won't let you touch him," Sidney said.

"It's worse than that, I'm afraid." Paul gave his wife a long look, then dropped his gaze. "I'm leaving regardless of your actions, Jilly," he told the lawn. "Because what we've got? Is unsustainable."

"Unsustainable" was punctuated by Sidney slamming the van's rear door. The door closed via her car remote, but Sidney had no patience for sitting through those interminable eight seconds.

"Time to go," Amanda said quietly, and slipped her hand through his.

"Look. Paul. *Look*." And then Jill Banks slapped herself, hard. Amanda could see a red handprint rise almost immediately. When Paul made no comment, she did it again. "See? Please. You can't leave me like this. Paul? Please?"

It's worse than that, I'm afraid.

As the three of them gaped, Mrs. Banks climbed the porch steps, steadied herself, and then smashed her head into one of the pillars. Twice. When she turned back to them, a knot the size of a walnut was starting to form. Then she took two handfuls of her shoulder-length blonde hair and yanked, yanked, yanked until tears were streaming down her pink, swollen face.

Oh, you manipulative cooze. Poor form, she knew. Mrs. Banks was clearly suffering.

Not her job. "In you go, Paul," Amanda said, and gently shut the door as Paul buckled his seat belt. She was trying to understand the self-effacing decency of a man who would tolerate his own abuse but not his wife turning her violence inward.

Then she got ahold of herself because they were breaking their own rules, not to mention losing time. "This is not a spectator sport," she hissed. "He's packed, we're loaded, it's time. To. Go."

"Um, should we call an ambulance?" Cass murmured.

"They're on their way," Paul called from the van. "Not even five minutes out. Thanks again for being right on time."

Damn. He's quite the planner. Sidney swung a leg over her Roadster as Mrs. Banks darted inside the house, no doubt on the hunt for a knife to stab herself or a fireplace poker to beat herself or paper to cut herself or poison to glug like it was a spritzer. Amanda and Cass climbed into the van, which pulled away from the curb even as Cassandra's door slid shut. Sidney swung out in front and put out her left arm, palm forward: *follow me.*

Paul let out a breath from the passenger seat and let his head thump against the headrest. "Whatever you guys get paid, it's not enough."

"That's what I've been saying," Cass said. "We should triple our fees. And then triple them again. And then quadruple them!"

"Ignore her," Amanda commanded. "We don't get paid."

"You're kidding." Paul turned around in his seat. "How do you fund your operation?"

"Mostly our own money." It wasn't any more expensive than belonging to a book club that met an hour away, given how expensive hardcovers and gas were. "Though we never say no to donations," Amanda continued. "There's a form you can fill out and everything. Warning: the proceeds of said donations go toward our debrief sessions at Muddy Waters."

"Seems fair." Paul let out another sigh. "Some advice? Don't get married. I know my experience isn't typical, but . . ."

"No worries" was Cassandra's grim reply.

"None of us want to get married," Amanda added.

"Excellent. Take me away, ladies. And thank you again."

CHAPTER
TWENTY-SIX

"Behold, the only decent member of the Manners clan."

Back in Prescott, jiggety jig. Amanda parked behind Sidney's van, popped the kickstands, made sure they were locked, and waited for (*sigh*) Beane to (*siiiiiigh*) remove his hands from her waist and hop off.

She'd been so angry that she had released the carrier strap and all but thrown Sidney's old helmet at Beane, which he caught with his belly like it was a medicine ball from a 1950s gym. "Oooof!"

Cass and Sidney exchanged looks. "Sean, you could ride down with us," Sidney suggested, with the air of a woman inviting a rattlesnake to hang out in her bathroom. "Pretty sure your safety might be compromised otherwise."

"He's riding with me," Amanda snapped, and glared in response to Sidney's arched eyebrows.

"It's fine; I'd love to ride with Amanda," Beane put in, and who fucking asked him?

"Put it on," she said as she straddled her bike and kicked the engine over.

"Happy to respect the law." He sniffed the helmet and probably got whiffs of Sidney's grape-scented hair spray and not a little rage, then plopped it on his head.

"Not the law. The rule," she corrected the former cop. "My rule. There's only a partial helmet law in Wisconsin. Eighteen and under must wear helmets. We're both older than that, but guess what? Put on a helmet. It's why we keep the old ones on hand."

"Gotcha."

Yeah, sure. You and your "gotchas."

"Buckle it."

"Yes, ma'am."

Then he climbed on, his arms coming around her waist to hold her firmly. None of those tentative grasps first-time passengers used, or the way-too-firm, argh-I-can't-breathe beginner's clutch.

While buckling her own helmet, she got the intoxicating scents of aftershave, cotton, and soap-clean skin as he leaned against her, which was infuriating. She felt him settle into the pillion seat, then kicked the engine to life.

They cut through side streets to get to MN-280, then hopped on I-94 east to shoot over to US Route 61. Soon enough, cities were replaced with strip malls, which were replaced with fields of corn, the tassels already hip high.

Cornfields always reminded her of detasseling stalks for local farmers, Cass and Sidney at her side. As usual, the route smelled like sunshine, fresh grass, and . . . Sean?

Dammit!

"Amanda, you copy?"

"Copy," she replied. *Gotta love smartphones and helmet mikes.* "I was just thinking about you guys."

"Naw, you were thinking about what a pain in the ass detasseling corn was. No wonder they hired mostly teenagers; adults know how much the work sucks. Hobbling around like you're in your eighties isn't as much fun when you're sixteen."

"I don't think hobbling is fun for anyone at any age. And you know better, Sidney. We weren't teenage detasslers, we were seasonal agricultural adjusters. I think that's where your hatred of euphemisms was born: in the lush cornfields of Wisconsin beside the Kum & Go gas station."

"Yeah, yeah. I didn't get you on the horn to reminisce."

"Sure about that?"

"I'm just checking in, and also, you're not gonna kill Sean Beane, right? When we're about to clear Cass? I get being mad at the guy—"

"I would hope so."

"—but I can't help feel that murdering someone who's investigating the murder of someone you had a motive to kill could backfire on you."

"*Could* backfire?"

"Well, nothing's for certain. I'm just throwing stuff out there."

Amanda sighed into her mic. "I'm fine."

"Good to know. Gotta admit, he's a sneaky fuck." This in a tone of mild admiration. "Not exactly an uggo to look at either."

"His looks are irrelevant," she said, thanking God that Beane couldn't hear the conversation.

"Suuuuuuure they are. I'm sure if he was short, obese, bald, incontinent, and in his sixties, you'd still be into him."

"I'm not 'into him.'"

"Uh-huh. Y'know, when he grabbed your wrists like that in the morgue . . . I've seen other men try that on you."

"What can I say? I bring that out in people, apparently."

"Uh-huh. Without fail, any guy grabs you without permission, the best they can hope for is a knee smash to the balls. The *best*. The worst hardly bears thinking about. Not Beane, though. You didn't even try to bite his eyelid."

"He caught me off guard."

"Bullllllllshiiiiiiiit."

"Sidney—"

"Oh, and book left before you get to Point Douglas Road. Construction. Take the detour."

Amanda was so relieved they were off Beane that she could have swooned. "I'm always happy to obey your road commands."

"No, you are *not*. And watch out for squids. One of those clueless fuckers almost clipped me when he was lounging on his bike like he was on his sofa instead of a highway."

"Thanks. Too bad hot weather really brings them out."

"If they stuck to riding in sunshine, it wouldn't be so bad," she griped. "God save us from sandal-wearing, knee-scraping, throttle-gunning, toolkit-ignoring, selfie-taking numbfucks who think riding in downpours is a good idea."

Ack! I have inadvertently awoken the beast! "You're so right," Amanda soothed. "They're annoying and dangerous. You have every reason to be repelled and horrified."

"*Very* fucking annoying. And yeah, dangerous, which is almost as bad. Swear to God, the worst thing about squids is how they don't know they're squids."

Squids were a hazard anytime but never more so than in summer. There were fewer things more dangerous than a young rider who overestimated his (she'd never met a female squid) skills and burned valuable time bragging about their (nonexistent) bike prowess. Usually just before they shredded their knees on pavement. Or their skulls.

A small price to pay for the pleasures of the road, but still a price.

It was normally a thirty-minute drive from Minneapolis, but later, she could never work out if it had gone too fast or taken forever. She'd never been so conflicted about climbing off her Triumph. She was still thrilled by the firm grasp on her waist and pissed that her libido wouldn't give it a rest. She kept thinking about his eyes and how he'd been in kissing/biting distance. And she kept reminding herself that turning around to kiss or bite him at sixty mph was a bad, bad, bad, *bad plan* at best.

Sidney had parked her minivan and was eyeing the shop Manner's Bikes—the grammatically incorrect "Manner's" on the sign never failed to irk Amanda—with arms crossed over her chest. "Haven't been here in a while, thank fuck."

"Same. But Sonny's okay," Cassandra said. "The best of the bunch, even."

"Low fucking bar."

"Well." Cass let out a giggle. "Yeah." To Beane: "Jonny Frank, a.k.a. Franklin Donahue, was shot, you said."

He handed the helmet to Amanda, who promptly strapped it down. "Shot and dumped," he agreed. "And found in the river."

"Wait, I haven't heard this," Sidney declared. "Beane, since you're sort of local, you gotta know that, around Prescott, 'the river' means two. So where exactly was the body?"

"The confluence of the Big Muddy and Saint Croix, five hundred yards from the bridge," Amanda replied.

Sidney smirked, and Amanda could almost read her mind: *My, my, look who has all the fucking deets from Hunka Hunka Burnin' Beane.*

"Right, the river. And I was your first suspect because . . ."

"You lost the coin toss?" Sidney guessed, and got a poke for her trouble.

"Because the killer might be a local, and witnesses saw someone on a motorcycle speeding from the scene," Beane replied.

Cass smiled. "See? Vindicated. I don't have access to my dad's guns, and I don't have a bike anymore. Everyone knows that."

The words were reassuring, and Cassandra's body language even more so. She wasn't fidgeting or avoiding eye contact or fiddling with her scar. Clear eyed and calm was her default, and due to her dreadful upbringing, she was a master of de-escalation—all of which had made her such a valuable foil and friend. Calm wasn't Amanda's default, and it sure as shit wasn't Sidney's.

"The dead guy was a coward to the end," Sidney said. "Killed his wives—"

Oh, hell, I keep forgetting about the first Mrs. Frank. Sidney's right; the system blows.

"—changed his name, snuck back into town . . . pathetic. I'm not advocating murder, but it's not like Jonny Frank's gonna be missed. No matter what name they bury him under."

Amanda turned to Beane. "Which reminds me . . ."

Beane sighed.

". . . here's proof that people *can* change their names. Not just murder victims. You understand this is a process that anyone can undertake, right? Even dead guys?"

"You might want to drop that," Cassandra said, kindly enough.

"I will *never* drop that." *Irritating him and pounding points into the ground is how I keep control.*

Wait, what?

Amanda turned on her heel and marched into Sonny Manners's shop, assuming Cass and Sidney would follow and not caring if Beane did.

Sonny had been sitting behind the cash register, but when he saw them, all six feet of him came off the stool in half a tic. (One of the reasons Jeff Manners was such a shit? A lifetime of resentment of being the runt of an extraordinarily tall litter.) His shoulder-length dark hair was pulled back into a low ponytail, and he was sporting his usual midsummer tan. Sonny Manners was a bronze god in the summertime and white in winter. Belly-of-a-frog white.

"Hi, uh, Cass. Sidney. 'Manda. And . . . er . . ."

Cassandra stepped up (figuratively). "This is Detective but not really Sean Beane. We haven't gotten around to hiring him yet, but . . . y'know. He's here anyway."

Sonny blinked, then let it go. "'Kay. Say, I heard from Kirsten Neumann the other day. She said to say hi, 'Manda, and you should call her if you want to go out, maybe talk about getting back together."

"Thanks, but no." They'd only gone out a handful of times, which came to an end once Amanda realized the sole impetus behind their relationship was Kirsten's determination to bring a date to her cousin's wedding. Amanda hadn't signed on to be a placeholder, so dumped her accordingly, then had to listen to all the reasons Kirsten thought *she* was the selfish user. "Nice of you to pass on the message, though."

"Her?" Sean asked. "Oh."

"I'm bisexual. Problem?"

"Nope."

"All right, then."

Sonny cleared his throat. "Anyways, I know why you're here."

Amanda doubted that very much. "Any*way*, singular." Pause. "You do?"

"Sure. C'mon back."

They followed him and had only gotten a few steps when Sidney clamped down ("Yow!") on Amanda's elbow.

"Fuck a duck, that's a Suzuki TM400!"

"I have eyes, Sid."

"Vintage!"

She pulled Sidney's fingers off her arm. "And dangerous."

"It's not that dangerous." Sidney's euphoria was to be expected, given that her bike was almost as notoriously perilous as the Suzuki. She circled the motorcycle like a passionate fan worried about getting too close to a star. "God, I love these older bikes. Beautiful and perfect. The older lines, the way they stand the test of time . . ."

"The way they're prone to leaks . . ."

Sidney was already shaking off the criticism. ". . . the skinny tires, the way they make your teeth rattle at speed . . ."

Amanda rolled her eyes. ". . . the absence of all modern safety features . . ."

"You want one, you fault-finding bitch."

"Do you want me to take a picture of you with your new friend?" Amanda smirked and held up her phone.

"I know you're being sarcastic, but yeah, actually, I'd love a picture with . . . oh, shit."

Sidney stopped suddenly, and Amanda did a quick side step to prevent a partial collision.

Then she saw what had startled her friend. No, friends, plural (right?). Cass had gone so white that her scar stood out as a vivid pink line slashing across her face.

"Oh, *shit*," Sidney said again. Amanda didn't blame her; "oh, shit" was about five times better than anything she could have come up with.

How long has Sonny been hiding a ghost in the back of his shop?

CHAPTER
TWENTY-SEVEN

Five years ago . . .

"You're leaving town? Just like that?"

"S'not just like that," Cassandra muttered. She was packing, though Amanda noted that she was mostly taking things from one box and putting them into another. Cass's apartment, messy at the best of times, was a tsunami of half-empty takeout cartons, dirty carpets, empty bottles, Noxzema, and despair.

"You just have to give it more time."

"I did. All summer. Nothing's better. Not. One. Thing." Cass laid still more tape across a box marked Regrettable Fashion Choices, and she did it over and over and over until it was more tape than box. "The opposite, in fact—things are so much worse. Because of us."

"You're using Scotch tape?" She knew it was the wrong thing to focus on, but yikes. It was so *glaring*. "Ye gods, you're bad at this."

"We can't all be lucky enough to be Air Force brats who are expert packers."

Amanda held her tongue, which was as unpleasant as it sounded. Like most military brats, she didn't think four schools in seven years was "lucky." Always being the new kid? Also not lucky. But given Cassandra's upbringing, complaining seemed crass.

Cassandra's apartment was three miles out of town, a two-bedroom, one-bath in pleasant (*yawn*) neutrals that looked like a twister hit, then came back for seconds. Or to put it another way, it looked the way it always looked. Except with loads of boxes in various stages of being filled.

OpStar was all over the place. With her mother currently serving a term in prison, and her father long out of the picture, Cassandra had been on her own the minute they arrested Iris Rivers. Except not really, because Amanda and Sidney wouldn't have it. Cassandra had sold her parents' house and much of the contents, but kept some of the furniture—the kitchen table, a bed, the hutch, a dresser. Some silverware, her mom's waffle iron, her dad's smoothie blender, a few photos.

None of the fake ones, though. None of the lovingly framed pictures of Cassandra and her mother and father beaming at the camera like all was swell. Those Cassandra burned along with her parents' wedding album and her baby book.

("What? Baby books are the worst. Even my mom thought so, though you couldn't tell because she filled it with useless garbage. Why would I want to look at a lock of my baby hair now? Or ever?")

Cassandra kept the pics of her friends and chucked the rest. "Oh God, here's the one from when I had chicken pox. I look like the Fly in the early stage of disintegration! And Sidney's eyes are closed." Ah, the chicken pox saga. Amanda's folks had really, *really* wanted her to catch chicken pox from Cass. It didn't work, even though it had been a slumber party weekend for the ages. And then Sidney was the one who caught the spots; her shrieks of outrage could have shattered windows.

"It's real," Cassandra had continued with interesting intensity. "We look real in these. Nobody's posed. Nobody looks stiff. Nobody has a frozen smile while hiding the pain of a broken wrist."

"True," Amanda mused, looking them over. "Nobody's doing those things in our pictures. Mostly we're giving each other devil horns and wet willies."

"That's all I want."

Then the three of them combed garage sales all over the Twin Cities metro area. The hide-a-bed couch? Liberated from a literal fire sale in Saint Paul; Amanda had attacked it with Febreze until it no longer reeked of smoke. The bookshelf? Sidney cobbled it together in her parents' garage. Same with the desk. Kitchen appliances? Silverware? Curtains? Donations from Sidney's folks, who were downsizing to a tiny house now that they were empty nesters.

Tablecloths, towels, washcloths, etc.? Cass crocheted them herself. Observing the lovely things that grew from Cassandra's hook, Amanda decided it was a good time to learn to crochet. Unfortunately, Cass was a crappy teacher: "It's easy, see?" This while her hook was flashing and her fingers were flying, and Amanda had *no* idea what was going on.

"I can't believe you're moving away over this. You can't blame yourself."

"Watch me."

Before Amanda could comment further, there was a no-nonsense knock on the door, followed by "Fuck me sideways, it smells like my alcoholic grandpa's closet in here."

Amanda had to stifle a chuckle. One of Sidney's finest qualities? How *specific* her insults were.

"Now what's all this shit?" Sidney continued, hands on her hips, eyeing the wreckage of Cass's life. Another fun fact about Sidney Derecho: she had no idea how cute she looked when she was scowling. Her curves, curls, liberal use of bronzer, and bright-black eyes gave her the air of an aggrieved forest fairy. "Well?"

"Cass is leaving for a bit."

"Yeah, that's not what your text said."

Cass looked up from transferring shoeboxes to another, bigger box. Her favorite black flats were on top. "You can both text till your fingers go numb—"

"Thanks, we will. Till they *bleed* if we want."

"—but it won't make a difference."

Amanda sighed. "Aw, man. I love those shoes."

Cass wordlessly tossed the box at her.

"Thoughtful! Except for the fact that you have feet fit for clown shoes, and I have squashed arches and cramped toes."

"Throw them out, then," Cassandra snapped, which was more pure goddamned insanity. "Jesus Christ with all the bitching and needling."

"Whoa. Okay." Sidney stepped between them by pretending she wanted to look at an empty box. "Take it easy, both of you."

"Hard pass," Cass muttered.

"It hasn't been that long. Maybe you just need more time to wallow in self-pity," Sidney suggested, which was code for "I love you and don't know how to help you, and I find that frustrating but please don't leave."

"Are you two reading from the same tedious script?"

"I also suggested she needed more time," Amanda said with a modest half bow. "Great minds and all that."

"Well, Amanda's smart, and I'm smart, and it's great fucking advice, and you should just shut up and take our fucking great advice already."

"Sure, I'll get right on that. Thanks for coming over uninvited, byeeeee."

"Oh. Now we need invitations?"

Nearly out of tape, Cassandra was trying to fold the top flaps of the box so they would stay closed, and failing because she always put the wrong flaps down first.

More disturbing than her complete inability to understand tape or boxes: all her riding gear was in a box by the front door marked "Goodwill." Amanda had nearly tripped over it on her way in. Not some gear. All. Not temporary storage. Donating.

She went back, easily opened the box

(How does Cass still not know how to fold a box closed?)

and beheld a dreadful sight: Cassandra's Easy Rider Mid Calf 35 motorcycle boots. By Tamara Mellon! A bargain at six hundred bucks. Her Cassini H2O gloves, another hundred bucks. Her Stella Dyno leather street jacket, three hundred.

Cassandra had spent years working and saving for all of it; it was how her writing career got started. The first piece of gear she bought— with a two-hundred-dollar kill fee—was a new helmet. And how often had the three of them debated the merits of the Ralph Lauren Everly riding boot (a dream of cognac-colored leather and a comfortable stacked block heel) versus the Michael Kors Kincaid boot (an homage to the classic equestrian boot in deepest black with striking cross-straps)?

So often.

"I remember when you got some of this stuff," Amanda said, poking through the box. "You were so excited about that kill fee. Who knew you could get paid for *not* publishing an article?"

"I think it's cool how she takes after her mom." At Cassandra's look, Sidney added, "In a good way. A writing way. Not a homicidal way."

"You're really leaving?" Silly question, given the boxes, but Amanda couldn't help it. "For good?"

"Yep."

"Really?"

"Yep."

"Really, really, really?"

"Jesus Christ."

"So no more Operation Starfish?" Sidney ventured.

Cass straightened up so quickly that she almost fell over. "*That* should have been obvious three months ago. Operation Starfish was done the minute they zipped Debbie Frank into a body bag."

There was a long silence, because . . . what could any of them say? But Cass wasn't done.

"Why? She was out; she was rich before they got married, and he wasn't entitled to a dime, and she was free!" Cass cried. She gave the nearest box a savage kick, then clapped her hands to her face and groaned through her fingers. "Why, you guys? Why did she go back?"

Sidney and Amanda traded glances, and Amanda took the plunge. Because for all their fretting and drinking and woe-is-me-ing, they hadn't really talked about the murder. Or their part in it. They'd been sidestepping around it for months. *I guess Cass is tired of sidestepping. But there's got to be middle ground here somewhere.*

"Cass, I know."

"You don't *know*, Amanda," she replied with such intense bitterness that she looked years older in that moment. "You can't. You can only intellectualize it. You can only study it, but you can't feel it. You're all theory and no practical experience."

"But in a good way," Sidney put in.

Ouch and double ouch. Nice try, Sid. "Look, it's awful, but Debbie wasn't really free. 'Free' isn't just about leaving the house or jumping on a bus or even a plane. In her head, she wasn't free. I'm sorry, I know that sounds inadequate."

"You just demonstrated my point. And 'inadequate' is the perfect word for this clusterfuck. We should have learned from our initial bad advice for Paul Banks and his crazy-ass wife, but guess what? We didn't. We just kept at it and kept at it and . . . Christ! The sheer fucking arrogance of it all!"

"Mistakes were made," Amanda allowed. "No one's saying otherwise."

"'Mistakes'?" Cass scowled and rubbed her scar. "Not only did we not save her, we probably pushed her asshole husband to escalate when we barged in."

Sidney sighed. "We didn't barge, we were invited. And she was happy to leave with us. What, we should've crept in like mice?"

"Yes!"

"Would it have made a difference, though? Because . . . c'mon. She went back. Not a few weeks later or a few days . . . she went back the same damned day. He must have really laid on the smooth talk once we dropped her off."

"We should have taken her phone away," Cass grumped.

"Oh, sure, confiscate her phone along with her autonomy. Great plan."

"My point is, we were naive idiots and worse. And you know it, Sidney."

"What's worse than 'naive idiot'?"

"I ignored every lesson from my childhood, and Debbie Frank paid the price for that conceit."

"My ass," Sidney snapped. "You didn't ignore every lesson from your admittedly fucked-up upbringing. You stood up to your dad how many times? And you did everything you could to get your mom out. Shit, how many times did you call the cops? How often did you pack a suitcase for Iris, only to have her unpack before your dad got home? Nothing that happened back then was your fault, just like this isn't your fault either."

Cassandra just looked at her. Amanda had no idea if any of this was working but crossed her fingers anyway.

"Your childhood is why we do what we do," Sidney added. "And look how many we saved! Shit, I just got another box of orange-rosemary jam from Dinah."

"Oooh, me too," Amanda said. "Only mine was blueberry-thyme."

"Dinah's onto a brand-new life now. She's happy now. And so are Barb and Roxy and Karen and Paul and Jill and a host of others. Because of us, because of Operation Starfish."

Cass let out a snort. "Perfect example. I mean, Jesus, even the name! Operation Starfish? Pure childishness. Girls playing games based on an apocryphal story."

"So you're ignoring all the ones we helped so you can sulk over the one we didn't?"

"Pretty much, Amanda."

"But . . . your bike?" Ditching the gear was troubling enough. Selling her Norton Commando? Unthinkable. No way. *No way* was she going to take that drastic a step.

"Riding made me think I could do things I can't. And I got you two sucked into my obsession. So why should I get to ride when Debbie never can?"

"By that argument, why should you get to go to the movies? Or go all in on a buffet? Why should you get to use two-ply toilet paper? Why not just live like a monk and eat newspapers for the rest of your life?"

"I—what?"

"What Sidney means is—"

"Do *not* fucking think you're my translator, Amanda."

"—how does hurting yourself help?" Amanda persisted. "Or solve anything?"

"It's not about solving," Cassandra muttered. "It's about getting out. The way she should have and didn't. The way my—"

"Yeah, it all comes back to that, doesn't it?" Sidney asked.

"Very astute, Dr. Freud," Cass snapped.

Amanda was still trying to grasp current events. "But you've wanted a bike forever. You started saving up when you were in, like, the third grade, for God's sake. You spent years window shopping—it's what got Sidney and me into motorcycles. And we love our bikes!"

"So?"

"So you opened up entirely new lifestyles for us. By accident, no less, which makes it cooler. Without you, we wouldn't know a foot peg from a Fig Newton. And as much as we love our bikes, you love yours even more. Because you fought so hard and worked so long to get one. Like how I'll feel about my bookstore once I get it up and running."

"Yeah, about that. Give it up, Amanda."

"Oh, charming. You had a bad day—"

"Not as bad as Debbie Frank."

"—so everyone has to quit their dreams?"

"It's too much for one person. And an independent bookstore in the age of Amazon? In a small town? Ridiculous and doomed to failure."

Thank God she's packed the knives. Though she's a shitty packer, so I could probably find them without much trouble. "I know you're upset," Amanda replied through gritted teeth, "so I'll pretend you didn't just say what you just said."

"There's your fundamental flaw, Cassandra," Sidney (!) put in. "Talking about Amanda doing it alone—she wouldn't have done it by herself. Won't, I mean. Just like you didn't furnish this place by yourself. Just like you didn't start OpStar by yourself."

"I know. That's something else I have to face. Without me, you guys wouldn't have gotten into any of it. You'd be safe. Well, maybe not Sidney."

"And now you're trying to take away our autonomy." Sidney sighed. "Dick move, Cassandra."

Amanda rubbed her temples and tried to think of ways to arrest what was happening. "But what about your mom?"

Cass straightened, and Amanda was startled to see she was crying. Unlike her giggles, you could never tell Cass was crying unless you were looking right at her. She'd spent her childhood swallowing sorrow.

"Cass?"

"What *about* my mom?" Quickly, almost savagely, Cass dashed away an angry tear. "Part of this is on her. The one time my dad laid a hand on me—"

"It was a little more than laying a hand on you. Don't downplay what that fucko did."

"—and she kills him? When she went to prison, she essentially orphaned me. Wouldn't let me testify, wouldn't say a word in her defense, took a *plea deal*, for God's sake. What was she thinking?"

"To spare you the ordeal of testifying," Amanda replied. "That's what she was thinking. Also, it's what she told me."

"If she gave one shit about sparing me ordeals, my dad would still be alive."

Sidney sucked in a breath. "Ooooof. Harsh."

Amanda was shaking her head. "So, wait, you're on your dad's side now?"

"I'm on no one's side." Cassandra pointed right at her and scowled. "And that's how it'll stay."

"If it makes you feel better, Jonny Frank's ass is going to jail."

"It doesn't, Sidney. Why would it? That shithead should have gone to prison the *first* time he killed a wife. No one bought his bullshit she-fell-down-two-carpeted-stairs-and-shattered-her-skull excuse."

"You're right," Amanda replied. "Everyone knew, but the cops couldn't prove it."

"He'll be out in less than ten," Cass continued. "Guaranteed. And she'll be in the ground forever."

"Fewer," Amanda said, because she was a slave to good grammar. *And it probably isn't a great time to point out that she was cremated.* "Fewer than ten."

"Thanks, grammar Nazi."

"Whoa! Can we not throw that word around?" Sidney demanded. "It cheapens the shittiness of actual Nazis."

"You're the one who doesn't like euphemisms."

"Yeah, well, I make an exception when it comes to Nazis. Call Amanda naive or tight-assed—"

Jesus Christ.

"—or a brainiac who isn't quite as smart as she thinks but still goes into lecture mode way too often—"

"Jesus Christ!"

"—but keep the N-word out of it."

Cassandra rounded on Amanda. "Why do you even care?"

"I—why? One of my best friends is freshly traumatized and moving away." Amanda took half a step in Cassandra's direction. "Why wouldn't I care?"

"No, I mean OpStar. Why'd you even get into it? You had a perfect childhood."

"Wow. Lots to unpack here." Amanda took a breath and tried to will herself calm but could feel her temples throbbing in time with her heartbeat. "Big number one, this isn't the first time you've hinted my lack of DV-survivor street cred means it's weird that I give a shit about survivors. But I think I've proved myself. Screw that—I *know* I have."

"No question," Sidney piped up.

"So why are you still acting like I should have auditioned, should have been vetted instead of jumping in? And number two, just because my dad didn't make a habit of beating the crap out of my mom doesn't mean 'perfect childhood.' It's not a contest, for God's sake."

"If there was, though, I think Cassandra would win."

"Not helping, Sidney," Amanda replied. "And third—and again, we've been over this—I'm in it for the same reason you are. We couldn't help your mom, but we can help others."

"But you didn't prove yourself. Neither did I. Neither did Sidney."

"I feel like I should jump in with 'Leave me out of this,' but it'd be a waste of breath."

Cassandra ignored Sidney's comment. "Case in point: Debbie Frank."

Amanda sighed. "So as I pointed out, you're choosing to focus on the one failure instead of all the other successes. Which isn't just insulting, it's shortsighted. Though it's nice to hear you sort of acknowledge that your street cred didn't make you any better at this than I am."

Ha! Direct hit. Cassandra didn't have an immediate rejoinder. Long seconds ticked by, giving Amanda enough time to wonder if this had been the best approach.

Cassandra tried to pull off another long strip of tape, but there was only an inch left. She cursed and tossed it aside. "Goodbye, you guys. It was a disaster, but only at the end. And the beginning."

"A stirring summation," Sidney said dryly. "Well, when you recover from . . . from whatever the hell this is, we'll be here."

"And when Frank gets out and comes home? And is walking around breathing the same air we are?" Cass kicked another box across the room; Amanda didn't know what was inside, but they all heard glass breaking. "What then?"

"Well, we could murder him," Sidney suggested. "Right in his fat stupid face! Starting with that cleft chin. Might as well be a bull's-eye. That might make you feel better."

"Yeah, let's shelve that plan for later. Out, now. Both of you."

"Don't act like you don't need our help," Amanda warned.

"I don't. Which is the point." Cassandra gestured to her apartment. "What you see is what you et cetera. I can move this by myself in an afternoon."

"Nice to see you embrace the lame joy of minimalism, I guess?"

"You'll be back," Amanda vowed. "Mark my words!" *Okay, I didn't mean for that to sound like a threat. But it is what it is.*

"Don't bet on it," Cassandra said, and gently shoved them toward the door. "You can mark my words too."

"Well, at least Sonny Manners is gonna have a good day," Sidney said. "Don't fucking push, we're going. He and Jeff have been lusting after your Commando for years."

"I'm glad someone's having a good day," Cass replied.

"You take that back, Cassandra Rivers! You don't *ever* wish nice things for *any* Manners!"

For rebuttal, Cass gently closed the door in their faces.

They stood there for a long few seconds, then looked at each other. "Well, fuck."

"Perfect encapsulation," Amanda agreed.

Sidney pounded on the door. "I meant what I said, Cassandra Rivers! When you wake the fuck up, we'll be here for you!" To Amanda: "I give her two months."

CHAPTER

TWENTY-EIGHT

"It's still here!" Cass whirled on Sonny. "Why is my bike still here?"

Excellent question, because there it was in all its classic glory. The isolastic frame, the vertical twin engine, the center stand, just a lovely pile of bright red and chrome, like an apple you know you shouldn't eat but will anyway. Amanda knew if she checked the bike's windshield bag, it would be full of crochet hooks, earplugs, a tire gauge, Starburst, and sunscreen.

But given that the bike would probably be exhibit A for a prosecutor at some future date, putting more fingerprints all over it wasn't such a great idea.

"Sonny!" Other than on the day she'd gotten her scar, Amanda had never heard Cass sound so horrified. "Why is it still here? And why is it in such good shape after all this time?"

It wasn't in good shape; it was in *great* shape. Cassandra's Commando was spotless, so well maintained that Amanda was sure if she started it, it would kick right over, and they'd all hear the delightful rumble of the OHV engine.

"I . . . what?" Sonny picked up a shop towel and was wringing it like a goose's neck. "I've been keeping it here for you. I knew you'd be back for it. Again, I mean."

"Back *again*?" Beane asked as Cass groaned and bent like she was about to barf all over the surprisingly spotless workshop floor.

"Well . . . yeah. Cass took it out a couple of times in the last week or so."

"Um." Amanda took a second to steady her tone. Probably wouldn't do to sound too shrill. Or accusatory. "What?" She turned to look at her (estranged) friend, who was currently so pale that her scar stood out in glaring relief. Guilt? Shock? "He thinks—you've been—*have* you been—?"

Sidney was studying Cassandra, her head tilted to one side like a— like some kind of—Amanda couldn't even finish the simile, she was so rattled. "Something you wanna share with the class, Cass?"

"Jesus, you guys, it wasn't me!" Cass was holding her hands up like someone about to be arrested, a stance that wasn't helping her case. "You think I've been secretly tooling around town under cover of darkness? That I—I killed Jonny Frank and then hit the Muddy for cheese curds? And I turned myself in and tagged along with you guys, ultimately leading you—and a former cop—here? Right here? This shop? All to— what? Throw you off the scent?"

There was a short silence, broken when Sidney cleared her throat. "It does sound out of character."

"Well, *thank* you."

"You're way too lazy to put up with any of that, Cass. I just don't see you doing any kind of premeditated murder. Crime of passion, sure. Road rage? You bet. But nothing that takes research. Nothing that takes more than half a day of planning."

"I did think you turning yourself in to the police was unfathomably stupid," Amanda added, because Sidney was right: the elements of this particular murder were beyond Cassandra. But that presented a bigger problem. "Maybe so stupid only an innocent person would have done it?"

"Not the vigorous defense I was hoping for," Cassandra sighed, "but I'll take it."

"But that means—" Amanda cut herself off. It meant that not only did someone specifically target Jonny Frank, but they also targeted Cassandra. Only she was to be a different kind of victim: the kind who went to prison for two decades while the true killer got to roam free.

Which made Cassandra's situation so . . . much . . . worse.

Beane stepped forward with a carefully blank expression. "You saw Cassandra Rivers take the bike?"

"Don't answer that!" Amanda screeched, startling Sonny into dropping his rag. The list of people who would want to frame Cassandra five years after Starfish disbanded was short. Which meant this shop was the very last place they should be talking about Jonny Frank *or* Cassandra's bike. *We have to leave. All of us. Right now.* "Let's . . . let's think a minute. Preferably somewhere else."

"It's okay," Beane soothed. "Cassandra wasn't Mirandized. She's not even under arrest. And I'm not a cop anymore, so I can't use any of this against her." He turned back to Sonny, and you wouldn't know he didn't have a badge anymore, given how he radiated calm authority. She couldn't decide if that went in the Like column or the Dislike column. "Now, Mr. Manners, did you see her ta—*mmph.*"

Amanda had seized him by the shirt, yanked him close, and kissed him.

Stupid, stupid, stupid idea, this will never work and calls my sanity into question, and it'll be awful because first kisses almost always are, no idea why, too many teeth or something . . .

It wasn't awful.

At all.

Even better, Sean Beane was on board. His arms came around her as he pulled her up on her toes. And kissed back. And it still wasn't awful. And he still smelled better than anyone had a right to. And he was breaking the kiss. Disappointing yet sensible. And she was beyond gratified to see the flush of arousal on his face.

She only remembered their gaping audience when Sidney smacked her palm on top of one of the tool cabinets. "*Wow*, do I feel silly. I thought finding out someone's framing Cass would be the most off-putting moment of the day."

Ha ha. Someone framing Cass for murder was *so much worse*. And it wouldn't be long before an actual investigator would be sniffing around and talking to a judge about probable cause for a search warrant.

No, that wasn't fair. Beane *was* an actual investigator. Giving up the badge didn't change that. The only thing that changed was who signed his paychecks.

"I'm confused," Sonny announced.

"Same," Cassandra replied.

"Shut up, shut up, all of you shut up! Especially you, Cass." Amanda realized she still had two fistfuls of shirt and forced herself to loosen her grip. "Sean, I need to speak to you privately."

"No doubt," Sidney sniggered.

"So, uh, Cass—are you saying you haven't been taking your bike out?"

Cass buried her face in her hands and shook her head, hard. She straightened and replied, "Sonny, I had no idea it was here. I brought these guys here to prove that. Only to find your inconvenient kindness really screwed me over."

Sonny blanched. "Aw, hell. It's just, I knew you didn't want to part with it. I mean—how could you? So I knew you'd be back. Didn't you notice I never sent you any money or a receipt from selling your bike?"

All eyes went to Cass, who flushed. "Nope. Never did. Which was careless and stupid."

That's maybe a little harsh. Cass had closed the door on all of it when she took off. She would have spent five years *not* thinking about what she'd lost, what she'd given away. So why would she be wondering about how much Sonny could get for the thing she didn't want to think about ever again?

"Shop's doing okay," Sonny continued, "so I could afford to store it for you. I sure didn't mean to cause you trouble."

Cass was rubbing her scar and found a smile from somewhere. "Ah, thank you, Sonny. I appreciate that. But this is the first time I've been in your shop in five years. If someone's taking my Commando out, it's not me." To the others: "I swear it's not me."

"We believe you," Sidney said immediately, which was presumptuous and true.

"How many times?" Beane asked at once, holding Amanda at arm's length to forestall more distractions. She had a clear shot at his balls, though. *No, no. Not the time for a sucker punch.*

"Uh, twice, I guess? Maybe three times? It was always back in the garage, and nothing was stolen or anything, so I just, y'know, assumed. I figured if it was someone up to no good, they woulda trashed my place or at least robbed me."

"I don't have the keys to my—to this bike," Cass reminded him. "I gave those up too. And I never had the key to your shop. So who's been coming here after hours to tool around town on my bike shooting randos?"

"Pretty sure this particular victim wasn't random," Sidney commented.

"Wait, who's been shot?" Sonny asked, alarmed.

"Fuck fuck fuuuuuuuuck." Sidney rubbed her eyes, hard, then answered: "Franklin Donahue."

"Who the hell is—"

"The guy they pulled out of the river who used to go by 'Jonny Frank.'"

Sonny digested this, blinking. "I thought he drowned."

"Well, he didn't; keep up, for fuck's sake. Anyway, Team Beane over there has kept the news of his richly deserved demise out of the papers so far, but that's gonna fall apart any second. Do you have security cameras?"

"Jeez, no, Sidney. Don't really need 'em. I've never had any trouble, and you know how it is here." Sonny waved his hand, gesturing to the bike and his spotless shop. Essentially, *Everything's righty-tighty, everything's where it belongs, everyone knows their place, this is a small town where most of us like each other, nothing to see here.* "We all know each other. So somebody shot Jonny and threw him in the river? You sure it wasn't an accident?"

Sidney rolled her eyes. "How do you accidentally shoot someone in the back of the head and then hurl them into a river? If you're not a cop, I mean. Yeah, that's right, Beane, I said what I said." To the others: "So now we're looking for someone with a motive to kill that killer. Preferably someone who *isn't* one of us."

"We're not looking for anyone," Amanda reminded her. "Remember your little speech in my Hole?"

"Gross."

"About how amateurs shouldn't try to catch killers?"

"Of course I remember, it was just a few hours ago."

"Though if this was a book or movie, Sonny'd be our red herring," Amanda mused aloud. "He's just too nice. Last-person-we'd-suspect nice."

"We've gotta do something," Sidney continued. "This gets stranger and stranger by the minute. If we just sit around, there's a chance at least one person in this room could end up bunking with Iris Rivers."

"I think 'stranger' is in the eye of the beholder," Amanda said. "It brings to mind something I read."

"Ohhhhhh God, here we go." From Sidney, who got a grin out of Cassandra for her theatrical moan.

Amanda ignored the interruption. "One of the reasons murders seem unsolvably weird is because investigators get misleading facts and run with them. Or they don't get enough info and jump to conclusions. If you don't have all the facts, even a smash-and-grab could seem mysterious."

"Everything you just said sounds made up."

"Well, Sidney, I can assure you it isn't. See, Sean agrees with me, he's nodding."

"He's probably still light headed from the mack you put on him, and who cares *what* his head is doing? Can we stay on topic? Just once, just to see if we like it?"

"I *am* on topic. This, all of this, it's like the severed feet that keep washing up on beaches."

Sidney groaned again. "Oh God, not the severed feet again."

"Whaaaat?" Cass raised an eyebrow. "I missed this."

"Count your fucking blessings."

"I've missed your know-it-all nonsense," Cassandra said, and Amanda wasn't sure if it was a compliment disguised as an insult or vice versa.

"Your own fault, Cassandra. For about twenty years—"

"Now you've done it. Now you've got her giving a goddamned lecture about severed feet. And we all have to hear it. And it's gross. It's just so incredibly gross."

"—for *about twenty years*, severed feet kept washing up on UK beaches. Not corpses—feet. And not partial feet—the entire foot, still encased in a shoe. Everything else, gone. And nobody could figure out why. Divers in trouble? Sharks chowing down but spitting out feet?"

Cass smiled. "Because sharks are known for being *such* picky eaters."

"A serial killer chopping his way through a cruise ship? A sign of the coming apocalypse?"

Sidney raised her hand like she thought Sonny's workshop was first-period American history and she needed to be called on. (Ironically, the only time she ever raised a hand in AH was to use the bathroom.) "I still say it's that last one."

"Hush, Sid. Anyway, big mystery—except not really. Not once you understand modern shoe designs and how bodies break down in saltwater."

"Please tell me you don't have pictures of that on your phone. Also, please don't take out your phone."

"Oh, Cass, you know she does. And you know she will."

"Will you two nix the interruptions?" Amanda cried. "I know your babble makes sense to you, but it's just another reason why side conversations are rude."

"Another reason?" Cassandra asked.

Sidney let out a long-suffering sigh. "Fine, fine, keep grossing us out with a lecture no one asked for and no one has time for due to pressing matters like the bike-shaped elephant in the room."

"So it turns out that when a corpse hits bottom, scavengers go to town on the body buffet. And they're lazy; they prefer soft tissue. So they nibble through ankle ligaments, and eventually, the foot breaks off from the body. Since it's in a sneaker, it floats. Since it floats, it's carried by the tide. Since it's carried by the tide, it eventually washes up: severed feet in near-perfect condition thanks to superior shoe design and lazy-ass scavengers."

"Nope. Apocalypse."

"Whatever the reason for all the strange feet, it's moot." Cass was shaking her head so hard that Amanda was getting a headache just watching. "You guys. You guys have done enough. More than, in fact. I left town because I got us all in trouble and needed distance. I'm back fewer than three days, and you might be implicated in a homicide investigation." She paused and Amanda heard her gulp. "I n-never should've come back."

"Don't say that, Cass," Sidney said, giving Cassandra her standard sideways hug with no eye contact. "It's a mess, but it's not your mess.

Well, it kind of is, but it's not your *fault* probably. Even if it is, you're gonna fix it, maybe."

"The world lost an angel when you decided not to go into social work, Sidney," Amanda said, and was more than a little proud that she managed the observation with a straight face.

"My point, *Cassandra*, since nobody's talking to Amanda, is you shouldn't have to face any of it alone. Haven't I always said so? Though that husband crack was below the belt, you rotten bitch."

"It's true." Amanda nodded. "About the crack and about how Sidney always said you didn't have to be alone. If I'm gonna be honest—"

"I'm not sure I'm up for more honesty," Cassandra said in a small voice.

"—I'm sorry to say I had no plans to track you down." *There, let that sink in for a few seconds.*

She couldn't, was the thing. Tracking her down would mean admitting she was incomplete without Cassandra Rivers. And she couldn't put her pride aside and admit that, because Cass clearly didn't feel the same way. How could she, when she had removed herself so entirely from their lives that she'd turned herself into a ghost?

Or so Amanda had thought, once upon a time. But now she wondered. Maybe it was time to give Cassandra a smidge of the benefit of the doubt. Maybe she hadn't left to protect herself, but all three of them.

She shook it off, all of it. Focus was critical here. "It was all Sid's idea," Amanda finished. "If I had my way, Dave would never have had to guard my Hole."

"I'm not alone. My mother—"

"Your mom kicks ass and bakes a mean apple pudding," Sidney put in, "but she's also locked up and no help to you at all. Not out here, not with a murder investigation bearing down on us."

"Bearing down on *me*," Cassandra urged.

Sidney waved away Cassandra's remark. "Face it, babe: we're it. Oh, and Beane, too, maybe; who the fuck knows with that sneaky shit?"

"I'm in the room," he pointed out. "In case you forgot."

"Who the hell could forget? We can't get rid of you . . . well"—Sidney gave Amanda some side-eye—"some of us can't. Every time we turn around, there you are."

"Where else would I be?" Sean asked, which was an odd question from someone they'd just met a couple of days ago.

Not so odd if you know his backstory, Amanda thought. *Because we didn't just meet him three days ago.*

"I'm still confused," Sonny reminded them, which was a sensible reaction to the madness he'd just stepped in.

"Join the lame-ass club. Now what?" Before anyone could answer, Sidney added, "Besides the obvious."

"The obvious?" Sonny asked, because he thought he was in this for some reason. Well, two reasons: this was his shop, and he was standing four feet away. *We need to stop having confidential meetings in public places with witnesses.*

"Yeah, that being we all strongly encourage Cassandra to get the fuck out of Dodge," Sidney finished. "With clubs and kicks if necessary."

Cass shook her head. "No way."

"I'll do it, Rivers!" Sidney smacked the tool chest again. "I'll find or make a club and go to fucking town on your selfless ass and boot you right back over the town line, you just *watch.*"

"I believe that. I meant 'no way' because I'm not leaving you guys holding the metaphorical bag again. And yeah, Amanda, before you jump in and point it out, I'm aware of the irony. Couldn't get out of here fast enough five years ago—"

"I thought we agreed this didn't need pointing out," Amanda sniffed.

"—and now you can't get rid of me."

"It's a nightmare, all right," Sidney agreed with uncharacteristic cheer.

"We've taken up enough of your time," Sean told Sonny. Amanda had no idea if that was true or just a platitude, but guessed Sean thought they should continue the gosh-who's-using-Sonny's-shop-to-frame-Cass-for-murder chat somewhere one of the (unlikely) suspects couldn't hear them.

Having finished wringing the towel, Sonny was now drying his dry hands with it. "Oh. Okay." To Cassandra: "I'm real sorry if I caused trouble for you. It's just . . . y'know. Your bike. You need it." This last phrase said as if he were talking about her liver.

"It is. Was, and is," Cass agreed. Despite the shock, Cass seemed delighted to see it again. *There's a rider for you,* Amanda thought. *Sure, the proximity of this machine will mean more trouble, but shouldn't we start it up and listen to that delicious-sounding engine regardless? And perhaps make a cream puff run?* "I appreciate you taking such good care of it."

"And if you don't leave, if you think 'er over and decide you're gonna stay in town for a bit"—as Sidney opened her mouth, Sonny rushed ahead—"you should swing by and see Becka Swanson. She hears from her sis all the time, and she'd love a visit with you."

Oh, boy. Becka and Bobby Swanson. There's a footnote from history.

"Thanks, Sonny. Maybe I will," Cassandra replied with a bright smile.

The smile, like "maybe I will," was a lie. For all that Operation Starfish was Cassandra's brain baby, once the battered spouse in question was out, Cassandra's focus was always on the next one; she never looked back, Debbie Frank being the notable exception.

"Becka and Bobby Swanson?" Sean asked.

"Rebecca and Roberta," Amanda explained. "Fraternal twins. Only one of them married well." Which was how Roberta Swanson ended up as OpStar's first client.

"I'd love to hear about it."

Yes indeed, Sean, I'm sure you would.

Too bad.

CHAPTER TWENTY-NINE

Operation Starfish: First run . . .

"So just a reminder—"

"Amanda, we read your dossier." Sidney was (probably) glaring at her. Hard to tell with the dark sunglasses covering half her face. "Your twenty-two-page dossier. Your twenty-two-page dossier which I had to read hungover, since we only graduated two days ago, and the booze has been flowing like wine."

"First, why are you narrating? I'm aware Friday was graduation. Second, the *r* in dossier is silent."

"Speaking of silent, let's all be that." This from Cass, who looked only slightly less DOA than Sidney.

Amanda took a breath and tried again. "But I think it's worth emphasizing—"

"We. Read. It."

"—that the most dangerous time for an abused spouse is the first ninety days after they leave," she finished in a rush.

"That sounds so familiar," Cass said, straight faced. She took a sip from a travel mug big enough to hold a half gallon of (*urgh*) Mountain Dew, her wake-up drink of choice. "I feel like I might have read that somewhere. Recently." To Sidney: "Cooler's on the back of my bike."

"Thank God," Sidney moaned, then hopped down from the minivan and helped herself to Cassandra's saddlebag. "I'm taking the V8, but I wouldn't touch the Pop-Tarts if you stuck a gun in my mouth."

"It makes sense," Amanda said as Sidney made half the V8 disappear in three gulps.

"Don't ask her any follow-up questions. Because she'll answer them."

"What makes sense, Amanda?" Cass asked with a grin.

"Dammit, Cassandra! Shit, my head . . ."

"That whole hair-of-the-dog thing," Amanda elaborated. "Like a Bloody Mary: it might be awful to contemplate at eight o'clock in the morning, but it's got vitamins C and B, electrolytes; it helps replenish your fluids . . . like that. The one thing in a Bloody Mary that won't help your head is the vodka."

"Thus . . ." Two more gulps. "It's a V8, not a Bloody Mary. But what're the Pop-Tarts for?"

"To elevate your blood sugar," Cass said. The "duh" was unspoken.

"Oh, sweet dear little baby Jesus in his holy onesie in heaven," Sidney breathed. "Do not chase your Mountain Dew with a chocolate fudge Pop-Tart. I will barf, Cassandra. And not just dry heaves. It'll be a lake of barf. And not a wimpy lake like Hiawatha. A Great Lakes–size lake of barf. The Lake Superior of barf."

"Leaving's a process, just like the abuse is a process," Amanda put in, because she needed to get them back on track and didn't want to giggle at a Superior lake of barf. "It doesn't start with the abuser slapping them on the first date."

"No, it does not," Cass muttered. "Who'd ever agree to a second date?"

"And sometimes leaving takes a few tries, also."

"We can't help that," Cass replied. In half a tick, empathy had been replaced with chilly pragmatism. "We're giving them a shot. What happens after is up to them."

Amanda and Sidney traded glances, but now wasn't the time to work on that particular flaw in Cassandra's logic/personality. "Okay, just a reminder. We're not judging and we're not confronting. We're not social workers and we're not cops. There's no paperwork and no bureaucracy. We're giving her a ride to the hotel-cum-shelter, where she can crash for a day or two and figure out what's next. And that's *all*."

"You know what I won't miss about high school?" Sidney asked. "The teacher making us read stuff and then telling us what we already read. It's exhibit A for why I've got no interest in college."

"Just for that, I'm not telling you about your V8 mustache. Okay, let's go."

After a short drive, they pulled into the half-mile-long driveway, Cass and Amanda on their bikes, Sidney driving her minivan. The house, which sat on three-quarters of an acre, was large enough to be intimidating—four bedrooms? Five? There was a barn on the property, the garage was big enough to be a house on its own, and there was a small cream-colored shed just a few feet away from the garage.

The closest neighbors were three miles away—Bobby had assured them her husband had an appointment and would be gone all morning. So they'd huddled up to talk about dossiers until it occurred to Amanda that they were stalling.

"We're supposed to be here," she reminded them. "We have every right to be here, in fact; we were invited by the homeowner. In writing, no less. So let's go to work." Even as she said that, the front door slowly opened, and Roberta Swanson peeked around the frame, then crept onto the porch.

For a long moment she just looked at them. "I—I can't believe you're here."

Cass spread her arms and smiled. "We said, didn't we? Don't look so surprised."

Bobby Swanson found a shaky smile from somewhere. "I—sorry. I've never done this before."

You're in good company, Amanda thought. "Are you ready? Overnight bag packed? Got any backup meds? If you've got extra bags, there's plenty of room in the minivan."

"Yes," Sidney said. "There certainly is plenty of room in *my* van, and this isn't even the first time my van came in handy. Won't be the last either; you can bet your ass on that. Thank God for my van!"

"We all have our, um, agendas," Amanda said even as Bobby was creeping down the porch stairs in a way that made her five-foot frame seem even smaller. "But if you're ready, we can hit it."

"It was . . . really hard—" Bobby said. She stopped creeping to dart around the corner, went down onto her hands and knees, and stuck her arm under the porch. She fumbled with something, then stood and hefted a small bag onto her shoulder.

Didn't dare keep it in that enormous house. Couldn't be sure he wouldn't find it. So he goes through her things on the regular. Christ.

"—because he's so nice—" Bobby was saying. She was digging around in her shorts pockets for something. "—to everyone. And me, too, in the beginning. He still is. A lot of the time, he's nice to me. It's just . . ."

"Yeah, he sounds like a real Prince Harming." At the eye rolls from her friends, Sidney shrugged. "Too soon? Okay then."

"It only started getting really bad when he decided in *this* century to jump on the 1990s start-up-tech craze, and it's been difficult. So he was just . . . there. All day. All night. If the tiniest thing went wrong, even if it was just a burned-out light bulb, he would—I mean, he didn't like that. And even after restrictions were lifted, his company figured they'd save on overhead, so they said everyone could just keep telecommuting. So there was nowhere I could really—I mean, it's not all on him, is the thing. Circumstances were, um . . . they played a part. They're as much to blame as—" She cut herself off.

We shouldn't be just standing here listening to her. She has one bag; we should be halfway back to town by now. But how do you cut someone off from sharing the harrowing tale of their life without coming off like an impersonal jackass? Especially when it was beyond obvious that talking about it was as cathartic as it was wrenching? Just . . . interrupt her? Or try to shoo her toward the van while nodding attentively?

Optics? Now? Really?

"He's always sorry," Bobby was saying. "After. And he's usually very . . . um, very careful. About leaving marks. It's one of the reasons people have a hard time believing me. He grew up here. Everyone knows him. The 'him' he wants them to see, I mean. And nobody knows me, so."

Sidney let out a frustrated sigh. "'No marks' is one of the biggest misperceptions out there. There's always a mark."

Some more apparent than others, Amanda thought, and made a conscious effort not to look at Cassandra. She realized that there was a reason Bobby had swept a hank of hair behind her ear and tilted her head toward Sidney.

"That's how you lost hearing in that ear, isn't it?" Amanda realized. "He did it."

A shrug, followed by the hiss of the inhaler she'd been digging for. She shook it, sucked down another dose, then put it back in her pocket. "Almost out."

"Don't worry, we—"

"Anyway, he didn't mean to pop the eardrum. It just . . . got away from him for a second. Like when he gave me a bit of a push when we were arguing in the garage; he didn't know I was almost out of albuterol."

Sure he didn't. He cut you off; he goes through your stuff whenever he wants but isn't keeping track of your inhalers? Bullshit.

"He ran right out to the pharmacist to refill my scrip."

Sidney was right: always a mark.

"Then I saw your guys' Facebook thing and . . . and . . . so I called."

"That's how you found out about us?" Good, that was helpful. Amanda wondered if, in addition to leafleting local shelters, she needed to whip up one of those online forms: How did you hear about OpStar? (a) Google, (b) mass mailing, (c) a battered friend, (d) pure luck.

"You called and here we are," Cass said. "That's just right. Pack up, ladies; let's get Bobby somewhere safe."

"She's already safe."

This from the man who had just thrown open the doors of the small shed beside the garage and was marching toward their small group.

Prince Harming, no doubt. A heavyset blue-eyed blond dressed in immaculate jeans and a pressed, cream-colored henley. Amanda figured he was sixty pounds heavier and at least four inches taller than his wife. He showed them a fixed smile, but as he got closer, she could see a vein throbbing at his temple. She put him in his early forties and figured Bobby was at least fifteen years younger.

Bobby shrank back, though he was still twenty feet away. "I—I—I—"

Oh, shit, look at this. Didn't go to work. Waited for us instead. So he's monitoring her screen time and her phone. Lovely.

"Good morning, ladies!" Prince Harming (who had an actual name, but who cared?) waved and smiled. "Roberta, invite your guests inside for some tea."

"I'm good," Sidney said, brandishing her empty V8 can. "And we were all just leaving."

Prince Harming sighed and shook his head at his wife. "All this? Over one little fight?"

"The fight where you popped her eardrum, or the fight where you deliberately stressed her into an asthma attack?" Cassandra asked with the charm and warmth of a concentration camp guard. "Well. Fights, plural. You guys tend to stick with what works."

His smile slipped. Just a bit, but it did Amanda a world of good and got her back on track. "Come on. We're not here to confront, defend, fight, or even have a mild disagreement. We're not here to talk at all. We're here to give Bobby a ride and that's all."

"I—I—I—"

"C'mere." Sidney reached out to Bobby, who took her hand after a long moment and let Sidney lead her to the van. "It's fine. We're going. You don't have to worry about him for a couple days, anyway. That's the point. That's the guarantee."

"Roberta! This is foolish. I apologized, and you claimed you forgave me." His wife looked back but kept going for the van. "But instead of the forgiveness I earned and that *you promised me*, you blabbed private family business, and now you've got these ladies all wound up."

"I'm not wound up," Sidney said. "Not even a little. How 'bout you two?"

"I'm whatever the opposite of wound up is," Amanda replied. "Wound down? Like one of those creepy mechanical monkeys that can't beat their cymbals when the battery's too low?"

"And for what?" Harming continued, clearly determined to whine them into submission. "A silly domestic squabble?"

"How silly could it have been," Cassandra asked reasonably enough, "if you had to lie to your wife and piss away half your morning hiding in a shed?"

"I was *not*—" He gritted his teeth. "I wanted to see if she was a liar. And she is. That's disappointing, Roberta. Your judgment of late has been suspect. Overreacting and then calling kids for help?"

"Hey! We're old enough to be drafted, to fight and/or die for Merika. We're adults in every sense of the word."

Harming ignored Sidney's outburst. "And all because you can't exert the smallest bit of self-control."

"I'll bet that's important to you," Cass said. "Control."

"Oh, look at the high school psychology student peering into my murky brain. How adorable." He flashed them a game show host grin. "But yes, it is. It's how I came up in the world. There's a reason I'm the fourth richest man in the county."

"Oh my God," Cassandra said with one of her helium giggles. "Who keeps track of stats like that? Fourth? Who's the seventh? The thirteenth?"

Bobby, to her credit, wasn't letting the conversation stop her from getting into the van. Also, *why the hell were they still having a conversation?*

Sidney carefully shut the passenger door and turned to Prince Harming. "Here's the thing. If you 7had to spend half your morning cowering in a shed, you're not controlling shit."

"I was *not*—wait! You can't leave. It's a medical imperative. Look at this, Roberta!" His Royal Harmness dug in his pockets and held up two inhalers. "The last thing you need is to run off and have another asthma attack without your meds. Remember last time? How awful it was for both of us? It wasn't easy seeing you in that state. Please stay here where your meds are. We'll work all this out, and you'll feel much better now we've cleared the air."

God, he sounds so reasonable. No wonder nobody believed her. Amanda half expected Bobby to hop out of the minivan and then climb up the porch steps to her husband. Instead, there was a decisive click as she buckled her seat belt. Then she leaned out and spoke to her husband through the car window. "I, um, asked these gals to swing by Walgreens and pick up my inhalers on the way." Pause. "I thought you might find my backups, so I explained the situation to my doctor, and she wrote me a new scrip."

For the first time, Prince Harming looked worried. "You explained . . . you told people . . . you dragged Dr. Bimmerman into this?"

"Yes. She's been worried about me for some time. So you can hang on to those. I'm all set." Longer pause. "Thank you, though." Longest pause. "Goodbye."

"Fucking masterful," Sidney said, then laughed so hard that small amounts of spit made an appearance.

"Roberta, you can't leave! Don't listen to these people; they just want to break up our family."

"Fair," Cassandra allowed. "And it doesn't make us wrong."

As Prince Harming rushed to the van, Bobby took another hit on her inhaler, then speared her husband with a dead-level look. "I can't dance," she continued, fiddling with her earlobe. "My balance is all screwed up now. From the—from what happened. I'll have to relearn everything, and I'll still never be any good. You shouldn't—"

"Roberta, I'm so sorry. I told you I never meant—"

"However it happened, you shouldn't have taken that from me." To Sidney: "Let's go. Please?"

Prince Harming made a lunge for her door handle, only for Cass to catch his arm and yank, spinning him into the side of the van. They all heard the thunk as he bounced off the metal.

Then he turned, cobra quick, and Cassandra's head snapped back as he connected. It was so fast that Amanda wasn't able to track his movement, just the resulting kinetic energy that rocked Cass on her heels.

Backhand, Amanda guessed. *Big and fast. Bobby never stood a chance in any face-off with this reasonable-sounding creeper.*

Cass wiped her mouth, looked at the blood on her thumb, and beamed like a kid on Christmas morning. "Believe it or not, I'm awfully glad you did that."

◆ ◆ ◆

"Are you sure this is how you want to spend a reasonable chunk of your adult life?"

Cass grinned through bloody teeth and batted away Sidney's hand. "This is *exactly* how."

"Sit still, you fucking maniac." Sid was dabbing at Cassandra's split lip with damp towels. They'd taken Bobby to the Port of Prescott, a boutique hotel owned by Anna Simmons, a friend of Amanda's parents and Cassandra's mother. They'd spoken with her about Operation Starfish, and Anna had offered them sizable discounts on a trial basis.

Bobby had brightened as soon as they pulled into the parking lot. Perhaps it was the knowledge that she was taking positive steps for herself, or perhaps it was the incongruous and cheerful bright blue of the hotel. It was once an office building, and the snug, comfortable rooms and overhead lighting reminded Amanda of big cubicles with proper walls. Which, now that she thought about it, was the definition of an office.

Decor aside, it was a safe place, and Bobby had flopped down in the middle of the queen-size bed and had begun making calls as they left. What happened next? No idea. But more importantly . . .

"We did everything wrong," Amanda fretted. They were at their table at Muddy Waters; after the morning drama, all three of them were famished, and Sidney wanted a semisafe spot to indulge her inner Nurse Ratched. "From the second we got off our bikes."

"Not everything. Kicking Bobby's husband in the shin hard enough to draw blood was pretty terrific . . . ow, Sid, that stings like hell."

"Ha! Yeah, he squawked like a bitch. And hopped like a pissed-off kangaroo. Now shut up and sit still."

"Ow!"

"You're neither shutting up nor sitting still, so reap what you have sown, you contrary jackass."

"It was all wrong!" Amanda insisted. "We weren't supposed to have a confrontation; we certainly weren't supposed to take sides—"

"How the *hell* do we not take sides?" Cassandra asked, all trace of teasing gone from her tone.

Amanda backpedaled. "My point was, we're supposed to be in and out and, at best, de-escalate. That was way more traumatic for Bobby than it had to be. We shouldn't have dillydallied in the driveway; we should have left immediately; we should have let her confide in us *on the way to the hotel.* We certainly shouldn't have gotten into it with Prince Harming."

Sidney grinned. "I'm so glad we're making Prince Harming a thing."

"We, Amanda?" Cassandra asked, good humor restored. "Look. This was important, and yeah, we can get better, but we *will* take sides, and we can't guarantee a trauma-free extraction. We just can't. Cops and social workers can't either. Damn, listen to me. 'Extraction'? I feel like a Marine or something."

"It was our first time," Sidney reminded them. "We'll get better, okay? Like with sex and math: the first time it's a clusterfuck; then you learn from your mistakes, and pretty soon it's awesome."

"That doesn't apply to math. And I'm just saying, someone could have been hurt."

"Ow! Jesus, Sid, are you dabbing me with barbed wire?"

"Yeah, Cass. I am dabbing you with barbed wire. It only looks like gauze."

"Hurt more, I mean," Amanda revised. "And I know you don't care, Cassandra, but we don't want you to get hurt either."

"Stop speaking for me, you silly, silly bitch."

"We should have anticipated that. We should have had a policy in place before we even got there. And we have to be really careful how we go forward. If we can learn from our grotesque errors—"

Cass snorted. "'Grotesque' is harsh."

"He dismissed us as kids pretty much immediately. That's something we'll have to work on," Amanda mused. "We look too young to look like we know what we're doing."

"Also, we don't actually—ow!—know what we're doing."

"We're lucky he didn't mistake us for the homecoming dance committee."

"We'll age, I promise," Cassandra said. "In fact, I guarantee it."

"And I can't believe we let Bobby talk us out of calling the cops," Amanda fretted. "We witnessed an assault! And one of us was the assaultee. Most of the time with DV, the only witnesses are the hitter and the hittee. But there were witnesses this time! Two of whom have impeccable reputations!"

"But we did promise," Sidney replied. "And we've gotta be as good as our word. If we say we're coming, we are. If we promise not to file a police report, we have to hold to that. Otherwise, nobody will trust us. And how does *that* help?"

"Now we know why she preemptively asked us not to call the cops. Shades of my mother," Cassandra mumbled.

Sidney shrugged. "So we'll figure out our stance on stuff like that. Y'know, like a contract. We come get the survivor in question, help him or her leave, help him or her pack and move, even, but if your scumbag spouse assaults any of us, we're legally allowed to jump on his face until he barfs up his brain."

"Jesus, Sidney." Cassandra was trying for shocked, probably, but couldn't hide the smirk.

"But pretty it up with legal jargon," Sidney added.

"Not better. Not really."

"Is this how you pictured it when you first hatched this plan, Cass?" Amanda asked. "All the way back when you were—what? Seven? Ten?"

"Nine." Cass stopped smiling and leaned forward. She moved so quickly that Sidney dabbed air for a second. "And no, it's not. I pictured me doing it by myself. Every time. And taking my lumps and getting right back in it. So this is way better than my fantasy ever could've been."

"Awwww."

"I'm serious, Sidney."

"I am too. I think it's great that we improved on the obsessive fantasy you've been nursing for the better part of a decade. Now sit the hell still or I'll make you eat your lunch before your dessert."

Cowed, Cassandra obeyed. "But that brings up another problem. And it's not that I don't love you guys, I don't want to seem ungrateful . . ."

Oh, boy. Hit me.

"But why are you in this with me?"

"This?" Amanda asked sharply. "Again?"

"It's just . . ." Cassandra spread her hands and shrugged. "I don't get it."

"Yes, you've made that clear. Why do I need a motive?"

Cassandra blinked. "Everyone does. For everything."

"Ohhhhh boy. Okay, one thing at a time. You know I'm an Air Force brat, right?"

"Are you really? Because you've never mentioned it. Oh, wait, you have. Twenty or fifty or ninety times."

"Not in a bragging way," Cassandra hurriedly put in. "More like in a complaining way. Or to highlight comparisons. Y'know, because you've seen so much of the country."

"Or to one-up us. 'God, the grocery store here sucks—you should see the stores in Minot!' 'Why don't we have more than one bank in this town?' 'There aren't *any* banks in . . .' I forget what you said."

"In Duncan, Arizona. No banks. Anywhere! Which is crazy to think about, right? Imagine having to drive forty miles to an ATM. Imagine—we're getting off track. My point was, we have to give back."

"Do we, though?" Sidney asked.

"Shush, you. Cassandra, why do you think my dad joined in the first place?"

"Free college?"

"Well, yeah. But also to give back. He's had fifteen years to get out but hasn't. And he's a volunteer fireman in his spare time."

"I remember when he hosed down our Christmas tree that year. I still don't get the fuss," Sidney griped. "It was barely even on fire."

"And my mom's been running the Christmas Meals on Wheels program for over a decade. For free. And she donates most of the food, so."

"So it's crazy that you guys spend all of Christmas morning and afternoon doing the Meals on Wheels thing and don't get around to presents until, like, nine o'clock at night on the twenty-fifth."

"I'm aware, Sidney. But it's fun! And it makes Christmas Day last forever. When you're a kid, you count the days and then the hours, and you open presents on Christmas Eve—"

"Nope! Only sociopaths open gifts on Christmas Eve."

"—*then the gifts are opened*, Sidney, on Christmas Eve *or* the next morning, and it's over. All the delicious anticipation is gone by nine o'clock in the morning on the twenty-fifth.

"But the way my family does it, the day goes on forever. By four o'clock in the afternoon, you've fed three hundred people who were going to be stuck at home, alone, on Christmas. That's—it's really just the best feeling. Sure, we have to start at seven o'clock in the morning, and the day ends with a splitting headache because all you've had are food scraps and coffee, but you don't mind because you've still got presents to look forward to."

"Sounds like madness," Sidney observed.

"Well, it isn't. It's more important than that. You've got to give back. Otherwise, you're just a parasite, or Jeff Manners. Or Donald Trump."

"Keep politics out of it," Cassandra warned. "We had to make that rule after the pudding wars."

"Oh, for—I throw *one* cup of tapioca, and you revise history and decide it was a war."

Cassandra ignored Sidney's irrelevant observation. "So that's what OpStar is for you? Giving back?"

"Sure. And it's way more interesting than making fifteen gallons of gravy, sucking down coffee, and sneaking stuffing. Also, do you even know you're insulting me when you ask that question?"

"You might have, um, made that observation before," Cass admitted. "I'm sorry. It's not that I think you shouldn't do it. I love that you're in this with me. It's that you don't have to put yourself in those situations, but you do anyway."

"By that argument, we should ditch Meals on Wheels because we don't have to put ourselves in those situations. And we shouldn't report a fire."

Amanda could see the second Cass surrendered, mostly because she threw up her hands and said to the ceiling, "I don't want you or Sidney to get hurt any more than you want me to get hurt, is all."

"Noted. Now let us never speak of this again. And something else— we should follow up with Dr. Bimmerman. You still do her clinic notes, right, Sidney?"

"Sure do. She's the unicorn of her profession: a physician with legible handwriting. I thought that was a cliché, but it's not. Every single doctor except Bimmerman has the messy scrawl of a serial killer."

"Good, that's your in. She helped with getting Bobby new meds, and Bobby told me she was going to call her back to tell her how it went. I know the doctor can't give us details about her patients, but we can give *her* details of what we do. She could be a good resource for us, or put up flyers in her office or something."

"See? We're improving already. There, Cass, you fucking toddler, you're all patched up. Or as patched up as I'm inclined to patch."

"*You're* a fucking toddler," Cassandra pouted.

"You may now indulge in your ten-o'clock-in-the-morning hot fudge sundae."

"Woo-hoo!"

◆ ◆ ◆

After they'd exchanged a few carefully selected words and phrases about that first OpStar run, the girls exchanged nostalgic smiles.

"That's it?" a clearly confused Sean Beane asked. "You're just going to drop heavy hints without actually telling me the story?"

"Yep. We all just reminisced about it, so there's no need to talk about it. That's what this was."

"I'm glad you tipped us off," Cassandra said, straight faced. "I almost reminisced about the wrong event."

"Ha! My favorite part of what we just reminisced about is how that fucker Prince Harming limped for a week and told everyone he got kicked by a horse."

"Which isn't entirely inaccurate," Cassandra giggled.

"C'mon, let's go back to my Hole. You can come, too, Beane."

"Oh, fine," he said, and sulked most of the ride, to Amanda's petty, triumphant delight.

CHAPTER THIRTY

"Look, Virgil Abloh does great work. Did great work, sorry, still can't believe he's dead. Anyway, his work is amazing, and not just the menswear he did for Louis Vuitton. I love his leggings, but I'm not dropping five hundred bucks on a dress that looks like it was made out of rusty tinfoil. I'm just not."

They were back at Amanda's store, still reeling from the strangest garage meeting ever. As they took their leave, Sonny promised he'd keep a close eye on Cassandra's Commando, a textbook case of locking the barn door after the motorcycle had run away.

Their choices were so narrow as to be almost nonexistent. Take the bike out of Sonny's garage? And then what?

Cass picks up where she left off and starts riding again? Too soon.

Turn it over to the cops? Bad idea, given how little they knew about what was going on. Even the innocent should hesitate to openly invite the police to investigate them.

Let Sidney store it at her place? Same problem, only in a different garage and, worse, could make her an accessory after the fact.

Throw it away? Sacrilege.

Blow it up? Give it a Viking funeral? Maaaaaybe . . .

"You guys know a lot about designers," Beane commented.

"No, we know a lot about designers with connections to Wisconsin," Amanda corrected. "Elena Velez, for example."

"Ohhhhhh, Elena Velez," Cass sighed. "Love her."

Beane was blinking like four or five eyelashes had dive-bombed his eyeball. "There are Wisconsin designers?"

Sidney sighed. "Jesus Christ, of course there are. Just because New York and LA assholes blow us off as flyover country doesn't mean they're right."

"We've been over this, though," Cassandra said. "We *want* them to think of us as flyover country."

Sidney nodded. "Point. Like we need to be discovered? Let the snobs stay in New York, where the island of Manhattan is eventually going to get swallowed by the Atlantic. And the entire state of California is just gonna drop off into the Pacific one of these days. We all know it! Wildfires and mudslides, and soon enough, mudslides on fire; those poor fuckers are doomed."

"Bleak," Beane commented.

"But not incorrect. D'you even know how many high-end stores have headquarters here?" Cassandra asked.

Sean rubbed his forehead. "You must know I don't."

"Lands' End, Bon-Ton, Harley-Davidson . . ."

"Harley-Davidson, Jockey International . . ." Amanda added. "And yet, you left, Cassandra."

Cass rolled her eyes. "Yeah, but not because of any local designers or the fact that Kohl's has their headquarters here."

"Where'd you even go? Sidney won't say."

"You never asked me," Sidney pointed out. "I would've told you, but I'm not a fucking telepath."

"Northfield," Cassandra confessed.

Amanda laughed. "You put it all behind you, gave up your life, and killed Operation Starfish, all to move for a fresh start . . . thirty miles away?" It was astonishing that they'd never run into each other. Amanda was in Northfield all the time, even before the teahouse opened. Was it just coincidence she'd never seen Cass? Or had Cass been avoiding her?

Cassandra shrugged. "I guess I suck at moving far, far away."

"Not really a surprise, though. We already established she had to stay close to her mother," Beane said, though nobody asked. "And we're talking about fashion instead of murder because . . ."

"There's no 'we,'" Cassandra replied. "Amanda and Sidney and I are talking fashion. You're just sort of standing there looking confused."

That is delightful. "Ha!"

"If you won't tell me about your first client, tell me about your next one. Or the tenth one. Anything!" Beane begged.

"Shaddup," Sidney said absently. Then, to Cassandra: "You're right to love Velez and wrong to love Abloh. His dresses are weird."

"You like Velez's weird dresses but not Abloh's?" Amanda cried. Beane had asked the important question but wouldn't understand the answer: the three of them often discussed fashion when faced with obstacles. Some women joined book clubs; some bitched over beet-root pesto with goat cheese pizza; the three of them plotted while they lamented the fact that Beverly Feldman didn't have a store within fifteen hundred miles.

Much more fun to debate the pros and cons of Abloh's unsightly holographic duffel bag than wonder when Cassandra was going to be indicted for murder. And for some reason, coming up with lists like "Worst shoes in the history of footgear" and "Ugliest trench coats of 2023" often helped them solve the problem they had shelved. Must've been a left brain / right brain thing.

"No, you do *not* like Velez's weird dresses over Abloh's," Amanda decided. "It makes no sense."

Sidney smacked her hand on the counter. "Abloh made dresses out of Gore-Tex! I'm not paying twelve hundred dollars to look like a sexy-ass Michelin Man."

"Better that than apocalypse chic," she retorted. "Velez does good drape, I'll grant you that. But all her dresses look like she cut fabric while blindfolded, then threw it into a washing machine with a bunch of razors. Her 2022 collection was a parade of disaster."

"Too harsh!" Cass insisted.

"Not harsh enough! One dress was essentially a volleyball net. A *volleyball net*, Cassandra. And not a nice one. A garbage net that was so torn up, college kids stuck it in storage and forgot about it."

"But the corset dress—"

Amanda groaned. "Oh, Cass, you're killing me. Corsets? Again? In this century? There's nothing innovative about going back a hundred years. Next, we'll be up to our butts in bustles and beehives."

"Could be worse," Dave Conner, faithful guardian of Amanda's Hole, said sotto voce to Beane.

"Jesus," Beane replied with a flinch. "I forgot you were here. You really do blend in."

"So they tell me. Like I said, could be worse." Dave nodded in the trio's direction. "They could be arguing about Crocs versus UGGs. So many pencils thrown that day. Y'know, it's amazing she hasn't put anyone's eye out."

"Okay, this could go on for hours—"

"Excellent! I've missed it," Cassandra admitted.

"—but we're just gonna have to agree to decide I'm right and you two are idiots. So now what? Beane? Any suggestions? And don't say Cass should turn herself in," Sidney warned.

Cass had wandered behind the counter to freshen her cup of coffee. Unlike Sidney, Cassandra did not turn hers into dessert. "Since we're back on that, quick question. You and/or Amanda didn't kill Jonny Frank, right? Just so I can check that box?"

Amanda stuck out her tongue. "Hilarious. And no, we didn't. I mean I didn't. I can't speak for Sidney. It's not like I watch her every minute."

"Fuck yourself sideways, Amanda. I wouldn't have shot him and dumped him. I would have cut off his face and fed it to him. But who has that kind of time?"

Cass looked around at their small group. "So now what?"

Excellent question. "We don't have any leads," Amanda admitted. "How could we? We're not investigating; we've been over that and over that. But sitting around hoping Cass doesn't get arrested isn't an option either. And it's not like we can start Operation Starfish again."

"Whoa!" Cass almost spilled her coffee. "Who even said restarting our fucked-up Underground Railroad was on the agenda?"

"Nobody," Amanda admitted.

"I can't advocate vigilantism," Beane said, "but you ladies performed a valuable service. You saved my sister from Debbie Frank's and Wanda Garner's fates. If you wanted to—I mean, I could help you. If you decided to take up the work again. There are ways to help without breaking quite so many laws."

"We're getting waaaaay ahead of ourselves," Amanda warned.

"And who's Wanda Garner?" Sidney asked.

"Frank's first wife," Cassandra and Beane said in unison.

"Oh, fuck, how awful is it that I couldn't remember her name?" Sidney sighed. "There's just so many."

"Okay, here's where we might have an edge on the cops," Amanda said. "Maybe we should look at Wanda's family and friends. And Debbie's."

Cass was already shaking her head. "Neither of them had any friends when they died. That's what they do. The abusers. They isolate their wives. Hell, Debbie left a good chunk of her money to us."

Dave looked surprised. "I didn't know that."

"Me neither," Beane said.

Well, no. They wouldn't. It wasn't common knowledge. And given how Debbie's murderous husband had gone to prison, Amanda wanted to keep it that way. "It's how I bought this building," she said. "Without Debbie Frank, my Hole wouldn't exist."

"It would have," Cassandra said at once. "It just would have taken you longer. You started saving up for your own store in middle school, for God's sake. You told me all about it the day we met."

This. *This* was why Cassandra's abandonment had been so hurtful, and why Sidney had needed to talk Amanda into poking their noses back into her life: Cassandra's utter, unflagging loyalty to friends. Cass had punched people in the face on Amanda's behalf. They had faced danger and inclement weather and carbs together; they had saved lives. Amanda would have bet Debbie Frank's fortune that they were indissoluble. The three of them had been a resourceful, loving unit. Right up until they weren't.

"That explains a lot. I always wondered how you made any money," Dave replied. "Your shop keeps erratic hours, and half the time, you're not even here."

"My shop keeps erratic hours this week," she corrected. "I don't normally have to run around clearing a friend of murder."

"Naw, Dave's right," Sidney said. "You're shut down a lot. You close every year on February twenty-second."

"Excuse me for thinking Edward Gorey's birthday should be a national holiday. No. *Inter*national holiday. I will eventually bend the world to my will, Sidney."

"And you close it for Night of the Radishes."

"Oh, so acknowledging another country's holiday is bad?"

"It's not a holiday," Sidney said. "It's a radish-carving competition on December twenty-third with a cash prize for the most elaborate radish. Ask me how much I hate that I know that."

"Which you only observe because you don't like being open that close to Christmas," Cassandra added. "Which is insane! Christmas Eve Eve is a gigantic retail holiday."

"It's also the best day of the year," Amanda replied with a happy sigh. "It's all the anticipation but none of the stress, because anyone sensible finished their Christmas shopping a week ago. You can just curl up with tea and read and watch it snow and wait for presents."

Sidney groaned but (uncharacteristically!) didn't say anything.

"You also close for Chocolate Mint Day," Dave said.

"Can we get back on topic, please?"

"Sure," Dave said. "I think it's great that you guys ran a network for abused wives. And I'm not the only one."

"Abused partners," Sidney corrected. "Husbands and boyfriends get beat up too."

"Right. Still neat, though. The network, not guys getting smashed by their spouses."

"But there's a downside to everything," Amanda pointed out.

"Aw, c'mon," Sidney teased. "Everything?"

"For every situation that highlights humanity's essential compassion, there's an opposite factor," Amanda insisted. "There was a reverse Underground Railroad, for example, I'm sorry to say. Treacherous shitheads would 'rescue' a runaway slave, only to turn around and sell them."

"Jeez," Dave said. "I didn't know that either."

"We did," Cassandra said. "We can give you the short version."

"There's nothing wrong with my version," Amanda grumped. "But it's moot anyway. OpStar is dead, and we don't have any leads, probably because we're not looking for any. Plus, no one's actually hired Sean."

"I don't care about that," he replied.

Sidney's eyebrows arched. "So are all your cases pro bono, or did you make an exception for us?"

"The latter. I promised myself I'd help you if I ever got the chance. I don't give a shit about the money."

"Huh. Okay. But like Amanda said, everything's moot."

"Not everything," she corrected.

"OpStar's done, and we've got no leads. We're leadless."

Beane cleared his throat. "We have a lead."

CHAPTER
THIRTY-ONE

"So we're not gonna talk about the kiss?!?"

"We are not."

"Not even a little?!?"

"Not even a smidge."

"Because it was incredible!"

"I'm aware. And you don't have to shout." Amanda put on her turn signal, then eased into the curve and left the highway. "Do you not understand how helmet mics work?"

Beane tightened his grip on her waist. "I know you're being sarcastic, but until this minute, I forgot about the mic."

"Hopeless. I don't even know why we're letting you tag along." A lie; she wanted him there. And she loved how he didn't hesitate to ask for another ride. It was stupid, especially for the twenty-first century, but there were plenty of men who didn't want to ride niche. (Years ago, the three of them decided "ride bitch" was unacceptable, so out came the rhyming dictionary. Not that "bitch" and "niche" rhymed. Close enough, though.) "Especially after the malarky at the morgue."

"Sorry," he said, because he had to be lying too. "I was only ninety-five percent sure—"

"Only?"

"—you guys didn't have guilty knowledge at that point. The percentage is much higher now."

"How much higher? Ninety-seven percent? Ninety-nine percent?"

"And you have to admit, even though I'm an ex, I lend some authority to your investigation."

"Oh my God, you did not just talk about 'lending authority.' And it's not an investigation. It's . . . it's sightseeing with questions."

He laughed so hard he almost slipped off the bike, which set off her own giggles. "Behave, you gorgeous dumbass! You're not dressed for a get-off."

"Wait, who's getting off?"

"Haul your feeble brain out of the gutter, please. 'Get-off' is slang for a minor crash."

"Oh. Because you 'get off' the bike."

"Clever man, you've cracked the code." They were approaching a stoplight, so Amanda rolled off the throttle, applied the brakes, and downshifted. "I've got no business letting you climb on. I've never ignored 'All the Gear, All the Time' in my life, but I'm breaking that rule because you're a good kisser. And also to help Cass clear her name. On the off chance it needs clearing. Which we've established it may not. Oh, good, the light's about to turn green; let's just ride in silence for the last mile, okay?"

"Or we could kiss again. You've got a few more seconds."

Absurdly tempting. Especially given how Sean was snuggled up behind her with his goddamned distracting aftershave and deliciously deep voice.

"Please shut up now."

"Impossible. I'm still wrestling with the knowledge that you think I'm a gorgeous good kisser."

"You caught me in a dry spell," she admitted. "It's been a while. For me."

"Also impossible. Nothing you can say will persuade me that you have *any* trouble getting laid."

She could feel her face heating up behind the helmet. "Dammit, Beane, that's absurdly flattering."

"Is that why you sound annoyed?"

"No, that's just her normal tone of voice. Sorry to rain on your weird sex parade," Sidney said in her ear, "but you're on a group com."

"Liar. You're not a bit sorry, Sidney Derecho."

"And are you taking the long way on purpose, you horny jackass?"

"Are you really?" Beane asked, delighted.

"I. Am. Avoiding. Construction."

"There's. No. Construction. Within. Fifteen. Miles. Nice. Try. Horny. Jackass."

Berkeley Breathed had it right: friends are the ultimate mixed blessing.

The light changed, thank God, so Amanda goosed the gas and didn't say another word until they were pulling into the MCF-Stillwater parking lot. Sidney pulled up beside them and hopped out. "How'd you like the ride, Beane?"

"Loved it." Sean unbuckled his helmet and strapped it down. Amanda double-checked from long habit, but it was righty-tighty.

"Ah! A new convert." Cassandra came around the van, as euphoric as Amanda had ever seen her. Who knew Cass was so excited to visit her incarcerated mom? Twice in the same week, even? "I got these two hooked on riding, so it's nice I haven't lost my touch. Time for you to get some leather and join a law enforcement motorcycle club. LEMCs are a real thing."

"Naw. I'm happy to ride behind Amanda."

"Presumptuous," Amanda sniffed.

"Gotta give you credit, Beane, your connections are making life easier. Usually, only two people at a time can visit an inmate, and the guards need more than an hour's notice."

"Tsk, tsk, Sidney. You mean 'individuals with justice-system involvement,'" Cass teased.

"I said what I said, goddammit!" Since shrieking could get them kicked out before they even got all the way in, she lowered her voice. "Sorry. I just hate euphemisms so fucking much."

"You do? Gee, you've never said so."

"Kindly die screaming, Amanda."

Twenty minutes later, they were sitting across from a bemused Iris Rivers, who greeted them with, "I do love surprises. Amanda, how nice to see you. Thank you so much for the copy of *Cooking with Deadpool.* And Sidney and Cassandra! Again."

"We're aware. Mom, this is former detective Sean Beane—"

Her perfectly plucked eyebrows arched. Did they let "individuals with justice-system involvement" have tweezers? And if they didn't, how did Iris create such perfect arches? Mysteries, mysteries. "Sean Beane? Truly?"

"There's an *e* at the end, but it's ridiculous, right? Don't worry, he's changing it."

"No, *he's* changing it," Beane replied. "Nice to meet you, Ms. Schmitt."

"It's Rivers, former detective Beane. I took my maiden name back the day after I murdered my husband. And I think you knew that."

Yeesh. Even after all this time, it was jarring to hear Iris confess to murder with such calm.

"And my daughter stopped using Schmitt on her sixteenth birthday." Iris looked around at their small group. Sean had worked more benign magic and gotten them their own room for the interrogation. Visit! It was a visit. "What is it? What's wrong? And please don't insult my intelligence with false assurances."

"Not even one false assurance?"

Iris speared her daughter with a level gaze. "It's just another way to lie, Cassandra. As you lied to me earlier this week."

"Oh. You, um, found out about that?"

"I run and write the *Prison Mirror*. I find out everything. Speaking of, how goes your own writing?"

"It's fine, Mom. So listen, last time you made a point of saying it was nice to see familiar faces."

"I did, yes."

"Inferring that you've been visited by strangers."

Before Amanda could open her mouth, Iris beat her to it. "Implying, dear. I implied, you inferred."

For her grammatical excellence, Iris was treated to a Rivers eye roll. "Right. Anyway, d'you mind telling us—"

"Marcus Garner."

And there it was. Right out there for all of them to ponder.

"Huh," Amanda commented. "I thought it would take more than twenty seconds to get a name."

Iris leaned in. "Tell me what's happened."

They had talked about this before the drive over. There didn't seem to be a way to find out what Iris knew without tipping her off about Frank's murder and Cassandra's suspected involvement. So Cass agreed they'd have to tell her the whole story.

Which Iris already knew, so it didn't take long.

"But you aren't under arrest, correct?" At their nods, Iris continued. "And former detective Beane, you're investigating at your own instigation, yes? Not officially?"

"That's correct, ma'am."

"So, Mom, we were wondering what you thought I—"

"Leave town. Tonight."

Amanda blinked. *Not the advice I was expecting.* But given what Cass had done five years ago, Amanda had to wonder if it was advice *Cass* was expecting.

"Mom, you caught the part where I didn't actually kill Frank, right?"

Iris looked at her remaining family member with terrible pity. "Oh, my dear. You grew up in an abusive home, something I still blame myself for."

"Or you could blame the dead guy," Sidney suggested. "Just, y'know, for a change of pace."

"You were abused, you have a documented history of erratic behavior, Operation Starfish routinely broke the law, you have a motive, and your mother rather famously committed mariticide."

"I always learn a new word when I come here," Sidney observed, but Iris stayed on point.

"Do not put yourself out there, Cassandra. Do not assume law enforcement will keep an open mind, share everything, and play fair. Leave town. Immediately."

Beane cleared his throat. "Uh . . ."

"Former detective Beane, I am aware hashtag 'not all cops.' I am sure nine times out of ten, or nineteen of twenty, perhaps even ninety-nine of a hundred, the police diligently do their jobs. But until that number is one hundred out of one hundred, it's too high a risk for a mother."

"Okay, great input; let's call Cass fleeing into the night plan B," Amanda said. *Jesus, we just got her* back. The thought startled her. Was Cass back? And was she staying, or was this a hiatus until she went back to her life in Northfield? A week ago, Amanda wouldn't have cared either way. "Can you tell us why Marcus Garner came to see you?"

"Which time?"

There was a pause while the group digested that.

"So . . . he's been coming to see you for a while, Mom?"

"Not lately, but yes."

"Why?"

Iris gave them a dry smile. "Why else? To commiserate. He knew what it was to feel helpless while a loved one is brutalized. Quite a charming man, in fact. A bit standoffish, but who can judge?"

"When was the last time you saw him?"

"Many months. He moved abroad last spring."

"Oh." Scratch Marcus.

"And you know this to be true because . . . ?"

"Because there was nothing for him here, former detective Beane."

"He's still a detective," Amanda piped up, surprised as anyone to find herself defending him. "He's just missing the badge."

Iris ignored the interruption. "He and his sister visited London when they were teenagers, and she always wanted to return. So he brought her ashes there and remained. He still writes me; I can show you the letters if you wish."

Beane opened his mouth, but Amanda cut him off. "That's okay, Iris, we believe you." Once her husband was in the ground, Iris had never lied again. She'd told Cass that after fifteen years of "I walked into a door" and "I tripped on the stairs" and "I'm taking up tinikling," she swore never to lie about her circumstances again.

Amanda still couldn't believe she'd been enough of an idiot to fall for Iris's tinikling excuse. Yeah, she'd only been fourteen at the time, but it was still galling. She'd looked it up and found out it was a Philippine folk dance where two people held bamboo poles and smashed and clacked them together as the dancers weaved back and forth between the poles, the goal being to avoid shattered ankles. A real dance; a fake excuse.

It was one of the reasons Iris would be in prison for so long: She refused to plead down to a lesser charge, to try and legally downplay what she had done. She wouldn't allow her lawyer to be even remotely disingenuous (within the boundaries of attorney ethics) on her behalf. And she wouldn't let Cass lie on her behalf, or even testify.

"Okay, Mom. Thanks for telling us. Sorry to barge in like this."

"You didn't barge."

"And don't worry."

"I *will* worry, be assured of that. To the best of my knowledge, I have only failed you once. Never again. Which, of course, means worrying as well as constant vigilance. Or as best I can manage behind bars."

"They're probably not called 'bars,'" Sidney muttered. "Probably 'confinement enablers.'"

Despite the gravity, Amanda and Sean laughed.

"Mom, what Dad did wasn't your fault." Cass reached out and took the older woman's trembling fingers in hand. "I never said otherwise, I never even thought otherwise. What *you* did was, but I'm older now. I think I understand a little better. You had two choices, and they were both unthinkable. I shouldn't have said what I said back then." Cass took a deep, steadying breath. "I'm sorry I didn't tell you any of this sooner."

"You were entitled to voice your objections."

Voice, shriek, scream, roar . . . Amanda was careful to keep a straight face even as she stifled an internal shudder. *Christ, what an awful, black day that was.*

"Though I'm gratified to see you grow in wisdom. Think how clever you'll be when you're as old as I am." Iris was smiling, but it was an old smile, one Amanda had seen many times when Iris had a husband still living. The I'm-fine-it's-just-a-cracked-rib smile. The I-shouldn't-have-provoked-him smile. But Iris was pale and shaky, and it wasn't just prison pallor or low blood sugar. However calm their tones, the room was fraught with heavy emotion, as it always was when the topic was the worst day of Iris Rivers's life, and the last day of her husband's.

"It was ages ago," Cass said. "I almost never think of it." She caught herself reaching up to fiddle with her scar, and put her hand in her lap. "Almost never."

Another lie. But for a good cause.

CHAPTER
THIRTY-TWO

Ages ago . . .

"Jesus Christ, why are you so fucking slow?"

Oh, I dunno, bad genes? Why are you such a fucking asshole?

"Coming, Dad." Cassandra Schmitt lugged the tackle box down the short hill to the creek, because God forbid Dad put his pole down to run his own errand. Like it was her fault he grabbed the wrong tackle box?

"Lunch in five," her mother called from the top of the hill.

"I told you, I need to switch out reels and check lines before I can get back to it!"

"Lunch in fifteen!"

For the millionth time, Cass wondered why her mom put up with the sentient bag of nail clippings that was Randy Schmitt. It was more than being Catholic; it went beyond "We're staying together for the kid." Did she lose a bet with God?

Once, her love for her father had been all encompassing and unconditional. Over time, that changed. The worst part? It didn't change *enough*. She still loved him. And he loved her. He loved her mother, even! Cass still went to him for advice; they had long talks about college and motorcycles and life. He could still make her laugh; his support could still be relied on. She looked forward to Friday Family Film Night; though the older she got, the lamer *it* got.

He could be kindness itself. When he found out she was saving for a motorcycle, he promised to match her dollar for dollar if she stayed on the honor roll. And every time she thought they were past the deadly drama of domestic violence—once, he'd gone ten months without hitting her mother—Iris would limp into the kitchen to fix breakfast. Or she'd pick Cass up from volleyball practice, and there'd be a splint on her finger.

And she never said a word against him. And she never fought back. And she always, *always* defended him. And the days went by.

It was flattering and shameful to know that Amanda and Sidney thought she was a minor badass, locking in the impression she'd made the day she kneed Jeff Manners's testicles into his throat. But wouldn't a badass call the cops each time her father broke the law? Or fight back on her mother's behalf? Or at least tell a school counselor?

Her friends weren't stupid; over time, they noticed her mother's tendency to have "accidents," but Cass didn't say word one and brushed off their concerns. That wasn't badass. That was chickenshit.

Maybe it would get better at home once she left for college. Maybe if it was just the two of them, then they'd get along better. Maybe the problem was her? Or the dynamic of the three of them?

Stop. Stop it.

If she didn't knock off the pondering, she'd get another headache. And she was determined to enjoy the day. Or at least get through it.

The weather was nice, so that was a plus. But unfortunately, it contributed to her dad's mood. There were always predators ready to deal death from above, so fish looked up. A lot. They also scooted away from shadows, so approaching the water with care, especially on a sunny day, was crucial. It didn't help that Coulee Creek was shallow and narrow, and the short dock poking into it seemed superfluous. But it was teeming with trout—brown, brook, and rainbow—which were wily and delicious and would make a terrific supper. Especially if her mom made those yummy tinfoil packets of potatoes and onions and butter and tossed them on the grill with the fish.

Please, please let trout be supper. Her father's temper, almost never banked, worsened when he got skunked. But to give the jackass of a devil his due, he was an excellent angler and didn't get skunked very often.

"Shit!"

Cass knew better than to ask what his problem was. He'd tell her quickly enough. He'd tell everyone within a ten-mile radius quickly enough.

"Goddamn, this line is a mess. Get me the eight-pound mono."

"Sure, Dad." It meant trudging back up the slope for yet another tackle box, and he'd bitch because she wasn't the Flash, but she knew better than to complain. He wouldn't hit her—she had no memory of him ever hitting her, though Mom claimed he spanked her once when she drew on the walls as a toddler—but there were plenty of nonphysical ways he could make her miserable.

"Tell your mom lunch has to be later!" he bawled after her.

You literally just told her. She's twenty feet away, for fuck's sake.

They'd parked the truck at the top of the bank, and her mom had the tables and chairs out and was elbow deep in lunch prep. She didn't fish anymore. Dad hated it when she put more on the dock than he did.

"He always grabs the wrong line," Mom said with a rueful smile. "Even if you try to anticipate."

"Right?" One of the worst things about Randy Schmitt was his inability to learn from his mistakes. Cass spotted the necessary tackle box and crawled into the truck bed. She pushed the kayak paddles aside

(The creek's only three feet deep at its deepest, why does he always think we can kayak?)

and grabbed it.

"Should I, uh, bring him a beer?" A tipsy dad was a slightly less shitty dad.

"I forgot to pack the beer."

Lie. Dad was a gold-medal control freak who didn't like it when anyone else drove. Cassandra could count on one hand how often he'd let her mother take the wheel. Mom accepted that, even as she refused to countenance any behavior that could endanger her daughter. This wasn't the first time she'd "forgotten" to bring booze. Risky as shit, but about some things, her mother was about as flexible as a mountain.

"Well, I'm not telling him," Cass announced.

"Wise," her mom replied with a chuckle. She was moving slower than usual. Cass suspected Dad had kicked her in the side again, but knew better than to ask. "Here." She tossed Cass a bag of M&M's, then quickly turned away, but Cass saw the wince of pain anyway. "To tide you over."

"Thanks." As usual, when thinking of the abuse her mother suffered, she had to deal with a roil of emotions: fury, despair, love, and, yeah, it had to be said, contempt. Mom could leave him. Divorce him. Fight back. Call the cops. Meet him at the door with a baseball bat. Just up and leave in the middle of the night. It wasn't 1955; she had options. But for whatever reason, her mother preferred her status as the official family punching bag.

But that was an old, tired thought, and it got her nowhere. So she tucked the bag of candy under her chin and hustled down the hill to where her dad fulminated. "Here you go." She set the box down and raised her chin, putting her hand out so the bag plopped into her palm.

He looked her over, frowning. "Lunch isn't for half an hour."

"It's just to tide me over."

"*Mmmmm.*" Dad did the sidearm-cast thing and let the line fly. Then he let a string of curses fly as well. "Son of a bitch!"

Cass swallowed a giggle. He'd misjudged the distance and was tangled up in the bushes across the bank. He stomped down the short dock, then back up, glanced around at the tackle boxes, and let out a groan. He halfheartedly tugged at the line; the bushes bent and rustled, but nothing came free.

"Well, at least I've got the range. Cass, scoot over there and free it up, wouldja?"

She was already in the water. Thank God it was August.

"And hurry up!"

Or you could get it yourself, but I'm assuming that's TOTALLY UNTHINKABLE.

She splashed through the water, entertaining dark thoughts. *To think I could've gone to the MoA with the girls to scope the new Kate Spades and gobble Cinnabons.* Amanda could eat two. One right after the other! And didn't even need a nap after. She was an insatiable miracle. And Cass had long copied Sidney's trick of triple frosting a mini Cinnabon. The bread was just a vehicle for the frosting anyway.

Cassandra reached the far side, saw his line, pulled gently; the hook wouldn't come. She cursed herself for being in such a rush to obey that she hadn't brought the nail clippers.

"Jesus Christ, in the time it took you to do that, I switched reels and put on fresh line and baited the hook!"

"Almost got it, Dad."

She straightened and turned ("See? Watch!"), and then something hit her eye and slashed a trail of fire all the way up her forehead and into her hairline. She screamed in shock and surprise, and clapped a hand to her face; her fingers were instantly wet with blood.

Then he set the hook.

Hard.

She screamed again. The pain was bad, but the surprise was devastating. Five seconds earlier, nothing hurt, and the only parts of her getting wet were her feet.

She fell to her knees and groped for the line. *Gotta grab it, gotta get some slack, it hurts, IT HURRRRRRTS . . .*

Her father's voice from far away, like, coming from Mars far away: "Cass? Cassandra? I'm—"

Then a splash she barely registered as she felt for the fishing line again, wound it around her fist, pulled hard, and snapped it off even as her blood streamed . . . everywhere. *I can't see! Oh God, did it rip up my eye?*

Get a grip, Cass. You're gonna scare Mom to death. Calm down. You snapped the line; nobody can yank it again, focus on that.

It took a minute, but right around the time she took her own advice *(Remember when you fell off the swing and cut your head? Remember how Mom said scalp wounds bleed a lot and look scary, but they're usually not serious?)* she heard more splashing. She wiped more blood out of her eyes and looked up to see a partial, blurry, red-tinged vision of her mother crossing the creek. In seconds, her cool hands were locked around Cassandra's wrists.

"Let me see."

The voice—the tone—calmed her as nothing else could have. "Is it bad? I can't see out of my left eye. Mom, I can't see!"

"You're not blind," the most beloved voice in the world assured her. "You can't see because the blood from your forehead laceration is streaming into your eyes. Hold still." Cass heard a sharp snip, felt a careful tug, and realized Mom had slowed down long enough to grab Dad's multitool. It wasn't the first time she'd had cause to be grateful for Iris Schmitt's unflappable nature.

Both pieces were now in her mother's palm. *At least it's an Aberdeen hook.* They were softer and quicker to bend, but the long shank made hook removal easier. God forbid if he'd been casting with a circle hook.

Also, where *was* Dad? She'd like a word. She'd like a whole bunch of words. *He'd better be working on the apology to surpass all apologies. And I want ice cream for lunch* and *dinner, dammit!* Her father did occasionally apologize, but never with words. He'd just be extra nice for a couple of days. After this, he'd better be nice for a week. *And maybe a pony! Made out of ice cream!*

"There. Keep still." Then blessed coolness as her mother wiped her face with a damp towel. "Don't worry, I'm using bottled water, not creek water."

Like she gave a shit. Cass would have wiped her face with dog vomit if that would've helped with the blood and pain.

"I must say I'm relieved," her mom murmured. "I thought you'd dumped out all your father's bait again."

Despite the pain, Cass laughed. Five-year-old Cass had felt so sorry for the worms her dad was using to catch trout, she had

(Fly! Be free!)

dumped them out in the garden behind their house.

"Is it bad? Mom?"

"You'll need stitches, but your eye is fine. I'll drive you to the emergency room."

"Dad's not gonna like that," she warned, then took her mother's extended hand and got to her feet. It seemed to take forever to stand, and the unexpected wave of dizziness made her lean on her mother's shoulder. The adrenaline was starting to ebb, leaving her weak and shaky.

Maybe Dad will make an exception to the driving rule this once. Or maybe he . . .

. . . he . . .

. . . maybe he . . .

"Mom?"

That's . . . that can't be what it looks like. I'm seeing things. The shock or whatever.

Her father was face down in the creek.

To clarify: her father was face down and motionless in the creek. One of the kayak paddles floated beside him. And it was so, so quiet. No birds. No traffic. Just her own harsh breathing and the quiet gurgle of the creek.

"Dad?" Then, like an idiot, she raised her voice. "Dad, are you okay?"

"Come along, Cassandra." She'd never heard her mother sound so calm and detached. Not even when she was high on Vicodin after Dad broke her wrist. "We need to get that wound seen to."

Pushed him. She pushed him off the dock, jumped on his back, pinned him with the paddle, and put all her weight on it until he stopped twitching. While I was bleeding and screaming, she was . . .

. . . she was . . .

"Oh, Mom," she moaned. She stumbled and her mother steadied her. "What did you do?"

"Don't look."

"Don't *look*? I'll see this every time I close my fucking eyes!"

"And watch your language. Now come."

Cass decided to ignore both commands. She pushed past her mother, grabbed her dad's shoulder, and flipped him over. Water streamed from his mouth as he bobbed. His staring, astonished gaze was a perfect reflection of her own feelings.

She struggled and pulled and splashed and finally hauled him out and up on the bank. She tried mouth-to-mouth as more of her blood streamed everywhere, and by the time she gave up, she and her father's corpse looked like they'd been in the same knife fight.

Her mother, by contrast, was still the very definition of calm serenity. While Cass labored to save her dead dad, Iris Schmitt packed the fishing gear, folded up the tables and chairs, loaded the truck, then came back down to the dock.

She jingled the keys. "Come along, Cassandra. We'll get ice cream after."

Worst birthday ever, and I didn't think anything would top my chicken pox birthday.

CHAPTER
THIRTY-THREE

An hour later, they were back in Prescott. Cass and Sidney decided to have dinner down the street from the Hobbit Hole; Amanda and Beane declined. When the others left, Amanda tugged Beane into her store and locked the door.

She looked up at him. "It's been a stressful week."

"It has. I'm sorry you and your friends have to relive so much misery."

"Can you stay?"

"Oh, yes. I checked my mail yesterday, so I'm good to go. Plus, my niece's birthday isn't for another seven months."

"Will you come upstairs with me and spen—"

"Yes."

◆ ◆ ◆

I can't feel my legs. Sean was spread out on Amanda's bed starfish style, staring at the ceiling. He would never move again. He would never leave this bed. Eventually, he would die here. Which was fine and more than fine.

He'd wanted her. Badly. From the instant he first saw her. Why he'd fixed on her but not the other two was a mystery he had no interest in solving. And he never would have tried to get her into bed so soon; to say he was grateful for the invitation was to say chocolate tasted good: beyond obvious. He was in such a hurry to tumble her into bed that he'd nearly trampled her on the stairs. Which made her laugh so hard she would have fallen if he hadn't scooped her up.

For all her petite frame, Amanda had been firmly in charge. From the kissing to the groping to the stripping, the way she'd gently but insistently showed him how she wanted him to touch, lick, suck, kiss. God, the *sounds* she'd made. And the taste of her: hot, salty honey. He thought he was fucked out, but his cock gave an interested twitch when he thought about her touch, her scent, and the amazing strength of her grip when she wrapped her legs around his waist and urged *more, faster, harder.*

He heard footsteps, and then Amanda booted her bedroom door open and came in, naked and smiling and carrying chocolate malts.

"Oh my God. That was amazing." He managed (somehow) to find the strength to raise his head. "I was incredible."

"No lies detected." She leaned over him and pressed one of the chocolate malts to his belly

(Gaaaaah!)

and he scrambled away from it with the speed and dexterity of a stunned tortoise, then flopped over on his back again. "That was mean. Also, you're incredible."

"Correct."

She took a slurp, waited until he struggled upright, and handed him his glass. "Consider this a reward for putting an end to my sex drought."

"Consider my profound gratitude for letting me. And thanks for being really fucking great in bed. And out of bed."

"Awwww."

"No, don't downplay. Gorgeous, brilliant, fearless woman fucks my teeth loose and then brings me a milkshake? Heaven. How are you still single? That's not rhetorical. I really want to know. It seems impossible to me."

She laughed like she thought he was kidding. "Deep emotional scars. And I might ask you the same. You smell great, you look great, you seem like a good guy. You're . . . reasonably intelligent. Why hasn't someone been able to chain you down yet?"

Chain me down? "I'm going to ignore the pause between 'you're' and 'reasonably' and take your question at face value. My folks split up when I was a kid, but not before years of fighting and stress and tension and tears."

She set her malt on a bedside table, then clambered back into bed and snuggled up beside him, all naked and sweaty and wonderful. (He was just naked and sweaty.) "Let me guess: 'We have to stay together for the kids.'"

"Nailed it. When has that ever worked? For the adults or the kids? And then . . . you know. My sister. She was in such a hurry to get out of that house that she went with the first guy who asked her."

"How's she doing?"

"Great," he replied with the happy relief that always came when he considered her vastly improved circumstances. "She loves her life and her new husband and her kid, and you're in her prayers."

"And you've been up to check on her."

"Many times."

"Because she didn't confide in you before. Not until it was over. So you had to make sure she was okay this time."

She's not asking. She's deducing. "Yes. That's right."

She nodded. "I would have done the same."

He let out a rueful chuckle. "She called it 'sweet spying.' But after the sixth unannounced visit in two months, she put her foot down." *And her boot up my ass.*

"I'll bet! And I'm glad," she replied, smiling. "I'm so glad. I feel like . . . you know, it all imploded when Debbie Frank was killed. It was hard to see past that. But it's nice to know we helped a few people."

He propped himself up on an elbow, leaned in, kissed her dimple. "A few? My sister, Cora Robinson, Shelly Perkins, Beth Reinhardt, Lori Carlson, Bobby . . ."

"Whoa." She leaned back and studied his face. "Okay, that's gratifying and a little frightening."

"I'm sorry," he said at once. "I didn't mean to come off like—I did some digging after I found out what you did for Dinah, who I called yesterday, by the way, and she sends her love."

"As long as she's not sending more jam. No, that's a lie; I'll eat everything she sends me, no questions asked. So you're on Team Pay It Forward, I take it."

"What?"

"It's a pool, I think. A deep, still pool. And then you drop a rock— plunk! And here come the ripples."

"I love your sound effects. It's like I'm standing on the bank of the pond."

"Shush. So Cassandra watches her dad beat up her mom and thinks up OpStar. Ripple. But there are other rocks and intercepting ripples: my family did Meals on Wheels for Christmas for years, another ripple. My folks instilled in me a hatred of olives but also a love of giving back to the community. So when Cass floats the OpStar idea, I'm in. And Sidney—I'm not entirely sure about her ripples. Well, she likes a good fight. But she likes breaking them up even more. And she loved Cass. And she loves Iris. So she's in. We help your sister, more ripples, because then you ran into us and were compelled to follow up. And possibly make an obsession board you don't keep in your bedroom."

"It's not a board. You're welcome to come over any time and see for yourself."

She pointed a finger at him. "I might take you up on that." He took her wrist, brought her index finger to his mouth, licked away the chocolate malt.

"Do you think you'll ever get married?" The shift took him by surprise, but it seemed she was honestly curious, so he answered in kind.

"I don't know." If not to Amanda—and what were the odds?—then someone just like her. Someone sweet and brave and lovely, a formidable woman incapable of turning away from injustice. "I hope so. I want to."

"Because I'm single. And you're single."

"Don't tease."

"Me, too, by the way. I know most marriages are violence-free. DV isn't the default. It's just . . . well. Cassandra's situation and all. I've gotta say, I'm amazed she told you the story."

"Me too." It wasn't the most harrowing tale he'd heard—he'd been a Minneapolis cop for four years—but it made the top ten. "I thought she was brave. And not just for telling a near-stranger about the defining trauma of her life." He tried to picture sixteen-year-old Cassandra Schmitt (now Rivers, as Iris was a Rivers the moment she drowned her husband), bleeding, screaming, fighting to save her father. Failing. And her mother's cold efficiency throughout.

"Cassandra's always been brave. And she'll always tell you she isn't." She took another gulp. "You want to know the worst part?"

"There's a worst part?"

"Of course there's a worst part; isn't there always a worst part? And here it is: Cass never could figure out if her dad did it on purpose or if it was an accident. He'd never hurt her before. Which just ramps up the awful, you know?"

He did know. Some people beat the shit out of their kids but left their spouse alone. And the reverse, of course. And some people beat the shit out of one kid but never touched the others. Some spouses abused their first wife or husband but not the second. And not because there had been a penalty like a police report or retaliation or a trial. No, they just . . . didn't beat up the other one.

A complicated creature was man, or some such bullshit.

He nodded. "Because she'll never know. Not for sure. And so it eats at her. Thoughts with teeth, just going around and around in her brain."

"Yes! That's just right. Do you know, she kept both pieces of the hook? They're in her jewelry box. Or they were the last time I saw her jewelry box. And Iris wouldn't let her testify. It's one of the reasons she pled guilty. God, Cass was *so mad* about that."

"Understandably."

"Yes. Now me, personally? I think it was an accident. I think Cassandra's dad was just trying to prove she was slow and he was fast, but he misjudged his cast again."

"That's a possibility."

"Except he was an expert angler. He'd even written magazine articles about it—Cass got the writing bug from both her parents. It was weird he overshot once, never mind twice. So who knows? After her mom went to prison, Cass told me Iris told *her* that he caught her scribbling on the walls when she was little and spanked her. Couple of whacks, nothing over-the-top abusive or anything."

"And?"

"Iris broke his wrist with a fish whacker—those little wooden bats people use to smack fish to put them out of their misery."

"Whoa."

"Yep. And he never touched Cass again. In fact, he left all the discipline to Iris after that." Amanda paused and looked away. "I'm—I'm not sure why I'm telling you all this. I shouldn't. I wouldn't, if Cass hadn't shared her story."

"My sister says I've got the face of a bartender."

"And the butt of a male stripper."

He grinned. "People tell me things. And I don't have to do anything with the info. I'm not sure if you heard, but I'm an *ex*-cop."

"Yes, it's come up a time or ten. Anyway, since she'll never know, and her mom might be an unreliable witness, Cass made a conscious choice to *not* think about any of it. Or to at least move on from it. And one of the ways she did that was to come up with OpStar."

"Because you can't save everyone, but it makes a difference to the ones you can."

"Excellent. Paying attention when I talk is a real turn-on for me."

"It's from the starfish story," he continued. "By Loren Eiseley."

"Oooooh," she mock-moaned. "Now repeat something else I told you. No, never mind, I don't think either of us is up for another round just now. We'll probably end up accidentally hurting each other."

"I'm game if you are."

Amanda's smile faded and her gaze shifted. "Accidents. I don't . . . there's something about that. I had a thought, but it slipped away." Then her gaze sharpened as she smiled at him. "Thanks again for coming up and staying over."

"Amanda—and I say this with every shred of sincerity I can manage in my exhausted state—you are most welcome. And the thought of leaving this bed anytime soon will probably induce a panic attack."

She laughed. "Let's try to avoid the panic attack angle and just be glad we're together right now. Also . . ." She wiggled her fingers in front of his face. "You're dreeeeeeeaming. None of this is real . . . real . . . real . . ."

"Don't even joke about that," he said fervently. "You've got no idea how often I dreamed of you. If I wake up—if none of this is real? I'm going to be pissed. Not least because it means I didn't achieve the goal I set for myself when you helped my sister."

"The goal of banging me?" she teased.

"Well, yeah, but also when I promised myself if I was ever in a position to help you, I would. Instantly. No holds barred."

"Surely *some* holds should be barred."

"Not one. Then I found out about Jonny Frank—"

"And it was the perfect opportunity to feed your obsession."

"Er, yes."

"I'm teasing." She leaned in and patted his thigh. He shifted; even that mild touch was waking up his sleepy cock. *The woman's a walking, talking aphrodisiac.* "I'm glad you reached out. Thank you for helping Cassandra. I'm embarrassed to be the last one to hop on the time-to-help-an-old-friend-in-trouble train."

"You had your reasons."

"And y'know what else? I'm *still* mad at her, even though I'm glad she's back. *If she's back.*" Her grip tightened on his thigh, and he let out a small yelp, and she shifted her grip. "Sorry."

"She abandoned you and that was it, right? Not a card or a letter or a phone call or a Facebook post in five years? If Frank hadn't turned up dead, she'd still be gone."

"True. But I could've reached out too. I'm hoping when this is all over, she sticks around: At least, I think that's what I want."

"She lives half an hour away," he reminded her.

"Yes, but you know what I mean. Sticks around mentally, I guess. That's a ridiculous phrase, but I'm too tired to fix it. Will we all go back to ignoring each other, or will we kind of rebuild the friendship? Operation Starfish is now in history's dustbin, but is there anything beyond that? What does a pack of vigilantes do when they stop being vigilantes, separate, and then come together again? Join the Y? Take up gardening? Write a memoir?"

"You could just . . . be friends. Like you were before OpStar. See what happens."

"Yes. Be friends and hope the cops don't follow a trail of bread crumbs to Cass, but regardless, never talk about the past. Is it still a viable friendship if it's different from what you had before?"

"Sure. People change, their lifestyles change. You're not the person you were when you were sixteen or twenty. Neither am I, neither are they. You can all turn over new leaves and forge a new path."

"You're killing me with the clichés."

"Tough. You'll just have to endure. And what about us?"

"We'll have to endure," she teased. "But c'mon . . . what 'us'? We haven't even known each other a week. It's too soon for 'us.'"

"You're right," he agreed, and wished he wasn't. "But I need to—I mean, I'd like to see you again."

"See me? You'd better watch those euphemisms around Sidney."

He almost shuddered. "I like her, but she's terrifying."

"Naw, it's all bluff and bluster. Sidney Derecho's biggest fear is that people will find out she's secretly a sweetheart. And moths. Those are the two big fears. Especially the big fat ones that land on lamps and flap their wings *really* hard when you try to shoo them away. Which I totally get."

"Have you ever seen one up close?"

"Why the hell would I do that?"

"They have cute faces."

"Moths and their faces are irrelevant since they're terrifying. And I'd like to, ahem, 'see' you again too. I've never been with anyone who knew about my baggage and my friends' baggage going in." She tittered. "No pun intended."

He rolled his eyes. "Finally, a flaw. Thank God; perfection gets old. And it doesn't have to be one sided. I'll tell you all the sordid tales from my childhood. The time I fell out of a tree and got a concussion. And all the times I fell out of a tree and didn't get a concussion. And the time I took up baking and decided flour and powdered sugar were essentially the same thing."

"Stop it," she giggled. "You're making that up."

"Nope. And the time a bat got into my apartment—how, I'll never know—and I dealt with it by screaming for twenty minutes. I'll tell you whatever you want to know about me. Everyone's got baggage, y'know? I knew that years before I pinned on a badge."

"Baggage." Her pretty brow furrowed in thought. He leaned over, poked his phone, and saw it was past midnight.

"Do you want me to go?" *Please say no.* "It's not a problem if you want me to leave. *I'd* want me to leave . . . Amanda?"

"Hmmm?" She looked at him, then bent to haul the blankets off the floor, and covered them both. "Don't be ridiculous, of course you should stay. You . . . hmm."

"Are you okay?"

"Hmmm? Sorry, I'm fine, I'm just . . . I'm thinking about what you said. About baggage. And accidents. It's right there in my brain, just a bit out of reach. I'd probably be able to put a thought together if you hadn't made me come about a dozen times."

"Sorry," he said, and got a poke in the ribs for it. He shotgunned the last of his malt and set the empty glass down with a determined thud.

"Uh-oh."

"Ice cream headache."

"I can fix that."

"Would you?" He opened obligingly, then caught her wrist and sucked on her thumb, and pulled her closer.

"Again?" she murmured, watching his face. He lightly bit her thumb, then pulled it out of his mouth and kissed her deeply, rolled her on her back, rubbed against her like a big cat, and kissed the hollow of her throat.

"If you wouldn't mind terribly."

"I try to be an accommodating hostess."

"And I, a grateful guest."

She laughed and wriggled beneath him, slipped away and straddled him. This gave him an outstanding view of her face, her riot of red waves, her small, sweet breasts, still flushed and marked with beard burn from his stubble. Seeing his marks on her pale, pretty flesh was as erotic to him as if she'd decided to drop everything and swallow his cock.

She reached back, found him already semihard, raised her eyebrows. "Oh, my."

"You're not the only one who was enduring a sexual drought."

"We really should come up with a better phrase for that. Hand me one, will you?"

He obliged so quickly that he nearly dumped the drawer out on her floor. When she'd invited him up and made clear her intent to fuck his brains loose, he'd had to tell her he didn't have any condoms on his person. Or anywhere. (He hadn't been kidding about the drought.) But that was fine, because she did.

Hearing a condom packet rip was Pavlovian; in fewer than thirty seconds he was fully hard, and she slipped the condom on, tightened her grip, and guided him into her. She was still slick from earlier, and as she groaned and started to rock against him, his eyes rolled back.

"Oh, fuck . . ."

"Bossy."

"Exclamation. Not . . . verb." He tightened his grip around her waist and thrust against her, then parted her damp red curls with his fingers and reached for her clit.

"Oh, that's . . . just a bit higher and a bit . . . a bit more to the . . . ah . . . yes . . . like that . . ."

"Like that?"

"*Just* like that." She rocked faster, and he tugged her down for a kiss and stroked the long line of her back, clutching her to him as they soared together, and it was every cliché in the world, and he didn't care, because it was Amanda, and she was a delight, and he had never felt more at home, not even when he *was* home.

CHAPTER

THIRTY-FOUR

When the penny dropped (stupid yet accurate phrase), she jumped out of the shower and ran to her bedroom, not even bothering with a towel, and skidded to a halt before she brained herself on her dresser.

"Baggage!"

Sean catapulted upright from sound asleep. "What? Are you okay? What?"

"Baggage, Sean!" She jumped on the bed. "That's how we'll catch him! Not that we're investigating! Because we aren't! I'm pretty sure none of us have gotten around to hiring you yet! But if we were!"

He blinked, shook his head. "Um."

Probably should moderate my tone. "Did you get that, or should I break it down?"

"What?"

"Sonny Manners told us someone's been taking Cassandra's Commando out. At night, when the shop is closed."

He rubbed his eyes. "Yeah."

"So who hates Cass and can ride and could lug a body to the river and would love it if she went to prison?"

Sean's gaze tipped up as he thought. "That's gotta be a short list."

"Really short. A list of one."

She grinned to see him come to the same conclusion. *"Problem-solving is hunting; it is savage pleasure, and we are born to it."* It was a line from *The Silence of the Lambs* and, in her opinion, much more interesting than the overused "ate his liver with some fava beans" passage.

"Jeff Manners," he said, and tossed the blankets aside to get dressed. "Brother of Sonny of Manner's Bikes."

◆ ◆ ◆

Sidney's minivan pulled up beside Amanda's bike, and she hopped out. "All right, where's the jackass?"

Cass got out, too, and the four of them stood at the edge of the parking lot like they were about to start a quest. The only things missing were a few hobbits and Sean Bean. "Is it me, or would that make a great podcast? 'Love true crime? Download the latest episode of *Where's the Jackass.*'"

"And I would listen to that podcast," Sean admitted.

"Thanks for meeting us, you guys," Amanda said.

"You kidding? How often do I get a wanna-come-to-a-state-park-and-ruin-Jeff-Manners's-day phone call?"

Amanda pretended to think about it. "Once, I'm guessing."

"It's true," Cass said. "She almost knocked me down when she went for her car keys."

"Your own fault for not getting out of the way."

"I wasn't *in* the way. I was buttering my toast. I wasn't even in the same room as your keys."

"Are we gonna bitch, or are we gonna throw Jeff Manners into a ravine?"

"No reason we can't do both," Sidney said as the four of them walked into Pioneer Park. "Any ideas where he'll be?"

"Men's room," Amanda predicted. "Which is next to the women's room, which is perfect since I have to pee."

"Can we track down one scumbag without having to hear about your elimination schedule?"

"What do you think, Sidney?"

"I think you've got a bladder the size of a flea."

"God, the snark," Sean muttered. "It's like *Sex and the City: Midwestern Edition.*"

Cass rolled her eyes. "Not this again. You're aware women who are friends like to do things in small groups, right? Candace Bushnell did not invent that concept."

"*Mmmm.*"

"Well, that was a noncommittal murmur if I've ever heard one. Come on, let's get in there."

Then, as Sean headed toward the restrooms, Sidney seized Amanda's elbow. "I know you fucked," she hissed.

"*Gah*, trim your talons, please," she said while prying Sidney's fingers off her arm. "You don't know everything about everything."

"That's true," she said with a smirk. "But I know you fucked. He's wearing the same clothes as yesterday, and he's *way* too relaxed. So he's either a disgusting slob, doesn't understand how washing machines work, or you fucked. Going by your glow, it was nifty."

"I'm glowing?" she asked, both delighted and concerned.

"Like a potbellied stove in January," Cassandra said.

"'Nifty' doesn't do it justice, you rotten nosy bitches, and can we keep to the matter at hand, please?"

"Sure," Sidney replied, but shot her a later-for-you glare.

"Priorities, priorities." Cassandra reached out and gave Amanda a hesitant pat on the shoulder. "Though I've gotta say, it's nice to see you smiling."

It's nice to have something to smile about.

"*Mmmm.*"

"Now who's noncommittal?"

Amanda ignored Cassandra's comment as the irrelevancy it was and hurried into the women's room.

She stopped short. "Manners, what the hell are you doing?"

Jeff Manners jumped like he'd been goosed and spilled several knotted baggies of what looked like dried basil but probably wasn't. "What the fuck are you doing here, Amanda?"

"Peeing. Any second now! And don't steal my line. Why are *you* annoyed to find *me* in a women's restroom? Are you that desperate to hook up?" She raised her voice. "He's in here! Hurry up, for God's sake; I hate being in the same room with him!"

"Who are you t—" He trailed off as Sean shoved the door open and came in, Sidney and Cass right behind him. "What the fuck?"

"Your confusion is understandable. I mean all the time, not just right now."

Manners's eyes widened as he spotted Sean. "Oh, shit."

"Oh, *Sean*," Amanda corrected. "Why'd you do it, Jeff?"

Fifteen seconds in, and Jeff was already so rattled that they could almost see the sweat breaking out on his forehead. He was the picture of guilty knowledge.

This is what the thrill of victory feels like, she decided. *Or the thrill of finding Jeff Manners in a bathroom.*

"How'd you find me?"

"It was easy. We just asked ourselves where a drug-dealing scumbag with delusions of awesome would hang out. And here you are."

"But if it makes you feel any better," Cass added, "we checked the dump and all the liquor stores first."

"Not the library, though," Amanda added. "Somehow, we knew that would be a waste of time."

Sean walked over to the row of sinks. "What's this?" he asked, indicating bags bulging with something that probably wasn't dried basil.

"None of your fuckin' business."

"Disagree. Marijuana's still illegal in the state of Wisconsin. Possession gets you six months and a fine of a thousand bucks. And that's just the first time."

"You can't prove shit," he insisted, scooping up the baggies, dropping them, then grabbing them again and stuffing them into his jeans pockets. Except the vain shithead wore jeans a size too small because he thought it accentuated his dick. Which meant he really had to jam those baggies in there. Amanda would never understand the human impulse to hide a flaw by emphasizing it. Comb-overs. Boob jobs. Botox. Did Madonna *really* think she was holding on to her youth by paying someone to jam botulism into her face?

"This is why you should eschew vests and wear flannel lumberjack shirts with big pockets. And chinos."

"Nuh-uh, Amanda. It's 'achoo.'"

"Again with this? 'Eschew' is not pronounced like a sneeze, Sidney!"

"The holy fuck it *isn't.*"

"It's 'es-*choo*,' I think."

In unison: "Shut up, Cass!"

"You can't do shit," Jeff was informing Sean. Well, at least *he* was staying focused, the disingenuous shithead. "You're an *ex*-cop."

"Oh?" Sean was now leaning casually against the far sink. "Who told you that?"

Good question. Too bad Jeff didn't feel like accommodating: "Fuck off, all y'all."

"All y'all"? He's aware he was born and resides in Wisconsin, right? Hmm. Maybe he isn't. He was never the sharpest knife in the drawer.

"You gave yourself away," Amanda said. *This is probably how Sherlock Holmes feels when he explains who did it: postcoital levels of satisfaction.* "You found Cassandra in the park too fast. We were barely there, and then *you* were there. This is a small town, and word moves at the speed of gossip. And Cassandra Rivers coming back is big news."

"Which is pathetic and ridiculous," Cass put in.

"I'm glad someone said it," Sidney snickered.

"So you found out she was back, and there you were, right here in this park," Amanda continued. "You wasted no time getting in her face. Why'd you even care?"

"I don't give a fuck about any of you."

Sidney let out a sharp bark of laughter. "Cut the shit, you've been crushing on Cass since middle school. And she did worse than reject you; she ignored you."

"To be fair, I had a lot on my plate back then."

"Shush, Cass! And you hated it when she helped me get the bike you wanted. You were acting like a jealous spouse despite the fact that you're single and, I imagine, will remain that way until you eventually succumb to hypothermia because you wear sleeveless vests in Wisconsin winters. When did you find out Sonny had been storing her Commando?"

Good question. The Manners clan stuck together, mostly because the rest of the town couldn't stand (most of) them. And Amanda found it telling that Sonny had kept that Commando a secret for five years.

"And when," Sidney continued, looking at Manners like he was a bundle of rotten eggs, nicotine, and denim, "did you decide to kill Franklin Donahue and frame Cass for it?"

"Who the hell is—"

"Jonny Frank, Jonny Frank, fucking Jonny Frank!" Sidney howled.

"*What?*" Jeff looked at them, now in a half circle surrounding him. "Jesus, fuck, I didn't kill anybody! And I didn't touch your piece-of-shit bike."

"It's a Norton Commando, and they're made in England, you clot," Amanda snapped.

"Beat me to it," Cassandra remarked. Then: "'Clot'? What is that, some kind of British diss?"

"I'll explain what clots are to you later, Cassandra."

"I know what a clot is, Amanda. I've just never heard you use it as an expletive."

"You don't know anything about anything, Mr. Manners?"

"Fuck right, I don't!"

Amanda managed to stifle her laugh. *Can't believe he said that out loud.*

"So if we dust the bike for prints, yours won't be anywhere on it. Right, Mr. Manners?"

There was a long pause while they all watched Jeff try to pick one lie and run with it.

"I—it's my bro's shop. I'm in there alla time, maybe I touched it or something, I dunno."

"Or something"? Eww. Also, that's just as good as a confession. At least as far as I'm concerned.

"But what was your motive for murder?" Amanda asked. "Just to bring weight down on Cassandra?"

"I told you, I didn't kill anybody. You think I give a shit about Jonny Frank or Franklin Jonny or whoever the fuck?"

"Maybe not, but you *do* give a shit about messing with Cassandra. And when you saw a chance, you grabbed it."

His hands were up like he was being arrested. Appropriate! "Swear to fuckin' God, I didn't kill anybody."

If it's an act, it's a good one.

"You were *seen*, Mr. Manners. There are witnesses."

Manners seemed to suddenly remember he wasn't on trial nor under arrest nor obligated to submit to an interrogation in a public restroom. He shoved his way through them until he reached Amanda, who felt grumpy and disinclined to move. His shoulder thudded against her, and she stumbled, then straightened in time to see Sean stretch out a long arm, catch Manners by the back of his shirt, and bounce him off a stall door.

"Touch her again," he said with terrifying calm, "and you'll be pissing blood all weekend."

Sidney smirked and glanced at Amanda, and as usual, Amanda knew what her friend was thinking: *Okay, that shit was pretty cool.*

She herself was of two minds: (1) she could take care of herself, (2) that shit was pretty cool.

"I'll fuckin' sue you!"

"Wonderful!" Amanda said, and clapped. "I can't wait to see you testify under oath about how you definitely didn't steal Cassandra's bike."

"Fuck all y'all."

"You're from the Midwest, cheesedick!" Sidney called as he stormed out. "You've never made it past Madison!"

Then they just stood there and looked at each other.

Sidney broke first. "Fuck that Bandido wannabe. Let's eat and plot."

CHAPTER THIRTY-FIVE

"So what happens now with our noninvestigation?" Amanda asked. "Do you make a citizen's arrest and haul Manners in by the mullet?"

"Not quite. I call the Violent Crimes Investigations Division commander and lay it out. They'll pick up Manners for questioning, and things will roll from there."

"I still can't believe being mad at Cass was the motive," Amanda said. "It's so tawdry and lame. Like a gossip blog or anything Tucker Carlson does."

"*No*," Sidney said. "You've gone almost a month without a political rant. Don't break the streak."

"But that's what you don't get; it's not about politics. It's not about Republicans versus Democrats. That's the fundamental flaw in your logic. It's about basic human decen—"

"No. No. No. *No.*"

"Say 'no' seven more times," Cass suggested. "It might sink in."

"Ugh, fine, I'll shelve that lesson—"

"Lecture," Sidney declared. "It's a goddamned lecture. Every time."

"I'll shelve that *lesson* for later. Let's hope Sonny doesn't mind his shop getting fingerprint dusted from roof to basement."

"Serves him right for having such a shithead for a brother," Sidney said, and stole another of Amanda's fries. They'd grabbed breakfast to go and were sitting on the barstools clustered around the counter in Amanda's shop. "I knew Jeff Manners was gonna be a problem the second he loogied me in middle school."

Cass nodded. "That was a sizable tip-off."

"Fuck that teeny weenie."

"We've got bigger problems than a teeny weenie with the charisma of a wet brick. We just did that thing where we tipped off the killer, who now has hours to make his escape," Cassandra pointed out.

Amanda was watching Sean. "You don't think Manners is the killer."

"Whoa!" Sidney yelped. "What? Then what just happened? What was the point? Why'd we convene in a bathroom? Not that I need a reason to ruin that fucker's day."

"I'm having trouble getting there," Sean admitted. "Stealing the bike, absolutely. He strikes me as the petty type. And he's definitely fixated on Cassandra."

"Prob'ly popped a boner the second he climbed on," Sidney chortled. "Greatest night—and ride—of his life, I'll bet."

Cass shuddered. "Memo to me: sell that bike. Or blow it up."

"Don't you dare!" Amanda cried. "You just got it back. Or will once the cops are done with it. That's like throwing away a Prada bag because someone you don't like borrowed it."

"Just slosh three or four jugs of Clorox over it until you're staggering and ready to pass out from the fumes," Sidney suggested. "Then you'll know it's been cleansed of all manner of Manners boners."

Amanda groaned. "*Please* stop talking about Manners boners."

Sean put up his hand. "Second that."

She poked Cass on the shoulder. "Listen. It's like a miracle you can get it back. It's a ghost come back to life. Like Jesus! When I saw it sitting in Sonny's garage, spotless and cared for and looking like we'd just seen you on it the day before . . . it was like a sign. The life-changing kind. I know you guys aren't all that religious—"

"Atheist." From Cass.

"Lapsed Presbyterian." Sidney.

"Practicing Jedi." Sean.

"Oh, for God's—never mind. Cass, you're getting a second chance. You don't have to shut yourself away from the things you love because Debbie Frank went into the ground. Sonny keeping your bike is a sign! One you should drop everything and heed."

"So you've said."

"Yeah, well, when you ignore my outstanding advice, I'm forced to repeat myself. I've also said you've had five years to punish yourself, which if you ask me—"

"No one ever does," Cass said. "Did you notice?"

"Shush. I'm just saying there's no need to torture yourself for the next few decades. Debbie's death was never on you."

"Or Wanda Garner's," Sidney added.

"Hey!" Amanda's sweet tea almost went down the wrong pipe. "Wanda's murder was *not* our fault. And neither was Debbie's, but Wanda really, *really* wasn't our fault. That's one hundred percent on the mercifully murdered Jonny Frank."

"It is, isn't it?" Sean said. He was standing close enough to Amanda that their hips bumped, ignoring Sidney's knowing smirks. "One hundred percent. No gray area there. But loved ones will still blame themselves. Like I did. Which reminds me, my sister's coming to town next month, and she'd love to see all of you."

"Of course—we're the hottest ticket in town. But who knows where we'll be a month from now." Amanda managed to deliver this observation without looking at Cass. *Not to mention: definition of "we," please? The three of us? The four of us? The two of us?* "You were saying about how loved ones blame themselves, Sean?"

They waited while Sean paused to figure out how best to articulate his thoughts. "Like I said, I can't see Jeff Manners enacting this elaborate plot just to make Cassandra's life difficult. Tracking a target, getting the bike, getting a gun, killing a stranger, transporting the body, dumping the body, and for what? The off chance it *might* cause trouble for Cassandra, who doesn't even live here anymore?"

"You make a good point," Amanda said after the short silence. "The only reason Sean figured out what was going on is because he's obsessed with me."

Cass raised her eyebrows. "Oh, wow. The vanity."

"Nothing at all to do with vanity." Amanda sucked down two more sweet potato fries.

"Amanda's right," Sean said, ducking his head.

"Aw. That's cute! And a little off-putting," Cass said.

"So if it's not Jeff, we're back to the first square. If we were investigating. Which we're not."

"Maybe it's nothing to do with Debbie," Cass speculated. "Jonny Frank was a scumbag and a half. It could have been anyone, for any reason. Drug deal, bad debt, botched mugging. Wrong place, wrong time. He killed two women, and that's just what we know about. There's no way he didn't make enemies outside this group."

Amanda nodded. "You're saying Wanda Garner and Debbie Frank weren't outliers."

"Outside," Sean said. "Hmm."

"You wanna elaborate on that 'hmm' or just sit there looking mysterious and a little constipated?" Sidney asked. "Oh, and we *will* be discussing you boning my friend, and your intentions. You might as well mark that in your calendar with permanent ink. If people still had paper calendars and wrote in them."

Amanda rolled her eyes. "Sidney, not now with this, all right?"

The frog over the door announced Dave's entrance, and he looked surprised to see them eating together. "So you guys are all friends again?"

"We're still working that out," Amanda replied.

Cass raised her eyebrows. If she kept it up, she'd pull a muscle. "We are?"

"Shush."

"God, I've even missed the shushing; what is *wrong* with me?"

"Nobody's got that kind of time," Sidney informed her. "But I can put together a list if you want. Might take a few weeks."

"It will not!" Amanda insisted, and got a quick hug from Cass for it. "Four or five days at most. Ow!"

Dave edged closer for a look at Cassandra's breakfast like he didn't want to spook an antelope at a watering hole. "I've never seen anyone eat meat loaf and gravy at nine fifteen in the morning."

"That's her thing," Sidney said. "Dinner for breakfast. It's how you know she's a raging sociopath."

"Huh. Okay. Amanda, if you don't need me to watch the counter, I thought I'd be a customer for a change."

"Yes, of course—I know what you're here for." Amanda went to the small bookshelf labeled with stickers of each letter of the alphabet, and pulled out two new tomes from the slot marked *C*. "I can't believe it took the publisher two weeks to get this to me. Thanks for not getting impatient and buying it from Amazon."

"That's okay. Gives me an excuse to come in and—"

"Awwww, Dave! I'm touched."

"—learn how to duck when you inevitably throw more pens at me."

"Oh, boo. And here's the other one, you're gonna love it."

"What'd she make you get?" Sidney asked, peeking over Dave's shoulder. "Oh. Wallach's *Rugged Road*. Yeah, that *is* a good book."

"It's about a pioneering motorcyclist—"

"He bought the book, Amanda."

"—who famously rode from London to Cape Town via the Sahara and through Africa. Without a compass!"

"He'll be able to read all about it, Amanda."

"And she did this on a 600cc single-cylinder Panther motorcycle! While hauling a sidecar and a trailer! She was also the only female engineering student at Northampton Polytechnic. She also—"

"You just have to let her run down," Sidney told Dave. "Booze doesn't work and neither do gags. Nothing on earth can stop her when she's midlecture. Sorry she's spoiling the entire fucking book for you."

"*She also* joined the Women's Engineering Society. And raced motorcycles. And was a mechanic in World War Two. Like Queen Elizabeth the Second!"

"Amandaaaaaaa . . ."

"And she was the only female dispatch rider in the British Army and was the ATS's first female tank mechanic, and that's all I'm going to say about her."

"Lookin' forward to it." Dave examined the other book, *The Way Things Work*, and smiled. "My niece is gonna love this one. She shadowed me last week and wants to start her own construction company."

"Sidney was telling me about your construction company too," Cass said.

"No, she wasn't," Sidney replied. "Cass is making small talk to make you feel included."

"Whoa! Not nice, Sid. Even for you."

"Fine, Cassandra, sorry, get over yourself." Sidney waved her apology away even as she made it. "What? If I go over the line, I'm mature enough to own it."

"Are you, though?" Amanda teased in the "Is he, though?" tone of voice made famous in *Thor: Ragnarok*. To Dave: "We were actually talking about Jonny Frank and why it's terrific that he's dead."

"I hate when we remember the scumbag's name but not the victims'," Cass said. "Can you tell me the name of even one of Bundy's victims?"

"Margaret Bowman, Kimberly Leach," Amanda said. *The Stranger Beside Me* was one of her desert isle books. "Nancy Wilcox. Brenda Ball."

"Okay, someone who isn't Amanda? Or Dahmer's victims, can anyone name . . . no, wait, that last is a bad example. Dahmer was from Wisconsin, so lots of people around here can name some of his vics. Steve Tuomi was one."

"Ray Smith's another," Amanda said. "Ed Gein was from Wisconsin too."

"Yeah, that's right. Gross. Anyway, getting back to it, let's say we were talking about Wanda Garner and Debbie Frank, *not* Jonny Frank," Cass said, soaking up meat loaf gravy with her last biscuit.

"Oh, yeah, Garner." Dave was carefully bundling the new books into his messenger bag. "He's gonna be happy Frank's dead."

Cass froze in mid-sop. "You're talking about her brother? Marcus Garner?"

"Yeah. He's pretty intense. Not that I blame him, but he's like a hermit in training. One of those guys who, y'know, doesn't really like people. Any people. Even before his sister died."

"She didn't 'die,'" Sidney snapped. "She was murdered by her fuck-stick husband. Don't downplay. Wait. What are you saying, Dave?"

Cass was still stuck in mid-sop. "You know Marcus Garner?"

"Sure. I'm building his mausoleum."

Amanda almost choked on a fry. "I'm sorry, Dave, could you repeat that?"

Dave blinked. "Mausoleum. Y'know, a tomb? One of those big marble boxes you see in fancy cemeteries? People have them built to hold their families' remains?"

"I know what a mausoleum is, Dave!"

"Do you? Because you seem super confused right now."

"Where?" Amanda cried.

"Where what? Oh." Dave's blinking intensified. "Forest Lawn. In Maplewood."

"Mr. Conner, just so I understand your meaning, Marcus Garner isn't in England?"

"Cripes!" Sean had come up on him so quickly and quietly that Dave flinched back.

"Serve you right, you're always creeping up on us," Sidney said.

"I'm not, though. You're all just really self-absorbed and keep forgetting I'm here." To Sean: "No, he's not in England; we've been working on his tomb for the last coupla months. He wants it done by September, y'know."

"Did he say why?"

"Naw. Didn't ask. Not really my business so long as the check clears."

"The contractor's code." Amanda already had her phone out. "Here it is. Wanda Garner was murdered on September first."

"A deadline," Cass breathed. Before she could elaborate, her cell phone pinged. She fished it out and went pale, then showed them the caller ID: MCF-Stillwater. "Mom *never* calls me. Almost never. I can count on one hand how often she . . . Mom? Hello?"

"Speaker!" Sidney commanded, and Cass obliged. Five years away wasn't long enough to gain the ability to ignore Sidney when she used That Tone.

"Mom? What's wrong?"

Iris Rivers cleared her throat. "I may have miscalculated."

"What?"

"I believe I was in error."

Amanda could see the tension go out of Cassandra's shoulders so quickly she sagged on her stool. "Jeez, Mom, you scared me. Listen, I'm glad you're finally ready to apologize for murdering my father, basically orphaning me—"

"You can't use 'orphan' as a verb," Amanda hissed.

"I can, actually; look it up and shut up!" She continued in a softer tone, "Orphaning me and gagging me to prevent my testimony, but now isn't the—"

"I will never apologize for that."

"That whole lack of remorse thing? That's gonna keep you in prison for a looooong time."

"I'm aware, child. But when you were here the other day, I told you Marcus Garner moved to England. Then I gave it some thought and took another look at his letters; they're all still locally postmarked. So he either, one, utilizes a forwarding service; two, I misheard him; three, he *did* go to England but never wrote me while he was there; four, he intends to go abroad, just not in the time frame he suggested to me—"

"Or he lied."

"Yes. My miscalculation was assuming he meant to move but hadn't yet. But once I started pondering, I realized there could be a more sinister explanation."

"Fuck a duck sideways!"

"Hello to you, too, Sidney. How I loathe being on speakerphone . . . as I was saying, once I realized I could be in error, I utilized my phone privileges. I have two minutes left."

"Don't worry, you won't even need two seconds. And your timing is amazing, gotta go, Iris, bye!" Sidney bawled.

"Mom, we'll catch up later, and I'll tell you the whole story—"

"What a delightful change of pace."

"I'll see you Friday."

"Ah, yes, the third visit this week. You've broken your own record of . . . one. I knew you were up to something, young lady."

"Yep, can't fool you, got it." Cass disconnected. "Holy shit."

"You're wrong, though," Amanda said.

"What are you talking about?" Cass asked. "It makes perfect sense."

"What I mean is, we don't 'gotta go.' And you all know why."

There was a short silence, broken by Cassandra's tentative, "We do?"

"Are we still pretending this isn't an investigation?" Sidney asked, exasperated. "Because it's definitely an investigation. Probably since the day whenever the hell this all started. So, yeah, we 'gotta' go. We've come this far; we're sure as shit not gonna stand down now. Right?"

Amanda turned to Dave. "Please tell us you have a meeting with Marcus Garner today or an address where we can ambush—I mean, go see him."

"He's kind of a loner," Dave warned.

Yeah, no doubt. And possibly a murderer.

"Why a mausoleum, though?" Cassandra asked. "That seems over-done, somehow. And why build it all these years later? And why does the September deadline matter? Wanda's dead, she's not going anywhere."

"Well." Amanda slid off her stool. "Let's go ask him."

CHAPTER
THIRTY-SIX

Sean led the way; he'd hopped in his car, and the rest followed in Sidney's minivan.

"Thought you'd be giving your fuckbuddy another ride," Sidney said. "No pun intended. Naw, that's a lie, pun definitely intended."

"I want to talk to Marcus Garner right now, not waste time working out who's riding with whom and in what vehicle. Plus, that's too long a drive without appropriate gear. ATGATT, right?"

"And you wanted to dish."

"I did not, in fact, want to dish."

"You're pro-dish and you know it! So you might as well spill the tea on Beane's boinking."

"'Boinking'?" Cass laughed. "Are you twelve?"

"No, but even if I was, show me a seventh grader who uses 'boinking' on the regular. You can't."

"I'm not dishing on anything," Amanda informed them. "Or anyone."

"But it was good," Sidney prompted. "You can fess up to that much."

"... very good."

"That is *quite* the sappy look on your face right now."

"It's not sappy! It's my ordinary smile. My regular, um, look of contemplation."

"Sure it is. But was it good because he understands the clit exists or because you haven't gotten laid in . . . what season is it again? And which year?"

"Oh, come on, Sidney. It hasn't been that long."

"That's not like you," Cass observed. "The casual-sex thing. Or it wasn't five years ago."

"True. But I'll be honest, I wanted him the minute I realized the dark circles under his eyes were the color of Godiva's salted-caramel truffles. I've spent the week trying to get my feral libido back on the leash."

"That's beautiful." Cass giggled.

"And he's tall," Sidney added. "You always get a wide-on for the tall ones."

"Sidney! Ewww!"

"I said what I said."

"But here's the crazy part . . ."

"He likes wearing your panties?"

"I wouldn't care if he did. What's crazy is that he said he wanted me the minute he saw me too."

Sidney and Cassandra, who was in the passenger seat, traded glances. "Why's that crazy?"

"You're super cute and smart and fun," Sidney added. "Why wouldn't he want you the second he saw the bundle of weird/cute/cool that is Amanda Miller?"

"I dunno, I guess I never believed in love at first sight."

"Oh, we're talking love now?" Cass asked. "Because you didn't say 'love.' You said 'want.'"

"Lust at first sight, yeah," Sidney announced. "No question that exists. But I'm with Amanda; love at first sight is not a thing. It's fucking impossible! It's like saying you don't have to know someone to love them. You don't even have to talk to them! You're just . . . just magically compatible in every way."

"Well . . ."

"Bull. Shit." Sidney nodded her head at "bull" and again at "shit," which had a near-hypnotic effect. "Doesn't exist. That he wanted to bone at first sight, sure. Love? Nope."

"Maybe some of it's gratitude," Cassandra suggested. "No offense."

"None taken, especially as that's part of it," Amanda replied. "The day we met him at Dinah's, when he was still in college? He promised himself that if we were ever in a jam, he'd come running."

"Promise kept," Sidney said. "Huh. That's . . . kind of cool."

"Right. So between that week, years ago, and this week, we all went about doing our separate things, only Sean kept his ear to the ground, pardon the cliché. But it's not just gratitude or altruism. He doesn't like being in debt. He's like Sidney and credit card interest rates, and no, I'm not getting her started."

"Fucking nineteen percent? And twenty-four percent for cash advances? You can get better rates from the mob! How do those people sleep at night? How many Ambiens do they have to suck down to knock themselves out? Two? Five? Thirty?"

"So are you gonna keep up with the boning or what?" Cassandra asked.

"That's up to him," she replied stiffly.

"It really isn't," Cass said. "Or at least, not just up to him."

"I think it's cool that this isn't about sport fucking," Sidney said. "And he seems okay. Keep banging, get to know him, have fun, maybe some babies in a bit."

"I'm getting married before I have babies. And for his own safety, I'll have to insist Sean take my surname. Sean Miller sounds much safer than Sean Beane."

"Good call."

"But we're getting ahead of ourselves." Amanda turned to Dave. "Don't you think?"

"I'm just sitting here pretending to read my niece's book because this conversation is making me uncomfortable." Dave slammed the book shut. "But listen. And I'm not just telling you this in a desperate ploy to change the subject. Marcus is a nice guy . . . well. Not nice exactly. Polite, though, and intense, like I said earlier. I'll get you in, but just . . ."

"Spit it out, Dave, time's not our friend. Lots to do; confronting a possible killer's only one item on a long list."

"What I'm saying is, if you get all up in his face, he'll shut down or he'll shut you guys down. Or he'll give you the boot, and then I'll have to explain why I brought a bunch of nosy strangers to ask him if he's a killer."

"Got it, got it," Sidney said. "Don't worry. We'll be so fuckin' cool, we'll be the definition of cool. Like a penguin chillin' on an ice floe cool."

"That sounds like a lie," Dave said glumly, but let it go.

"Amanda." Cass turned her head, then reached back. "Gimme your hand."

"I told you I don't believe in fortune-telling," she replied even as she obliged. "My palms are not a gateway to my past, present, or future. Their main function is to facilitate high fives."

"Naw, I just wanted to check . . ." Cass reached out, took Amanda's hand, grinned at what she saw. "I thought I saw you with this. Never change."

"No worries. I'm far too lazy."

"Why? What's wrong with your hand?" Dave asked.

"Not one thing. You've seen me use this at the store." Amanda showed him her fingers. She was wearing a thick steel ring; one side of it was smooth save for a small bump. She pushed the bump, and a tiny razor slid out.

Twine cutter. She'd gotten the idea from an Andrew Vachss novel; the DA working with the main character routinely carried one to discourage any potential scumbag with a grudge. Slice it across someone's face, Vachss had posited, and you were playing "got your nose!" for real.

"What's Beane think about the fact that you sometimes walk around with a razor on your hand?"

"He doesn't care; he was glad it wasn't a wedding ring. This'll sound nutty, but he seems to like everything about me."

She waited for mocking laughter and/or one of Sidney's bitchy observations. Instead, she got silence.

"You guys heard that, right?"

Sidney caught her gaze in the rearview mirror. "You're awesome, you silly bitch. Didn't you know? Sorry, I know the word's overused—"

"'Bitch' or 'awesome'?"

"Both, but I meant 'awesome.' Of course the Beane Machine thinks you're nifty."

She laughed. "Swear you'll never call him that again."

"Nope. That's the new nickname. But listen, is it just that he looks hot in Dockers? Not that there's even one thing wrong with that; he's a great-looking fuck. But . . . is that all there is? Maybe it's too soon to tell."

"He gets it," Amanda said. "That and a big dick are all I require. Not that I'm a size queen. It's all about the aesthetic."

"Excellent. Keep it simple."

Cass turned around. "Sidney's right, y'know. You're great. And you deserve whatever happiness you can grab. And since we're talking about overused phrases: go for it."

Absurd, but Amanda could feel her eyes fill with tears. It was nice being reminded that people valued you not in spite of your quirks but because of them.

And yes, she'd been lonely. And not just because there'd been a Cass-size hole in her life for five years. Being part of OpStar had made her feel important and safe. When Cass left, she took those things with her.

It would have been difficult even if they were ordinary women with ordinary friendships and ordinary stories. No one likes being abandoned, no matter how drama-free their adolescences and relationships were. But they'd comforted Cassandra when she wept over the damage inflicted on her mother. They'd talked her out of patricide more than once. They'd taken her in after her father's ignoble death. And after Cassandra had been, for all intents and purposes, orphaned, they'd packed his shit and gotten it out of her life.

"Fuck you both," she replied, because she'd rather hide behind sarcasm than acknowledge how much their words meant. How much *they* meant.

"Anyone in here have something else I can read to kind of mitigate how awkward this is for me?"

"Shut up, Dave," she said kindly.

CHAPTER
THIRTY-SEVEN

Years earlier . . .

"Whoa."

Well put. Amanda and Sidney stood in Cassandra's (former) living room and took in the chaos their friend hath wrought. She'd gone from her follow-up clinic appointment to her family's now-abandoned home, a cream and brown split-level, the kind where, when you come in the front door, you immediately have to go down eight stairs or up eight stairs. Downstairs—two bedrooms and a bath. Upstairs—living room, kitchen, master bedroom.

At first glance, it appeared Cassandra was intent on tossing/blowing up her late father's belongings. And a few of Iris's things were in the pile too. Notably, the framed physician assistant oath that once hung in the kitchen. It was peeking out from a pile of DVDs, so all Amanda could read was the first line: "I will hold as my primary responsibility the health, safety, welfare, and dignity of all human beings."

"Uh. Need some help?" Sidney asked.

"Clearly," Amanda answered, though the question wasn't directed at her. "Is this a time-to-pack-up-the-deceased's-belongings thing or a time-to-blow-up-the-house thing?"

"The former, prob'ly," Cassandra replied. "I mean, it's gotta be done, right? He's gone. He'll never come back for any of this. And it's not like they're gonna let my mom out of prison to take care of it, so."

"What'd the doctor say?"

Cassandra touched her stitches. "It's too early to take them out, but I don't have to keep it bandaged anymore. This is the air-will-help-it-get-better-for-some-reason phase. But hey! It's not like they're noticeable or anything, right?" She forced a smile, then burst into tears.

Horror and compassion tussled for control, and compassion won. "Cass, Cass, it'll—" Be okay? No. Be the death of her? Please, no. Never be over? God, no. Be awful for years? Yep. She crossed the room and put her arms around her wounded friend while Sidney stood there and shifted her weight from foot to foot and said nothing and did nothing. Cassandra didn't return the hug, just stood like one of those Native American totem poles. "There, there. By the way, me saying 'there, there' doesn't make me feel inadequate at all. I'm going to pat you ineffectually on your shoulder too. And somehow, you'll magically feel better."

Cass snorted, then pulled back. The stitches were noticeable, sure. And while the contrast was livid between the deep black of the thread against the raw, red flesh of the healing slash—there was no swelling, no indications of infection—it was . . . almost striking. *She'll always have a scar, but maybe it'll be one of those cool scars.*

"It's just . . . I look around . . ." Cassandra flapped her arms, then let them drop to her side. "And there's so much to do. And when I get one thing done, five more pop up. After I get rid of Dad's things, I'll need to get rid of a bunch of other things. And when that's done, I've gotta sell the house, which means researching real estate agents and hoping they won't screw me. And the garage! I keep forgetting about the garage. I don't even know where to start in there."

The two-car garage housed one car. Mr. Rivers's truck took up one side. The other was for fishing equipment. Soooo many rods, reels, tackle boxes, and tons of stuff Amanda couldn't identify because the list of things she would prefer to do instead of fishing was long and distinguished.

Iris's Ford Fusion, by contrast, was in the driveway in all weather, and occasionally needed a jump in winter.

"You shouldn't just get rid of that stuff," Sidney ventured. "I'll bet you could sell a lot of it for good money. Your dad kept his equipment very fucking immaculate."

"And maybe sell the truck, but keep your mom's car?"

Cass nodded. "Uh-huh. Sure. How? How does a teenager do all this shit? I don't even know where to start! And when everything gets tossed or sold or sorted, then I've gotta sell this place. Which means doing a buttload of paperwork since I'm a minor emancipated by murder. Oh, and I should probably finish high school. That's on my to-do list too."

Sidney, now that the tears had subsided, tentatively joined their small huddle. "Yeah, it's fucked up that a sixteen-year-old has to deal with this all alone, but—*aaagghhh, Jesus!*" Sidney took a hopping step backward. "Dammit, Amanda! I think you just shattered my ankle."

"She's *not* alone." Amanda tried to remember the last time she was this furious but couldn't. "She hasn't been alone since the day Jeff Manners loogied all over your palm. She'll always have us and our families, and unlike some parental units I could mention, we will *never* abandon her. Get it?"

"Fuck fuck fuuuuuuuck." Sidney hobbled in a small circle as she clutched her ankle. "You'd better start running before I get the use of my shattered ankle back. Cassandra, there's gotta be a cane here some-where. Bring it to me so I can knock 'Beat Amanda silly' off *my* to-do list, then limp home."

Cassandra tried and failed to suppress her giggle. Despite the circumstances, Sidney smiled; it was the first time they'd heard Cass laugh in days. She shot Amanda a later-for-you glare as Cassandra put a hand on Sidney's elbow and maneuvered her to the only seat in the living room not piled high with belongings.

"Sit tight," she said, then wound her way through piles of belongings into the kitchen.

"Sorry," Amanda whispered. "I guess that was harder than I meant."

"You guess? Stay away from me, you flame-haired psychopath. And why aren't you running? You should definitely be running." Sidney lowered her voice. "It's possible I'm making more of a fuss than warranted to give Cass something else to focus on." She cleared her throat. "Ow ow *owwwww*, this is a pain I've never felt before! Stop grinning, you unrepentant cow. And I'm still waiting on that cane."

Cassandra returned with an ice pack. "Nobody's running anywhere," she said mildly. "Amanda's right, I'm not alone. I'm kind of embarrassed I forgot that for a minute." She knelt, pulled off Sidney's shoe and sock, revealing her surprisingly delicate foot and plump toes, then plopped the ice pack on her ankle. They all pretended one of her tears hadn't fallen on said ice pack, because the only thing Cassandra hated more than crying ("It's never solved anything. Not once.") was someone pointing out she was crying.

"There. Sit still for a bit. Don't you dare move that ice pack for at least five minutes."

"But it's coooooold," Sidney whined. "Can't you make me a room-temperature ice pack?" She caught Amanda's gaze and winked. "Soooooo coooooold."

"Oh, stop it. And thanks. For coming over, I mean. And other stuff. Everything, I guess. Thank you both for everything."

"Thank *you*," Sidney replied. "Your shenanigans got us out of school again. My parents told me I've only gotta worry about two things this year: helping you and passing geometry. But I think only one of those is gonna happen."

"I keep offering to tutor you," Amanda began.

"And I keep telling you that's my worst nightmare. One of them. Having to sit through an hour-long geometry lecture is as dreadful as that dream where all the snakes are yelling at me and chasing me out of the reptile house on their little snake bicycles. I still don't know how the hell they could ride . . ."

"I'm trying not to be insulted," Amanda replied. "And failing. Plus, I thought moths were your worst nightmare."

"It's a long list," Sidney snapped. "Right now my subconscious is taking a break from the nightmare about moths taking over the radio station and is dishing out snakes on bikes. Do I know why? Fuck no. Do I care why? Nope. I just have to get through it. We all have our trials, Amanda!"

"But why would moths even want to be on the—never mind. It's not just you guys," Cassandra said. "I owe your folks, too, Sidney. They've basically had to adopt another kid at the last minute. And not just any kid. A PTSD-laden brat with a dead dad, a jailed mom, and a need for ongoing medical care. Who showed up with no warning, lugging a pile of literal and figurative baggage."

"I don't think your example works," Amanda began.

"You're right. It's not like an adoption, since I was forced on them."

Sidney shook her head. "Nobody's forcing shit; they love you and always have. You can talk and feed yourself and wipe your own ass."

"Wow! Great! Congratulations on finally attaining those goals," Amanda deadpanned.

Sidney glared. "My point is that it's not like taking on a newborn or a toddler or a senile octogenarian. Like it's that much harder to cook for five instead of four? Mom doesn't even have to wake you up for school; you take care of that yourself. You're no trouble. Y'know, comparatively speaking."

"Now that we've got that settled, let's make a plan. I know it looks overwhelming," Amanda said, poking through a pile of flannel shirts. They all had pockets; Cassandra's dad only liked shirts that accommodated a pack of cigarettes, despite the fact that he'd quit smoking five years ago. One of the rare arguments Iris won. *But why would she want him to live longer?* Yet another question about the dichotomy of loving your abuser that Amanda couldn't answer.

"Sure, sure. Just make a plan and . . . ta-da! All fixed."

"Ugh with your attitude, Sid. It's doable. It's like that old joke about one person eating a bear all by themselves."

"Don't ask," Sidney muttered. "Cassandra. Cassandra! Look at me. Do. Not. Ask."

Cass cleared her throat. "What old joke?"

"Dammit!"

"So a young woman—"

"Which young woman?"

"Dunno, Cass, just some random young woman. Anyway, she declares she can eat a gigantic grizzly bear all by herself. So her family laughs at her. But she reiterates that she can do it. Gobble up a whole bear on her own. So when they ask how, she says, 'One bite at a time.'"

"What a touching yet stupid story," Sidney said. "But at least it was short."

Cassandra cut off Amanda's rebuttal. "Since we're all here, let's get started. Many hands make light et cetera. Sidney, you can supervise. Cassandra, command me."

Her friend unearthed a Kleenex box, blew her nose, tentatively dabbed at her stitches. "Fucking tears. Useless *and* sting like crazy." She balled up the Kleenex, glanced around at the chaos, focused on her friends. "Okay. One bite at a time. Today we'll just concentrate on his clothes. There's a lot of stuff that's barely worn we can box up for Goodwill."

"Me," Sidney said at once. "I'll put the boxes together and seal them. I love you, Cass, but a blind orangutan can pack a box better than you can."

"Don't you love the specificity?" Amanda spotted a roll of masking tape on one of the end tables and grabbed it. She gave it to Sidney, who promptly began strapping the ice pack to her ankle. "Not a member of the ape family—an orangutan. Not an ordinary orangutan—a blind orangutan."

"I do love the specificity," Cassandra replied, smiling. "I love all the weird things you guys do." She sighed. "Let's get to it."

CHAPTER THIRTY-EIGHT

Dave's meeting with Marcus Garner was, appropriately enough, at the cemetery . . . inside his brand-new, custom-made mausoleum with a creepiness factor of eight plus.

The five of them had clustered briefly by the gates, then walked into the cemetery. Sean took Amanda's hand, for which she was profoundly grateful.

". . . yeah, so we started as soon as the ground thawed enough, and she's just about done. Coupla weeks at most. I don't get it, but it's not the first time I've built something I couldn't see the point of. Man's writing the check, he can have a bathroom with a basketball court or a basement greenhouse or a mausoleum."

"And you've been here during the construction, Mr. Conner?"

"Welp, I'm mostly in the office these days, but I try to get out here coupla days a week, and I'm meeting Marcus today to talk about if he's good with the angel carvings and the trim or wants more."

"It's hard to imagine someone's notes consisting of 'Not enough angels.'" Sidney's everyday scowl was intensified as she pressed her lips together.

"Sid?" Amanda asked. "You okay?"

"I'm counting up all the horror movies with cemeteries or mausoleums. I'm up to seven. We're acting like every basic bitch in every horror movie in the history of the genre."

"Want to go back?"

"Did I say I want to go back? Whoa." Dave had led them past neatly tended graves to a short building that could only be the future Garner family mausoleum, small but gorgeously detailed. "Jeez, it's like a toy Taj Mahal."

It was a small white building, about eight feet by ten, with three steps leading up to the entrance and two pillars flanking the double door.

"Holy flying duck shit." It was rare to see Sidney so dazzled. "Guys, you should do this for me when I die. But bigger. At least two stories. And maybe an extra pillar. And a gag buzzer. Something that plays the theme from *Friday the 13th* when you press it. Or the theme from *The Good Place*."

"We'll get right on that," Cass muttered.

"And don't spare the marble!"

"Huh."

"Problem, Mr. Conner?" Sean asked sharply.

Dave was frowning. "I don't see any of my guys around."

"How many horror movies feature a doomed idiot saying something along those lines?" Amanda asked Sidney.

"I dunno, all of them?"

"It's almost lunchtime, though," Cassandra observed.

"Yeah, okay." Dave went up the steps to the double doors, paused, then pushed them open. "Marcus, you in here?"

They followed, and saw that Marcus Garner was, indeed, waiting for them in the cool gloom.

He was a slender man of medium height, dressed in a spotless black suit, black dress shirt, and black dress shoes; his face was a pale oval floating five and a half feet off the ground. His dark-brown hair—the same brunette as his sister's—was cut brutally short; his dark eyes missed nothing. He was standing before a small pillar on which rested an elegant silver urn, arms behind his back at parade rest.

He inclined his head. "Hello, David. I was unaware this was a group meeting."

Dave cleared his throat. "Yeah, well, something came up. Hope you don't mind. You okay? You look a little weird."

"I'm fine. Especially as you've brought Operation Starfish to see me."

Well, that's *not alarming in the slightest.*

"Ladies, I am in awe of your past efforts. And David, thank you for bringing us together. And you, sir, I . . . have no idea who you are."

"Sean Beane."

"Truly?"

Sean ignored the question he probably got every time he introduced himself. "I'm looking into the murder of Jonny Frank."

Amanda noted the careful "I'm looking into" as opposed to "I'm vigorously investigating." Nor did Sean mention his law enforcement background. Kid gloves?

Marcus smiled. Or his lips curled up. Probably a smile. Or a toothache? "Good. Justice must be pursued, isn't that what we're taught? We don't find out the truth until years later."

"Yeah," Cass replied cautiously. "That's a bummer, all right."

"Please, ladies, tell me about yourselves. Or perhaps David can elaborate?"

Dave picked that moment to run out of words; maybe the chill of the building got to him, or Marcus Garner's off-putting demeanor, or he thought they could introduce their own damned selves.

Amanda let go of Sean's hand and stepped forward.

"Hello. So sorry to barge in. Your mausoleum is lovely. This is my friend Sidney Derecho; this is my other friend, Cassandra Rivers—"

"Amanda only has two friends," Sidney said with a straight face. "She caught her limit back in high school."

"And I'm Amanda Miller, small-business owner."

"Yes, you own the Hobbit Hole, a play on words regarding your little bookshop; how clever," Marcus said in a tone that indicated he thought it was anything but clever.

Amanda hated clichés, but when he casually dropped that nugget, she felt her pulse stutter. *He knows about OpStar, he knows about my Hole, and he's been visiting Iris. Have I been wondering about the wrong man? Sean has been watching out for us for years, which could have easily been misconstrued. But how long has this politely blank stranger been slithering around in my life? Our lives?*

"I am Marcus Garner, as you know. This is my sister, Wanda," he added, indicating the small, elegant urn, which had a silver background and delicate gold bands at the neck. She'd assumed it was silver, but given Garner's obvious wealth, Amanda was now willing to bet it was platinum. "I will join her here eventually."

"Oh. Well." Cass cleared her throat. "That's . . . something to look forward to?"

"She hated being alone."

Sidney was studying the urn and pillar. "You're building this great big thing—this great big, gorgeous thing—when all you need is about a foot and a half of space?"

"It's what Wanda would have wished."

Amanda doubted Wanda would have wanted her brother to obsess, murder, and piss away hundreds of thousands on a small marble building and a platinum urn, but kept her mouth shut.

"And how is your dear mother, Cassandra?"

"Fine. In prison, but . . . fine." She paused. "It was nice of you to visit her."

"I am not nice. And I regret—many things, now I think about it. Among them, that I was unable to assist in her legal defense, then and now."

Okay, so he didn't know Iris until recently. But . . . now?

Cassandra obliged her: "Now?"

Garner nodded. "My last two visits, I suggested a new attorney and a new strategy, but she was adamant. And thus remains imprisoned. Doubtless, she wishes to keep punishing herself for a crime that was no crime."

"Er, yeah. Doubtless." Amanda could see Cass was equal parts puzzled and uneasy. "She's, um, doing good, though. Y'know, relatively speaking."

"Doing well," Amanda whispered, then hissed when Sidney pinched her.

"Though she was bummed about losing her appeal to reinstate her license—"

"Seriously?" Sidney asked. "Iris thought they'd let her keep being a physician assistant? I owe her huge for turning me on to transcribing clinic notes from home, but I could have told her they'd never let her keep her PA license."

"—but she cheered up when they let her run the prison newspaper. Is that how you found out about Operation Starfish? My mom told you?"

"No, I took an interest in your work after my brother-in-law murdered Debbie Frank. I regret not knowing about you prior to your disbanding. I would have been an asset; my not inconsiderable funds would have been at your disposal."

Amanda had a sudden vision of Marcus as a voice on a speakerphone, funding the three of them and their missions like a sinister *Charlie's Angels* reboot. And why did people use "not inconsiderable" instead of just "considerable"? Ridiculous.

She cleared her throat. "Yes, that's too bad."

"I think you might have the wrong idea about what we were doing," Cassandra said warily.

"Not at all. Your efforts to rid the world of domestic abusers were laudable. You simply lacked the will, organization, and funds to take it far enough."

Oh, great, another man who wants to take women "in hand" so they can enact his agenda instead of theirs.

Cass was already shaking her head. "That's not what we were trying to do."

"Oh, no? You weren't trying to effect a cure?"

"We were never the cure. We were just the Band-Aid. That was always the problem."

"Better a Band-Aid than nothing at all."

"Depends on the injury," Sidney observed.

"It's nice of you to say that, Mr. Garner," Amanda said.

He gave her a thin smile. "I am not nice. What a pity you gave up. I would have thought outlaw bikers had more staying power."

"Oh, fuck me, another guy who bought into the all-bikers-are-Hells-Angels trope."

If Sidney's outburst had offended him, Garner didn't show it. "You . . . aren't?"

"Nope. The vast majority of MCs—"

"'Vast majority' is redundant," Amanda put in, then moved out of pinching range, because she was a willing slave to the great god Grammar.

"Eat it, Amanda. Like I was saying, ninety-nine percent of MCs are super legit. It's like most things; the fucking one percent ruins it for everybody else."

"So, what?" His tone skated right up to the line between light teasing and bitter mockery. "You did it for awareness?"

"Shit, no, we don't—I mean, we didn't do it for awareness. Christ, it's the NFL's Breast Cancer Awareness sop all over again. Show me a functional adult who doesn't know breast cancer exists. Or domestic violence."

"Hmm. I won't deny, it's invigorating to run across such impertinence."

This is him invigorated? Also, "impertinence"? Who talks like that? Besides me?

"Then it's your lucky day, pal." Sidney spread her hands and grinned. "Impertinence is my fucking moniker."

"Sidney?" Amanda didn't finish; there was no need. Sidney heard the words even if Amanda didn't say them: *You wanna ease up a little on the unstable killer?*

"And while we're educating you on shit you don't actually understand—"

Huh, maybe I did have to say the words.

"—that whole trope about how MCs are all about rebels and free spirits is another teeming pile of bullshit."

"'Teeming'?" he asked, and—whoa!—smiled. Or grimaced. His lips moved, anyway.

"You've never seen people more invested in enforcing their hierarchy. There's *rules*, Garner, so many rules. Hierarchy rules, codes-of-conduct rules, whose-turn-to-bring-a-slow-cooker-full-of-chili rules . . ."

"They're like the House of Lords that way," Cassandra added.

"Yep. And if you're late to the party? Try to copy anything from an MC, like using the same name or the same cut design, and see what happens."

"Violence?" Marcus asked, and it was downright creepy how he perked up.

"Worse. Lawsuits. MCs like the Hells Angels and the Bandidos are as vigilant—"

"And litigious," Amanda added.

"—about copyright infringement as Disney. And nobody in their right mind ever, *ever* fucks with Disney."

"This is disappointing," Marcus admitted.

Sidney shrugged. "Sorry. You bought into the hype. It happens."

"He killed her," Marcus said. "He bullied her and belittled her and beat her, and when I finally talked her into leaving, he shattered her skull like it was a ceramic plate, and *nothing happened.*"

"Nothing happened" was still echoing when Sidney cleared her throat. "We're aware. And it fucking sucks. But here's the thing, Garner, because I guess it's the theme of the week: it wasn't your fault."

"Don't presume, Ms. Derecho."

"'Presume' might as well be her middle name, Mr. Garner, so you can forget about her taking that advice."

"Kindly die on fire, Amanda."

"Plus, she's right," Cassandra added. "It wasn't your fault. You didn't have to spend years punishing yourself. You can't think that's what Wanda would have wanted." She glanced sideways at Amanda and muttered, "I'm aware of the irony here; don't you say one word to me."

"What Wanda would have wanted is both moot and irrelevant."

"Aren't those kind of the same thing?" Sidney asked.

"No," Amanda and Marcus replied in unison.

Marcus continued: "Wanda is dead. Cut down like a rabbit hiding from a lawn mower. I will never see her again. She will never see me again. She will never *anything* again. Speculating about what Wanda would have wanted is an infuriating waste of time and energy."

Yes, it's almost as futile and wasteful as pissing away a fortune to build a mausoleum years after the fact that, by your own admission, your sister will never see or even know about.

Amanda wrapped her arms around herself. She knew it was her imagination, but the mausoleum was getting colder by the moment.

Marcus had been keeping himself so still, Amanda almost jumped when he broke the silence with, "Why have you come to see me? I expected a couple of members of Saint Paul's finest, not . . . whatever you are now."

"To belatedly offer our condolences?"

"Do not lie to me, young lady."

Sidney cocked her head to one side. "Pretty sure you're not even ten years older than we are."

"Okay, then, we're here for your mausoleum-warming party."

Marcus let out an elegant snort, which was amazing. It was like someone letting out an elegant sneeze: it sounded impossible until you saw it happen.

"Nothing from you, sir?" he asked Sean. "I don't believe you've spoken since you introduced yourself."

"This is their show. I'm the tagalong."

"Ah. How nice that we all know our place." Marcus picked up the urn, examined it, then started to . . . unscrew the top? "As for the mausoleum-warming soiree, if I were hosting such an absurd event, it wouldn't be until September. But I won't see September."

"Because you'll be in England?" Cassandra asked. "That's where my mother thought you were when we—"

"I know why you're here."

Later, Amanda would have trouble parsing the events of the next thirty seconds. Marcus upended Wanda's ashes, and a small pistol clunked out with them—a .38, maybe? Amanda felt someone grab her and haul her backward, and then Sean's broad shoulders were blocking her field of vision. She heard the clang of the urn hitting the floor, a gunshot (deafening in the small space), and Sidney's moaned "Oh, fuck" even as she craned around Sean to see.

Marcus was still alive. Blood streamed from his ears and dripped on the flawless marble floor; the left side of his head had a curious bulge, which wasn't curious at all. He was leaning heavily on the pillar, and

Wanda Garner's ashes were a cloud. Somehow, he opened his mouth and brought the pistol back up.

"Don't!" Sidney screamed, just as Sean shoved her aside and reached for Wanda Garner's last living family member.

The second shot did what the first couldn't.

CHAPTER
THIRTY-NINE

"Pretty sure I'm done throwing up now."

"I didn't know you *could* throw up," Cass observed. "Remember when you got blasted on vermouth and chocolate milk? When you didn't barf then, I figured you never would."

"And if you tell anyone," Sidney said, wiping her mouth on her sleeve, "*you'll* be drinking vermouth and chocolate milk."

"Everyone all right?" Sean asked. He'd checked Marcus Garner's vital signs, an exercise everyone in the mausoleum knew was futile, and followed them out to the fresh air. "Physically, I mean?"

Amanda opened her mouth to answer, then cocked her head when she heard sirens. "You called for backup."

"No, I *came* with my backup." Sean brushed some of Wanda Garner's ashes off her cheek and shoulders. "I just called for reinforcements."

"Oh. Good. That's good. That's. Um." She burst into tears and clutched at him, taking comfort in his arms and from Cassandra's gentle pats on her back and Sidney's "Aw, don't cry, or you'll get me started, and I hate crying as much as I hate puking."

"You're all idiots," she sobbed as sirens drew closer and the corpse in the mausoleum cooled.

CHAPTER FORTY

Cassandra Schmitt's sixteenth birthday . . .

She heard them before she saw them.

"Don't look at me like you're measuring me for a straitjacket! We're allowed to be here! My folks are right behind us. We're taking her home!"

Then approaching footsteps and a different voice: "Ma'am, you can tell us the room number or we can just start opening doors. And I don't mean to lecture, but you shouldn't put all your faith in the chubby unarmed guard who's old enough to be our grandpa."

She could have smiled if she hadn't been so numb. She'd never been hooked up to a Valium drip before, but it was pretty nifty. "Down here, guys," Cassandra called. "Room two seventeen."

She heard the wheeze of the pneumatic door opening, and then Sidney and Amanda all but galloped into the room.

"Oh my God!" Amanda cried, which was bad enough.

Then Sidney made it worse (Cass would have thought that impossible at this point) by bursting into tears. "Oh, Cass, your poor face!"

Cassandra gestured at the bandages and the IV. "Yeah, fishing today was not fun."

They rushed up to the bed and then stopped, as if reluctant to touch her, or even get too close. "Is—is it true?" Amanda whispered. "Is your dad . . . I mean . . . did your mom . . . ?"

"They took Mom," she croaked. "They arrested her."

Sidney edged closer. "Yeah, we know. Listen, my folks are here; they're talking to the attending about signing you out."

"That's nice. I hope they let me finish the IV first. I like your parents. They always pretend we can't stay up late or snack, but then they let us stay up late and bring us snacks."

Sidney was studying the IV bag. "Yeah, well, there'll be snacks aplenty. Except maybe you'll stay here overnight with this shit in your system. Either way, it's up to the doc, but you're gonna come home with us, okay? If not tonight, then tomorrow. Okay? Just for a couple of days. So don't even worry about it. Okay?"

"No," she replied. She'd thought she was done crying, but nope; she could feel tears beneath the bandages, knew her sinuses were filling like a bathtub. "It's not okay at all."

"We're sorry," Amanda said, her lower lip trembling. "Oh, Cass, we're so sorry."

"D'you know who isn't?" When they looked at each other but didn't answer, she went on. "My mom. She doesn't care that Dad's dead. I don't think she even cares that she's going to prison."

"Maybe she won't," Sidney suggested. "Maybe she can . . . I mean . . . self-defense? Or something." It was strange how her hesitancy, so out of character, made the nightmare worse.

"She kicked him in the balls, shoved him off the dock, then jammed a kayak paddle between his shoulders and drowned him. You wouldn't think someone her size could overpower someone his size, but . . ."

"Once he was down, he couldn't get any leverage," Amanda said. "Plus, your mom had the whole lifting-a-car-off-her-child adrenaline rush going for her."

"Yeah."

"We'll testify."

Sidney grasped that straw. "Goddamned right we will! We can tell the judge about the bruises and the black eyes. We'll tell them *everything*. Are you mad at us?" she added in a small voice.

"What? No. Why?"

"We could've called the cops. I mean . . . we knew. Nobody's that clumsy. It was the Thing We Didn't Talk About. We could've . . ."

Sidney trailed off and looked at Amanda for help. "It didn't have to get this bad," she finished.

"Not your fault," Cass said firmly. "We're teenagers, for God's sake, we don't even have driver's licenses yet. This isn't on us. Or at least, it's not on you guys. And calling the police doesn't work. Mom just sits there and sits there and denies everything."

There was a shocked silence, followed by Amanda's tentative, "We didn't know that. That you called the cops."

"Twice."

"Fuck," Sidney muttered, staring at the floor. Then she looked up and gestured to Cassandra's face. "Is your eye okay?"

"Yeah. It's just swelled shut; that's why it's bandaged over. No permanent damage. Doc says it'll go down in a few days. And a mere twenty-eight stitches." She managed a laugh. "That's what 'mostly superficial' means around here."

"Sure," Sidney said, wide eyed. "Just what I was thinking. Superficial."

"And nobody's testifying. Not you guys, not me, not even Mom, because there won't be a trial. Mom confessed. She told the police *everything*. If the hospital hadn't called the cops, she would have."

"Why'd he do it?" Amanda asked abruptly. "That's what I can't figure. It's such a horrible random thing to do, I mean . . . a fishhook?"

"I don't know," Cass said flatly. "I'll never know. C'mere." She reached out and, when they each took one of her hands, hauled them closer. Amanda let out a yelp of surprise, and Sidney almost stumbled.

"This shit," she told them in a low voice. "This awful shit cycle. I'm done. I'm not putting up with it, not for a minute, not for a—a—"

"Nanosecond?"

"I'm gonna keep saving, and I'm gonna get my bike, and I'm gonna help women like my mom."

"You mean . . . killers?" Sidney asked, sounding not a little horrified.

"She means battered significant others," Amanda said. "Don't you, Cass?"

"Yeah. I'm gonna make a place for them. It'll be theirs. Not a shelter or anything like that. I don't want to try and reinvent the wheel. This would be something short term, like an ER visit. They won't have to fill out a form or talk to a social worker or any of that bureaucratic bullshit."

Sidney blinked. "So . . . *not* like an ER visit."

"I'm not following what you're—"

"I'll set up a system, and they can call, and I'll come get them, no questions asked. Like, the *second* they call. Then I take them somewhere safe so they can figure out what to do. You know that stupid starfish story Sidney did for Fogarty's speech class?"

"Hey! It wasn't stupid."

"I'm gonna do this, the starfish plan, because saving one or two or five is better than saving none."

Amanda's eyes widened. She was usually quicker on the uptake; must have been the stress of seeing Cass's mangled face. "Because your mom got left on the beach."

"I'm gonna do it so some poor lady doesn't spend sixteen years soaking up rage, only to drown her husband during a family fishing trip and then take her copiously bleeding daughter to Dairy Queen for Peanut Buster Parfaits."

"Oh, fuck," Sidney exclaimed, sounding amazed and repelled. "That's what she did?"

"She was *very* determined to buy me ice cream."

Amanda clapped her hands over her mouth, her eyes going wide as she tried to stifle all sound.

"I won't get mad if you laugh."

"Well, I will," Sidney snapped. "Handle your shit, Amanda."

And that got Cass started, which got Sidney going. The tears stung, and giggling hurt her throat, still sore from all the screaming, but it was fine. Well. Not fine. But . . . a little better?

When they'd calmed down and Sidney had found a box of Kleenex and was handing out tissues, Cass elaborated on the plan that had begun to form when the lidocaine kicked in and the doc started stitching.

"It's not gonna be a full-time job or anything," Cass cautioned.

"Good, because we've also got to make a living."

We?

Yeah. We.

"Anyway, I'm doing it. Even if it's just part time. Because, again, part is better than none. I'm gonna make a plan and then implement a plan."

"No, I'm gonna make a plan," Amanda retorted. "Long term isn't your strong suit."

The relief was like a wave. Not that Cassandra would admit it out loud and give Amanda an opening to comment on clichés. She hadn't doubted her friends, but she also knew this was asking a lot. "So . . . are you guys in?"

"Of course," Sidney said. "Like you needed to ask, you bandaged bimbo? Ow!"

"Too soon," Amanda said, and kicked her again.

"Fuck! I get it, jeez."

"It'll be like Meals on Wheels, helping the communi—no! It'll be better than MoW, because it'll be our thing. The three of us." Amanda had gone from tentative to tearful to glowing in a shockingly short time. "Not something we do with our parents, or that we have to do for school. It'll be *ours*."

"That sounds good. I'd love the chance to lecture an abusive husband with a two-by-four to the forehead. And, y'know, rescue their battered partners."

"You don't fool me," Cass said, smiling a little.

"Me either," Amanda said at once. "Um, in what way is Sidney not fooling us?"

"You like to mix it up," Cass continued. "You like to get in there and get a little bloody or muddy. So do I. But as much as you like a fight, you like preventing one even more."

"That sounds like something you made up on the spot," Sidney replied.

"I note you aren't actually refuting Cassandra's point," Amanda teased.

"Did you also notice Cass can barely keep her eyes open? We should prob'ly go."

Cass stifled another yawn. "It's been a long damn day. But yeah, you guys should head out. It's nice your folks are here, but I'm hoping the hospital keeps me overnight. I need to think. I've gotta figure out the starfish plan. I've got two years until graduation to work it all out."

"Like Sidney said, we'll help," Amanda said. "If Leonidas could take on the Persian Empire with three hundred men, we can help a few battered spouses."

"But Michael Fassbender and all those other hot guys died. Every last one."

"Shush, Sidney!"

That almost got her started again. They talked for a couple more minutes, and then Cass accepted hugs, yawned, and politely kicked them both out so she could start plotting the rest of her life.

CHAPTER FORTY-ONE

Hours later, after police and paperwork and it was just the two of them back at Amanda's store, Sean led her upstairs, ran a warm shower, undressed her, stripped, and followed her in. Together they washed Wanda Garner off their skin and out of their hair.

"Too bad we can't wash away that mental image," Amanda said, standing beneath the hot spray with Sean's arms around her. "Have you ever seen something like that? Silly question—of course you have."

"Not right in front of me like that. I only ever saw the aftermath. Poor guy. He's exhibit A for why you don't use a .38 to kill yourself. At least the cops have the murder weapon."

"I mean . . . I'm trying to put myself in this guy's shoes. But I can't. I—aaaaaah, don't stop." Sean was giving her a back rub while washing her back. Points for multitasking. "I can't imagine spending the summer supervising the construction of my own tomb, killing my sister's killer, then speeding up my suicide timetable once I realize I'm about to get caught." She shook herself like a dog; drops flew everywhere. "I think I finally feel clean again. You?"

He kissed her by way of answering, and she admired the silent efficiency. She returned the kiss, running her hands over his broad chest and the light dusting of dark chest hair as they sighed and groaned and touched and rubbed.

"Wait!"

He backed off so quickly that he almost lost his balance. "Did you not want—"

"No, I mean the sex in the shower thing only works in the movies. I mean, it's fun for a few minutes, but then the logistics get to be too much. C'mon, there's something I've always wanted to do."

Which is how they ended up kissing and groping in the calendar section of Amanda's Hole. "See? Paper calendars do exist!"

"I'm not the one who needed convincing."

"Shut up," she panted. "Let me have this."

She gasped as he got rid of her towel and his own, then reached behind her, gripped her thighs, and started to lift her onto his cock. Something else that only happens in movies? Instant, easy penetration in such a position. It took some maneuvering on his part, and some wriggling on hers, but *X* eventually marked the spot.

Christ, he's strong. He's not even leaning on anything!

"Don't mind . . . telling you . . . this is . . . impressive . . ."

He chuckled and nuzzled her neck but kept the pace slow and delicious.

She loved that he was holding back for her sake, but it wouldn't do. "No, it's . . . okay. Remember? It's okay."

She'd been blunt: *I can't come in that position. You come like this, then guzzle an energy drink or whatever and go down on me until I come and then fuck me from behind.*

"You're kind of . . . a miracle . . . you know that?"

"And you're easy to—ah! Dazzle."

She held on as he sped up, carrying her to the counter and leaning against it for leverage. *Gaaaaah, he's so deep I can almost feel that glorious cock in my throat . . . maybe later . . .*

Then he was shuddering like he had a fever, and she watched for the telltale sign she loved to see in a partner: eyes rolling back. He groaned into her neck and staggered.

"Ack! Don't drop me, and definitely don't squish me."

"Oh, Christ, don't make me laugh."

"I'm not trying to make you laugh! I'm giving you instructions that will keep us both safe!"

He groaned and staggered like a drunk as he lowered her until her feet touched the ground, then collapsed to the carpet.

"Clean up on aisle . . . fuck it, I'm too tired to finish the joke."

"Good, it's overused. Am I the only one who wants a malt?"

She chuckled. "You are not."

CHAPTER
FORTY-TWO

"Huh. Well, I've got to give you credit for honesty if nothing else, Sean. This is not a bedroom, and that is not an obsession board."

"Honesty but nothing else, huh?"

"Depends on what you cook for me."

It was the next morning, and Sean had politely yet reluctantly begged to take leave of her so he could go home, shower, change his clothes, check his mail. *I must reek. I need clean clothes for sure; she's sweet to pretend not to notice.*

Amanda had made them both chocolate-banana milkshakes, which they drank/ate while chatting about their plans for the day. Amanda's smoothies were like Dairy Queen's Blizzards: one could hold them upside down and nothing would come out.

"Checking the mail is a big thing for you, huh?"

"You've got no idea." He chewed more smoothie, swallowed, continued: "I missed most of my niece's birthday party because I failed to notice the invitation when it showed up."

Amanda was getting dressed, which was almost as delightful as watching her undress. She got dressed the way most people cleaned out their garage: This? No. Pitch it. How about this? No, that sucks too. In next to no time, she was ankle deep in rejected jeans, leggings, shorts, and T-shirts. "Ouch."

"And my sister will keep reminding me of that until I'm on my deathbed, and then she'll remind me and throw a bucket of ice water on me, so."

"Well, shit." She'd run a brush through her red waves and piled the (clean) clothing rejects into an empty hamper, which she booted into the corner. "We'd better get over to your place and check the mail, don't you think?"

"We?" He paused, then found a more casual tone. "I mean, sure, okay."

"Nice try keeping it casual, but you should see how delighted you look right now."

He ducked his head. "Never mind how I look. What about your Hole?"

Amanda grinned at his deadpan question. "My Hole is closed for the holiday." When he looked at her expectantly, she added, "Lipstick Day."

"You're making that up."

"Nope—every July twenty-ninth."

So he gave her a lift to his place, relieved that earlier in the week he'd cleaned out his car, which was occasionally mistaken for a garbage barge. Fifteen minutes later, they were pulling up to Schoolhouse Square.

"Wow. That's quite a coincidence," Amanda said, eyeing the row of town homes that used to house former OpStar client Jen Johnson. "But not really, I'm guessing."

"No, not really. Once I'd graduated and joined the MPD, my sister recommended the place. Jen Carroll—she's back to her maiden name since she divorced the scumbag you liberated her from—was my neighbor."

Amanda snapped her fingers and pointed at him. "I think she was talking about you when we picked her up! She said her neighbor helped her pack and would be surprised when he got home and found she was all moved out."

"Yeah, Johnson must have escalated. When we talked about it, apparently he'd only 'accidentally' pushed her hard enough to sprain her shoulder. Christ, that's two women in my life who were being abused, and I didn't know a thing until it was all over."

"It's insidious," Amanda agreed. "And everywhere. It's why we—ack!"

Benny Sol had smacked into the passenger-side window, then clung like a six-foot-six barnacle. Which made sense; barnacles probably couldn't skate either. "Hi, Sean! Hi, person in Sean's car!"

"Jesus," Amanda muttered. "Do I roll down the window? Or should we keep driving? I can't tell if this is an ambush or a nervous breakdown or a cry for help. Or all three."

"Same. Looking good, Benny!" Sean lied. "Introduce yourself to my—to Amanda."

"Nice to meet you," he replied as she rolled her window down.

"Are you okay?" she asked. "You look pretty scraped up."

"This is nothing. You should've been there when Sean had to take me to the ER. Six stitches! It would've only been four, but I slipped again after I slipped. Again."

"Well. Er. Keep up the good work?"

"Back away from the car, Benny; I have to pull in."

Benny, who had finally regained his balance, pushed away from the car window and fell on his ass on the grass. Which was all they could have hoped for. "Nice to meet you!" he hollered as Sean pulled into the garage.

"Believe it or not, that kid is a certified genius. That's literal. He showed me the certificate."

Amanda laughed. "I believe it. Lots of smart people are foolish about ordinary things. Like Richard Dawkins and Sherlock Holmes."

He checked his mailbox, then brought her up into his kitchen. "Just magazines," he said, relieved.

"Cooking magazines. Some I've never heard of, for all I run a store that sells them. *Gastronomica*," Amanda read aloud, peeking over his shoulder. "*Cherry Bombe?*"

"Nosy," he said affectionately.

"Oh, look who's talking. Go on, then. Let's have the tour."

It didn't take long. And it ended where it had to. He'd stood back while Amanda studied the wall, poked at some of the articles, walked back and forth, read every word, and finally stood in front of it with her hands on her hips.

"I'm gonna go ahead and posit the obvious: you haven't had a chance to take it down."

"Busy week," he pointed out with a smile. Since she didn't seem horrified or even put out, he slid an arm around her waist. "But I promise to tear it all down."

"*Mmmm.*" She looked at him. "It was brave. Showing me this."

"I'm—I'm glad you're not mad." He'd imagined this scenario more than once. And more than once, imaginary Amanda had taken one horrified look and run off, shrieking. Imaginary Amanda also kicked him in the balls a few times. So, yes, this was definitely a dream.

"Oh, I didn't say that," Amanda teased.

Explain yourself. If you can. "I'm not unaware I've been living an incomplete life."

"Okay."

"And if I *was* unaware, my sister would remind me. She mentions that almost as often as the botched b-day party. And maybe you won't believe me, but until recently, I hadn't posted anything for a year. I only come in here to vacuum."

"But then you updated." Amanda tapped the newest article pinned to the wall. "When you found out Jonny Frank had been murdered. Which kicked things off all over again."

"Yes."

"Hmm."

"But we're done now, so." He went to the closet and grabbed an empty Amazon box, then turned back and reached for the newest article, destined for the shredder.

"No. Leave it up." She turned to look at him. "I don't know what's going to happen next. Or what we're going to do. But people still need help, whether from the system or OpStar or what have you. So leave it up for now. All of it. I have to think about this for a while."

This is amazing. So, again, it can't be real. Could I have a fever? Has this entire week been the greatest fever dream of my life?

"Oh. That isn't what I . . . um . . . okay. Sure."

"Aw. You're cute when you're discomfited." She hooked an arm around his neck, pulled his head down, treated him to a slow, sweet kiss, then pulled back and nipped his lower lip. "Dear me. I can't seem to remember the way to your boudoir. Refresh my memory?"

"Only if you never call it a 'boudoir' again."

"Fine, take me to your fart palace—ack!" He'd swept her into his arms, carried her down the hall, and plopped her into the middle of his bed. "Whoa. Nice sheets."

"Thank you. You're the only—I mean, I haven't had many women here."

"You sure? Because you are an above-average fuck, to put it mildly. Can't learn that in a vacuum or from the internet."

He grinned. "I didn't say I didn't fuck. Just that I haven't had many overnight guests."

"Ah." She was already wriggling out of her shorts and "Reading Is Lit" T-shirt. Always the gentleman, he gallantly stepped forth to relieve her of her panties. Then she crooked a finger at him, but when his hands went to his belt, she shook her head. "Naw. Now and again I like to indulge my CMNF kink. Clothed male, nude female," she added before he could ask.

"Far be it from me to complain." He settled against her and groaned as she started wriggling against him.

"I thought about fucking you in front of the obsession wall, but that would have been weird."

"Weird is a sliding scale." He sucked in breath; it had taken her about two seconds to unbuckle his belt, pull down his fly, and reach for him. She squeezed, smiling as he stiffened in her hand. "Which is something I never thought I'd say during foreplay."

She laughed. "That's okay. 'Fuck you in front of your obsession wall' was something I never thought *I'd* say."

"A week of firsts" was all he managed before his eyes rolled back, and he was wholly hers, as he always had been, but never dared hope for.

CHAPTER
FORTY-THREE

The next morning, Amanda was trying to figure out if they should fuck in the mystery section or test preparation section, as Sean did his best to distract her, which he was damned good at. They were both coming off long dry spells, and she'd probably be sore tomorrow, but who cared?

Just when the kissing and groping had started to get interesting, they were interrupted, which she should have predicted. "Knew I should've locked the door."

"At ten o'clock in the morning on a weekday," he teased. "Dave was right, how *do* you make any money?"

They heard an aggrieved sigh and left the shelves to find Sidney helping herself to coffee. "D'you two think you can stop eating each other's faces for ten seconds?"

"Easily. Go ahead, Sid, start the countdown."

"Rhetorical question, you horny dope."

"How are you feeling, Sid?" she asked sweetly. "Need a barf bag?"

"Yeah, actually."

"I set myself up for that one," Amanda admitted. She pushed past Sidney to get her own coffee as Sean, adorably sex flushed, adjusted his clothing. "And ohhhh, poor Dave. He was almost as much a wreck as Sidney."

"Fuck you, it was traumatizing as shit."

Sean nodded. "You'll get no argument from either of us."

"At least now we know how Marcus came to hire Dave to build his monument to murder . . . he'd been poking around Prescott. Just another way to keep an eye on what was going on, I suppose."

"Efficient but creepy. Marcus Garner in a nutshell."

The frog croaked again, and here came Cassandra with a smile so big and bright Amanda wondered if Iris was getting early parole. "Hi, guys! What's up?"

"What's up is why aren't you still traumatized?"

"I am. If it makes you feel better, my normal night terrors are on a much-deserved vacation. This morning I screamed myself awake because of Marcus Garner."

"That's the upside to trauma," Amanda said. For all Cassandra's light tone, Amanda had the sense the woman was telling the truth, and she couldn't resist setting her coffee down and giving Cassandra a hug. "You get all-new night terrors instead of reruns. So what are you grinning about? I've seen smaller smirks on jack-o'-lanterns."

"Okay, well, now that we've cleared my name—"

"Which never needed clearing."

"—I can share my big fat news. I sold a book!"

"Aw, good for you, Cass. I mean, I sell books every day, but you go right ahead and feel proud of yourself."

"No, jerkass, I wrote a book, and it's being published."

"Hey, that's great!" Sidney said. "Good for you."

"I didn't know you even finished it! You've been working on that book since graduation." *Also, I thought you gave up that dream when you gave up on us.*

She would have said that out loud earlier in the week. How odd and wonderful that such changes could be wrought in a few days.

"I got the news a couple of weeks ago, but I couldn't . . . whenever anything good happens to me, I want to tell you guys. And when something bad happens, I want your advice." She paused. "My own fault I couldn't, though."

"Yep!" From (who else?) Sidney.

"And then when I saw you at the police station, it seemed stupid and vain to greet you with 'Hey, great to see you, I sold a book! And someone was murdered or whatever.'"

"Super-*duper* stupid and vain."

"Amanda, give her a break."

"I'm sorry I ran away from you guys." Cass took a breath, let it out slowly. "I was chickenshit. I thought I was protecting you, but . . . well. Everyone in this room knows who I was really protecting." She glanced at Sean. "Maybe not everyone."

"No, it seemed pretty obvious you were thinking mostly of yourself," Sean teased. Then: "Ow," as he got a pinch for his pains.

"Did you tell Iris? I bet she flipped right out," Sidney asked.

Cass ducked her head and smiled. "She was really happy for me."

"Is that what she was whispering about when you and I left Stillwater the other day?"

"Yeah. She knew I hadn't told you guys yet, so she was something you will never be, Sidney Derecho."

"A murderous Virgo with a great haircut and a killer apple-pudding recipe?"

"Discreet."

"Yeah, fuck off and tell your mom to fuck off. No, don't do that last one. What's the book about?"

"It's a history of women bikers and motorcycle clubs. I'm basically turning all my articles into a book. Pub date next summer."

"Yay!" Amanda jumped up from her stool. "We'll have your first book signing here. Don't worry, I won't double-book you and Edward Gorey."

"That comes as a great relief," Cass replied, straight faced. "So what about you two? Still bangin'?"

"Clearly. Though we're taking it to the next level by dating; pardon the overused phrase."

"At least you're not doing it totally backward or anything," Sidney snarked.

"You remember you married a man you never met, right?"

"And pretty soon I'll be divorcing him," Sidney vowed. "I've just gotta find him first."

"Road trip to Canada?" Amanda suggested. "I'll make a rare exception and close the shop for a few days."

"Your work ethic blows. How have you not starved to death?"

"Debbie Frank."

"Oh. Yeah, makes sense. D'you know, I haven't touched a penny of what she left me?" Cass said quietly.

"And yet you didn't use any of it to hire Sean," Amanda teased.

"Well, I did," Sidney said. "Touched the money, I mean. Paid off my school loans and my van, put a down payment on my house."

"Good. She didn't leave it to us just so it would sit in a money market account."

"No, she left it to us to spite the fucko she married. Which was awesome," Sidney said, "if I haven't made that clear. Ha, he was so mad!"

The memory made Amanda smile. Jonny Frank had lunged at the three of them when he found out the woman he'd foully murdered hadn't left him a cent. His shriek when Cass cracked his patella could have been a hymn; it was such a joyous sound to their ears.

"So I was thinking maybe we could . . . start something? A charity or whatever? The three of us?"

"That depends. Are you going to keep asking me why I'm in it? And are you willing to stick around?" Amanda asked. "In the spiritual sense. Not necessarily literal."

"Well, shit, we thought you'd never ask!"

Sidney's being a bit liberal with "we." But Amanda didn't feel like saying anything that might trash the mood. "I'm on board. And whatever new project we're going to start together, if we need a reasonably priced private investigator, I know the perfect guy."

"We won't," Sidney snarked.

Sean laughed. "Ouch."

"Almost forgot." Amanda dug something out of her back pocket, handed it to him. "Here."

"A new Cold Stone Creamery card!"

"Better than new, see? I've had it for three months, so now you only need two more punches to get a free Like It serving." To Sidney and Cass: "He's got this huge thing for ice cream."

"Amanda." Sean was staring at the card like it was one of those giant checks they make for lottery winners, then looked up at her with shining eyes. "Do you like burgundy or seafoam? You've seen teal, and taupe's in the wash."

Cass blinked. "Uh, what?"

Sean looked around. "And does anyone else smell tomato sauce?"

"Spaghetti and meatballs," Cass said, indicating the bag she'd brought with her.

"At eight thirty in the morning, barf."

Cassandra shrugged, unmoved by Sidney's revulsion. "Sean, you didn't get into trouble or anything, right? Once Marcus was in the morgue and the cops got through all the paperwork?"

"I got chewed out but no real penalties. But at the risk of sounding like a male chauvinist oinker, I shouldn't have let you come to the mausoleum with me."

"'Let.'" Sidney snickered. "Ha."

"You guys know things could have gone off the rails, right?"

"Welcome," Cassandra said, "to our lives."

"So, what?" Sidney asked. "Everything's fixed? The killer's dead; the guy who killed the killer is dead; we're all friends again; Amanda's gonna have regular sex, and I'm gonna do my best to become a widow? And we all just get on with it?"

"Nice recap. Forget about transcribing clinic notes," Amanda suggested. "I've said it before, and it bears repeating: go write for the AV Club."

Cassandra shrugged. "This is real life. Problems aren't always solved and then neatly shelved."

"Right? Loose ends all over the place. Like Jeff Manners. Cass still has to decide what to do with him. He wasn't the killer, but that doesn't make it okay for him to steal your Commando. It's still operating a vehicle without the owner's consent. It's a felony, in fact."

"That's not a loose end. C'mere, you guys."

She led them to the alley, and Amanda let out a squeak when she saw Cassandra's Commando parked beside Amanda's Triumph parked beside Sidney's Roadster. "I had my doubts about Sonny's security system, so I went over and liberated my bike."

"And the thing is, Cassandra owning a bike again isn't as shocking as Sidney *not* driving her minivan over here."

"Just for that, I'm pushing Cass's bike over. It'll hit Amanda's and mine, and they'll fall over like gigantic, ungainly dominos."

"I'll call that bluff," Cassandra said.

Sidney opened her mouth, then let out a groan. "Dammit. Can't do it. Guess you'd better paint the 'No parking except for the Bobber, the Hardtail, and the Tuck' warning again."

"The what, the what, and the what?" Sean asked.

"It's biker slang," Amanda said. "A stripped-down bike with bobbed fenders like Sidney's is a bobber."

"A hardtail is a bike with a frame but no rear suspension, like mine," Cassandra continued. "And the tuck is when a rider sort of ducks down low to be aerodynamic, like Amanda does."

"Because 'Private parking, keep out' was too much trouble?" Sean asked as he put an arm around Amanda's waist. "Since I'm sticking around, I'll need to make a few purchases, won't I? No offense to Sidney or her helmet."

"Hey! Your hair never smelled better than after you wore my old helmet."

"That's what I'm afraid of," he replied, straight faced. "Becoming even *more* appealing to Amanda."

"Jesus Christ, the mouth on this guy." Which was just about the most ironic observation Sidney had ever made. "You guys wanna ride?"

"I should probably keep my Hole open for more than two hours this week. Suppertime road trip? I can have steak, Sidney can have pasta, Cass can have oatmeal, and Sean can have me."

"Lame," Cass commented.

"Soooooo laaaaame," Sidney agreed. "But doable. The food parts. I've got no comment on the fuck parts."

"Not that lame," Sean said, and kissed her right there in the alley, surrounded by the ghosts of her past and the promise of her future.

EPILOGUE

Six weeks later . . .

"I'm so pissed Edward Gorey blew me off."

"He didn't blow you off, hon. He died."

Amanda crossed her arms over her chest. "You always take his side."

Sean smiled. "Is that what I'm doing?"

A bark from the back cut him off before he could elaborate. "Hey! Let's keep the line under control, okay? Back up, don't crowd the author. Yeah, I'm talking to you, sunshine. Good God, kiddo, that lollipop is bigger than your face. Jeez, no, don't *offer* it to me. It's way too shiny with your spit."

Amanda dropped her head and groaned into her palms. "Tell me Sidney isn't yelling at a first grader in my graphic novel section."

Sean pushed the cup of pens out of reach. "Sidney isn't yelling at a first grader in your graphic novel section."

"Unfortunately, my ears work perfectly, but thanks for trying."

"Anytime, hon."

"I'm not yelling!" Sidney shouted. Then lower: "Ma'am, thanks for coming, and also, you'll be purchasing every book your daughter touched with her sticky hands. So I hope you're into European history and graphic novels and at least one cookbook."

"She's terrifying," Sean commented with no small amount of admiration. "Are all book signings like this?"

"This isn't a book signing," Amanda reminded him. "It's a combo prepublication date, author's night, bake sale, date night, and drinking game, because among other things, I'm awesome at multitasking. It's practice for when Cassandra's book comes out next year."

"You just wanted an excuse to talk about Gorey while eating brownies you didn't have to pay for because you're the hostess."

"What? Sorry, couldn't hear you over all the brownie in my mouth. No! Don't you dare take that one, it's the last one. Hey! Let's make smoothies out of the leftovers."

"Naw," He looped an arm around Amanda's shoulders, kissed the top of her head. "But I'd drink a milkshake made out of the leftovers."

"I thought that whole crumbling baked goods into a beverage was an awful idea, the way stuffing is an awful idea. Stale, damp bread jammed up inside a turkey corpse . . . what the hell were they thinking?"

"That wasting food was sinful? And that they were lucky to be alive at all?"

"Learn to recognize rhetorical questions, please. You spending the night?"

He grinned. "You have to ask?"

"I always ask. And I appreciate that you never assume." She went up on her toes to kiss him. "Also, take it easy! Don't trip when you race up my stairs. It took three Band Aids to take care of your skinned knee last time."

"Worth it."

"Idiot." She rolled her eyes, but the hell of it was, Sean was (probably) telling the truth. He loved the building she loved best and usually spent at least three nights a week with her. But he was careful never to assume, and he reciprocated invitations. Which was how they'd ended up fucking on all fours in front of the obsession wall. Which, in turn, led to acknowledging that having sex while Iris's and Jonny's mug shots looked on was (1) weird, and (2) an experiment that didn't warrant repeating.

Sean had spent the last several weeks cooking for her any number of times and was a bit abashed when he presented some of her favorites: spinach *palmiers*, carbonara, butterscotch custard. With a mouth full of *palmier*, Amanda said, "Also known as pig's ear or palm heart. Oh, yum! Unrelated, do I want to know how you know I love carbonara and pudding? Because we've talked a lot but never about pudding."

"I followed you on Facebook for a while," he admitted. "You knew that. But I stopped last year. My sister kept reminding me I was living an incomplete life."

"Ah. Then you also know I love Oreos and smoked oysters. And gazpacho and deep-fried Snickers, but only in small doses. And never together."

"Next time," he vowed, making her giggle.

It was far too early to be talking cohabitation, but it wasn't too early to start talking about talking about cohabitation. Anyone who could put up with her weird life (and, even better, thrive in it, as Sean was) and her weird friends and her weird . . . everything else . . . that person was a keeper.

Sidney rushed up to them, more agitated than usual, which was horrifying. "Can you believe the turnout tonight? Over half a dozen! And they all took one of those little posters—"

"Cover flats," Amanda corrected.

"—and bought cookies and brownies."

"That's great, Sid—"

"But we're out of snickerdoodles!"

Sean, who had eaten three, had no comment.

"And this was great, Amanda, excellent test-run plan." Sidney began to prowl back and forth as she pondered. "But y'know, when the book comes out, we need to do some kind of bike-themed thing. And maybe something with designer jackets or whatever? In keeping with the theme that female bikers can be into Elena Velez *and* Ducati?"

"Motorcycle cupcakes?" Sean asked. "Served on a bed of designer denim?"

"Don't be stupid. Wait." Sidney's gaze went to the ceiling as she considered. "Only if the little bikes on top of the cupcakes are made out of sugar instead of plastic. And it better be buttercream frosting. The real stuff, not that colored Crisco shit."

"Or we could just sell books?" Amanda asked. "Because we're not a bakery?"

"You know you're saying that with a mouthful of brownie, right, you sugar-laden bitch?"

"Sugar-laden." Damn. Amanda smiled to see her oldest friend's enthusiasm and looked forward to Sidney losing her damned mind at the actual book signing next year. If Cass ended up getting rich and famous, Sidney was going to be the friend who was also the heavy.

("Hey! Back off, don't crowd her—oh, you know this person, Cass? Here, have a seat. Sorry about throwing the garbage can at you.")

"It's possible Sidney's more excited about the spring release of *Riding Bitch* than the author," Sean observed.

"I had the same thought," Amanda replied.

"Thanks for doing this, Amanda." Cass ambled over to the register to liberate an M&M cookie from the plate and into her mouth. "A pre-pre-book-signing bake sale. Though I don't think we sold many—"

"Good practice. How's your talk coming?"

"That's right; that's coming up next month, isn't it?" Sean asked. "Are you nervous?"

"*Mmm.*" She took another bite, chewed, swallowed, answered. "Haven't given a speech since Speech in seventh grade."

"I remember," Amanda replied. "'How to Traumatize Your Children.'"

Cass laughed. "You remember the title?"

"How could I forget? How could anyone?"

"Anyway. I'm nervous, but it's not the speech, or the people. I've talked to lots of . . ." Cass looked around, saw Sidney was on the other side of the store, and lowered her voice. "I've talked to lots of individuals with justice-system involvement—"

"This is a euphemism-free zone!" Amanda hissed. "Are you *trying* to get us all killed?"

"—when I visited Mom. They're mostly regular folks who had bad luck and followed up with bad choices." When Sean opened his mouth, she cut him off. "Please let me stay in that idealized bubble. Obviously, some very terrible people are also locked up."

Amanda knew all about the bubble. Though her feelings about her murderous mother were conflicted, Cassandra didn't want her to get hurt or worse. So at first, she was nervous about visiting the prison facility, which was why she and Sidney had accompanied her the first time, and several times after. To see Cass chatting up other inmates and befriending guards was to see her relief that, like so many things, prison wasn't like in the movies.

It helped that Iris Rivers had valuable skills, not least her background as a physician assistant. In exchange for a lack of hassle, Iris offered free medical advice. She'd also noticed when one of the guards was in the first phase of a heart attack. ("No, it is *not* normal when your left arm suddenly hurts like hell and you can't get your breath, now sit down.") And she saved the life of an inmate who tried to kill herself by jamming a sharpened toothbrush handle into her own throat. Amanda had been saddened but not surprised to read that the number one cause of death in prisons was suicide, a terrible tidbit she had not shared with Cassandra.

"Anyway, my point," Cassandra was saying, "I just don't want to embarrass Mom, y'know?"

MCF-Stillwater occasionally invited professionals to give inspirational talks to the residents, and Iris Rivers had suggested her daughter. When the invitation came, Cassandra had assumed it was a joke until a phone call disabused her.

"How would you even embarrass a murderer?" Amanda wondered. "Especially that one. Make fun of her hair?"

"I'm sure I'll find a way," Cass replied drily. "Drop a few f-bombs, maybe start a riot, instigate a cafeteria sit-down, steal all the toilet paper, whatever."

"Well, I look forward to it."

"I wish you were kidding."

"Except, you know I'm not. It's almost ten, I'm going to close. You want to come up for the drinking game?"

"*Hell*-o!" Sidney, freed from keeping books away from the child who was more lollipop than girl, bustled up front. "Drinking game? Here I thought it was gonna get dull."

"Cass is going to practice her speech at us—"

"'At'? That's an odd way to put it."

"Shush, Cass. She's going to practice, and we're going to drink every time she uses an unnecessary adverb—and most of them are. Also any run-on sentences or plosives."

"Plo—wait." Sidney started to reach for her phone, then realized it was easier to ask. "Isn't a plosive just a word that starts with p or t?"

"Uh-huh. And k."

"But how the hell is she—"

"That's Cassandra's problem," Sean deadpanned. "Ours is keeping the Brandy Alexanders flowing like wine."

"Oh, fuck me sideways, you and your ice cream obsession."

"An improvement over my OpStar obsession, don't you think, Sidney?" he teased.

"Barely," Sidney sniffed, but Amanda wasn't fooled. Sean was growing on her like a benign fungus.

Cass was scrolling through the Notes app on her phone, skimming her speech as she frowned and fretted. "I don't see how I can take out all the plosives. What a ridiculous rule."

"It's a drinking game. By definition, all the rules are ridiculous. Like strip poker or reality TV."

"Just for that, you—" Before she could finish the thread, the frog croaked, and Dave came in, holding hands with a slender brunette with a slight limp.

"Too late! We sold all the snickerdoodles and most of the brownies," Amanda called. "Nice to see you as always, though. Who's your friend?"

She wasn't just happy to see him; she was relieved. Dave had had to deal with the traumatic fallout from Mausoleumgate, as had Amanda, Cass, and Sidney, which he'd done by distancing himself for a couple of weeks.

When he'd started coming around again, he'd confessed that he, too, was having nightmares about that scorching-hot day and the tragedy that had unfolded in the cool gloom of the mausoleum.

("I dreamed about it again, except instead of shooting himself, he blew up the mausoleum and us with it. But I didn't die. You guys all did. Then I tried to rebuild using my blood for mortar."

"Jesus Christ, Dave!")

The fact that Marcus Garner had paid in full had come as a relief. Dave's late, lamented client had wired two-thirds in advance, then apparently set up an automatic balance payout on September first, the day he'd planned to die. It gave Dave a cushion—he'd turned down several smaller jobs to focus on the mausoleum—and, better, he didn't have to immediately worry about rustling up new clients to make up the shortfall.

"This is Lola," Dave said. "We went to high school together, and she just moved back from Vancouver."

"Welcome back! I'm sorry most of the baked goods are gone. Dave's chronic tardiness has screwed you, but it's not his fault. Comes with the job."

"That whole thing about all contractors are chronically late, unreliable, and constantly over budget is a gross generalization," he replied amiably.

"Is it, though?"

"It was my fault, really," Lola said in a low, pleasant contralto. She was thin and, considering it was a chilly September evening, underdressed in a sleeveless summer dress. Her hair was pulled back so tightly she looked perpetually surprised, and there were shadows beneath her brown eyes. Her elbows were pale points. "I ran into some . . . it's my fault."

Dave cleared his throat. "Anyway, I just wanted you guys to meet. And to support Cassandra's new book. But mostly the first one."

"Hello," Sean said.

Lola smiled and looked at the floor. "Hello," she murmured. "Nice to meet you all. Dave talks about you all the time."

"Nice to meet you; please ignore the fact that you're surrounded by idiots," Sidney said, shaking Lola's hand. "And don't listen to anything Dave says; he's an infuriating moron. Whoa! Cold hands. D'you want a sweater or something?"

"Or something," she replied.

Amanda took a closer look at Lola. *Underdressed. Limp. Wouldn't make eye contact with Sean.*

Oh-ho.

Dave's gaze was as level as his tone. "I don't know what you're doing these days, or if you've got plans to—I know it's only been a few weeks, is my point. You're still figuring things out. And maybe nothing will happen; maybe you'll decide you don't want to jump back in. Which would be understandable. I just . . . wanted you guys to meet. Just in case."

There was a short silence, broken by: "I can't offer you snickerdoodles, but there's still plenty of coffee and hot water for tea. I was just going to lock up. Why don't you guys join us upstairs for a drink? And also to mock Cassandra's speech?"

"Kindly drop dead, Amanda."

"Aw." Amanda poked Cassandra in her annoyingly flat belly, then gave her a noisy kiss on the cheek. "*Mmm-wah!* I know you love me."

"Irrelevant! Also, you smell like chocolate. A lot of it. How many brownies did you cram down your gullet before—"

"Come on, come on. Time and milkshakes wait for no man, so to speak. Sean, you want to show Dave and Lola up to my place?"

"Will do. Follow me, and don't be alarmed by all the jelly she keeps in the cupboard." That got a giggle out of Lola, which was nice to hear. "Are you laughing because you thought I was kidding?" Sean teased as he led them up. "Because I wasn't kidding."

The three women looked at each other as they listened to the receding footsteps, then waited until they heard the door at the top of the stairs close before speaking.

"So . . ."

"So . . . ?"

"So!" Cass finished her tea and set the mug down with a thump. "Guess we'd better go listen to her story."

"You sure?" Sidney was studying Cassandra with surprise. "Because of the three of us, you were the last one I thought would say that."

"I'm not saying start up again. I don't know if we should, or if it's even possible. I'm saying we hear her out. It doesn't have to be OpStar 2.0. It doesn't have to be anything. We can just . . ." Cass shrugged. ". . . read the terrain and act accordingly."

"Sure, sure," Amanda replied. "Great plan. What's the worst that can happen?"

Cassandra snorted. "Too soon. No. Wait. Y'know what?"

"It's *not* too soon?" Sidney guessed.

"Guess we'll find out."

They went up, once friends, once OpStar, now a sisterhood.

BIBLIOGRAPHY

"Early Women Motorcyclists," https://www.sfomuseum.org/exhibitions/early-women-motorcyclists.

"The History of Women Motorcycle Riders in the US," https://blog.chopperexchange.com/motorcycle-life/lady-riders/the-history-of-women-motorcycle-riders-in-the-u-s/.

"History of Women Riders," https://ctrideguide.com/women-riders/history-of-women-riders/.

The Rugged Road, Theresa Wallach.

"Ten Pioneering Female Motorcyclists," https://www.goodwood.com/grr/race/historic/2021/4/ten-pioneering-female-motorcyclists/.

"Women's Motorcycle History: Female Legends," https://femmefatalemoto.com/blogs/news/womens-motorcycle-history-female-legends.

WIMA World: https://www.facebook.com/wimainternational/.

"Women Riders—History," https://www.shorelinehd.com/About-Us/ Women-Riders-History.

ABOUT THE AUTHOR

MaryJanice Davidson is the *New York Times* and *USA Today* bestselling author of several novels and is published across multiple genres, including the Undead series and the Fosterwere trilogy. Her books have been published in over a dozen languages and have been on bestseller lists all over the world. She has published books, novellas, articles, short stories, recipes, reviews, and rants and writes a biweekly column for *USA Today*. A former model and medical test subject (two jobs that aren't as far apart as you'd think), she has been sentenced to live in Saint Paul, Minnesota, with her family. You can track her down (wait, that came out wrong) on Facebook, MaryJanice Davidson; Twitter, @MaryJaniceD; Instagram, @maryjanicedavidson; and www.maryjanicedavidson.org.